LT /
FIL
MANBURY

W9-CSB-903

Dark Star

Anne Maybury

Thorndike Press • Thorndike, Maine

Library of Congress Cataloging in Publication Data:

Maybury, Anne.
    Dark star / Anne Maybury. -- [Large print ed.]
      p. cm.
    ISBN 1-56054-025-7 (alk. paper : lg. print)
    1. Large type books. I. Title.
[PR6025.A943D37   1990]   90-36324
823'.914--dc20   CIP

Thorndike Press Large Print edition published in 1990 by
arrangement with Random House, Inc.

Large Print edition available in the British Commonwealth
by arrangement with A. M. Heath & Company, Ltd.

Cover design by Catherine Minor.

The tree indicium is a trademark of Thorndike Press.

This book is printed on acid-free, high opacity paper. ∞

"No one knows the end of those who are born under the Dark Star. It is said they are born to some strange . . . destiny. Some are fey . . . or . . . madness comes upon them."

—William Sharp

(

I could remember even now, ten years after my college days, the beautiful line I once read. "God gave us memory so that we might have roses in December."

But I didn't want roses; I wanted no remembering. For several weeks I had fought against it. What I needed, I told myself, was some heavenly magic that would charm me into forgetting.

Everyone gave advice. My mother, writing from New Zealand, where she had made her home after my father's death, pleaded with me to join her.

Antonia, my mother-in-law, urged me. "Judith dear, please try to see that the thing that happened to you was something absolutely isolated. Lewis never meant to harm you. Every marriage has its difficult moments and like many gifted people, Lewis is very temperamental – perhaps more so than most. He lost his head. But it has obviously shocked him terribly. You must see, Judith, that it could never happen again."

My friends were unanimous in their point of view. "But he *couldn't* have meant to hurt you. Not Lewis . . ." They told me about people having blackouts when they were overwrought and afterward having no knowledge of what they had done. "Dreadful things, Judith," they said. "And in a way, such people are innocent because they never know what they have done."

It was all beyond the understanding of relatives and friends. Lewis Mullaine, brilliant pianist, charming and apparently devoted husband, adoring father of a seven-year-old son — how could he have attacked his wife and left her for dead unless he had suffered some emotional paroxysm? With the wisdom of hindsight I realized that since I had kept silent about the growing frequency and violence of Lewis's rages, outsiders could not be expected to understand.

Since that appalling night Antonia and I had spoken of it seldom. Beneath my own trauma at what had happened, I could sense the terrible distress the tragedy must be causing his mother. Her brilliant son — who at the age of thirty-five had been called by the critics "a musician of genius" — her adored only child, was the subject of television, radio and newspaper headlines:

Famous Pianist Attacks Wife
Mass Hunt For
Lewis Mullaine

A warrant was out for his arrest.

Leaning against the centuries-old door of Mullaine Castle, I watched my son's bright head darting about across the tall wild grass as he kicked a football around with more zest than ability.

The peace of the small sparsely populated island of Cathair Mor was folded gently about me. Yet that peace was an exterior thing. Inside me, where it didn't show, I was desperately afraid. For although the police believed that Lewis was far away in hiding, this was his island, the crofters and the fishermen were his people, the moors and the hills belonged to him.

Upon the death of his father, Lewis had become Laird of Cathair Mor. The small Hebridean island south of Mull was only six miles wide and four miles long; it had no shops, and unlike Iona and Staffa, was entirely private and closed to tourists.

Scottish lairds were very often called by their surname. Lewis was "The Mullaine" to the islanders — a small contented community who had not wholly moved into the twentieth century and seemed happy not to.

It was a very beautiful place, and I had often seen, when staying there, boatloads of tourists passing as close as they dared to the tall guardian cliffs. From the sea, Cathair Mor must have appeared very romantic, with its towered Castle and its Abbey against the background of moors and sky.

A shaft of late-afternoon sunshine poured from the edge of a purple cloud onto my face. It came like an arrow shooting a message at me across the gilded sea, defying all the good and kindly advice I had been given. All those injunctions not to be afraid, to give Lewis time to think over what he had done and then to realize that he must come out of hiding and give himself up to the police. "Of course he will," my friends had assured me. "Try to forget it all, Judith. Time resolves everything."

That was the way the people around me talked. And I let them. Their consolation and their optimistic advice were kindly meant, but they didn't know Lewis as I knew him. He never admitted to a mistake; he was, to himself, a young god above reproach. He would not come humbly out of hiding. He was not somewhere meditating on his guilt. He would be planning to turn his actions against me, to put himself convincingly in the right. How that would be, I didn't dare think about. But the shaft of sunlight was like some symbolic message confirming my fear.

You are still in danger. Face it. Don't try to forget or you will become careless. And you dare not ...

Because of Lewis's last words to me before he disappeared, I needed to keep constantly watchful, constantly remembering. He had said, "Get one thing clear. At whatever cost, *I will have my son.*"

I looked over the stretch of deep-green grassland down toward the glen where the wildflowers grew. Some few years ago Lewis had shown me a rosebush growing deep in the shelter of the glen. We were staying at the Castle in high summer and the little bush had put forth three fragile pinkish flowers.

Lewis had picked one and tucked it into my hair. He had said, "There's a superstition, you know, about this wild rose. It's said on the island that if the bush bears no flowers, then the Laird will be chief for many years. But if he sees flowers, then he must count them and that will be the number of years he remains Laird of the island. Three roses ..." He had stood laughing before me, his hair like a bright red flame, his deep-blue eyes on me, his hands, which could crash or caress piano keys, reaching out to tilt my face. "I hope it doesn't mean that in three years' time I'm to, er, 'Look my last on all things lovely' – on you and my son and my piano."

I had cried to him to stop talking superstitious nonsense, and laughing, we had raced together down through the glen to the sea.

I needed to keep it all in perspective – the happy golden days, the excitement of a concert, the long hours of listening to Lewis practicing, the social whirl that he loved. I must remember the charming moments in the early days of our love, for those were as important as the bad times. Like everyone else, Lewis's bad times were no more his "true self" than the good. Only, with him the former had been so violent and so devastating.

I forced my thoughts back to the good memories. "You laugh with your eyes," he had said. And when a musician friend had composed a piece of music for our wedding day, it was Lewis who supplied the title. "Call it," he had said, " 'Serenade to a Summer Princess.' For it's a summer's day and in a way my wife is a princess, since I am heir apparent to a fragment of Scotland."

I could hear the music now, elegant and nostalgic, gliding through my mind.

The happy times, the laughter . . . But equally I must recall the times of violence. I needed to hold every memory chained, like a rogue tiger, in my mind. For I feared that Lewis could carry out his threat to take Paul, even if it meant destroying me.

That had been what he had demanded — his freedom and his son. He could have had the first, but I could not give him sole right to Paul. I knew that even if I could bring myself to make that altruistic sacrifice, great damage would be done. For though Lewis could be the perfect companion, capable of understanding a child's outlook, if he had Paul entirely to himself and the little boy crossed him or pitted his will against his father, then Lewis's rage would flare up to bewilder and shatter an impressionable child. I had asked myself many times if I was a possessive mother. In all honesty I knew that I was not. But I needed to be a protective one which was a very different thing.

Would another wife have held Lewis's outbursts in check? I doubted it, for the sickness was inherent. I had molded my life to suit him without letting myself be a doormat for him. He was away a great deal, giving concerts, and although he liked me to be there when he played in London, he did not want me with him on his foreign tours. I respected that and it made it easier for me to keep my own independent life.

I turned from the sunlight and shadow of the summer afternoon and walked through the arched doorway and into Mullaine. As in most medieval castles, the Great Hall, as it was called, was the most important place in the Castle.

The sound of my heels was sharp and swift and intermittent, for as I went toward the staircase, I trod sometimes on bare ancient stones and then on Antonia's soft, beautiful Tabriz carpets.

I climbed the first flight of stairs, past the gallery where dim portraits of Mullaine ancestors hung on the walls, up the next flight, past my mother-in-law's suite of rooms and then to a narrow, circular stair that snaked around a stone pillar. On it was carved the mark made by the stonemasons who had built the Castle in the fifteenth century. The worn steps were very steep and a crimson rope was slung against the wall to steady those who climbed the tower. At the top was an archway, and beyond it, the room that had been Lewis's ever since he was a small boy.

As I entered, the force of his personality still met me and I shook with the terrifying fusion of remembered love and present fear. I went shakily over to the west window and looked out over the wild and lovely island, the heather-tinted moors, the Brenlorn hills that cut Cath-air Mor almost in two. To the left, beyond the glen, the sea was a glitter of silver and primrose light.

Then I turned and looked about me, filling my eyes and my mind with Lewis.

Here were the things he loved. In one corner of the room stood the piano he had played as a boy. On the other side was a deep armchair and on it lay a half-open score of a Beethoven sonata. There was fishing tackle and a green sweater, an old address book and sheaves of letters that probably had never been answered.

I could hear, on the floor below where I stood, a typewriter clicking away unevenly. My mother-in-law was busy collecting material from old letters and diaries for a biography someone was going to write about her life as a concert singer. Antonia Wells . . . Antonia Mullaine.

I wondered if her sudden strenuous effort at this was in part an attempt to find a release from her own anxiety over her missing son.

Immediately in front of me was a wall mirror. Lewis had once said in the early days of wanting me, "I like girls with long dark hair and golden eyes." And as I stared at my reflection, pulling at my hair, it was Lewis who seemed to be looking over my mirrored shoulder, as if his image had been summoned by my own thoughts of him.

Lewis Mullaine . . . He had a beauty that was entirely masculine: a lean and splendid slim-hipped body, a fine straight nose and a

15

mouth sculpted in sensuous lines. His hair was wavy and brilliantly red. He was a vital and passionate man. But beneath that stimulating and charming personality there was no depth of feeling except where music was concerned. His father had been killed in an accident while hunting in England, and Lewis had spent most of his young life at boarding schools.

He had once said to me, "There was my mother, spending most of her life going from concert hall to opera house. But even from a distance, her influence was strong. I suppose it was because she was such a public figure and I enjoyed a kind of reflected glory."

For Antonia was a very fine mezzo-soprano, and her voice, her looks and her charm made her a favorite for Verdi and Puccini opera. She adored the applause, the bouquets, the rave notices and the fans.

Her mother, Lewis's grandmother, had also been a singer, and Antonia had once told me that even before Lewis was born she had made up her mind that whichever it might be – a boy or a girl – her child should follow the musical line of the family. And there was no one to challenge her will, for when the time came to plan his career, his father was dead.

In one way, Antonia was fortunate – although she didn't realize it in those early days of clashes of will, tears and tempers between mother and son. Even as a little boy, Lewis showed himself to be the stuff good pianists were made of and a music teacher had told her, "It's too soon, Mrs. Mullaine, to say for certain if Lewis can ever become a pianist. Even though he has broad, strong hands and a gift for reading music very easily, I'm afraid he is not particularly interested."

"That," Antonia had said, "is a matter I will attend to."

But if she had believed in early success with her son, she was too optimistic. There were years of heartbreak and resentment while Lewis practiced with deep rebellion.

He had told me on that first occasion when he brought me to Cathair Mor that there had been times when he hated his mother. "I loved sports. I wanted to be out riding and swimming and climbing, but I was shut in that London house, in the huge room with the piano and made to practice. I wasn't allowed to go to camp in case I might do something to injure my hands. I wasn't allowed, when I came here, to go climbing. And how could a small boy spend his holidays on a rocky island without wanting to climb rocks and search caves for — oh, God knows what boys look for. Treasure, I suppose, since ships had sunk for generations off that wild coast and Tobermory Bay was so tantalizingly near."

It was Lewis himself who achieved what he called "the transmutation." One day, so he told me, practicing a Chopin nocturne, which until then he had detested, he suddenly felt an odd burning sensation in his body. He said it was like a flame that reached out to his hands. And he knew, not just that he could play the nocturne, but that he desperately wanted to play it more beautifully than anyone else. It was as if he had suddenly come alive, had taken a great leap from childhood into knowledge of his exciting fate.

I glanced around the room at the piles of the much-studied music he had used during his student years and had now discarded for more ambitious works, the symphonies and the concertos. I looked at the few photographs of him, of friends and his favorite snapshot of me, laughing and with my hair blown across part of my face.

There was also a small and beautiful painting of Lewis's one-time horse, Falconer. He had loved it and called it a devil. Antonia had warned him soon after he had bought the stallion that one day it would throw him and he might injure his hands, so he sold it, on her advice, and was depressed for days. I looked at the painting. I had always feared Falconer; he had an evil eye and a devilish nature.

Everything in the room seemed to stimulate a

memory of people we knew — people who were Lewis's friends, my friends and those who knew and liked us both. What were they thinking, feeling, saying?

I could remember so well occasions when Lewis was abroad giving a concert and friends invited me to dinner. I knew that they were secretly, vaguely sorry for me and yet envious. "He doesn't take Judith with him these days. Is their marriage on the rocks?" . . . "Did you know that Baroness X or the Contessa Y is traveling with Lewis Mullaine? How *can* Judith shut her eyes to it all?"

And I would know and answer them inside myself: "Because I love him; because I know that I can only hold him if I give him his freedom. Because I know he will come back to me."

Only much later, so very much later, did I realize that it was not to me that Lewis returned, but to Paul, his son. That was what held him to me, obsession with Paul. And I, blinded by my own love and my own sense of wonder that Lewis had married me, had been too trusting to see.

I came from an entirely different world. My father had been a successful farmer in that part of Devonshire where the Otter valley rises to the rich hills, with strange, secret Dartmoor on the horizon. I had loved my childhood on the farm with parents who were completely contented.

My home was a beloved and familiar place to me, which I left only after the art teacher at the college where I was educated told my parents that I possessed an original sense of line and pattern and persuaded them to send me to a London art school.

I studied for two years and eventually landed a position with a large textile manufacturing company in the West Midlands. Two years after my father died, my mother married a New Zealand farmer and my two brothers emigrated to Canada. The Devonshire farm was sold. I never went back to visit it − I couldn't bear to.

The company I worked for was well established. It had begun its trade when silks and cottons and wool were the only materials of any consequence. Since then, man-made fibers had come into their own and Thorburn Ltd. had begun to produce them. The company, however, had been reluctant to give up the old silk and cotton materials and had maintained a smallish area for their manufacture.

For the first eighteen months at Thorburn's, I had worked on cotton fabrics, and at the time of my meeting Lewis, had been promoted to the more beautiful and delicate silks. I spent my time traveling from London to Avonleigh, where the great mills and factories were, and after we were married I only stayed nights up there when Lewis was away on a concert tour.

So often it is the small, almost infinitesimal chance that changes a life. When a friend in London invited me for a weekend, I was merely told to "bring a long dress in case we go to a party." I took my favorite green chiffon with the swirling skirt, even though it was so difficult to pack. It had been one of those wild and unnecessary extravagances I felt I would regret for a long time.

That evening changed my life. The friends I was staying with were Scottish and I was taken to a large party in a London hall to celebrate the Scots famous Burns Night. The Scots were letting themselves go with reels and sword dances, raising their whiskey glasses and singing their songs.

There were some very fine exhibition dancers, and sitting in an audience of guests watching them dance the Highland Fling, I marveled at the delicacy of their foot movements. I wasn't particularly aware of the man on my right until he spoke.

"Are you Scottish?"

"No."

I turned and met laughing dark-blue eyes.

"Then you probably don't know how that dance got its name."

"No."

"Nor do a great many Scots," he said.

"Do *you?*" I waited, and saw him nod. "Then tell me."

"A shepherd watching his sheep was playing on his pipes to keep himself amused. Looking up, he suddenly saw the horns of a deer bouncing up and down over the top of a hedge, cavorting with the joy of spring. The farmer was so amused that he began to imitate it, flinging his arms up to represent the horns. That was the first Highland Fling dance." He paused, watching me. "Do you believe it?"

"It's so crazy that yes, I do."

"Who are you?"

"A friend of the Murrays." Then, while the guests applauded the dancers, I explained. "They brought me here tonight." I looked about me. "It's a lovely hall, isn't it? Maybe I have odd taste, but I like all those garlands and cupids and gilt."

"It's not so pleasant to play in as the larger hall adjoining it. It's a matter of acoustics, of course."

"Play in. . . ?"

He nodded, flexing his fingers, his eyes amused. I had a feeling that he expected me to know him and that I was unsophisticated not to. "I play the piano, as a matter of fact. I'm Lewis Mullaine."

Even I knew that name. I murmured a

crushed "Oh," and then added, "So I don't suppose the sort of music they play for this dancing really interests you."

"On the contrary, my Scottish blood stirs with it. But if I tried to dance as they do, I'd probably fall flat on my face."

A wild, swinging reel followed and we said no more. Later, however, he was introduced to me and asked me to dance. While we jigged along to the tune of "Scots Wh' hae," he said, "I asked to meet you. This is quite a night for me and I intend to enjoy it to the full."

At the end of our third dance together he suggested dinner one night the following week.

That was the beginning.

I stood pressed against the cold stone wall of the round tower, Lewis's voice in my memory, asking, "What is your second name?"

"An odd one. Clea."

"Then I shall always call you Clea. Never let anyone else use it. It's my name for you. Clea . . ." In those early days he said it as if it were a caress.

II

The brilliance of the sunset drew me back to the window. The sky was like an abstract painting in gold and saffron and lavender-blue. The distant sea was tawny where the sun caught it, and nearby, to the left of the loch, waves exploded in white spray against the huge boulders.

The windows were closed and I couldn't hear the sound of the sea. It was very quiet in the high, circular room, for on Cathair Mor there were no roads to take cars, no horses except the one kept by Jock MacCulloch, whose fat dappled mare and brightly painted cart were used to take anything heavy from one place to another. Not that distances were far, for the islanders all lived around the loch. The rest of the island was too wild and too lonely in winter and the coast around the other three sides — east, west and south — too rocky and dangerous and inhabited only by cormorants and gulls and shearwaters. I had never been at Cathair Mor in winter, but they told me it was then that the barnacle geese flew in with "a great singing in their wings."

I watched Paul down in what the islanders called "the parkland," which was in reality just large stretches of grass interspersed with birch and rowan trees and little wind-stunted bushes. The Castle had no splendid "grounds." I saw Paul jump up to a low branch and shake it, and a shower of recently spilled raindrops fell onto his face. I knew the curious pleasure of that because I had often done it myself, letting the tiny needles of rain flick my skin. Paul rubbed his cheeks, turned and found his football again.

Lewis . . . Paul . . . I had stepped so far into a different world. I hadn't come slowly, cautiously, able to take stock of every unfamiliar situation as it came along. I had plunged into Lewis's dazzling world without in the least knowing how I got there. A farmer's daughter and a great pianist. A girl who knew what she liked in music but had no deep understanding of what she heard. And a young man already destined for greatness. Not that it was a Cinderella story, for I had been the happy daughter of a happy family; I had started on my own highly promising career and I was having a good time, anyway, before I met Lewis.

But I was no beauty who had overwhelmed an impressionable man, no rich girl who could further an already remarkable career, and no authority on music.

Then why had Lewis married me?

He had said, in those early days, "I fell in love with you while I was telling you the story of the Highland Fling."

But years later he was more truthful. He had said in that ice-cold voice I had learned to dread, "You were new; you seemed to be practical and level-headed. I decided that you were not the type to ever be possessive or to make scenes. Those things all added up to the chief one. And that, my dear Clea? *I saw in you the type of woman who would produce the kind of son I wanted.*"

So, in a few words, Lewis had coldly and calculatingly both explained and destroyed.

I was drawn to the window again. Someone was talking to Paul over the low stone wall. I could see, even from a distance, that it was not one of the islemen. His clothes were different. He wore a russet-colored sweater and his hair had a gleam to it.

I picked up the binoculars from the window aperture and focused them on the man with Paul. He was a stranger to me, and any stranger talking to my son alarmed me. I linked unrecognized faces with Lewis, who dared not come himself to the island but who might, with bribery and sweet talk, use a friend or an acquaintance for whatever he wanted done.

The typing in the room below had stopped. A few minutes later I heard footsteps and then Antonia appeared in the doorway. She was wreathed in late-afternoon light as if a stage electrician had focused a spotlight on her.

My mother-in-law was unique. She was small and slender, with hair that had turned white when she was in her twenties. It was short and curled like swans' feathers. She had an enchanting face, and Lewis had inherited her straight sculpted nose, her large mobile mouth and the extreme, and I believed, quite unconscious sensuality. She was a very feminine woman, temperamental in her profession, calm and controlled in her private life. Only where Lewis and Paul were concerned did her serenity forsake her. She adored them both.

"Judith dear . . ." She looked about her anxiously. "Why? Why come up here? It must only distress you."

I said, without preamble, holding out the binoculars to her, "Who is that man talking to Paul?"

She ignored the field glasses, went to the window and looked out. "That's Shane Kilarran, Rory's brother." She remained at the window, frowning. "Nobody told me he was coming back. And he surely wouldn't arrive without warning — well, unless there was some crisis. But what? The Kilarrans can't have

27

suddenly lost their money and Rory isn't ill."

I said, scarcely listening, "So *that* is Shane — Lewis's friend."

"Oh, it was years ago," Antonia said quickly. "I doubt it they've been very much in touch, if at all, since Shane went to Iran. That was just before your marriage, wasn't it, Judith? It's odd, though, that no one told us he was coming home." Then she laughed and shook her shoulders as though shaking off a thought she didn't like.

She held out her hand to me. "Come along. I've had enough researching for today. I'm tired of reading old gossip. Let's go downstairs. It's rather early for a cocktail, but we can sit and talk." There was still anxiety in her eyes as she looked at me.

"It's all *right*," I assured her. "I'm not being morbid coming up here."

"Then . . . ?" she glanced about her.

"Why *did* I?" I tried to explain. "Because I need to face up to things. I've been trying to push away all the fear I feel, to behave as though it's over. But it isn't, and I've got to look at it clearly. It's important for me to get everything in perspective."

"Oh, Judith," she cut in, "there *isn't* any perspective about what was done! Lewis lost his head, it was a moment's madness. And wherever he is, he'll be suffering torture be-

28

cause of it." Her voice shook. "Don't make efforts either to remember that night or . . . or to forget it. No mother believes her son is evil, but I *know* Lewis isn't. Dear, let's help each other to ride this storm. Sometimes the temperament of an artist is a frightening thing, but they can't help it, and it all blows over."

Listening to her, I thought, We are both magicked by the enchanter — her son, my husband . . .

If I didn't take care to keep the harsh facts to the forefront, Antonia would persuade herself that nothing much more than a lovers' quarrel had happened that July night when Lewis left me for dead and escaped.

Because I had to jolt her into facing the truth, my voice was clearer and colder than I would have wished. "Lewis tried to kill me, Antonia. He *did*."

"Oh God!" She turned her face away.

"We have to remember that," I said. "We dare not bury the truth."

"Ugly things *should* be buried."

"Not until they are faced and resolved. This isn't. Lewis is missing, the police are searching for him."

Her pale hyacinth-blue eyes watched me despairingly. It is never easy to understand another's reactions to something personally deep and distressing. Helpless to bridge that gap, I

29

watched Antonia pick up a small silver medallion from Lewis's desk, curl her fingers around it and then drop it back.

"If we only knew . . ." I said.

"Knew what?" she asked.

I had held back for so long from saying what I was now certain had to be said that the words came on a breath. "Whether Lewis is . . . alive . . . or dead."

"*No!*" Her loud denial rang around the room. "Lewis would never kill himself. Judith, I've tried so hard to make you understand that what happened in that room was terrible and quite out of character. Lewis's disappearance *is* in character. He has gone into hiding in order to work out for himself how he can recompense you – and even, in a way, me – for what he did. You know him; you must see that. When Lewis comes back –" She swallowed as if her throat pained her.

"Let's not talk about it." I leaned forward and kissed her cheek, understanding her as I needed her to understand me. The shock was mutual. My husband, her son . . . But there was no man close enough to us to bring a masculine reaction to what had happened, for both Lewis's father and mine were dead and there were no brother or cousins near enough for either of us to go to for help. On this issue, too, Antonia avoided her professional associates and her legal advisers, all of whom saw only the hard facts and could not feel emotional involvement.

I said gently, "Yes, we'll go down and have that drink. But first I must fetch Paul. He has been out on the moors with the children all afternoon and he's probably covered with bits of bog myrtle and heather and mud." I smiled at her. "I'll join you in a few minutes."

Antonia left me, walking with the light swishing movement of silk, leaving behind her the faint scent of sandalwood. I heard the rattle of the gilt links that joined the stair cord to the wall staples as she gripped it.

I made no attempt to follow her. I needed more time.

Remember ... remember it all — the laughter and the tenderness, the violence and the shock and the appalling unreason.

Six months after that first meeting, Lewis married me.

I walked in a golden dream, questioning nothing. Lewis loved me; our different backgrounds seemed no longer important. I was only vaguely aware of the furor the whole love affair had caused among the countless women, some linked to Lewis by mutual musicianship, some moving in the social circles where he was so sought after. They were all incredulous that "this slip of a girl" had netted a genius.

Often, after my marriage, friends had said to me, "Your life seems to be a kind of mixture of the social whirl and a perpetual honeymoon, the sort people dream about."

It had been so for a long time. But then, in a way, it was I who kept on that even keel of happiness because in my desire always to please Lewis, to be what he would have me be, I never crossed him. Not that I had damaged his character by indulging him. That had been done long ago.

I insisted, however, against Lewis's wishes at the time, that I keep my job as a textile designer. Even in the beginning, in spite of Lewis's heady love affair with me, perhaps I had a subconscious feeling that the marriage would not last and I would one day need my independence. As it happened, working as I did was the very best thing for both of us. My steady hours and Lewis's irregular ones gave him, so I discovered later, the freedom he needed.

A year after our marriage, on a March evening, Paul Christopher Mullaine was born, tiny and yelling and fair-haired. The other thing we celebrated on that night was Lewis's first invitation to play with the London Philharmonic Orchestra at the Albert Hall.

Champagne had been drunk at the hospital meeting over a newborn, sleeping Paul, and flowers were everywhere in my room. Lewis had hung a sunburst of aquamarine and small diamonds on a platinum chain around my neck. It made me look, I thought as I studied the effect in a hand mirror, like a woman who had been put tipsily to bed still wearing pink chiffon and jewels after a riotous party.

Looking back, I realized that our wills had first seriously crossed over Paul. While he was a baby, Lewis did not take very much notice of him. It was only when Paul could walk and talk and learn that his father's real interest began. And then he became totally possessive and adoring. Paul must understand and love music; Paul must experience life early. Lewis was impatient for him to grow up. He planned so much for his son and himself.

I tried to keep quiet about these great dreams; I thought that perhaps as time passed he would accept that our son would one day be an adult with his own views and his own ambitions. But I became increasingly anxious as Lewis hurried his plans for Paul. I used to protest that he was a very little boy and he must not be rushed into experiences beyond his understanding.

It was these protests of mine that began our quarrels. At first, that was all they were, and also, at first, I kept my own protests in low-key. This was because I believed I understood

Lewis's way with Paul. It was the direct result of Antonia's treatment of him when she had kept him from the natural development of a little boy's experiences from childhood into adolescence. I believed that the memory had sparked off Lewis's determination that Paul must know the world. What he could not see, though, was that it was his own choice of experiences he wanted for his son. And Lewis's ideas of suitable experiences were far too sophisticated for a seven-year-old boy.

When Paul was much younger, it was easy. On the few occasions when Lewis and I were at Cathair Mor, he encouraged Paul to fish and climb. Once, when we were walking over the Brenlorns together, he said, laughing, "I often slipped off, unknown to my mother, and went fishing in the streams or climbing. Shane used to help me."

"Shane?"

Lewis pointed to three arches rising from a building beyond the pine trees. "Inverkyle Abbey. The Kilarrans live there. Just two brothers — Shane and Rory. Rory is the eldest and lives permanently on the island. He's a bit simple, though if you want to learn the folklore of the island, he's the one to ask. He's a teller of old tales. Shane is seldom, if ever, there now. He's a civil engineer and has been in Iran for the past eight years on some enormous building schemes. Shane was my one friend here. There's only our place, Mullaine Castle, and theirs, Inverkyle Abbey. You'll meet Rory, of course, and Shane, if he gets back while we're staying here. We still write occasionally."

Gradually, the arguments between us spread to things apart from Paul. In fact, we quarreled whenever my will was opposed to Lewis's, even in small ways.

Anxious and bewildered and exhausted by his rages, I wrote to Antonia. At the time she was giving a series of concerts at the Fenice Theatre in Venice. I told her that Lewis's growing violence worried me.

Her reply was almost airy: "Judith dear, bear with him. He is probably working too hard. It will pass."

I had "borne with him," not out of duty but because in between the rages we enjoyed happiness together. There were times that were still wonderful, times like those during a particularly successful concert, where I had sat tense with pride, watching and listening and feeling a sense of reflected joy at Lewis's achievement. Then his eyes would turn my way and smile as he accepted the storm of applause. Later, when it was all over and we were home, I knew another, and deeper, kind of joy when, keyed to a kind of ecstasy by his success, he would make wonderful love to me.

I tried to hold on to the memory of those magic hours. But I remembered, too, the fury at being crossed in any way, the rages that became progressively more violent.

I had sometimes wondered whether he was trying to free himself of me because of another woman, wanting me to be the one to leave him and so allow him to keep his lovely home . . . and Paul. But I was fairly certain there was no permanent woman in his life. I knew that when he was away giving concerts, there were women who were passing affairs — there had to be, with someone as charming, as gifted, as restless and volatile as Lewis. But it wasn't marriage he wanted; it was his freedom from all marriage, all ties, all responsibilities except the ones to his music, and to Paul.

I told myself that Lewis, too, was suffering. That to be unable to see the extent of his own crazed temper and its effect on others, to be unable to save himself from his demon, must be dreadful for him.

I knew that the most exasperating reaction would be for me to behave like a patient and martyred angel. I needed to keep cool and quiet and yet not allow myself to be crushed or humiliated by the vicious violence of the things he would say to me. But the effort to keep my own balance had its effect on me. I developed a frightening habit of forgetfulness. One morning we had a scene over the fact that I had taken the newspapers to read the critics' reviews of a concert of Lewis's the night before. That I had taken them because he had not appeared for breakfast was not the point, according to Lewis. The papers should be by his place at table.

The whole business was so petty that I had laughed. "You sound like a Victorian husband," I had said. "Oh, Lewis! As if it matters whether I had read the reviews before you! Here, take the papers. The critics are raving again. They call you a superb artist."

He had sat very quietly at the table, his hands tight on the arms of his chair. "And what do you know about critics or music? A farm girl I've brought into a world she will never understand —"

"Oh, I understand very well."

"So you think you do?"

I got up from the table in silent fury at the sneer in his voice. Lewis caught me at the door, swung me around and gripped my chin with his powerful fingers. "Listen to me when I'm talking to you . . ." Then began the flood of fury.

I had listened as I always did because he held me in a vise. He was strong, and fighting him physically was pointless. But when it was over, I walked away from him. I left the house and went to my small room in Thorburn's offices in Berkeley Square. When I returned that evening, Lewis had left for a concert in Paris.

The pattern was always the same. After such scenes, I forgot dates, forgot messages, mislaid things. Even now, all this time later, I still could not remember the dates having been made or the messages given. My only vivid recollections were of the trouble that followed each time.

Once Lewis had apparently telephoned and asked me to give a message to his agent, as he would be involved all the morning in rehearsal. I had no recollection of any such call from him.

He had said that night, "You are frightening me, my dear. I'm beginning to wonder what, in God's name, you'll do next."

I had even made an appointment to see a doctor whom I knew and trusted to tell me the truth. But before that day arrived, the last and most terrible rage of all had struck Lewis.

I told myself: *Remember, most of all, that last night . . .*

III

Lewis and Paul and I were staying for two weeks on the island. Antonia was away visiting friends, and Lewis, who sometimes enjoyed fishing, had gone out that morning with one of the boats.

At lunchtime that day one of the island women called on me. Morag MacAil was a powerful and friendly woman who was the dominating personality among the fisher folk and the farmers. She had a large family of children and grandchildren, but her heart and her cottage were warm and welcome places for anyone on Cathair Mor.

To most of the people on this tiny island, I was considered a "foreigner," but not to Morag. The door of her croft was always open for me, tea and scones ever ready; gossip about the islanders came richly from her wide mouth in a mixture of English and Gaelic. But whenever she broke into that she would always laugh and say, "Oh, *mo ghaoil,* but you don't understand, do you," and then tell me in English. I was *mo ghaoil* (my dear) to her since the time some few years ago when I had seen her small granddaughter walking with an ugly bow-legged gait. I had suggested that the little girl wear a brace on her feet when she went to bed. "A friend of mine did this with her daughter and she grew up with beautiful straight legs. It won't hurt Mairi," I had said.

Morag was too typically Hebridean not to be suspicious of these "new damty city ideas," but I kept on at her, and in the end, with the help of a doctor on Mull, I obtained a brace and brought it to her. Morag could not stand out against the Mull physician and me. Two years later, when I visited the island again, Mairi's legs were elegantly straight. From that moment I was no longer "The Mullaine's wife." I was *"mo ghaoil."* And whatever happened, I had her loyalty for ever.

Children were her passion, and it was largely thanks to her that Paul had become quickly integrated into the island children's lives. At first they saw him as utterly foreign, with his strange talk and city ways. But soon he had become one of them and he knew far more Gaelic than I. So when Morag thought Paul was threatened by unnecessary exposure to what she believed were the wicked ways of "them that come from the south," she visited me one morning because she "felt it rightly"

40

that she should warn me to watch "that wee laddie," my son Paul.

"Angus tells me this mornin' that he be goin' to Mull late tonight. I asked him what for would he be going past midnight, and he says, 'I wasn'a to tell no one, but it's nae good, I'm thinkin', to take The Mullaine an' his son to Mull when good folk should be asleep. 'Tis a party they be goin' to, all wild like, I'm guessin', they wi' their gamblin' an' all, but 'tis to be secret. That's why them as live at the Castle must all be asleep when he takes the laddie with him.'"

I knew the people who had the house on Mull. They were rich Londoners, Jonathan and Lucia de Rainze and her brother, the Earl of Harvel. I had nothing in common with them and even Lewis was a cautious friend. He knew that if he had a concert to work or a tour had been arranged for him, he did not dare accept an invitation to one of their parties.

"I know they've come to spend a month at their place on Mull," I told Morag, "but I hadn't heard about the party tonight. If my husband is going, then I'm quite certain he won't take Paul."

"Aye, so ye think. But I'm telling ye, ma lassie," she shook her head, her black hair falling a little from its nest of pins. "From what I hear, that hoose is nae place for a wee laddie."

41

I said, "If my husband goes, he would be going to dinner, and he has said nothing to me."

"He will. Aye, he will." She went on then to tell me that Angus was taking Lewis to Mull for dinner. Then, at one o'clock, when we were all asleep, Angus would fetch Lewis and bring him back to Cathair Mor, where Paul would be roused and dressed and taken to Mull for the rest of the night.

It was too far-fetched to be true. And yet, in some curious way, I believed the story. More than once he had said to me, "It's never too early for a child to know his way around. I don't want an innocent for a son."

All that afternoon, while Lewis was out fishing, I thought, *But he wouldn't do this . . . It's too crazy . . .* Deeper down, beyond the protests, I answered my own thoughts. "But people *do* crazy things."

I had to cling to the belief that when he returned from his day's fishing Lewis would tell me he was going to the de Rainzes' party. He would probably suggest that I might like to go also, and laugh, as he did, when I would refuse, saying, "You know that I play backgammon badly, and I don't like having to fight off men who believe that at the end of a party the wife should never go home with her husband, or the husband with his wife."

42

As I expected, when Lewis returned from his fishing he told me about the dinner party. "I forgot to mention it to you this morning before I left for the fishing. The de Rainzes felt that it was useless to ask you."

"That's right, it is. I suppose it will be a very late affair."

"Yes."

"How will you get back?"

"By boat, my darling." He had laughed at me. "Did you think I'd swim?"

"I just wondered what state you'd be in to guide the launch."

"Have you ever known me to be drunk?"

"No. But very tired, very drained. And judgment isn't at its best in the early hours of the morning."

All Lewis said was "Don't be silly," and turned away, adding, "I'll sleep in the Armour Room so that I won't disturb you when I get back."

I kept silent about what Morag had told me because I was certain she must have misunderstood. Her English was better than most of the islanders', but even so, it was by no means perfect. Many times in the past we had laughed over sentences that, translated from Gaelic into English, made cheerful nonsense. The same language problems sometimes arose with our two servants, Rosheen and Duncan MacDer-

43

vin. They were custodians of the Castle and looked after us when we were there, with the help of two daily women, wives of shepherds on the island, who had the unenviable task of cleaning the huge expanses of stone floors.

All these people were good solid Hebrideans, beyond reproach except for a little secret poaching during the salmon season. We knew that sometimes part of a beautiful lush salmon would find its way to the kitchen table while the Laird and his family were eating lamb chops in the dining room. It was a kind of honorable and accepted deceit.

On the night Lewis dined with the de Rainzes, the Castle was very quiet, and after dinner Rosheen and Duncan tidied up and went to their own quarters, Paul and I tried to watch television, which was never successful, since the Mull mountains shadowed Cathair Mor so much. I played Scrabble with him, and after he went to bed I read for a long time. Tossed on a chair was a scarf of cinnamon silk Antonia had meant to pack earlier when she went to visit friends on Mull. She had found that the hem had become unstitched, and left it behind. I mended it for her. Then, at eleven o'clock, I undressed, put on a housecoat and took off my makeup. I told myself I was behaving idiotically in not going to bed, but I curled up in a deep chair in the small sitting room in the suite that Antonia had given us in the wing of the Castle. I would wait until one o'clock, the time when Lewis was supposed to fetch Paul.

The clock down in the Great Hall struck the quarter after one when I was roused by a sound. My heart plunged, and all belief that Morag had her facts wrong vanished.

Lewis had come for his son.

I quickly turned off the lamps in the drawing room and went down to meet him. He was crossing the great Hall, and at the turn of the staircase I reached for a switch that would light the huge chandelier. Lewis looked up quickly, blinking, and saw me. "What the hell?"

"I was waiting for you."

He glanced ostentatiously at his watch. "And may I ask why you are standing there like some suspicious, demented wife?"

"Because I *am* suspicious – and I hope I'm wrong. One o'clock, they said, one o'clock was the time you had arranged to return for Paul."

"And who had the damned impertinence to tell you what I intended to do? Or no, don't tell me. It's obvious. Angus. I'll deal with him in the morning. Tonight I need him. Now get out of my way." He had reached my side and put out an arm to thrust me away.

I was ready for him. I tore up the stairs, but before I could reach Paul's room, Lewis had

45

leaped forward and caught me. He flung me roughly into our sitting room on the floor above the Great Hall.

Fear usually dissolves all clarity of memory, but such was the horror of that night that I had almost total recall. I could remember the moments of Lewis's rage in the dark room – first my coolness, then my pleading, and through it all, like a sinister thread, Lewis's deadly quiet voice. It was always like that when he was angry – a kind of running whisper of vitriolic words, a white-hot anger as ominous as the first rustle of trees before an earthquake.

Searching my memory, reliving the terrible night, I remembered my first words: "Turn on the light."

Lewis made no move. His powerful fingers gripped my shoulders.

I ignored the pain, trying to talk to him calmly. "Lewis, don't take Paul with you. Oh, I know that's what you intend. But not at this time of night."

"He's not growing up thinking that he has always to go to bed at – what is it? – ten o'clock? He's going to know that men have a longer night to live."

"A little boy of seven . . ."

"Yes, a little boy of seven," he mocked in that soft, harsh whisper. "And it's time he got the taste for amusements, male amusements. What do you want, a mother's boy?"

"That's the last thing I want and you know it."

"All he's going to do, *my darling,* is to watch men and a few pretty women playing backgammon – or whatever we choose to play. Learning the ways of the world. And if a few get a little drunk, that's the way of the world too."

"That is a lesson he must learn when he's old enough to judge what he sees for himself. Lewis, please try to see it my way. He'll be half asleep, and bewildered. But he'll feel that he *has* to enjoy the party because you are there and he must model himself on you."

"That's right, he must. And he must learn, too, not to make the mistakes I did."

I could just see, from the hidden moon giving a faint glow through the windows, that Lewis's head was bent to me. For a few moments there was silence in the room and I heard the wind outside, fretting and sighing like muted harp music around the Castle walls.

"For God's sake," Lewis exploded with his whispered venom. "Don't you understand? *I don't want you* . . . God damn it, I made a mistake when I married you. Do I have to tell you?"

"Please, let me go . . ."

He moved his hands to my shoulders, tightening his fingers, catching a nerve somewhere

47

near my neck so that I had to hold on to myself hard in order not to cry out with pain.

"Impulse bedeviled me. You intrigued me. You never joined the huntresses. I thought, This is the one. She won't try to possess me. With her I'll be free, but I'll have a son. And I have, haven't I?" He seized my hair and pulled my head back so that I was forced to look at his shadowed face. "I have a son. And I'll have my freedom too. Do you hear? That's my other need — freedom."

I said, "The prison door is open. You can walk out."

"With my son."

"No!" the single word had seemed to be thrown against the walls and to ricochet back.

Lewis laughed and the sound was as sinister and sibilant as his speech. It chilled my heart. "Try and stop me. Just try. If you do, I promise you, I'll break you."

I found sudden strength and I fought him, dragging at his arms. He struck me and I stumbled and fell.

Lewis moved swiftly as I got to my feet, reaching over to a small Georgian bureau. I had no idea what he took from it until I felt the cold edge of metal against my throat.

"I warned you, Clea . . . I warned you." His face was against mine as if in a caress. But as I jerked away from him the steel caught my shoulder. I felt the rip of silk and a sharp jab of pain. I reeled back and before I could find my balance, Lewis hit me again, his knuckles like steel against my mouth. As I slumped choking, the back of my head caught the sharp carved edge of the bureau and a blinding pain seared through me. In those moments before I lost consciousness, I heard Lewis's voice — still soft, still quietly lethal. "Just get one thing clear. *Whatever happens, I will have my son.*"

Through the unendurable pain, a terrible thought ran through me. *He wants me to die . . . he wants me to die . . .* And then the raging pain was too much and I knew nothing more.

It was much later that I learned that I had nearly died from the wound at the back of my head and that the stab on my shoulder was caused by a pair of gilt scissors Lewis had snatched from the bureau.

When I lay in the hospital at Salen on Mull, I was able to recall the scene. It was like some outrageous nightmare. But one thing nagged and tormented me, making that night all too terrifyingly true. The throbbing of my head, the pain in my bandaged shoulders were nothing compared with the memory of a sudden, half-blinding light that had struck my eyes just before I lost consciousness.

Someone had entered that Castle room. Paul, small and hunched in his striped pajamas, had stood in the doorway, his eyes wide and frightened, his finger frozen on the light switch.

I discovered that no one else knew that Paul had left his bed that night. When he came to see me in the hospital he never spoke of it, and since he wandered around my room with a bright, monkey curiosity about everything he saw, I did not test his memory by questions. Nor did I tell anyone, not even Antonia.

As soon as I was well enough, the police came to my bedside, but I did not mention Paul. This secrecy was in order to protect him, for I had no way of knowing how such police questioning would affect him. Anyway, I decided that the state I was in when I was found was sufficient evidence that I had been attacked and my word as to who had left me for dead in that Castle room was all that was necessary.

I had learned from Rosheen that Duncan had heard sounds and come to investigate. He had found me, bleeding, unconscious and quite alone. Rosheen had gone to Paul and found him curled up in his bed. Sure that he was asleep, she hadn't wakened him. I had a feeling that Paul had been lying there in a state of shock. But not once, since that night, had he spoken of his father or of that moment when he had switched on the sitting-room light.

The story of what followed the attack on me was now clear. Lewis had raced from the castle to the loch, where Angus MacAil, who sometimes acted as ferryman for the *Midir*, the Castle launch, was waiting with the boat. Lewis had explained to him that he had changed him mind about fetching Paul, and Angus had taken him back to Mull and dropped him at the little jetty there.

"Aye," Angus had replied when the police questioned him, "an' he told me to go an' fetch him around five o'clock. He seemed fine, and I never guessed there's been trouble at the Castle. So I just said I'd be there for him. An' I thought, 'Tis no time to be goin' to bed. But then, he were the Laird."

Lewis had not been seen at the party after he left to fetch Paul. But the people there had been too absorbed in their poker and backgammon and had merely assumed that Lewis had decided not to return. Later a boat was missing from a small private jetty at Carsaig and all evidence showed that Lewis must have taken it and escaped to the Scottish mainland. Also, his car, which he always left at Oban, was still in the garage there.

The case had been put into the hands of Scotland Yard, since the search for Lewis had become international. Inspector Hartwell, who came from London to see me, was kind, courteous and shrewdly perceptive.

The police had searched Cathair Mor very

51

thoroughly, probing the hollows in the hills, the clefts in the great organ-pipe cliffs. The few shallow caves that could have been a sanctuary for a fugitive were deserted. They had even taken the police boat around the tiny, sibling island of Cathair Beag and found that they could not even land. Very much later I learned that a storm had ripped through the sea in the early morning and the huge waves had covered the guardian boulders and the thin strip of beach. "So," they had said, "no one could land on that hell's island."

I was still in the hospital when the police had satisfied themselves that Lewis was nowhere near the island and gave orders that when I was well enough to leave, I was to go to Mullaine. There were far too many opportunities in London for a small boy to be kidnapped. "And for you, Mrs. Mullaine, it would be too easy for someone to waylay you on your way home. The front gardens of the houses in the street where you live have too many trees for your safety."

They were right, of course. The great trunks of the planes and the sycamore trees in our London street would be a perfect cover for a man waiting to attack.

As soon as Antonia received the news of Lewis's attempt on my life, she had rushed back to the Castle, shattered and bewildered, and when I was ready to leave the hospital, she fetched me.

There was no need for me to fear Mullaine. Antonia had had all my clothes and personal things moved from the bedroom I had shared with Lewis to another on a lower floor. Here I slept in a huge fourposter bed with intriguing hidden places where the medieval Lairds had kept their ancient weapons ready for a sudden attack.

Apart from our splendidly furnished bedroom, where Lewis's clothes still hung, there was another room which I seldom entered. The door to our small sitting room in which Lewis had attacked me was invariably closed. It was like a haunted room where the victim had become a ghost. Only, I was still alive.

And so, the police believed, was Lewis. His friends, his agent, his manager – everyone who had any known connection with him, including the many women friends he had in England and abroad – were questioned. Nobody could throw any light on his whereabouts. His concert engagements had to be canceled; impresarios and agents all over the world were in a turmoil of indecision.

IV

As I stood at the door I watched Paul kick the football, and it soared across the grass into an archway through the trees which he was using as a goal. I saw him stand perfectly still in sheer amazement at his unexpected prowess. Then I heard my own sudden laughter. It was the first time in so long that I had found anything to be amused at that I was as startled at that happy sound as Paul was by his accurate kick.

One obvious result of that traumatic night in my balanced son was that he had become afraid of the dark. On the other hand, he was neither withdrawn nor nervous. It was just that some strange, protective film seemed to have screened the memory from his mind. At the same time, he was now subject to nightmares.

When I spoke about it to Antonia, she said, "Oh . . . but, Judith, children acquire odd ways. You must remember that he is used to the night sounds of London."

"He has stayed here before and not been afraid."

"It was different then. Lewis—" She began and then abruptly stopped speaking.

"Yes," I agreed quietly. "His father was with us at those times."

Antonia had said quickly, "He seems perfectly happy to me. I can't see any change in him. Let it go, Judith. Stop worrying."

But I had to talk to someone I could trust to understand. I went to see the doctor who lived on Mull and looked after the islanders.

First I swore him to a secrecy he was not happy to agree to. But he eventually saw my point that to bring Paul into any further court hearing might be bad for him and certainly could not add to statements already proven.

I told him about Paul's nightmares. Could they be connected with what he had seen that night — a kind of dream memory that had been closed to the waking one?

The doctor agreed that it could well be. But he advised against trying to waken Paul's conscious memory, particularly since no use could be served by it.

When I had protested, "He's been used to camping in lonely places with his friends, and he has often slept in one wing of our house when Lewis and I were out and the servants

55

were on the floor above. He was never once afraid."

The doctor listened and let me talk.

I asked, "Shall I treat him like an adult and tell him everything? Might bringing it all into the open help to stop the bad dreams?"

The doctor had shaken his head. "He's *not* an adult, Mrs. Mullaine. He's a little boy and a very balanced one. Give him time. He had a terrible shock and didn't know how to cope, so a shutter came down over his immediate memory. His mind refused to acknowledge what he saw. These nightmares probably occur because there is something his subconscious tells him he knows and has chosen to forget. When he's alone at night, in the quiet and the darkness, this memory he can't really remember nags at the back of his mind. He'll come out of it in his own good time. But whatever you do, don't show fear yourself. That way, he will learn from you to overcome his own."

I turned and left the high tower room, ran down the flights of worn stone stairs, through the Great Hall and out into the sunlight.

"Paul . . ." I called.

He was up to his waist in the low wind-dwarfed bushes.

"Paul . . ."

He came at that second call.

"Heavens," I said, "what have you been

doing? I mean before you were in the garden?" I gave his streaked face a light tap. "Playing in the bog?"

He gave me a long, serious look. "We don't play in bogs," he said. "They're dangerous, didn't you know?"

I said on laughter, with mock humility, "I'm sorry. Of course. Then where did you get all that mud?"

"We saw some toads over there" — he pointed to a valley — "and we got down on the ground and watched them for a bit. The heather was all wet."

"It was probably bog myrtle. Go and wash and change. Go on," I urged, "it will soon be dinnertime."

"There were millions and millions of toads and they were all watching us," he said, trying to outstare me, dramatizing as children did at that age, and daring me to moderate his enthusiasm. "Toads have beautiful eyes," he added and leaped up the stairs to his room.

Antonia always changed for dinner. Even here, in this remote place, she managed to look the part of a "resting" star.

It was good for my morale to have her there. Left to myself, I would probably have gone to dinner wearing the sweater and slacks I had worn all day.

The light was still clear over the island, and from my window only the eastern mountains of distant Mull were shadowed. Cathair Mor was a mere quarter mile from it, and between us was Cathair Beag, or little island. It stood some three hundred yards away, a bird-haunted rock less than a quarter of a mile wide — a cluster of needle-sharp columns where the sea pounded and hissed and roared into caves. None of these could ever be inhabited even by men wanting to escape temporarily from the hustle of modern life, for they were partly submerged and the sea here was man's great enemy. Nobody ever went to Cathair Beag except the birds, but once Lewis had told me that he had discovered a way to climb onto the cliffs. It was dangerous and exciting.

"In a place like ours, once someone knows, then everyone does — and that includes Mother, who would probably have a heart attack at the thought of the damage I might do to my hands. So I never told her that on holiday once from University, I climbed the Cathair Beag cliffs."

I had asked him to take me. I had said, "I'm tough. I'd love to try."

He had given me a firm refusal. "I doubt if I could find the way to land there now — it's hidden and very tricky — and certainly I'm not the mountain goat I was once. The best thing

to do with Cathair Beag is to leave it to the birds. Certainly no one could live there, and I wouldn't like to camp for a night on it." He had laughed at his memory. "Even when I managed to get there, I was scared to death of it. Reckless though I was in my youth, I vowed never to try again."

I finished making up my face, clasped a gilt chain set with pearls around my neck and made up my mind that now I knew precisely what I must watch for — I must carry on with my life. The police had given me instructions to remain on Cathair Mor. Gerald Farrar, who was my immediate employer at Thorburn Textiles, had promised to keep my London job open for me, and the headmaster of Paul's school held his place there for him until such time as it was safe for both of us to return to London.

A small teasing breeze, which always seemed to find a myriad of entrances into Mullaine, whipped lightly around me as I crossed the Great Hall. Flemish tapestries hung on the walls. Over an arched door was a long gallery with a beautifully carved oak balustrade. It was a place where in earlier centuries musicians would play for the Laird and his guests. In the center of the gallery stood a Celtic cross carved with worn, mysterious letters. The four tall mullioned windows set high in the vaulted roof let in a soft primrose light. The elaborate oak chandelier swung slightly on the long iron chain suspended from the shadowed roof.

A fireback carved with the date 1646 and a coronet stood in the enormous empty fireplace. Lewis's grandfather had had central heating installed in the Castle, and although it was never adequate, no one had lit a fire in the Great Hall since I had known it. Jutting from the wall were two ancient banners. One was the green, white and purple of the Mullaine family. The other was an oriflamme of crimson and gold, so old now that it was in places almost as transparent as a spider's web. It had been carried triumphantly at Agincourt by Sir Colum Mullaine, the bravest and most reckless of them all, after he had wrested the banner from a French prince.

The Castle always smelled of old stone and sea spray except when Antonia was nearby, and then her lovely perfume defeated all the rest. The many small rooms off the Hall were never used now, except for one which Antonia had turned into a playroom for Paul. It had his gum boots and fishing tackle, a rather warped ping-pong table, cricket bats and books — much read, much loved.

Antonia was at her piano, which stood on a dais at the far end. In earlier days the Laird and his family would dine there while his servants sat in the main hall; now, only the splendid

Bechstein stood against the seven-paneled screen which protected the Hall from drafts.

Antonia was playing softly to herself and obviously had not heard me come down the stairs. I stood listening and enjoying the music, which I recognized, for Lewis had taught me a little understanding of music and a great love for it.

Although she was playing a Brahms love song, Antonia made no attempt to sing. This was her particular tragedy and the reason she had temporarily closed her London house and was staying in the Hebrides. She had known for months that she might never sing again and she could not bear to be surrounded in London by the pity of her friends. So she hid at Mullaine Castle.

At first her doctors had thought it was only a vocal collapse following a prolonged bout of laryngitis. They had warned her, phrasing it in flattering terms, that she was giving too much of herself to her public. But the last throat specialist she had consulted had given her a much more serious warning: "You must prepare yourself for the possibility that you may never sing again. It distresses me to tell you this, but I would be less than honest if I gave you false hope."

The shock to someone like Antonia, whose very pulse was the limelight and whose heartbeat was applause, was desperate.

Standing very quietly now, listening to her playing, I remembered the day when the news was broken to her. Lewis and I had gone to lunch at her Knightsbridge house. We were already in her cream-and-gold drawing room waiting for her when she returned from the specialist.

Standing in the center of the room, as if it were a concert platform, wrapped in furs, elegant and slender, she was quivering with fierce anger. Before she would tell us his verdict, she had demanded, and drunk, two martinis. Then, lifting her glass, she had smashed it against the wall with a wildly dramatic gesture, as if she had come from old Russia instead of a not very exciting suburb of London. I could hear now, as a background to her playing, the tinkling splinter of crystal.

"There he was," she had stormed in her unusually throaty voice, "that wretched man, Sir Temple Cawse, sitting leaning toward me, the mirror fixed on his forehead, staring into my throat, grasping my tongue, spraying, tut-tutting . . . then warning me." She raised her voice with an obviously painful effort. "But I *will*. I – will – sing – again." She had blazed at us as if we were her doctors depriving her of her life force. Then, with complete unexpectedness, since she had no love of the island, she

announced that she intended to spend the spring and summer at Cathair Mor.

Lewis had laughed. "You'll be bored in two days. You know you don't like living away from cities."

She had given him her little secret-cat smile. "We'll see."

He was right. Antonia was bored. But she stayed.

I watched her fingers move lightly over the piano that Paul hated so much. I knew that I was going to have to face trouble here at Mullaine, for Antonia nursed a passionate interest in Paul's future. He must follow his father and his grandmother. He must, also, be a musician. I knew that if Antonia had her way, Paul would be trained and petted and spoiled and bullied into the way she would have him. She wanted for Paul what she had achieved for Lewis, inducing him with rich rewards to live in the artistic cell she created for him.

Quite often, in London, when she had been between opera performances or concerts and these times coincided with Paul's school holiday, she would plead with me to let him come and stay with her. At first I did so, but I soon discovered that her plan had always been to bring along a fine teacher she knew to hear him, and in between the visits, to force him by bribes to practice. A chess set that he wanted was given him as a prize for two hours of practice a day, a fine set of adventure books for three hours. In the end Paul had rebelled, and Antonia had come to me in despair.

"Paul must work at his music."

I had said, laughing, "Poor Paul. He has no talent."

"Lewis didn't know that he was gifted when he first began to play. *I* made him gifted; you could say that I molded him from not very exciting material. You can, you know. Persistence, dedication – you see how it paid off with Lewis."

I had thought, but not had the heart to say, *At what price?*

I had replied that with Lewis there was great potential, but that I saw none in Paul. I said that Paul had a strong streak of determination that would rebel against anything forced on him. I attempted, carefully and kindly and without antipathy, to keep control of my son, to give him freedom to live a normal boy's life. It had not been difficult in London, where we lived separately from Antonia. But here at Cathair Mor, I knew I would have to face many tugs of war over him.

Antonia crashed a note on the piano so suddenly that I jumped. I had a feeling that she had stopped in the middle of a bar, but my thoughts had wandered too far to be certain.

She sat, head bent. Then after a long pause her hands, which had fallen into her lap, reached out again for the keys.

All who had ever visited Cathair Mor must have heard that tune she began to play. It had originally been composed many centuries ago for the Scottish bagpipes. Just as the island of Skye has its special song, "Seagulls and White Wave-crests," as Eriskay has the "Love Lilt," so Cathair Mor has its own music.

As Antonia played it, I said the words over to myself, each one coming reluctantly into my mind, because although I couldn't help myself, I didn't want to remember them.

> *"In the twilight of the morning*
> *The fiery man came*
> *Out of the mists on the heathered hills*
> *That brooded over Mullaine.*
> *'I am he returned to you,*
> *I, who you thought was dead.*
> *And I am the Laird of Cathair,'*
> *The red man said."*

Lewis was red-headed . . .

V

The music had stopped, yet it raged like a fire
in my head. It was as if every word was meant
for me.

"Why did you play that?"

She looked at me over her shoulder, surprised. "Do you know, Judith, I have no idea.
In a way I didn't play it, my fingers did."

The silence between us was too long. In a
stone alcove off the hall a clock struck. I
counted the hours. Six. Outside, the light was
still strong and clear, gilding the elaborate
stonework of the windows. Sunset and twilight
lingered long in the Hebrides.

Out of the huge hall's silence, Antonia said,
"I wonder if Lewis and Shane kept in touch
with one another after Shane left for the Middle East?"

"I believe they could have. But Lewis never
talked of him."

Antonia's fingers touched the piano keys
lightly. "I disliked their friendship when Lewis
was young. Shane encouraged him to skip

66

piano practice and go climbing and wasting his time with the fishing people down at the loch. He is a very strong character and, I felt, a bad influence."

I thought, And were you a very good one, Antonia? Was Shane, perhaps, giving Lewis relief from the burden of a piano he only later came to love? I could imagine her linking us, Shane and I, because we were the spoilers of talent, he in Lewis's youth, I because of the police involvement and a subsequent ruined career.

I said, "So he's not like Rory?"

"Almost the complete opposite." She got up from the piano. "Rory is gentle and rather simple, as you know, and drowned in island legends. Shane Kilarran is a civil engineer and has no time for fantasy. So many years away . . ." she said thoughtfully as she came slowly down the steps from the dais. "I wonder *why* he is back now?"

"If it's his home . . ."

"Since Rory is incapable, as you must have noticed, of running the house himself, Shane has done it – and very effectively – from a distance all this time. It's Jeannie and Dru McColl who look after the place." She turned to the stairs leading up to the drawing room. "Let's go and find that martini. By the way, I saw Paul just now slipping out of the door."

"Trying to keep that boy indoors," I said lightly, "is like trying to harness the wind."

"He will have to learn to *be* harnessed," Antonia said. "Talent needs it and —"

I was out of hearing. It was better than arguing all over again that Paul had neither musical talent nor any liking for the concert grand on the dais.

The heavy door was ajar. I pushed it open and stepped outside.

Paul had changed and had probably washed his face, but he was down by the larch wood getting dirty again.

I called to him and he turned, saying, "I lost one of my puzzles here."

"Then you can look for it in the morning. It hasn't got legs, so it won't run way. Come along in."

He plunged his hand to the ground and held up a small object that shone in the light. "I've found it," he said. "And now my hands are dirty again." Blue eyes dancing, he started to run past me.

I caught his arm. "What's this sudden interest in water?"

"It's nice to be clean."

"I don't trust it." Then I added, suspicious, "What have you got in the bathroom?"

He gave me a sideways look. "It's only a *very* little tadpole."

68

"In the bath?"

"Well, yes."

"Then get Rosheen to find you a jar. It will be just as happy swimming in that."

"It wouldn't have much room to stretch itself, though, would it?"

It wasn't an intelligent remark from an intelligent child. I knew my Paul. He was using every way he could think of to keep us talking outside, because that was where he always wanted to be, always the open air, never enclosed spaces.

I said firmly, "Take that tadpole out of the bath."

He grinned at me and ran into the Castle. I heard him calling Rosheen, his voice making hollow sounds among the arches of the Great Hall.

I wandered a little way over the roughly cut lawn. In the distance, across the glen, I could see the grey line of Inverkyle Abbey, the other great house that dominated the island — Shane and Rory Kilarran's home.

I stood looking at it, and remembered my first sight of that fine three-arched roof when Lewis had brought me, upon our engagement, to Mullaine Castle.

He had said, "The Kilarrans have been at Inverkyle Abbey as long as we've been at Mullaine. For centuries there were feuds between the two families as to who were the real lairds. We won." Then he had added, laughing, "With Shane always away on one of his engineering projects and Rory a sweet-tempered simpleton, it's a good thing that the Mullaines won the island."

I learned something about the Kilarrans' Abbey home on that visit. Originally built in the fifteenth century, it had been planned as a monastery for a breakaway order of monks. They had run out of money before the Abbey was completed and their religious order became absorbed by one on another island.

Soon after the monks left, the first Kilarran took over, bringing his family and his fortunes from Tobermory after a brief and bloody battle to annex lands from a brother chieftain. The outer shell of the partly built Inverkyle Abbey was retained, but the inside was adapted as a home. It was then that the feuding and dueling between the two great families of Cathair Mor began.

"Though," Lewis added, "why they wanted to fight over a pint-sized piece of land populated by a handful of people, I'll never know. In any case, it's mine now, Clea darling, for what it's worth."

On that misty September morning, as we sat together on my first visit to the island, Lewis told me more important things. I remembered how, as he spoke, the clouds hovered over the Brenlorns like formless ghosts.

"You'll have to know, Clea, that the legal side of ownership of the island is laid down very clearly. If the Laird — and that's me now — is ever away from Cathair Mor, then — should his mother be still living (and Antonia most certainly is) — she must act as Laird in his place. But if I should drive my car into a tree or do anything that shortens my wonderful life, then our eldest son will inherit the title. In that case, if he were under age, you would act as a kind of regent for him. It's nothing to alarm you. Cathair Mor runs itself."

I had said, wildly impulsive, blindly in love, "You're young and strong. You'll live forever. We'll both live forever."

I turned from the dark Gothic outline of the Abbey across the glen and looked at Lewis's towered home. It is said that probably no country in Europe has more castles than Scotland.

Well guarded by the sea, Mullaine was built of pink granite, heavily darkened over the centuries but still with the faint flush of its original color showing through. The experts had said that at one time, centuries ago, a small seam of the stone must have run across a corner of Cathair Mor. They had discussed how it could have appeared, like some changeling,

71

among the dark basalt forming the crags that almost ringed the island.

The Castle was built on a rise above the glen, so that although I went upstairs to it, my bedroom was on the ground floor at the back. It would have been fairly easy to crawl through the deep aperture in the four-foot-thick wall and land on the grass outside. Paul's room was above mine, and countless small rooms led from flights of stone steps. Antonia's suite was in the tower above and just to the right of my room.

There were only three really large rooms, the enormous and stately Great Hall, the drawing room and the dining room, created by a previous Mullaine who had torn down the walls.

When I first saw Mullaine against a pale-green evening light, it was like a castle of legend. A friend of Antonia's, who had come to visit her had exclaimed, "It's King Arthur's Camelot all over again!"

But Camelot had had its dark side, its mysteries and its violence. So had Mullaine.

It had not been built as a military castle, like Edinburgh or Stirling, but as a fortified home. It was a place of safety for the Laird and his family and his servants in the turbulent times of Scotland's fiery past. Mullaine was therefore not large, but the splendid tower thrust upward and the Gothic windows were arched oblongs of light where the sun caught them. Grass grew almost to its walls, and for most of the year the grounds surrounding the Castle were tinted with shades of green. Flowers were scarce. Antonia and Lewis and I were so seldom there, and Rosheen and Duncan, with typical Hebridean thrift, would not, as they would put it, "be wasting time on such things as flowers when there's only us most of the year to see them."

Growing flowers on the raised ground of Mullaine Castle would be a formidable task, anyway, unless care was taken to protect the beds from the winter storms and the salt tang of the air. Wild flowers did bloom, however. They waved like proud, defiant little banners among the grass, but they had to be sought and clusters of them were few and far between. It was different in the glen and on the *machair* — the grassy place above the beach. Here buttercups and speedwell and marsh marigolds flourished in the hollows, and it was said that in early summer the cows had clover-scented breath.

The wind had risen in the last hour and was breaking the translucent quiet and pushing strongly against me. I sensed that it was the forerunner of rain, but for the moment the world of Cathair Mor was rich with summer. From where I stood, the rocky islet of Cathair

Beag looked so close that the narrow strip of sea dividing it from us seemed to have ebbed away and the two islands, Big Cathair and Little Cathair, were one.

While I was on the island, there was no pressure from reporters wanting a story, no well-meaning friends "looking in" to see how I was. The police had merely given out a rumor that I was "resting in the country." I was also guarded by the bulky figure of Ulad MacNeill, who lived in a cottage by the landing pier on Mull, built as a tie-up for the launches, the *Midir* belonging to Mullaine and the *Lennonan*, which was the Abbey's boat. He was a kind of self-imposed coast guard, for in winter the crossing, though very short, was difficult.

In spite of this temporary security, I felt a sudden chill as I stood in the Castle grounds, and even when I turned and went inside, it was without any sense of warmth or belonging. Mullaine sent out no signals to me that it would ever become my beloved home. It was beautiful and remote and medieval and loaded with atmosphere. It was Lewis's home – and my uncertain refuge.

Antonia and I dined on lobster, freshly caught. Rosheen disliked doing "all that fancy stuff," so although Antonia was addicted to French cuisine, she had to put up with

Rosheen's simpler cooking at Mullaine. When the ice cream course came, I passed it over to Paul, who lapped it up as if I had starved him for weeks.

After dinner Paul left us. He and Duncan played wild games of table tennis, each of them possessing more zest than skill. Their shouts and yells of triumph and defeat could be heard only dimly through the great thick walls of Mullaine.

Antonia had always said that without the telephone as a link to the mainland, she could never have remained even for a week on the island. Some years ago a cable had been laid under the sea, and the two great houses, Mullaine and Inverkyle, were linked to Scotland.

The telephone bell rang sharply as Antonia and I went into the drawing room and she rushed to answer it.

I stood at the drawing-room window. The light was still rich and clear over the island and everything was so quiet that when I heard a sound coming sharply out of the peace, it startled me. It was distant and unidentifiable, a beckoning finger of sound which I could only interpret as a call of distress.

I stood very still and heard the sound again. It was human and yet unlike any other voice I had ever heard — long-drawn and primitive.

Footsteps sounded behind me and I swung

around. Hands in the pockets of his jeans, Paul said with wicked delight, "I made you jump, didn't I?"

"No. But you've saved me coming to look for you."

"Can I go down to the beach?"

"It's too late."

"But I won't go to bed for hours yet," he said reasonably. "I don't like bed here. It's too big. Castles shouldn't be lived in. I like little places."

"But you're happy here?"

"Oh yes." He was very matter-of-fact about it. "It's fun in daytime. What were you looking at when I came in?"

"Just a lovely sky."

"It's funny." He was at my side. "It's sort of come alive, hasn't it?"

"What has?"

"Over there —" He pointed to a place just beyond the small larch wood.

He was right. Small specks of crimson burned steadily where the wind swung the lower branches of the trees. It was as if a cluster of enormous fireflies had taken up positions for a camera shot.

"It's not a sunset," I said sharply. "It's a fire . . . over by Inverkyle. Inverkyle Abbey —"

"That's built of stone," my son said scornfully, "and stone doesn't burn. Didn't you know −?"

"You can give me a lesson later on," I called back as I raced to the door. "They may need help there. Stay where you are. Stay indoors."

"But I *want* to come." He darted in front of me.

I gripped his coat collar. "No, Paul . . ."

"But if −"

"And no 'ifs,' " I said, holding onto my small, squirming son.

Antonia was on the stairs. "There's a fire," I called to her.

"I heard. They have a loud cry here, one that carries, and they make it to warn each other whenever there is a crisis, like a fire or a flood. I was just going to see Duncan, but he must have heard it too."

"I'll go and see if I can help," I said. "There may be something I can do − save furniture, fetch buckets for water . . . Keep Paul here, will you?"

"Of course."

He wriggled out of my grasp. "I don't see −"

"No, darling, you don't. But just for once I can't waste time explaining." I shot away from him and heard Antonia talking to him.

As I ran I thought, I couldn't explain to you, anyway. Because what crossed my mind as he darted ahead of me was that perhaps both the fire and the call were an enticement, a decoy. Perhaps Lewis was somewhere out there with a plan for abducting his son.

But as I went across the lush grass I knew perfectly well that I was indulging in an extravaganza of black fear. When one is afraid, imagination has to be carefully controlled. No one was lurking out there to trap me. This was a genuine fire.

There were two ways from the Castle to the Abbey. I took the one through the larch wood. Although it was still light, the midsummer green of the pointed trees had become huge shadows. I could see that the fire was coming not from Inverkyle, but from a small stone cottage just in front of the pines that guarded the Abbey.

An old man, Murdo MacClaut, lived there. He had once been ferryman for the Cathair Mor boats and was now pensioned off, the money provided jointly by the Mullaines and the Kilarrans. He spent his time with his goat, his cow and his few hens.

I kept stumbling over the tufts of coarse bracken and slipping over last year's larch needles that carpeted the ground. Once I paused, wondering if I should go on. The red glow in the distance was fading quickly. Then, out of the silence around me, I heard a movement. I darted behind a tree, tense and waiting. Once again I fought the flash of fear, telling myself that this was imagination gone crazy and that, as I could see nothing, the sound must have been merely a squirrel or a pine marten, more disturbed by me than I was by it.

I left the shelter of the tree and began to run. The wind swung in the tops of the trees and the branches curved like the arms of dancers.

After a few more minutes through the pathless wood, I was near enough to see figures moving in the distance, but too far to hear voices. The glow had almost disappeared and the wind must have blown any acrid fumes in the opposite direction, for all I could smell was the scent of wild thyme and the tang of the sea.

Almost at the edge of the wood was a thick juniper bush. It stood blocking my way, and as I went around it my arm brushed the upthrust branches.

The man before me appeared suddenly, as if he had been waiting for me. We met head-on, and I took a swift step backward, half stumbling into the bush. The hurricane lamp in his right hand swung.

"I brought it as a precaution," he said, and his voice had only a slight Scottish burr. "It was just possible that the blaze would take longer to put out and we'd be at it at nightfall."

I said to the stranger, "Murdo is very old. Did he fall while carrying a lamp?"

"That's about it. But he's quite unhurt. Our housekeeper, Jeannie, and her husband, Dru, spotted the fire almost as soon as it started. By the way, I'm Shane Kilarran. And you are Lewis's wife? Am I right?"

"Yes."

He stood looking down at me, his back to the western sun, his face shadowed by the tall larch trees. "Judith Mullaine," he said. "You're not Scottish, are you?"

"No. I was born in Devonshire."

"The West Country," he said slowly. "So very English."

"Antonia told me today that you had just returned from the Middle East."

"Iran."

"After years —"

"Eight, to be exact. But there comes a time when a job is done."

"Building beautiful places —"

"My very first job," he interrupted with a hint of impatience, "was an enclosure for polar bears at a zoo in Switzerland. I build functional things. I've missed the era when palaces were created for kings and marble stairways for film stars."

"And now you've returned to live here at the Abbey?"

"Good God, no! A man doesn't retire at thirty-eight. I'm going to work in the London

80

office for a while, on a big project scheduled there. But it's necessary for me to return to my island now and again."

His island, Cathair Mor. His home, Inverkyle Abbey.

"Of course," I said, and glanced across at the mauve- and charcoal-tinted hills and the gleaming sea. I could understand. I could love Cathair Mor too, if only the shadow of its Laird did not stalk me.

"Is there much damage at Murdo's cottage?"

"Only in his shed, where he keeps all the newspapers anyone on the island has ever read. He's up at the Abbey swearing and mumbling. Tell me, why did I startle you?"

The change of conversation caught me off guard. "I thought you might be . . . someone else."

With an unexpected swiftness he reached out and gripped my wrist, drawing me from the edge of the wood into the rich western light. "That's better. Now I can see what you look like. Well! So you are Judith."

"You've heard . . . ?"

He did not even pretend to misunderstand me. "Of course. Even before I came home, I knew all about it. I read the story the newspapers carried."

His voice was no less pleasant, and yet I could have taken exception to his choice of words. It was possible to take them two ways. That he accepted what he had read. Or, more probably, that behind what had been written about the case, he guessed there were inaccuracies. I chose to ignore that implication – we were strangers and my own anxieties were far too great for me to add to them by probing Shane Kilarran's mind as to whether or not he believed the printed stories.

Instead, I said with interest, "You and Lewis were friends, weren't you, when you both lived here?"

"Yes."

"Did you write often to one another while you were in Iran?"

He said, "If by 'writing often' you mean did we keep up a once-a-week correspondence, no."

"But you did keep in touch?"

He paused before answering, and then I saw his eyes narrow as if I were guilty of some intrusion.

"I mean –" I added, and knew there was absolutely no reason why my voice should sound so hesitant and apologetic. "I mean the friendship was . . . was never really broken, was it?"

"No."

"Lewis always said he hated writing letters . . ."

"What are you trying to ask me, Judith?" His eyes were fixed on me, silver-light, curiously impersonal, as if, although he asked, he didn't really care whether I answered or not.

I did answer. I said, "I just wondered what he told you about our life together."

"Oh, odd bits of news. Lewis was never close to his father, and Antonia was so often away, absorbed in her concerts. I was static in Iran. He knew he could always contact me there."

"He had so many friends."

"Ah, but I understand him. I don't think many people do. Do they, Judith?"

I felt that it was not so much a question as a subtle accusation. I said in quick defense, "Do any of us really understand anyone else?"

"That's too deep a question for the moment." He took a step away from me as if the conversation were over. "And now I should get back, if I were you. There are plenty of helpers salvaging the remains of MacClaut's collection of rubbish. Goodnight."

He left me so quickly that it seemed, as I stood watching, that mere moments changed him from a stranger with a personality that had made an immediate impact, to an anonymous shadow vanishing through the pines that formed a semicircle around the eastern ring of Inverkyle Abbey. Only the lamp he carried seemed real, shining like a small, fiery orange between the tall black trunks of the guardian trees.

VI

It was obvious, now that it was too late, that there were important questions I should have asked Shane.

"Have you heard from Lewis?" . . . "Is there anything at all you can think of that might help the police?"

And if those questions brought no response, then the final plea: "Not for my sake, but for Paul's. Because Lewis intends to take him from me; he is no longer sane when crossed. If you can, help me, *please help me.*"

I had said none of the important things. Instead, we had talked almost as if we were strangers possessing a mutual acquaintance. And that was exactly what we were.

Shane had been perfectly polite, yet as I went through the glen I had a feeling that had I asked the questions I had wanted to, Shane would have avoided them adroitly. Remembering the strong, remote face that had looked down at me out of the melting primrose light, I doubted if Kilarran would ever offer me anything more than cool courtesy.

I turned and walked toward Murdo Mac-Claut's cottage. Three men were carrying piles of boxes from outside the charred mass of wood that was once his lean-to and disappearing with them into the stone cottages. Bundles of half-burned newspapers, their edges curled up like dry brown leaves, were piled by the stone wall. A rusty bicycle, a saw and a wooden chair lay on the rough high grass inside the low stone wall with which all the crofters guarded their small territories.

Now that I was on the scene, the smell of charred paper and chemical from an extinguisher, probably brought from Inverkyle Abbey, was strong.

Crofters and fishermen were hovering everywhere, talking among themselves in Gaelic, eying the shambles inside the shed and then looking covertly toward the Abbey, as if expecting old Murdo to appear and perhaps accuse them of looting his untidy two-room home. For his reputation as an acquisitive miser had been known and laughed about for years on Cathair Mor.

It was obvious that my help was not needed and that the excitement for the islemen was over. But they hung around, just watching, as an excuse for doing what they loved — meeting and gossiping.

The islanders were poor, judged by city standards, but though they were free to leave, few did. They clung to Cathair Mor partly out of habit, partly because they were a closed community which had grown together through generations and could not visualize a life apart. I saw their cottages dotting the lowlands around the loch. With all the lonely expanse of Cathair Mor, the islanders clustered together for companionship, their homes always welcome places, the kettle always boiling for the incessant cup of tea.

Rory Kilarran was squatting on a box outside Murdo's cottage, cramming papers into a plastic bag. I had met him many times and liked him. He had a deep affinity with the island, and even as a boy, had not been sent away to school. His father, Neil Kilarran, discovered that Rory was quite incapable of learning and had more or less discarded him, leaving him to his mother and the servant.

Rory was simple, guileless and charming. His only learning was the folklore of the Hebrides. He had heard, since he was a child, all the old stories of faery people and of what the islanders called "The Sight" – the second sight of the Celts. Strangely enough, Rory could learn and remember these tales as if they were part of some old memory. It was sad that there were so few island children born on Cathair

Mor for Rory to delight with his tales.

I found him peering closely at a small sheet of notepaper, and he was so absorbed, I thought with amusement that he had probably found another folklore tale to tell us all.

His hair was bright; his ears stuck out like two little pink wings, their naïve quality offset by his eyes, which had a slanting, pagan look. Unlike Shane, Rory was short and thick-set, and yet every movement was curiously graceful, as if a dancer was hidden inside him.

"Hullo," I greeted him. "I came to see if I could help, but it seems it wasn't much of a fire, after all."

Rory pushed the sheet of paper he was holding into his pocket in his typical flustered way. When something or someone surprised him, anything he held would be pushed into pockets, as if, like a squirrel, he had to hoard and hide whatever was in his grasp. So much found its way into Rory's pockets that they always bulged.

He picked up the plastic bag and scrambled to his feet. "Oh, Judith." His smile was broad and kind. "How good of you. But it's just some papers in the shed that caught alight. There's no window in there and Murdo went in carrying a candle, tripped and fell. That's what began it."

"So many bundles of papers!" I looked about me.

Rory chuckled. "And he's not one for reading, either." The Scottish burr of his voice was much stronger than Shane's.

"I've just met your brother," I said.

"Ach, is that so?" The lilt became more prominent. "Well, you had to do that sometime." He set the bag down just inside the cottage door. "Murdo won't miss what's got burned." He pointed to a bundle of scorched newspapers that had been swept into a corner of the small plot of walled-in land in front of the cottage.

"Antonia was surprised when she heard that Shane was home," I said. "I'd have thought the islanders would have all been talking about it — so little happens here."

"They didn't know he was coming. Even I didn't know until the cable arrived the day before yesterday."

"So after all this time away, he just appears."

Rory was picking up odd scraps blown over the ground. "Yes."

I had no good reason for persisting, but I did. "He left, then, in a hurry?"

"Oh, his work in Iran was finished, so he said."

"I see . . ."

But I didn't. After eight years away surely the

matter of departure wouldn't be a sudden cable home? Antonia had said, "I wonder why he has come back?"

I said, searching for something behind Rory's vague answers, "You must be very glad to see your brother again."

Rory didn't give me a direct answer. "Oh, Jeannie and Dru are wonderful in the way they look after the Abbey, but there's so much to be done. Because, you see, I'm hopeless. I can't even check the accounts properly. Do you know, I still add up figures on my fingers just as I did at school?"

I brought him gently back to the subject of his brother. "It will be company for you to have Shane here."

"We've never been together much. Shane is too clever for me. It was always Lewis —" He put his hand quickly over his mouth, stifling his words, as a child would do. "Oh, Judith, I'm sorry. I —"

"It's all right," I reassured him, and glanced around for some diversion to ease Rory's embarrassment.

Two men came out of the charred shed carrying a motley of spades and hammers and boxes of nails. I knew them both; I had watched them down on the beach mending their nets.

"Good evening," I greeted them. "I saw the

fire from a distance."

" 'Tis all out now, that fire. I've been after tellin' MacClaut it's time he cleared that shed." Logan MacRobert was one of my favorite islanders. It was said that he could sing the island songs so loudly that they could be heard on the far side, where the rocks stood stark like those on the famous pillar-island of Staffa. The other man, Alec Jevon, fished for a living and supplied the Castle with rich turbot and sole, and sometimes with oysters found in the far bay of Du-i-linn.

Logan went on in his rich island voice, "Well, 'tis for the best. Now he's rid of that lot, there'll be more room to store his peat for his winter fires."

While Logan was talking, Rory had been watching me. "You shivered, Judith. You're cold. Go back. There's nothing to be done here. We'll take the rest of the stuff into Murdo's cottage and he can sort it out himself when he's finished the whiskey he'll be lapping up in Jeannie's kitchen." Then he added almost shyly, "Will I see Paul tomorrow?"

"He's looking forward to it. He tells me you're teaching him to fish."

"Down just beyond the loch, with an old rod of mine. It's a fine rod for beginners."

"Paul is thrilled, and I'm so glad. There isn't a lot for a boy to do here, away from all his friends, and he loves being with you."

"You're so kind, Judith. And I like having Paul around. He listens."

I knew what he meant. Adults weren't inclined to pay much attention to Rory.

I left the others to the final clearing-up, and as I passed small groups of people I smiled at them and they called a greeting in their soft Gaelic voices.

I took a different way back to Mullaine, walking where the buttercups were like tiny suns and the grass was green as emeralds after recent rain. I could have felt such peace had it not been for the tension that was now my perpetual shadow. And when I heard a sound that rose in a moment of quiet between the rhythmic swish of the sea against the rocks, I was as alert to fear as I had been earlier in the wood.

It came again — an odd, pagan sound, at once lonely and mocking. But I breathed freely, realizing it was Murdo's goat probably protesting at being disturbed by the men clamoring around the cottage. She had a name — Aithne — and like all the goats of the islands, she was descended from the originals that came from Asia.

I reached the Castle. Down by the clear rushing stream that branched off just before it came to the glen, a heron stood patiently awaiting an unaware trout. It was tall and slender and deadly — and as it heard me it soared into the air with a great sweep of wings.

As I pushed open the Castle door, I could hear Antonia on the telephone. She was saying, "Just a minute . . . Judith is here. There's been a fire — such an excitement here, where nothing happens! — and she went down to see if she could help." She covered the mouthpiece of the telephone and turned to me. "It's Faith Lynton giving me the London gossip. Was the fire bad?"

"No, just some newspapers in Murdo's shed."

"Oh, good." She turned back to the telephone.

As I passed her I whispered, "Where is Paul?"

"In his playroom, I believe. He wanted to go out and I knew that you didn't want him to, so I told him to stay where he was . . . Oh, Faith? . . . Sorry . . . I was saying something to Judith."

Paul was not in his playroom off the Great Hall, nor was he in the kitchen coaxing a meringue out of Rosheen. I ran to his bedroom. It was reasonably tidy — and empty. I searched the garden, calling him.

Antonia had finished her telephone conversation and was at the door.

"I can't find Paul," I said.

"Don't worry. As soon as I took my eyes off him he probably slipped out to see the fun of the fire." She added with a little shudder, "Children are so gruesome."

I turned without a word and ran back through the wood. It was longer this second time, like a dream-run that never comes to an end. All the way I tried to fight a small panic. When Paul was with the children nearby, or with Rory, I felt no fear for him. But if he was somewhere alone on the island, in spite of police assurances that we were in the safest place, I could not stop the sense of someone watching and waiting.

A small group of men and women were still sitting on Murdo's wall, kicking their heels and talking. They hadn't seen Paul. Should they go and look for him?

Out of breath, fighting fear, I said, "Thank you, but let's just wait. He may have gone to the Abbey to see Rory."

He hadn't. Jeannie shook her sandy head. No, he had come that morning to go fishing with Mr. Rory, but she hadn't seen him since.

"He's missing," I said, "and it will be dark in a little while, and —" I stopped. It was not for me to tell strangers that my usually brave son was afraid of the dark. Nor why I was afraid for him.

Jeannie called to Dru, who came through the

93

door from the cloister, wiping his hands on his striped apron. "Are ye be after lookin' for me?"

"No, Dru. It's Paul. He's missing. I wondered if you had seen him."

"The wee laddie? Ach, but he'll no be far. There's nothin' daft aboot him." He looked keenly at me from under pale eyebrows.

Jeannie said sharply. "Ye'd better be oot, *bodach*, searchin' for him an' not standin' there."

"Thank you, Jeannie," I said quickly, "but I'll go back to the Castle first. Paul could have returned by now from some place where he was hiding. If he isn't, I'll let you know."

"Aye, ye do that, lassie. Use that telephone thing and we'll go oot, and don't ye worrit now, he'll no be far away."

It was kindly meant, but I did worry. I went back through the bright, beautiful evening — stumbling, running, pushing forward toward the flushed pink stone that was Mullaine.

Paul had not returned. Duncan and I searched all the likely places while Antonia and Rosheen combed every odd, dark corner of the Castle. Antonia said, "Some of the doors to the very small rooms are difficult and sometimes jam."

When the telephone rang, it was Rory asking if we had found Paul.

"No," I said. *"No . . ."*

94

"Then I'll collect some of the men who are hanging around the loch and we'll start a search."

"Oh, Rory, if you would —" My voice broke.

"You'll see us soon coming your way," Rory said, "and the men will do what they do when they've lost a sheep or a goat — they fan out over the moors. It's bad on the moors when it's really dark."

"I'll see you outside," I said and replaced the receiver.

It was a warm evening, but I had no idea how long our search would be, so I slid into a thick sweater, white so that it would show up if Paul was looking out for us. I put on heavy shoes and picked up a flashlight from a stone ledge near the door.

Antonia wouldn't be coming with us. I didn't want her to, anyway. She would be very likely to twist an ankle or get tired after the first half-hour of walking. Half an hour . . . an hour . . . I didn't dare think further than that, for when it was dark in the valleys Paul would be afraid.

If he was alone . . .

"You mustn't worry, Judith. You really mustn't," Antonia said. "I'm sure he's just hiding from us out of sheer mischief. Anyway, I'll be here."

I ran out to await the men, whom I could already see across the glen. Logan MacRobert's voice carried over the hiss of the sea. "Coo-eee . . . Coo-ee . . ." I didn't wonder whether, wherever he was, Paul might hear that sound. I was too afraid that he might not be alone.

VII

There were ten of us spread out in a line, fanning from the cliffs on the right to the last ridge of the moors on the left.

I joined the searchers, walking between Rory and Dru McColl. Shane was not with us, and for some reason I couldn't explain, I was glad. The men carried either flashlights or hurricane lamps, for in such wild country we could still be searching when darkness fell.

We passed the scattered cottages of the crofters and the fishermen. Most of the houses were low in order to protect them from the fierce winter gales. But in summer all the doors were open, and as we passed, the women came out, leaning on their low dry-stone walls and calling reassurances. The grapevine that relayed information was even more powerful here than in English villages. Everyone knew that the Laird's son was missing.

Highland cattle watched us; sheep, with their heads lowered, skipped out of our way. The men were so spread out that it was impossible to talk to them, but the voices of the searchers calling, "Paul ... Coo-ee ... Paul, laddie ..." warmed me with gratitude.

The rolling treeless moors seemed all too still except for the occasional cry of a disturbed bird. We had left the sheep-grazed grass and the smug homesteads. Here the moors, known as the Brenlorns, stretched out, treeless and remote.

"He'll not get far," Rory called. "Maybe he's back at the Castle now, and Antonia can't get word to you."

His reassurance did nothing to cheer me. I was wrapped in a fear that was entirely different from that of the rest of the party. I knew they believed my son had lost his way. I wasn't even in a state to think — only to feel. I was staring into a nightmare created by my demon fear. Against the background of the purple heather, the swaying cotton grass, the gilded beauty of the marsh marigolds in the damp hollows, I imagined the newspaper headlines:

MISSING PIANIST'S SON DISAPPEARS
KIDNAP FEARED

For now that he had ruined his career, Paul was not Lewis's only need. He had earned large sums by his music but he had spent lavishly. He would know that I had little money of my own, but Antonia was rich. And Antonia would pay. Ransom money would enable Lewis to escape, taking his son — my son — with him.

I stumbled through the tough ridges of heather and scree, and glanced at my watch. It was nine o'clock and the sun, easing its way to the northwest, was still brilliant. I scanned the silver-blue sea. Lewis could have been waiting somewhere out there with a boat. But the sea was wide and empty, and that could merely mean either I was too late or that the escape route was on the eastern side of the island, hidden from us by the last rolling shoulder of the moors.

I hurried and caught up with Rory. "Were the two launches down at the pier?"

"I don't know. I didn't look."

"If Paul —"

He said, "But Paul could never manage either of them by himself. He loves the sea, but the boats are far too big for him to handle."

"I didn't mean —"

"Hey, be careful!" Rory steadied me as I slipped over a rock concealed by a cluster of white bell heather. White heather for luck . . . *Oh God, let that small, innocent superstition be true.*

"Paul . . ." Their voices came, ringing over the moors. We climbed higher, peering into gullies and clusters of bracken.

I thanked heaven that it was a small island and that these men knew every path trodden by the Blackface sheep, every curve and dip of the way. We soon left the scattered cottages behind. Now all we could see were the moors, rich with heather and grey with the treacherous scree which trapped unwary feet, so that if I didn't look where I was going, I slithered and stumbled.

I had never before been so far across the moors, but I cared nothing for the hazards, the danger of a peat bog or an unexpected pool where water lilies grew. Minutes seemed to become hours, and I had to keep telling myself that panic helped no one.

The sky was streaked with color, pale green and primrose, like a field in spring; the wind had died down and a gentle melancholy lay over the moors.

"He could have fallen somewhere and not be able to get up," Rory said. "But he'll hear us calling and then he'll answer."

In the distance, the last birds to seek their nests in the cliffs — the cormorants, the gulls and the oyster-catchers — rode the light current of air. The harsh grass whipped my ankles and heather moths rose like little flurries of thistle-down. The green whirls of bracken hid the rabbit holes and in the boggy places the air was peat-scented.

I was listening all the time.

Rory began to talk, ambling by my side, his brilliant blue eyes looking all the while ahead of him, missing nothing. "There's a place here on the Brenlorns that's the real 'Land of the Ever Young.' You know, they call it Tir-nan-Og. All Scottish islemen know the story. But no one has ever found the spot. We'll look for it together one day, shall we, Judith? You and I. We must look for a hollow hill. That's where They live, the lordly ones. They say that you'd know the place because it's always ringed with blue butterflies that never sleep."

"Yes ... Yes ... You told me once before. But *please* keep on calling. Paul ... Paul..."

Rory said sadly, "I only wanted to take your mind off all this."

"I'm sorry, but it won't." I stopped to get my breath, and stood looking out over the wide valley that lay between the moors we had just climbed and the wide needle-sharp rocks that guarded the southwest corner of the island.

Etched against the background of the sky was a lovely ship, a three-masted schooner. Her russet canvas billowed in the breeze and she was gliding into the sunset like something out of a Gaelic dream.

"Aye," Rory said, also watching the ship, "she's fine, isn't she? She belongs to Kieran

101

MacBuie. He's a Scottish millionaire whose great-great-great-grandfather owned clipper ships that sailed the China seas. It's MacBuie's hobby, that ship, and he lends it out to young lads who want to learn to sail her."

On a different occasion it would have so fascinated me that I would have watched the ship until she disappeared.

"And they do say that —"

"*Rory!*" I cried, emotionally exhausted. "I can't listen to your stories now. It's Paul —"

He took my hand. "Do I talk too much?" he asked like a child.

"No, of course you don't. But I'm too worried to listen now."

We continued our nightmarish search, walking slowly, alert for any movement in the dips and hollows of the moors. The sun slid very slowly northwest, but it would be some time before twilight and the "gloaming" was over and night fell. And before that, we had to find Paul.

Blind to the beauty around me, I stumbled on, down from the moors to the valley, brushing away the summer midges that plagued us.

I was seeing the last of the sailing ship when the shout came — rising and falling, carrying over the quiet land.

"They've found him, Judith. That's Logan's

voice and when he calls like that, it's good news."

Rory began to run, and I, less sure-footed, floundered behind him, pitched forward once as I slithered down the steep drop toward the strips of bright green *machair* that lay between us and the cliffs. Logan's cry was all I cared about. They had found Paul.

I could see the men ahead of me moving one by one, tucking in their stomachs, tensing their shoulders as they edged between an almost hidden cleft in the soaring precipices of rock. I saw something else, too.

"Rory, look . . ." I pointed, shaking with joy. Something dear and familiar and bright scarlet waved in the wind. It was tied to a rock in a place where the cliff fell from a high point to one only a few feet from the ground, and it waved cheerfully in a breeze I couldn't feel.

"That's Paul's scarf," I said. "Oh, Rory . . ."

The men had all disappeared, as if the great cliff had swallowed them up. Then, free of the moors, Rory and I raced over the *machair* toward the cleft in the rock. I heard the men laughing and talking, and I heard a young voice — Paul calling, "Hi. I'm here . . ."

"And Hi, I'm coming," I shouted back, adding, under my breath, angry and happy all at once, "You little brat, giving us this scare."

"It's awfully narrow," Rory said as we approached the cleft in the rock. "I wonder how Jaimie MacDonald managed. He's like a giant." He gave his little giggle. "The sea seems to be some way away, so that opening in the rocks must be quite a long one. Do you think Jaimie has got stuck in there somewhere?"

I said, with both my hands reaching out to the hard grey rock, "If he is, I'll climb over him." I began to squeeze my way through the spurs and ridges of rock that stuck out in all the most difficult places for a human body to manipulate, and began to have frantic fears that a little boy could have squeezed through a cleft that was impossible for adults. I was cheered by the fact that men twice my width had managed it. But what happened around each hidden corner I had no idea. They could have piled up like a traffic jam, unable to go any further.

I paused by a lip of rock that was jabbing my stomach and called loudly, "Is Paul hurt?!"

"*Ha Nyall . . . Ha Nyall . . .*" they called back, and the Gaelic "No" was sheer joy to my ears.

The passage between the tall cliffs was angled first one way, then another, so that only a few feet were visible at a time. There was an occasional sharp cry of a startled bird and the sound of the sea pounding on rocks became clearer. Men's voices called to one another, but even they could not drive out the sense of the utter loneliness and the uncanny feeling that we were trespassers in some forbidden reserve.

Then, suddenly, I was free. I had heaved and edged myself around a particularly vicious jut of rock, achieved a bigger and better graze across my left leg, stepped down two small ridges and found myself in the place the cliffs were guarding so well.

It was a tiny bay, scarcely more than twelve feet wide. The beach was made of minute pieces of shell pounded to silvery dust by the unceasing action of the Atlantic over centuries. The boulders that lay at the foot of the cliffs were covered with lichen; those nearer the sea were clothed with gleaming brown seaweed. Sea anemones lay in bright pools and a little green crab shot from under a stone by my feet. In the tall cliffs were the nesting places of hundreds of birds.

Gulls and redshanks and oyster-catchers wheeled around us on their last flights before sleep. The sea was silver and green and turquoise, as if the shell sand needed the sea's color to set off the bay's beautiful symmetry. It was a tiny and enchanted place, and it appeared that someone, or rather something, had staked a claim there before we came. On a shelf of rock, near an inlet of water, a grey seal lay on its back, flippers folded, its enormous eyes watching us without fear.

Paul was standing close to it, fascinated and quite unheeding of us.

"Paul," I reminded him. "We aren't invisible."

He said, fair hair blowing, his eyes screwed up against the low sunlight, "Oh, hello. I thought you'd get here."

"I doubt if you thought any such thing." Relief that he was safe made me angry that he had disobeyed me. "I asked you to stay with Antonia."

"You only *asked*," he said with absolute reason. "You *told* me not to go down to the fire. I didn't. But Antonia was talking so much and I went out and I saw the ship — Did you see it?"

"Yes. But why go all this way?"

"Watching the ship." He sounded surprised that I had to ask. "I've only seen ones like that in pictures."

"And now," I said, "we'll have to get you back, somehow. Though how you managed to walk this far —"

"Ah, but he didna'," Jaimie said. "He didna' tak this way, did ye, laddie?"

"No. I went along by the sea. It wasn't far — at least I don't *think* it was." He was watching the seal with longing eyes.

"It's nae half as long," Jaimie said. "I ken it. But I didna' know of this cove. 'Tis beautiful."

"And you tied your scarf to that rock so that

someone would come and rescue you? Really, Paul!"

"But I didn't. I tied it because – well, you know, you fly a flag on a place to tell people it's yours. We've got a flag at Mullaine. Why doesn't Antonia fly it?"

"I don't know," I said quickly. Then I bent and picked up a shell, holding it out to Paul, anxious to take his mind off the flag, a little alarmed that he had forgotten what he must know, that the flag was flown on Mullaine Castle only when the Laird was in residence.

The cliffs that made a crescent around us were bare of plant life, their tips serrated like giant's teeth. The sea rushed at the cove in great waves and the spray was light and springy on my face.

Rory said, "Did you know that up here, in the Hebrides, they say that seals are men under magic spells?"

Paul was not impressed. "My seal is a seal. I like him that way."

"Let's not stay here talking," I said, too aware of the low sun and the night gathering in the east. "We must go back now."

"But not the way we came," Jaimie said. "Ye'd have to be carried, wouldn't ye noo, laddies? There's that way by the cliffs once we get out of here."

"Don't go so far from home ever again at this

time of evening," I said to Paul.

"Why not?" The voice came from behind us.

I swung around. Shane stood on a strip of rock just above us.

"Because," I said, and refused to show that I was startled, "Paul could have lost his way, and if a mist had come down, it would have been difficult to find him. Mists muffle voices, so even if he shouted —"

"There's little likelihood of a mist this evening," Shane said, not moving from his place on the cliff. "But then, you don't know the island as I do, so perhaps you can be excused for being anxious. You really did muster a search party, didn't you?"

"Rory did that," I said.

"Ah, yes . . ." He glanced at his brother.

"And mist or not," I went on, "I would still have worried. Paul is young and there are so many places where he could have wandered or fallen, and we might not have found him before nightfall."

"I'd have thought risks and chances were the things that it's normal for young people to take."

"But you haven't got a child to be worried about."

"No," he said calmly, "not yet. But I've been young and I know the importance of freedom."

"I'm not talking about freedom. I'm talking about stupid risks," I said hotly, "and —" I broke off. I couldn't shout the truth against the sibilant hiss of the waves. I couldn't say, "I'm not being an overprotective mother . . . I'm afraid for Paul's safety. Don't you understand?" But of course he didn't. He was free and cool and uncompromising. And he was Lewis's friend . . .

"Come on," I said again to Paul. "Let's be going."

Shane hadn't moved from the rock, and I had the sensation of something intimidating about him. I felt certain that it was not deliberate, he could not help the power of his personality. The low, vivid sun was on his face and I could see in the very clear light that his eyes were the color of the sea behind him: silver-grey.

I called up to him, "Did you know of this place?"

"It's quite something, isn't it?"

I told myself it was quite unimportant that he didn't answer my question. I crossed to Paul, who was crouching down by the seal.

"Does he know I'll come back?" he asked, looking over his shoulder at me, his eyes intent and longing.

"He's young, so I doubt if he's ever seen a human being before."

"But I *want* him to know me." He planted his

feet apart and his eyes flashed. "I've never had a seal before."

"We'll have to see," I said lightly, aware that just as Shane had not answered my question, I was not reassuring Paul.

He bent to touch the seal.

"Be careful," I said quickly.

"He's a young one," Jaimie told me kindly. " 'Tis affectionate they are so. 'Tis only the old grey seals as get the vicious ways."

"We'll leave him in peace on his rock," I said. "Come on. Home." I gave Paul a little prod.

He clambered up a ridge of rock, untied his scarf and scrambled down again, tucking it in his belt, where it flapped like a trapped red bird.

Waiting for him, I could understand how Paul must feel about this small, enchanted place, far from the great stone walls of Mullaine, far from Antonia and the dreaded Bechstein grand piano – or even from my watchfulness.

I put my hands on his shoulders and walked him firmly to where the men were already squeezing their way through the narrow cleft in the cliffs. We wriggled and edged and heaved through slowly, tossing comments to one another. The crash of the sea softened to a distant hiss as the cliffs curtained the sound, and the wind that had sprung up soughed through the pinnacles of rock like faraway tuning of instruments.

When we reached the green valley on the other side, I thanked the men. I knew they were anxious to get back to their fishing or their animals and I told them to go ahead. Jaimie insisted on remaining with us.

"It's nae easy across the rocks," he said and glanced at my low-heeled Gucci walking shoes. "You'll no mind gettin' them a bitty scraped on the rocks?"

It didn't matter. I'd throw them willingly in the sea out of gratitude for Paul's safety. I laughed. "Show us the way."

He loped off across the *machair* toward the sea, leaving the bay to the enfolding cliffs. Behind me walked Paul and Rory, Paul singing a Hebridean song Rory had taught him: "Seagull of the Land-under-Waves."

On this side of the shore the rocks were a tumbled mass and it was obvious that centuries ago some huge subsidence had caused the rock fall. The shore route that Paul had taken was a harsh matter of climbing over boulders, sinking into sudden patches of wet sand, losing one's balance on loose rock and slithering down into sea pools, scattering the tiny microcosms of life swimming there. Sea pinks and sea holly gave color to the dark-grey rocks and gleaming wet seaweed clung to boulders, the strands lifting and falling as the waves teased them, like blown hair.

We clung as closely as we could to the cliffs, Jaimie and Paul in front, Rory walking with me.

I looked about me. "Shane hasn't come with us."

"Oh, he'll be back in his own good time."

Paul stopped, turned, nearly overbalanced on a mound of loose sea-sprayed rock, and said, "Shane won't hurt my seal, will he?"

Rory reassured him, "Of course not. Why should he, laddie?"

"They kill seals," Paul said. "They say there are too many round our coasts and they take the fish."

"Your seal will be quite safe as long as he stays where he is. Shane never hunts or kills."

Ahead of us, the unneeded hurricane lamps the men carried swayed from side to side as they climbed over the boulders along the edge of the shore.

Once I paused and looked back. "Those cliffs are exactly like the ones at Cathair Beag," I said.

"Oh aye, and they are so." Jaimie lifted his tough brown hand in a half salute and bade me "Goodnight" in Gaelic.

VIII

Rory and Paul and I made our way through the slow Hebridean twilight.

Rory asked. "Have I ever told you, Judith, of the tale they tell — "

I laughed. Suddenly I could laugh so easily. "I've heard many. Which one?"

"About Dalua. They call him the Faery Fool, though he's no fool, really. They say that when you hear his voice calling, you have to beware."

"Yes," I said too quickly. "Oh yes, you told me that one." For I, who had no superstitions when I was in London, was suddenly afraid of the folklore of the Hebrides.

The sea made background music to Rory's chatter, the waves lulled by evening into gentleness so that they barely lipped the sand and the rock pools.

More than once I looked around for Shane, wondering if he was still there in the hidden bay. I was relieved not to see him, for he had become, for no reason except his long friendship with Lewis, part

113

of my caution and my fear.

The lights from the crofters' homes glowed in the distance and I realized why Paul had not been exhausted, as I had been, by the long anxious walk over the moors. At last the round tower of Mullaine came into view, dark and crenelated against the sky.

When we arrived at the Castle, I said goodbye to Rory and thanked him. I would have to think up some practical way of thanking those who had joined the search. It would have to be something that was not too obviously a "Thank you" gift, for they were a proud people and not even their Laird's wife was allowed to patronize them.

I gave Paul a little push toward the Castle door, and Rory did what he always did when we parted. He leaned forward and kissed me, shyly, for there was an entirely sexless quality about him.

Down by the low wall that encircled the Castle grounds I caught sight of a cricket bat Paul had left out. I crossed the lawn to get it and as I did so, Shane came in sight.

I said, with forced lightness, "Do you have wings? If you don't, how did you get here so quickly? You didn't come our way, and the way over the moors takes a long time. So –"

He said, "Remember I was born here." It was an answer and yet no answer.

"Thank you for helping me to look for Paul."

He turned away, giving a slight lift of his shoulders, and I wondered why I had said that to him. For he hadn't been around when the scare and the search was on, and so, unless he had heard us calling Paul, he couldn't have known that he was missing. I had an uneasy feeling that Shane had not appeared at the bay because he cared about our safety. But I had no idea whether it was that he was a "solitary," like Kipling's "cat that walked alone," and just happened to be walking there, or whether he was watching my movements for reasons of his own.

He had been walking away from me. Suddenly he swung around. "Let Paul breathe, Judith."

"I *do*. Oh, I do." I was angry with myself for the pleading I heard in my voice. What right had this man —?

"Words mean different things to different people," he said. "Just think about that."

I don't know what I would have said to him had he given me a chance to speak, but he didn't. As on the first occasion we had met that evening, he was gone, melting into the night.

Antonia was in the Great Hall, berating Paul with words of love. "Darling, don't ever do that again. I couldn't bear it if you were out all night. You're so important to me – Paul, are you listening? Please don't ever frighten me again."

When Paul was embarrassed his voice was jerky. It was jerky now as he said, "I didn't mean to scare anyone."

"But you must have known –"

"I wasn't lost. Grownups fuss so."

I laughed. "You sound like a tetchy old man," I said.

"What's tetchy?"

"Cross. Irritable."

"Oh. Did you like my seal?"

"Yes. *Go to bed.* I'll be up soon to turn the lights off. And, Paul . . ."

He waited, his eyes bright, not yet ready for sleep.

"Don't ever go out late in the evening by yourself."

"Why not?"

I took his face between my hands. He wriggled, but I held on firmly. "Instead of arguing" – I forced him to look at me – "you'll promise to do what I ask. Promise . . ."

"Oh, all right." His eyes danced in the lamplight. Then he grinned. "I wouldn't like you to get lost looking for me."

"Go to bed."

I sat with Antonia, who was curled up on the crimson sofa. A lamp shone on the ruffles of her marvelous hair and on her fair skin. She wore a peony-pink dress and small ruby earrings and looked as if she were waiting to go to a party.

I sat opposite her. On my lap, Saturn – Paul's Burmese cat – was curled into a ball. He had been brought from London because Paul had said, "He'll be so unhappy if I leave him behind." The cat now lay, sleek and bronze, pawing my skirt and purring at his own dreams.

We put on a record of a Paganini violin concerto, turning the volume low so that we could talk. Lewis's name was seldom mentioned, but Antonia must have had him in her mind when she said suddenly, "Paul seems perfectly happy, doesn't he? I mean, it doesn't seem to worry him that he is here in a more or less all-woman household."

"There's always Duncan; Paul likes being with him just as he enjoys Rory's company."

Antonia sighed and changed the conversation. "You never met Rory's parents, Helen and Neil Kilarran, did you? Helen died some ten years ago of pneumonia caught because she would go sitting by the sea in a flimsy dress with a gale blowing. She was a most impractical person. Shane's father died suddenly of a heart attack in London. Early on, though, Helen and Neil spent far more time at Inverkyle than Robert and I did. But then, Robert was easily bored, and remained mostly in London. I think the longest period he spent here was when we were first married and he inherited the Castle. Robert was a man of very strong impulses and passions – I think I was the only one who could really handle him. But I was so often away, and although he didn't like it, he could do nothing about it. I was stronger-willed than even he. So he would come up here with marvellous plans for making beautiful grounds and heaven knows what. But there was no social life for him and he'd get restless. Neil Kilarran was a London banker and seldom here, and when he was, they hadn't much in common. It wasn't much fun for Helen, but she was a pretty, frail woman who seemed to spend her life making patchwork quilts and entertaining her cousins from Inverness."

"Shane and Rory were brought up here, though?"

"Oh, Rory was. Since there was no point in sending him to a good school, he went with the island children over to Mull. Shane, who was very bright, had rather a splendid education, but he spent most of his holidays here and that's how he and . . . Lewis became such friends." She put her hand to her face as if the thought went through her like a pain. "I really can't think why Shane doesn't sell this place.

118

He's so seldom here and he could easily find a smaller house on Mull for Rory, with Jeannie and Dru to look after him."

"Roots," I said. "Strong ones, perhaps."

"Then let's hope he doesn't become too deeply rooted," she said with some asperity.

There was a sound outside the door and then it creaked open. Duncan stood in the doorway. "I'd like a word wi' ye, ma'am."

"Yes? Well . . . ?" She waited, giving him a smile of encouragement as he hesitated.

"It'ud be better if ye came oot," Duncan said.

"All right, if it's so secret, I'll come." She shot me an amused glance, and as Duncan left, she passed me, saying in a low voice, "I suppose staff quarrels happen sooner or later. I've never known Rosheen and Duncan to row, but there's always a first time."

I sat leaning my head against the upholstered back of the chair, stroking Saturn. Although it was summer, the eternal drafts of the Castle played around my ankles. I slid off my shoes and tucked my feet under me. Saturn gave a soft yowl at being disturbed, turned full circle and settled again.

Antonia came back after a few minutes, her charming face darkened with anger. She flung herself onto the sofa. "Shane Kilarran times his return very aptly." Her voice was tight with fury.

"How? Why?"

She gave me a blazing glance. *"He wants Cathair Mor."*

"But how can he? Lewis . . ."

"Yes, Lewis is the Laird, and Lewis is *still* the Laird. But he's not here – God knows where he is – and Shane Kilarran would like to take advantage of that. It's odd, isn't it, Judith? There must be such a thing as telepathy, otherwise why was I mentioning him just before Duncan came in?"

"Was it Shane who called just now?"

"Oh no. He's much too arrogant for that." She shot me another of those blue, penetrating glances that people connected with her profession had learned augured trouble. "Oh no," she said again. "He took on himself a responsibility he had no right to. He intervened between two of the crofters, each claiming the same piece of land. Shane came upon them fighting over it and acted as arbiter. The man who lost came here to protest, and that's who I saw just now. He wanted me to overrule Shane's decision. He said that as acting head in Lewis's absence, it was I who should be the judge."

"What can you do?"

"Do? Why, make my own judgment, of course. Whichever side has a right to the land doesn't enter into it. I intend to quash Shane's judgment."

120

"But if the other crofter really has a right – "

"I don't care. What I do care about, however, is Shane taking upon himself to play Solomon." She picked up a magazine and riffled through it angrily, and flung it down. "It seems that with his coming, we're back with the old feud that's been dead for centuries. Dear heaven! I won't play medieval games with the Kilarrans!"

"Shane *can't* just take over."

I doubted if she heared me, for she said slowly, following her own thoughts, "Shane was bad for Lewis. He kept him away from his piano; he was devious in his ways of getting Lewis out to go sailing or climbing." She shivered. "I'm cold."

"Shall I fetch you a scarf?"

She shook her head. "I'll get it myself. I want a word with Rosheen. The women get together and chat over everything, so I'll lay the foundation for one piece of gossip. I'll make it quite clear to her that there's going to be no takeover by Kilarran of Cathair Mor. And the sooner that news gets round the island, the better."

I dreamed that night that I was walking in the Brenlorns, looking for a hollow hill, avoiding the great peat bogs with miraculous ease. In my dream it was I who discovered the magic hill. I saw it ringed with blue butterflies and I ran toward it, crying, "Rory . . . Rory, I've

121

found it. I've found the place you told me about."

But another voice answered me, calling me by that special name. "Clea . . . Clea . . ." it said. And I awoke with a pounding heart.

IX

The following morning, sitting on a rock down by the tiny quay, I watched the fishermen bring in their herring catch. I had learned to be glad of windy days in summer, for they relieved the Hebridean islands of the everlasting midges that haunted the coast. The wind was soft, blowing from the southwest, bringing with it light clouds that were tossed like feathers over the moors.

I sat, hunched up, my fingers clasped over my knees, listening to the Gaelic voices of the men as they hauled in their nets. But my mind was on my own problems. The relief of last night when I had found that Paul was safe did not release me from my basic anxieties. How long did the police intend us to remain here at Cathair Mor? And if our exile from London continued for many weeks, how about Paul's education? We had already discussed the possibility of his joining the children who crossed to Mull for their schooling. I was certain that though going to school "over the water" would

123

seem fun to him at first, it would soon pall. He would fret for his many friends in London and his lively life there.

Apart from Paul, I knew that if Lewis was not found soon and the police advised me to remain on the island, I would have to find something to do. If I didn't, Cathair Mor would be as great a wasteland to me as it was to Antonia. I also missed my friends. I, who had been born and brought up in the country, had adapted to town life so easily that I missed the stimulus of people who talked my language; I missed theatres and concerts; I missed the streets and the splendid parks of London.

I would have liked to have asked friends to stay, but I couldn't. Only a few trusted people, very close to me, knew where I was, and the circumstances made it inadvisable, according to the police, for even the closest of friends to visit.

The more I thought about it, the more I realized that for whatever work I did to be worthwhile, it would need to include others. Working on my own wouldn't help. I wanted to bring the islanders into any scheme I chose. And I believed I had found a project that could help us all.

The women wove their own tweeds and wove them beautifully, but the patterns were very limited and the colors dull and uninteresting.

Instead of the complicated zigzags of Fair Isle woolens, the ones on Cathair Mor were of interlocking diamonds, in greys and blacks and browns. I wrote to Gerald Farrer, my immediate chief in London, suggesting that perhaps I might start a weaving industry on the island. I explained that the output would be limited, but now that good tweeds, woven in attractive patterns and colors were popular again, a small industry could be started that would sell to one exclusive London fashion house. I would do the designing and train the women in any detail which their own simple patterns had not required. I asked if I could go ahead, at least experimentally.

"We could try," I said, "and it would be rather fine to have an exclusive haute couture house lure their fashion-conscious clients into wearing Cathair tweeds."

Gerald's reply had been prompt. He was all for experimenting and he liked the idea. We discussed it over a long telephone conversation. His only doubt was that I would remain long enough on the island to be able to train the women in complicated designs.

I had said, "How do I know? I may be here for months."

"I hope to God you're not," he had replied fervently.

"And when I'm allowed back in London,

then I could still keep an eye on the women. I could fly north every month for a few days to see how everything was working out."

In the end, I won. We arranged that if the women agreed to try, the dyes and everything we needed would be provided, even new looms. I doubted, though, if this would be necessary. On his fiftieth birthday Robert Mullaine had made a splendid gesture and given the women of the island fine new looms capable of more complicated weaving and patterns.

The first step was to win the women over, and I knew that my wisest move would be to speak to Morag, Angus's wife, who was the acknowledged leader of the island community.

I told Antonia of my plan and she was enthusiastic. It was obvious that she would cling to any reason to keep me on the island while she was there suffering her self-imposed isolation. She had already set aside one of the countless small rooms in the Castle for me to work in. Duncan had found a long trestle table for my drawing board and the paraphernalia of the work I had planned: paints and brushes, pencils and rulers.

I could not go to the women until I had something to show them and it was time I got down to a few designs and color sketches. I unfolded myself from the rock on which I was sitting, and the gulls, startled by my sudden movement, soared away from around my head and screamed as they circled the herring catch.

Working again was a joy. It was also therapeutic and meant that I could lock away my fear – at least for the moment. I had found ideas for my designs in the island itself, in the heathers, the grasses and the strange formations of the great cliff peaks. There was such a wealth of potential design all around me, and with my colors and charts and drawing board, I lost all count of time.

I was dragged away by Antonia for lunch and then wheedled by Paul to take him over to Mull to buy some boots he wanted for fishing in one of the streams that ran clear and sweet from the wet highlands of the Brenlorns.

The police had insisted that if I wished to leave the island, even for an hour or so, I must be accompanied by someone who could be trusted. For the time being, I must not travel alone even to Mull. Duncan would be my adult companion, ferrying us across in the *Midir* and coming with me while I shopped. On our return, Paul went triumphantly to the Abbey to show his new boots to Rory.

I was walking on toward the Castle when Rory came after me, calling. He had what looked like a large envelope in his hands, and Paul was racing to keep up with him. "I must show you this," Rory's voice was excited, and he pulled me down on to the grass and spread out what I now saw was a homemade map of Cathair Mor. Paul crouched, peering over his shoulder.

"I can't read that writing."

"It's very old," Rory said. "I remember my father showing it to me. It's always kept in a desk drawer in what was his library. Look at the names —"

Tiny, ancient writing, the ink brown and faded with age, was scrawled over the map of the island.

"I had no idea there were so many place names here," I said.

Rory laughed. "Everyone has forgotten them now." He pointed. "Nobody ever calls that western bit there the Seven Hounds. You see, there are seven little hills. And that huge rock you see from the east end of the moors is called Cormac — and Cormac, you know, was a lord of the north isles. But this is what I wanted you to see. Look —" He pointed excitedly to the southwestern tip of the map and looked up over his shoulder at Paul. "Here's your bay and it has a name. See? The Bay of the Dark Star. I wonder why it was called that? Everyone here has forgotten — if they ever knew. It's all so long ago," he said sadly. "But it's a strange name to call a bay, isn't it?"

"Perhaps," I said, "some astronomer searching the night sky saw a new star from there." I spoke lightly, not really believing in what I said.

Rory didn't either. "I'm sure it has to do with an old legend," he said. "I seem to remember being told something about people who were born under a dark star, but I don't recall what it was."

"Well," I said matter-of-factly, "I can't believe that any family ever lived in that bay or that anyone was born there, except perhaps a seal."

"*My* seal!" Paul said. And added, "There's our place marked. And yours, Rory. The Abbey. Look. It's all very, very old, isn't it?"

We sat poring over the map, trying to read names of places that were almost indistinguishable. In the end, a cool wind sent us back, Paul going with Rory and I returning to my drawing board.

I told Antonia about Paul's bay. "I wonder if the islanders even know about the names that were once given to some of the places on the island?"

"I shouldn't imagine so." She wasn't particularly interested. "None of them go much further than the moors and their sheep and cattle," she said, "or to visit one another and drink tea or hold *ceilidhs*."

It was true, and anyway, it didn't matter.

Even Paul, who had annexed the bay, hadn't been interested. It was "his bay," "his seal." And yet the name fascinated me. Somewhere, back in the somber history of the island, lay the reason for giving that tiny place such a name.

Antonia had picked up a newspaper lying on the low table by her side. She held it out to me, and I took it and scanned it. Politics, a small bank raid, a lion had escaped from a private zoo . . . Then a brief paragraph.

There is still no news of the missing pianist Lewis Mullaine. The police are following up the many clues. His wife and son remain in seclusion somewhere in the country.

I laid the newspaper down. Antonia reached for it, folded it into a small square and tucked it out of sight under her chair. "Now, Judith dear, mix us both a strong martini."

I heard the hopelessness in my voice as I cried, "How can it go on?"

"The police are obviously doing all they can. I've told you what I believe, and what I *still* believe. The more I think about it — and God knows I can't stop thinking — I'm sure my son, with his great gifts, his marvelous career, *my son* had a breakdown. And he has gone into hiding, frightened and full of remorse."

"Someone could be sheltering him, someone

in England perhaps."

She nodded. "It's possible. Or he might be somewhere alone, hiding from everyone. We don't know. Dear, it's hopeless to play guessing games at something so . . . so terrible."

I sat back, trying to relax, to loosen the tightness of my shoulders, my back, my knees.

Antonia continued, "You are here with me and Paul, and I know you can't come to any harm while at Mullaine. By the way, where is Paul?"

"He came back from fishing some time ago," I said, "and I sent him to bathe. He fell into a rather muddy pool."

Antonia said on a note of impatience, "He spends altogether too much time with Rory."

"Oh no. They enjoy each other's company."

"But that man is as full of fairy tales as a child, and Paul is too intelligent."

"It isn't like that. I believe that they balance one another. And it's good for Paul –"

"It would be better if he would stay indoors and practice the piano rather than go out and have some accident climbing those rocks he seems to love, or fishing and falling into the water."

I said, shaking the cocktail mixer, "If he does, he'll survive. He's tough and he's sensible. He'll have a good many falls in streams while trying to catch the fish that got away. But I think I'll have to go over to Mull tomorrow and arrange for him to join the school there, as well as do something about my own job."

"Oh, that!" She made a light, dismissive gesture with her hand. "I'd forget about it."

"I can't. I'll need my salary. Thorburn's are keeping my place open for me, but they can't be expected to do that indefinitely. Textile manufacturers need to be fed with designs for their materials, and I'm one of their chief designers."

"My dear, I know. And you must be exceptionally clever at your work. But if they won't wait for you, then some other company will snap you up when the police decide you can return to London." She gave me her enchanting smile. "You don't have to worry about money, and it's so good to have you here."

I thought how strange and changed were circumstances. When Lewis had first taken me to meet Antonia, home from a wildly successful concert tour, she had welcomed me, had behaved charmingly, but behind it I could read her mind: *Out of all the women who wanted Lewis, he has chosen a farmer's daughter, a girl who probably doesn't know Mozart from Handel . . .*

Secretly, hiding behind a mask of pleasantness and pride, I had pleaded for her to love me. Every time I met her – glamorous and with the world at her feet – I prayed for something more than just to be tolerated. To her credit, Antonia never made me feel that I came from a lesser world than hers. She knew how to charm, how to hold the balance between open-armed love and cool restraint. I had entered the rarified world of professional music and inside myself I was humble.

Suddenly the balance of roles had changed. Now Lewis was a hunted man and Antonia was the one who, behind her beauty and her pride, was pleading with me to stay.

Living with her, in her home, meant living her life to a great extent, never quite free to do as I pleased, and having to learn tact with a possessive and adoring grandmother, for Paul must not be made the target for a tug of war.

Antonia broke the silence. "Paul still never mentions Lewis, does he?"

"No."

"I really thought that by now he would remember and ask. Lewis and he adored one another."

"It's as I said, and as the doctor told me. His memory is blocked. It's a kind of protection against something that, without realizing it, he knows would hurt him to remember. And perhaps it is easier for him now because Lewis was so often away on foreign engagements."

Antonia always shuddered slightly whenever

133

she had to mention Lewis's name, as if there were a fever in her heart. She drew the glimmering shawl more closely around her shoulders. "And now you have your weaving project, Judith."

"I haven't spoken to the women yet," I said. "I'll go tomorrow and see Morag and get her to call some of them together."

Antonia spread her hands and looked at her pink nails. "It will give the women here something to do besides their housework and their hens. During school, when the children are away on Mull and their husbands fishing or crofting, there's little life outside their household chores. I'm afraid if something isn't done soon to give them an outside interest, the next generation will go off to the mainland and Cathair Mor will become a ghost island."

"People will always love coming here. It's so beautiful."

"The odd thing is that beautiful scenery only brings happiness in imagination. In reality, you can become extremely bored by it. I have. Oh, Judith, what are we going to do?" She looked suddenly tired and drained.

"I think," I said, "that we should go to bed."

She laughed suddenly. "Lewis once told me that you were essentially practical. Lewis ..." Again I saw her shudder.

"If by calling me practical, you are paying me

a compliment, I'm not certain that it's deserved," I said dryly. "Our London home has run well because Lena Cruse is such an efficient housekeeper; Paul is very little trouble because he's at a school that teaches him discipline." I rose and looked for Saturn. "I'll go and give the cat his evening milk. Goodnight, Antonia."

As she raised her face to be kissed, I caught the scent of Fleurs de Rocaille.

I called Saturn and found him curled neatly on the staircase, head lifted, green eyes watching me.

"Milk," I said and went past him to the kitchen.

He followed me, gliding like a brown silhouette by my side. There was about him none of the exhibitionism of the Siamese cats. Burmese were quiet and highly intelligent.

The kitchen was empty, the servants having already gone to their quarters in the wing of the Castle that plunged like an arm into the Norway spruces – one of which for years was nursed as the island's Christmas tree.

While Saturn drank, his fastidious tongue making no sound, I opened the door. It gave onto a flagged courtyard surrounded by a broken line of ruined stone outhouses that had been left in their devastated piles because they formed a windbreak for those who worked in the enormous kitchen.

As I stood in the doorway the rain was like the brush of wings against my face. The Brenlorns were invisible and the only sound was that of the sea pounding the pillar rocks of Cathair Beag.

I looked away into the darkness on the left where I knew the *machair* sloped gently to the loch. To my right, the distance was dotted with occasional lights from cottages. They glowed steady and unwinking – except for one. It was far away from the cluster of cottages, moving very slowly as if carried by someone who was picking his way cautiously. But it was no light on Cathair Mor – a far greater distance separated it from the others. For a moment I thought it was curiously suspended over the sea. And then I knew where it came from.

Someone was walking over the needle-sharp rocks of Cathair Beag – the inaccessible island – so wild, so small that no human being could live there. I knew it was not a farmer searching for a lost sheep because no animal could stray across that strip of water dividing Cathair Mor from its sibling island. Nor could anyone fish there, for the wild sea would break a line. Lewis had once told me that only the birds lived there – the great solan goose, the petrel and the golden eagle that built eyries in the high gullies of the sea cliffs and roamed, proud and aggressive, around the shores of the Hebrides.

My heart pounded and I slammed the door, leaning against it as exhausted as if I had been running hard. Every nerve-end tingled.

I closed my eyes and remained, trembling, until I heard Saturn's soft yowl of protest that I had shut him out. I opened the door sufficiently to allow him to squeeze through. Then I fled to find Antonia.

She was not in the drawing room. I raced up the curving stairway that led to her rooms in the tower and my heels clattered on the worn stone slabs.

"Antonia." I knocked on her door.

"What is it? I'm just about to have my bath."

"Cathair Beag. I saw a moving light over the cliffs there."

"So?" Her voice came impatiently through the closed door.

"But no one knows the way onto that island . . . except Lewis."

The door opened. Antonia's robe was royal-blue edged with fine silver embroidery. She had taken off her makeup, but she still looked absurdly young to be a grandmother. Her eyes, however, were impatient.

"My dear, do please stop this fear that Lewis is lurking somewhere and waiting to harm you. Of course he won't! I've told you often enough that when he has got over the shock of what he did, he'll come back and face — and face — whatever he has to."

I leaned against the lintel of the door, shivering, finding no comfort in her words.

"How could you possibly imagine that Lewis, or anyone, could be on Cathair Beag?" she persisted, watching me closely. "There's no way of building a shelter, no way of getting food. And I'm not at all certain that Lewis ever found a way onto that mass of rock. I'm told that there are no caves there and the sea boils round it. I think it was just a kind of fantasy he had. Or," she added slowly, "it could be that Shane found a way. He was always climbing and exploring when he was young."

I wanted to telephone the Abbey and find an excuse to speak to Shane, but I could think of no reason. I could not call a man I scarcely knew just to say, "Were you walking on Cathair Beag tonight?"

"Go to bed," Antonia was saying, "and forget about it. What you saw was probably a fisherman out on the sea, or even, er, even a falling star."

"No star fell on Cathair Beag tonight," I said and walked away.

The lighting was inadequate along the gallery because the great stone walls absorbed it and gave none back. My own elongated shadow was thrown at angles just ahead of me like a teasing, catch-me-if-you-can child. There was a tall arched window at the end of the gallery and the thick stone embrasure made a wind tunnel which bore on the breeze a sound like a name calling: "Clea . . . Clea . . ."

But no one was calling me. My imagination was soaring like an untamed bird; the light I had seen earlier on Cathair Beag had frightened me. And those two enemies — fear and imagination — were the things human beings broke their lives on. I must not break. I dare not, for Paul's sake and my own.

I paused outside my son's room and opened the door. The small shape in the big bed didn't move. He slept in obvious peace, tousled and healthy after a day in the open air with the island children who laughed at his accent and sought him out because they liked him.

"Goodnight, darling," I said softly and closed the door.

In my bedroom the jade curtains muffled the wind, but they could not shut out the tiny, insidious spattering sound of rain. I lay in bed listening, turning restlessly, willing myself to stop remembering. The Hebridean islands lay locked in night. I pulled the blankets up to my chin as if I were cold, and closed my eyes again.

My door had a way of creaking slightly when

opened. I heard it, and suddenly alert, I started up and switched on the bedside light. A small figure stood shivering and watching me.

"Paul! What is it?"

"I'm scared."

I got out of bed, wrapped my robe around me and went to him. "What scared you?"

"It's awfully dark."

I led him to the window and pushed aside one of the curtains. "Yes, it is, isn't it? And cloudy. It's been raining."

"There are always lights somewhere in London."

"I know, darling, but you've been on the island long enough now to be used to the dark nights here. Look —" I leaned with him through the deep aperture to the window. "There are just the trees and the moors. I expect there are a few night animals running around looking for food, but that's nothing to scare you." (And from this side of the Castle, no sight of Cathair Beag and the moving light.)

"I had a nightmare," Paul said.

So that was it.

"But since you know that it's only a nightmare, there's nothing to be afraid of, is there? I'll make you some warm milk. It may be summer up here, but the nights are cold and you didn't put your slippers on."

"There's a funny noise outside, like someone talking."

"It's the wind, darling. You're not living in a fine modern house in London. The Castle is full of big, badly fitting windows. You know that. And the wind makes sounds like voices. I've heard them, too." *("Clea," they had said. "Clea . . .")*

Paul's eyes were troubled, as if he wanted to believe me but couldn't.

I said, "Lots of people actually enjoy walking in the dark. Rory does."

A small light of hope lit the blue eyes watching me. If Rory could be brave . . .

"He has absolutely no fear of night and so you don't need to, do you?"

Paul shook his head.

"Just leave the light on in your room while I get you some milk."

This time when I went downstairs I didn't look out. I turned my back to the door and avoided the window.

Up in Paul's room I waited while he drank the milk and assured him that if he heard voices in the wind again, he was to listen hard and he would hear them just telling old tales about the islands.

"There are hundreds of wonderful legends that have been told down the centuries," I said, "and those stories remain for always, for anyone to hear. If you listen hard, you might hear the one Rory told me when we went walking on the moors. It was about Dalua, the Faery Fool. Long ago his story was set to music. This was before you and even I were born, but the story is a very old and beautiful one. Ask Rory to tell you."

Paul's drowsy eyes watched me from the pillow. Then he smiled faintly and his lids fell. I heard him give a little sigh as if with contentment. The comfort I had been giving him had worked with a sleepy boy who just wanted easy assurance that the wind was kind.

X

Morag's croft stood just above the patch of *machair* that led down to the loch. Wild pansies and yellow iris grew in the shelter of the low dry-stone wall which every crofter built around his plot of land.

As I walked through the glen I kept looking across at the rocky crags and sea-carved columns of Cathair Beag. Only the birds, the gulls and the redshanks and the green cormorants wheeled, riding on the wind; the sea struck the tall columns of rock like organ music. Once I paused and studied Cathair Beag. From where I stood, there was no possible way a man could land there. Only the grey seals might find resting ledges. Certainly even if a boat could tie up on one of the low rocks, there was no way of gaining a foothold on those white pillars or saving the boat from the seething sea. If any island resented visitors, Cathair Beag did.

Morag's cottage was cluttered but very clean. Fishing nets hung from hooks in the ceiling rafters and pots gleamed on the stove.

She had collected all the women she could cram into the kitchen to hear my suggestions for a weaving industry on the island. Although I had only mentioned it casually, I knew the women well enough to be quite certain that by now there was not a single one from nineteen to ninety who hadn't heard of the proposed plan and discussed it.

"My goodness, 'tis pretty ye look this morning," Morag greeted me. "Come on in. The kettle is ready for tea."

Of course there would be tea, I thought with amusement – day or night, visitors were offered tea.

About twenty women were crowded into the low-raftered kitchen, its double walls lined with dry peat, a wonderful insulation against the raging storms of winter. The smell of wild fowl came from a pot simmering on the kitchen range.

I had been nervous of the women's reaction to the suggested weaving industry because I knew how conservative they were. But my spirits lifted when I saw lengths of cloth, skirts and sweaters they had woven laid out on the scrubbed kitchen table. It was as if they had decided among themselves to give it a try and were showing me what they could do.

I smiled and said warmly, sweeping my hand

toward the table, "That looks like a good sign to me."

Although there were nods of agreement, a few women sat stolidly and looked at me without smiling; I singled them out, slowly turning from one cautious dissenter to another. "Don't you like the idea?"

A lean lugubrious woman said, "It's no so fine for us. If we weave for ye doon there in London and no one wants our cloth, what do we do about it? There's no call here for fancy things."

I said, "You'll be paid just the same, Glynis. This I promise you. The responsibility is mine and my company's. We won't let you down. But I can assure you that real handwoven wool is beginning to be fashionable again in London and Paris."

Morag turned and spoke in Gaelic to the women. Like all Hebrideans her "s's" were soft and sibilant, her "r's" slurred. It was said that the island women had the softness of the sea mists and the rain in their voices. But that did not affect the power of Morag's personality.

I had no idea what she had said until suddenly she addressed them in English, and I was certain she was translating for my benefit. "The dear knows why ye sit there pretendin' that weavin' won't be good for us. Ach, but ye're dim an' all!"

145

I pushed the advantage she had given. "I know you spin in the winter, but you've already got the wool from your sheep up in your lofts, so why not start now?"

"Aye, and isn't that true?" cried Morag. "And hasn't Mrs. Mullaine been just after tellin' ye that ye won't be out of pocket?" Morag demanded.

"Oh, aye, but —"

"No 'buts.' Just listen." Morag lifted the kettle and filled a huge earthenware teapot. Then she pointed to her spinning wheel set near the window. "That's what we're here to talk about. The Mullaine's lady is here to talk, and listen ye're goin' to."

I explained how often, in a large store near where I lived in London, I had seen people lift a pure woolen garment and rub their faces against its softness. "Synthetic fabrics don't *live*, like pure wool," I said. I told them that my employers were certain that given good designs and colors, they could sell attractively woven material to some exclusive house. "We intend even to name it Cathair Wool," I said, "so that anyone who buys it will know it came from here."

"Aye, and we'd know how to work our patterns with our eyes closed," one said. "So it'ud be easy."

"But you're not going to work your own

patterns. I'm going to design new ones for you."

Their faces dropped into stern, obstinate lines, " 'Tis no other pattern we can do."

"You can, if I teach you." I moved some of the skirts and jackets from the table, opened up the bag I carried and laid my few designs on the table. "These are some," I said. "I have to get them passed by the London office, but I'm quite certain they'll approve and then we'll get to work."

The women fingered my paintings, passed them around and shook their heads.

"Just look at what I'm wearing." I fingered my blue skirt and blue-and-emerald sweater. "I designed these, and this is what people want — attractive designs; rich subtle colors."

"Ours —"

"I know what you're thinking. That yours are good. They are. They only need to be adapted to different tastes."

"We'd never be able to weave anythin' fussy."

"Not fussy," I said, "but perhaps more colorful. And with my help, you could do it. If you've got the wool, the dyes and the looms, there's nothing to stop you. I don't want the old tapestry weave, it's too heavy. We want to make lightweight woolens that could be sold exclusively to a London couturier or a Paris one, or to elegant Americans for their autumn wear." I half turned toward a loom in the corner, and as

I did so, saw movement in the open doorway.

Shane stood leaning against the doorpost. "Hello," he said pleasantly. "I'm just here to see fair play."

"It will be fair. I've got a scheme."

"Are schemes automatically fair?"

"Mine is," I said shortly.

"Go along with what you were saying. I'll just stay quietly by."

I crossed to the loom. "You think I'm trying to tell you how to do something that I can't do myself, don't you?" I said to the women. "Well, let me prove you wrong. Morag, can I use this wool?"

"Aye, you can."

I sat down at the loom. The women watched me, at first in silence, and then, as I shifted the shuttle, they began to whisper among themselves in Gaelic. I started to work the yarn already on the loom.

Before I was entrusted with designing, I had served an apprenticeship in both block printing and weaving so that I would know the difficulties I might be forcing on those who carried out my designs.

The pattern of the weave on Morag's loom was a simple traditional one known as Rosepath, which I had learned in my apprentice days. There was a slight variation in the use of a fine twisted thread of purple, the island's

148

traditional color, through the dull brown and grey of the cloth. The scent of heather still clung to the wool and the inevitable knots would be removed when the piece of tweed came off the loom and the process of "burling" began.

I was aware as I worked of Shane watching me. The women crowded around, waiting for me to make a mistake. But I had been too well grounded for that, although I didn't push my luck too far. I knew that anything done by hand held the individual impression of the touch of the particular weaver, and mine could not possibly resemble Morag's. This was something that I would have to watch when the women began, for the material must be evenly worked yet retain the individuality of handweaving.

I stopped, rose and turned to the women, laughing. "You see, I'm not trying to get you to do something I can't do myself."

Morag handed me a cup of tea. I took it and glanced toward Shane in triumph. He gave me a light handclap. Then he turned and went out, and I saw him sit down on the low broken part of the dry-stone wall, his back to us. I felt that he was waiting for me.

I had my first twinge of doubt that perhaps, with their simple looms, I was asking too much of the women. But I dismissed the fear quickly. I would take them step by step from their simple designs to the ones I knew would be more difficult, but quite possible, on their looms.

"Of course," I said, sipping tea, "since some will be working on the same design, we'll have to have somewhere where you can all be together. We'll need to find a place we can use."

They liked that. But they were still hesitant about the designs, eying them like unknown enemies as they lay between us on the table.

In the end I said firmly, "I'm afraid it's a case that either we adapt the designs or we scrap the whole idea. Scrapping —" I explained and made a cutting gesture with my hands. "Finish."

They understood that. Swift, low Gaelic began again, filling the room with a jumble of sounds. I waited.

A large, untidy dog ambled in. Barby, whose husband owned a flock of sheep, said, "Jessie here knows how to weave her own tartan, the MacGregor. Maybe —"

"Oh no. No clan tartans," I said firmly. "If you'll trust me, it will mean extra money for you all and no responsibility if the scheme isn't successful. Is that fair?"

"Aye, indeed, it's fair," said Morag.

"You see," I explained, "there will be so few of you that our production won't be large enough to make big profits. But I promise you'll find it interesting and you'll like working together once we've found a place. Does anyone know of one?"

They looked at one another in silence. I could sense at last that they were almost entirely with me on the idea. I hoped to heaven I wasn't being too optimistic in telling them they could do the work. I wanted the success of the scheme for them and for myself. But as I waited and they tried to think of some suitable place, I felt a sudden humility. I was standing in front of those women, all of whom were older than I, and the last thing I wanted was to be arrogant or dictatorial. But this was an honest plan which would benefit everyone and I needed them to make my enforced stay on the island bearable. I felt that once started, they would find such pleasure in their more complicated weaving, *they* would need *me*.

I left the women to talk among themselves and to find out if anyone had a shed in good state of repair that we could build onto and use. I glanced at my watch and found that I had been with them for more than an hour and a half. The women of Cathair Mor wanted all their "*i*'s" dotted and their "*t*'s" crossed before they would change their life style even for their own benefit.

Outside Morag's cottage, the sunlight poured onto an empty landscape. Shane had gone.

After the night's rain, the morning was glorious. A mist like amethyst gauze swept across the rhythmic switchback of the Brenlorns. I went down and walked by the sea, crunching on the white shell sand. The Atlantic was gentle, quivering with sunlight. I saw a lobster among the rocks and around me the redshanks piped, flitting among the crags. The two small motor launches rocked gently at their moorings by the tiny stone jetty.

I turned inland, climbing over moors rich with the white blossoms of ling. On such a morning I could almost laugh at fears, pushing back the shadow that stalked me of threatened death. Absorbed in the details of my plan for the Cathair women, I wandered with a new-found aimless happiness that had been alien to me for so long. I skirted known boglands where orchis grew and asphodel, and a field of daisies beyond which horned cattle grazed.

I had no idea how far I had walked or what the time was, for my watch had stopped. Eventually I turned back and made my way over the *machair*, watching the gannets plunge, wings folded, to snare some unsuspecting fish. The limpid air was soft and the sea pools were the color of chrysophase. In the distance I could see an osprey, that beautiful white-crested eagle that was only now returning to nest in Scotland. The lovely birds were carefully protected now and I stood watching this one until it disappeared.

Then a shadow crossed my path. I swung around, my heart beating in fear.

Shane stood behind me.

"I always approve of people who climb ladders from the bottom rung," he said, "instead of being hoisted halfway by influence."

I must have looked utterly bewildered, for he added, "Oh, I watched you from the cottage door while you worked that loom. You know your job."

"Someone in our village in Devonshire," I said, "had a loom and she taught me how to use one. I had more training at the London School of Art before I started to design fabrics."

"I wonder if you realize what you are doing to these women?"

"Of course I do," I said, startled. "I'm giving them a chance to have an interest in their lives and to earn a little money."

"Oh yes, the money . . . the golden lure . . ."

"No, because their production will be small, the money won't change their life style."

"Oh yes it will. The next move will be tourists —"

"This is a private place."

"So were Longleat and Chatsworth and Knole. But the tourists came."

"Those great houses welcome them. This is

different." I stood quite still and faced him. "Are you trying to stop me from going ahead with this project?"

"How can I?"

"But you would if you could."

"Oh yes." His eyes met mine, coldly and steadily. "Why do you think these people are still here, on a tiny island?"

"Because they're happy —"

"Go on."

"What is this?' I demanded. "A cross-examination?"

"If you want to put it that way. But you were saying 'because they're happy,' and then you hesitated."

"I think they're also happy because they are content."

"Put it another way. They've never been up against competition."

"I've no intention of being competitive. I don't want to spoil what they have."

"Oh, but it's a merry-go-round. You won't be able to help it. From the moment you start to sell the cloth they weave, it will begin — faster and higher."

"You are misconstruing what I'm trying to do."

"Am I?"

"All this" — I brushed wind-swept hair out of my eyes — "all this is because you resent my

154

plan. How do *you* know that the islanders won't be happy turning out lovely material?"

He stood quite still, making no attempt to answer, as if he knew I could give my own reply.

"Does it occur to you, Shane, that perhaps I know far more about the women's needs and their happiness than you do. For one thing, you've been away so long and I've been coming up here every year. I'm sure they'll love working together and having a little extra money to show for it at the end. It's a fine aim —"

"Oh no. It's a Pandora's box, my dear Judith. What you are proposing to do will bring in elements they know nothing about. Competition . . . envy between them and the people of the other islands."

The wind persisted in blowing strands of hair across my face. I pushed them back impatiently. "Oh, what's the use of arguing? I'm sorry if you dislike what I'm doing, but if I succeed, I don't believe I'll be harming anyone. And if I fail, I shall hurt no one, either. Even for my employers, the financial risk is very small. Only my own pride will be damaged. And I can live with that."

In the moments of silence between us, Antonia's words flashed through my mind: "Shane is strong — and devious. Be careful of him, Judith."

And here, in the bright sunshine, he was warning me of the very thing I needed so badly. Could it be care for the islanders? Or some personal resentment? But why resent me? Simultaneously with my question, my mind supplied the answer. He was Lewis's friend. And for all I knew, he still was . . .

Shane was standing very quietly, as if waiting for me to continue speaking. I told myself it didn't matter whether or not he understood what I was trying to do. Yet I heard myself rushing into an even deeper explanation. "I'm bringing together women who live lives that are isolated when their children are away at school and their husbands out fishing. These cottagers don't have neighbors round the corner. There aren't terraces of houses here where they can gossip for a little while over a garden fence."

"And if there is trouble between them — well, you won't be here then, will you?"

"What do you mean?"

"It's obvious, surely. If the scheme fails, then you'll return to London. You weren't planning to make this your home, were you?"

"Planning to stay *here?*" I took a long breath, and said in a carefully controlled voice, "You must know *why* I'm here. You told me that you had read the circumstances that led to — to this —"

As he stood before me, his black hair ruffled,

shining with copper lights, I saw the lines of his deeply tanned face and remembered what someone had once told me. "People who are not old but have deep facial lines are either very strong-willed – or very cruel."

"Of course I know. It's a terrible story – whichever way it is."

"*What do you mean 'whichever way it is'?*" I burst out. "Shane, please tell me. What did you mean by that?"

"How do outsiders know the truth?" He looked away over my head. "When moments of great happiness or tragedy lie between two people, only they can know. That's it, isn't it, Judith? Just you and Lewis –" His eyes turning to look down at me, were coolly uncompromising, his expression ungentle.

"What are you suggesting?"

He said, "How do I know? I've told you, only you and Lewis –"

"Then you don't believe me," I interrupted. "So what *do* you believe? *What?* That I lied in court? Under oath?" I watched him, trembling inside, feeling my face on fire. "What *do* you believe? That Lewis and I fought and I injured myself because I wanted him blamed? That suggestion even came from some journalist. I saw it in a newspaper that digs into every possibility – the murky, the lying, the squalid ... Did you see that newspaper and did it convince you that I had lied in court?"

"Oh, God in heaven!" he said under his breath, and walked away from me.

I stood swaying slightly with the wind. Without realizing it, I had turned my back on Shane as he strode toward the moors. I stared at the sea until my eyes ached with the blue dazzle. A kind of fury had risen inside me.

I could prove to you, Shane Kilarran, that Lewis attacked me. It was not a tragedy between two people, but between three. *Because Paul saw* . . . But whatever you think about me, I'll never tell you; I'll never bring my son into this to prove a truth to you. You're nothing to me — a man I don't know, a man of whom Antonia said, "Shane wants Cathair Mor."

I began to walk fast, in the opposite direction from Shane Kilarran.

XI

I turned inland, rounded a windbreak of Japanese larch and came face to face with a Blackface sheep quite obviously as startled as I was, for he turned, flicked his rump at me and galloped off to join the herd.

I had no idea how far I went. I resented Shane's intrusion into my life. But returning to Mullaine, I was plunged into another emotion.

Whenever Paul protested about something, the sound was always loud and clear. He never mumbled or sulked. He was protesting now. I heard his voice carrying over Mullaine's ill-kept lawns as I neared the Castle.

"I *hate* those stupid exercises. I like playing *my* way. One finger . . ."

Oh, not again! I thought, and crossed to the open door as Paul raced past me toward the larch wood.

"Where are you going?" I called.

"To see Rory," he shouted back at me.

"Paul . . ." Antonia was at the door. She was dressed in a sapphire skirt and a crimson silk

159

blouse, and was quite out of keeping with a Hebridean landscape. Every pose she took would have been blatantly artificial in anyone else. In her, all had become natural. Wherever she was, her manner had a touch of the theatrical, yet it was without vanity. She had trained herself to an unselfconscious elegance. She stood calling Paul a second time.

"He's gone," I told her, and asked, although I already knew, "What's the trouble?"

She walked ahead of me into the hall and strolled to the dais where her piano stood. "It's the same tussle I had when you were in hospital and Paul was staying with me. But that time he did what I told him and he really made progress with his music. I've tried and tried to get him to practice here. But he refuses. Judith, you really must insist. If only you'd take more interest in this gift of his!"

"Gift? Paul? For music?" I burst out laughing. "He has the agility of a mockingbird for copying a tune," I said. "But that's no great gift."

"I think, my dear, you should allow me to know a little about it. Music has been my life. I know a potential musician when I hear one."

"At seven years old?"

"Yehudi Menuhin," she reminded me. "Mozart . . ."

"Paul is no genius."

"But he could become a good pianist. Judith, don't you understand? He's very much my grandson — he has my looks, my mother's looks, my grandmother's looks. We are all musicians. It's *there!*"

I crossed the Hall and knelt on a window seat, looking through a small low circular window west toward the hills. "Please, Antonia, just leave him alone, will you? This is his holiday. I want him to be out in the air and with the other children as much as possible. There's time enough for learning when he goes back to school."

"Music isn't learning." Her voice was heavy and dramatic. "Music is art —"

"Oh God!" Exasperation was torn from me.

"— and not to be sworn at," she retorted. Her fingers moved automatically to the piano keys.

I said, more gently, "Oh, Antonia, I love music too. You know that. But Paul has got to come to it when he chooses, *if* he chooses."

"For any art," she said, "you need to start young. It's *now*, and not in ten years' time, that we have to think of my grandchild's career."

"*My son's*," I said quietly. "And unless he comes to me begging to stay indoors and play that piano, he's just not going to. Please try to understand."

"Children don't know what they want. It's for

us, the adults, to tell them, to teach them. Paul must —"

"Paul must do nothing under protest while he's on holiday," I said clearly, "except get up when I tell him and go to bed when I tell him, come in to meals when I call and try to be polite. That's all I ask of him for these weeks."

"You would throw away such a wonderful chance for him? Judith . . ."

Whatever she intended to say was suddenly caught back. She turned away from me.

I fought my rage against her. Antonia had done this before, in London, and it had resulted in harsh words between us. I had thought that would be the end of the matter. But here, at Mullaine, it had started again.

I had to stop the argument, but as I walked away, the Hall seemed to be waiting for me to make some other move. I paused and turned. Antonia was still standing on the dais, one hand resting limply on the piano keys. For the first time since I had known her there was an aura of defeat about her — an isolation.

It was very quiet. Around us on the walls were ancient tapestries that even Antonia, who had no interest in the past and saw no beauty in antiques, dared not remove, for they were the oldest and most valuable things in the Castle. The clear light from the tall windows shone on the carvings of the minstrels' gallery and outlined the Celtic cross. On either side of the dais the high arched doors seemed to accentuate Antonia's isolation.

On an impulse, I began to run toward the dais, warmth and compassion for her flooding back. I went up the three steps and took her hands. Her scent flowed around me, but her expression was unforgiving.

"Antonia, I'm sorry if I seem to cross you. Please try to understand."

She drew away from me and ran her fingers through her hair, closing her eyes as if to shut me out.

"I know you love Paul," I persisted, "and I'm glad that you do. Perhaps one day your dream for him will come true and he'll be a fine pianist. But so far, you must see for yourself, he has shown no real gift or any interest. Leave it for the moment, please, let him be free."

"He *is* free." She caught her breath, and then added bitterly, "I only ask for an hour or two a day of his time. That's all. And not for myself, for him."

"No, that's not quite true," I said and waited. Antonia remained silent. "Very well, let's be frank about it," I continued. "You want —"

"I want Paul to have his great opportunity."

"Perhaps you do. But I don't think you want it for *him*. You want it for yourself."

"Judith!" She was outraged. "How can you

say such a thing to me."

"Because it's fairly common. In a way it's natural — we all want wonderful things for those we care about. But *see* it like that, please. You want Paul's success for yourself so that when you have retired, you can live your triumphs all over again in his. It's a very personal thing."

She said faintly, "If Paul is a success, we would all be happy — and proud."

"His life belongs to him, and he's no infant prodigy. He's just an ordinary small boy who happens to be my son."

She turned angrily away from me.

"Antonia, please just stop and think. He's only seven years old and quite suddenly his father vanishes."

"Judith, don't . . ."

"I'm trying to make you understand."

"It's brutal to remind me."

Her hardening attitude invoked fresh anger in me. Thoughts that I had kept to myself rushed out in rapid sentences. "You had your own experiences of Lewis's unbalance long before I married him. You did, didn't you?"

"You talk about him as if he were mad. He's not!" She leaned against the piano and her hands accidentally touched some notes. They jangled through the Hall, echoing like bells far up in the vaulted ceiling.

164

"Why? Why has life done these things to me?" she cried in the throaty sound that came whenever she tried to raise her voice. Then she ran down the steps and walked quickly away through a tall archway. I heard her swift footsteps going toward the tower.

In spite of the warm day, it was cold in the Hall, but I didn't realize it until Paul's voice startled me. I jumped up and went to find him.

"Rory wants to take me over to Mull with him," he said. "I can go, can't I? I *can* go? He wants some more fishing tackle and he is going to buy some new shoes and he wants lots of chocolate — he loves chocolate. And —"

"Hey, take a breath!"

"But I *can* go?" Eyes dancing, he looked up at me. The freckles on his face were little gold splotches.

Rory was good with a boat and the distance was very short. The sea between Cathair Mor and the island of Mull was gentle, except during the gales of winter. And there was the everwatchful Ulad MacNeill on Mull.

"Yes," I said, "of course you can go."

"Wow!" said my son and shot like an arrow through the door.

At lunch we ate strawberries packed and sent by Fortnum and Mason's in London. Antonia said, "I'm asking Shane Kilarran to dinner. Joe and Catherine Torrens are coming over from

Mull and also the MacCallums, who are from Edinburgh but are staying with them."

"Shane Kilarran . . . ?"

She held a strawberry between her fingers, peering at it as if she were searching for an imperfection. "Sooner or later I'm going to find out why he's here. I've told you, I suspect he came for some purpose connected with the island and . . . and with Lewis's absence."

"He must surely come back occasionally?" I made it a question, needing reassurance.

"Of course. But after eight years, why just *now?*"

I had no answer to that, and the more I thought about it the more I echoed her questions. Why now?

I tried to think how I could escape from Antonia's dinner party, and faced the fact that short of taking to my bed with a migraine, there was nothing I could do. It cheered me, however, to remember that I had met and liked both the Torrenses and the MacCallums in London when the families were on holiday there. So I would have four people to talk to while Antonia played special hostess to Shane.

Late that afternoon, after Rory and Paul had returned, I went to take Morag's small granddaughter a birthday present. I had found a fold-up doll carriage, which she had longed for after seeing a child with one on Mull.

Morag told me that the parson of the church on Mull, which they attended every Sunday, was coming over on one of his visits.

" 'Tis God-fearin' folk we are," she said, pouring me out a cup of scalding tea.

God-fearing, I knew, but with a dash of paganism thrown in, for the islanders believed in the "faery people" of their legends. Still, I sat listening to talk of "that fine parson wi' his black beard an' his prayin' hands."

When I left Morag's cottage and her delighted pale-haired grandchild, I walked along the beach. The puffins and the guillemots were swinging overhead in agitated circles and screaming in a way they did when coming bad weather disturbed them. Clouds were piling up like purple smoke on the southwestern horizon. The sea seemed suddenly to spring out of its indolence, and the wash of some violent storm far out at sea broke in white foam at the base of the cliffs.

Morag had said, just as I was leaving, "It's been too good a day to last. Likely we'll have rain."

But the sun and the turquoise sky would be over the island for some time yet and I lifted my face and closed my eyes, feeling the warmth on my skin.

I thought, How like music the sea is when the tide is high and it beats against the rocks.

And then, still listening, I realized that what I heard was in fact music. My body became tense and I held my breath for fear I might miss a sound that would prove to me that I had misheard. But I hadn't.

Someone, somewhere, was playing the bagpipes, the strange, haunting, plaintive music that had a beauty of its own when heard in the open air.

I swung around. There was no one behind me and no one within range of me. Besides, the sound came from over the strip of water that divided the island from Cathair Beag. For one moment I wondered if the pipes came from somewhere on Mull, but the wind was from the southwest, which would have blown any Mull music away from me and I could never have heard it from that distance.

Someone was playing the bagpipes on Cathair Beag.

Once, when I came to Mullaine, I had been told that it took seven years to make a piper who was sufficiently proficient to play the traditional pipe airs. They said on Cathair Mor, "The Laird is the only one who can play the pipes here."

I stood, taut and alert, listening and watching. Out there, across the strip of sea, someone was playing the song of the island, "The Red Man."

The wind, carrying the purple clouds nearer, blew against me. I put up my hands and covered my ears. But nothing shut out the sound:

"I am he returned to you,
I, who you thought was dead.
And I am Laird of Cathair,"
The red man said.

I turned and fled.

XII

Crouched in a hollow in the heather above Mullaine, I tried to remember if I had heard of anyone else on the island who had learned to play the pipes.

From where I huddled, I could not see Cathair Beag, nor could I be seen by anyone there. The larks sang and the mountain linnets darted low over the furze. The heather had a hot, dry scent; the sullen clouds drew nearer.

Words came back. Lewis saying to me as we sat looking out to sea, "No, Clea darling, I can't take you climbing on Cathair Beag. It's far too dangerous. Anyway, there's nothing there but sea birds, and even the place I've found is treacherous and only accessible at certain times. Mostly the sea fumes and rages round. Anyway" – lightly teasing me –"I need a secret place where even you can't follow me."

I had laughed, happy and in love.

Then a memory. Lewis saying, "I'm going to give my set of pipes to Rory. He has always wanted to play them. He never will, of course.

170

He can't learn, that's his tragedy."

Rory had been shown the hold for the pipes and the preparation, but the first sounds he made were such piercing banshee wails that Lewis fled, dragging me with him.

I had protested, "Now you've hurt his feelings. He was so delighted that he could make a sound at all."

And Lewis had laughed. "Well, let Shane teach him when he comes home. I won't."

"Can Shane play?"

"A bit. At least what he plays is recognizable — if only just."

But the tune I heard this day was absolutely recognizable . . . perfectly pitched, perfectly played.

I lay back in the rough heather, remembering.

Gradually I became calmer. There must be pipers on Mull, and perhaps someone from there had come across, found his way to the top of the cliffs and practiced his pipes there in peace. But why "The Red Man"?

On an impulse I started up and ran down from the moors, past Mullaine, through the glen to the Abbey, to see if the bagpipes Lewis had given Rory were still there. If so, then I could relax, for it would be some stranger who had found his way onto Cathair Beag.

The door to the Abbey was very elaborate, its

two columns supporting carved arches. Above them were twelve figures representing the twelve apostles, their faces and robes worn away by centuries of storms.

I pulled the huge bell at the side of the door but I was trembling so that the sound was weak. When no one answered, I ran around the side, past the circle of rowan trees and the curious rough formation of stones that were the foundation of the uncompleted transept. Grass and flowers grew among the tumbled rocks, and I crossed the abandoned place to what was now the kitchen quarters of the Abbey. The door was open and Jeannie was at the table slicing the rind off a lemon, absorbed in making one continuous whirl of peel.

She gave a start as I knocked on the door, turned and saw me. "Oh dear." She looked flustered. "Ye rang the bell for sure, and I didna' hear ye. Now what for could I have been so deaf?"

"It doesn't matter. I want to see Mr. Rory."

"Oh, he's maybe after catching a trout at the burn."

But Rory wasn't. He came into the stone kitchen rubbing his hands. "I heard the doorbell but I was right up in the gallery. There's a place where the rain comes in and Dru is sealing it. I went up to watch. Was it me you wanted, or Shane?"

"Not Shane. Rory, do you remember the bagpipes Lewis gave you some years ago?"

"I remember." He shook his head. "I tried many times, but I can't play them. So I shut them up in the chest."

"And they're still there?"

He gave me a curious look. "Why shouldn't they be? No one seems interested here in playing them."

"But I heard some just now — over the sea. Someone on Cathair Beag was playing them."

"Not *my* bagpipes. A piper from Mull perhaps."

"I thought there was no place to land on Cathair Beag."

"No," he said slowly. "I've never heard of anyone —"

"Except Lewis," I said quickly.

His face changed and a kind of naked fear crossed it. "You don't mean . . . you couldn't mean . . ."

"I don't know what I meant when I said that," I said gently, as if it were Rory and not I who needed reassurance. "Suppose we just go and see if the pipes are where you put them."

"But of course they are." He took my arm and led me through the long, lofty hall which had been the skeleton for the nave of the Abbey. Although the place was unfinished, the vaulting was exquisite. I had the same thought here as when I had stood at the door. While the builder monks were busy with the solid foundations, the walls and the floors, the fine artists among them must have been absorbed in the intricate carvings. The hall, as it was now known, was an empty, columned place. The only thing that could take away the sensation of hollow space and give it a lived-in look would have been to have built a false ceiling over the fan vaulting. But no one down the centuries had dared to do that. The hall was, therefore, never used except as a place to walk through in order to reach the Kilarran living rooms. There were steps up to what had been planned as an altar and on which stood a long refectory table of oak so old that it was almost black. There were no chairs around the table, for no one ever ate there. At each end were wrought-iron candlesticks as tall as a man. From the pillars, sconces bearing electric fittings had stone carvings around them. Here, too, I supposed that while the builder-priests were at work trying to finish the Abbey, the artist masons had carved the faces of saints.

Rory went to a huge leather chest with brass fittings that stood near a side door to the cloisters. Through the short twisted columns that supported the roof, I could see the small square cloister garden where Rory grew flowers. It was beautifully sheltered and iris and early roses were already blossoming.

Rory was having difficulty with one of the locks of the chest, muttering to himself. I stepped through the door and glanced along the cloister. There was a stone trough where, I had been told, the monks went to wash their hands and faces. In it were planted nasturtium and calceolaria, brilliant splashes of color against the grey stone.

I had been to the Abbey before and Rory had shown me around. While the nave was too vast for domestic use, the other parts of the building had been made into comfortable rooms. The chapter house was the Kilarran living room, the refectory their dining room, the day room of the novices was Rory's bedroom. I had no idea where Shane slept.

I was told that the bell that should clang for prayers had been hung in the belfry by an enthusiastic Kilarran some years ago, but for some reason I had not heard of, it had never been rung. As I stood in that secluded place by the cloister, I could even hear, in imagination, the Gregorian plain-song that might have echoed through the Abbey had not money failed the monks.

"They're not here."

For a few moments I had been in another century. The transition back to the present was almost like a shock. I asked

175

stupidly, "What isn't where?"

"The set of pipes. My pipes . . . they're gone."

The past was completely extinguished. The present was suddenly frightening. I said, "Perhaps you put them somewhere else."

"I haven't touched them. When Lewis gave them to me, I remember saying to him that I'd keep them here. And he had laughed and said, 'Well, don't let them molder. Play them.' "

We stared at one another, and I felt that the dismay on my face was as great as that on his. Above the troubled blue eyes, his forehead was creased and his hair stood out, as it usually did, in little tufts. His lips trembled like a child's.

"Someone *was* playing the pipes," I said. "Out there on Cathair Beag. Rory, I *know* I heard them. Come on . . . perhaps whoever he is, is still playing them."

Our feet clattered on the stone floor as we ran. Outside, the storm clouds had crept almost to the rim of the sun and the hills were already turned the color of charcoal. The sea was like oily steel.

We stood, heads raised, turned toward Cathair Beag, listening. There was no sound of bagpipes.

"It must have been the sea you heard," Rory said. "You aren't used to our noisy waters, Judith."

"I know the difference between waves crashing and someone playing 'The Red Man.' "

"Oh God, you heard *that?*"

"Yes." Rory's sudden fierce alarm startled me. "Why, what's wrong with hearing that particular song? I mean ... why are you so upset?"

He pulled himself together quickly and smiled. "Oh, I suppose I'm jealous. I'm upset because I can't play the pipes. And I don't understand how anyone could have taken mine — if those you say you heard *were* mine."

"I don't understand any of it, either," I said.

We stood for some time, listening. But there was no music.

Rory asked in anger, like a child robbed of a toy, "Who took my pipes, Judith? Who could . . . ?"

"Perhaps Shane borrowed them."

He shook his head. "Oh no. Shane went over to Mull. Besides, he wouldn't remember how to climb onto Cathair Beag — I think he did once, but it's so long ago. And now — Oh, Judith!"

"It's all right," I said, calming him. "Perhaps what I heard was a piper from Mull. After all, if Lewis could find a way onto Cathair Beag — and perhaps Shane did once — so could others. You'll find your pipes, Rory, somewhere around."

The wind was rising, eddying around the

cloisters, and I felt suddenly cold.

Rory turned to me with a wide smile. "You're right. I expect the pipes are somewhere — I can be quite absent-minded, you know. And there are often sounds like music around the island. I sometimes think music is being played here inside the Abbey. I once showed you our old harp, didn't I? I used to think a ghost was playing it. But do you know what it *really* was?" He chuckled. "The wind humming in the cloisters."

But the wind hadn't played "The Red Man."

The gulls screamed at the purple clouds, and far away, on the Brenlorns, I could hear the bleat of sheep. Rory walked back with me across the glen as the first rain began to fall. At the door of the Castle he said, "It's so nice to have you here. And Paul, too. I wish you'd stay forever."

"It's very beautiful," I told him gently, "but I have my life in London and my work there."

"And soon you'll all be gone, you and Paul and Antonia."

"Not Antonia. She may stay for a while."

"But she doesn't bother much with me. She thinks I'm stupid."

"Of course she doesn't!"

He nodded. "She's right. But it's odd, you know. Stupid people don't usually know they're stupid. I do."

178

"That shows that you aren't."

He gave me a long strange look. "I wish things were different for you, Judith. I wish" – his eyes became curiously inward-looking – "I wish you could take a huge jump over these next few weeks. Because I like you so much . . . and then you'd be safe." His eyes suddenly lost their tranced look and became startled, as if he had frightened himself. He added quickly, "I must go . . . I must go," and ran from me.

Antonia came around the side of the Castle. She was carrying a sheaf of rowan branches. "There's so little here that one can pick," she complained. "But I can't stand my room without flowers." She turned the rowan branches to one side and showed me the few marigolds and blue iris she had managed to find. "Rosheen and Duncan just aren't interested in flowers, and I really can't think how these survived without any attention. I suppose they're wild. Even in the old days, when Robert came here so much, though he liked to garden, he was lazy. So Mullaine was always more or less all shades of green."

She glanced down ruefully at what she had managed to find and the ragged light piercing a storm cloud shone on her.

"Someone was on Cathair Beag –"

She swung around to me. "Oh, Judith, not

again! You told me you saw a light there. Now . . . now you say you saw someone there. But how could you? It's too far away for that."

"I *saw* no one. But someone was there playing the pipes and I knew the tune. It was 'The Red Man.'"

I was watching her too closely not to see the almost imperceptible start she gave. But she said lightly, "Oh, a piper from Mull was probably sent over there by his family because they couldn't stand the sound of the pipes. Even some Scots don't like them, you know. Come along in, it's raining."

"Do you remember that Lewis gave his set of pipes to Rory?"

"Did he? No. It must have been sometime when I was away on tour. Anyway, Lewis wouldn't want them any more. I'm glad he gave them to Rory. He'll never be bright enough to play them but he can have fun with them."

"They're gone."

She had been walking in front of me. She stopped, turned and said, "What do you mean?"

"Rory put them in a safe place, in the chest they have near the cloister door. But they're no longer there."

"No one has ever broken in or stolen anything on the island," she said, "but I suppose there's always a first time. Someone coveted them and knew that Rory would never be able to play."

"I wonder where the thief practiced, then," I said. "Because the island is so small, someone would have been bound to hear him and the news would have been all round the island that they had, at last, a player of pipes."

"Then someone must have stolen them and sold them in Mull. And the buyer was playing. That is" – she turned and walked on, adding, with her back to me – "if you really *did* hear pipes." It was almost a throwawy line and yet it hit me with a sense of shock. Antonia didn't believe what I was saying.

"You think I imagined them?"

She was at the door. "Come in quickly. I hate the rain on my hair."

Inside, with the door closed, I halted her, calling as she walked away from me, "Antonia, *do* you think I imagined hearing the bagpipes?"

"I really don't know. I hope you didn't, my dear."

"Why 'hope'?"

"Well –"

"*Why*, Antonia?"

I was at her side, forcing her to pause and answer me. She stood playing with the rowan branches. "Well, I think sometimes when someone has had a . . . a terrifying experience, they . . . they sometimes get overwrought and –"

"And imagine things?"

"Yes, Judith, I think it's possible."

For a moment her eyes met mine, and it flashed through my mind that she doubted far more than my thinking I had heard pipes played on Cathair Beag. How much did Antonia doubt of what had been done and said? Last evening's moving light, certainly. But before that — *long* before that — did she really believe my account of what happened on the night of Lewis's attack?

"You know," Antonia was saying, "when they were much younger, Lewis and Shane and one or two of the boys here all tried those pipes. One of them could have wanted to try them again somewhere where he thought no one would hear him. It could have been anyone."

"Except Lewis," I said.

She didn't answer me. Her expression was quite blank, as if she wanted me to know that I had made an unnecessary remark. She lifted a pewter jar down from a niche in the wall. "I think the rowan would look lovely in that, don't you? I'll just get some water."

Someone was pushing open the great outer door. I went to it, and Paul burst in, saying, "I'm wet." He lifted a streaming face. "Are you cross?"

"Why? Did you use magic to bring down the rain? Of course I'm not cross. But I hope the children all got home before it rained so hard. They may not have all your changes of clothes."

"Oh, I wasn't with them. I was down with my seal. You know, you saw it the other day when you thought I was lost. I didn't know what to call him. I couldn't keep saying, 'Hello, you,' could I? So I called him Rinn. Do you like it?"

"I've never heard the name before."

"It's the name of some prince or other in one of Rory's tales. Something about" — he wrinkled his nose in a way he had when puzzled — "something about a place called the Isle of Apple Trees — Rory always calls them by funny names — but he says it's all true. And Rinn was the prince of that place." Sudden caution shadowed his face. "You won't tell anyone, will you? It's *my* place. I made Duncan promise to tell the men who came to look for me not to tell either."

"And," I said, "you're dripping all over Antonia's beautiful carpet."

Very wet and laughing, kicking up his heels on the hard stones, Paul ran. Watching him leap up the stairs, I sent a silent message after him: *Don't go too far from me.* Yet I couldn't say it to him. All I could do was pray that when he was out of my sight, he was safe. In spite of the fact that remaining on the island was our best protection, I knew — by senses other than sight or sound — that danger was near. During those uncertain days I was very close to understanding the instinctive watchfulness of animals — the turn of the head at a shadow, the swift alertness at a sound.

I could, of course, defy the advice of the police and take my son with me to some remote place abroad. But what safety would I have anywhere in a world of easy air flights and diminished frontiers?

I leaned against the cold stone wall — nothing, *nothing* ever warmed the great blocks. The chill seeped through my sleeves, but I didn't move. I was still listening to Paul's feet above me, thudding as children's feet do. A wry thought crossed my mind: He'll be an awful athlete if he can't get some spring into his leg muscles.

I went back over the seven years of my son's life. At no time could I remember him as being excessively angry or losing control of his temper. He was argumentative, cheerfully stubborn, sometimes matter-of-fact, sometimes swept with wild fancies. But he was an utterly and completely normal boy. I heard his bedroom door close with a slam that echoed, and I sent a prayer after him: *Oh, God, let him be sane . . . Let him develop into someone dull and matter-of-fact and not in the least brilliant. I wouldn't care. But let him be sane.*

XIII

Rosheen was in the huge medieval kitchen, where the modern gadgets which had been installed from time to time looked entirely out of place. By the side of the ancient ovens and the roasting spit above them, hung gleaming copper pans. No one ever used them these days, but Rosheen would sit in the evenings listening to the radio and polishing them until they shone like fire.

She was standing at the scrubbed kitchen table slicing a fresh pineapple, which Antonia ordered regularly, along with strawberries and lichees, from London.

I perched on the edge of the table, watching her. "Does anyone on the island play the bagpipes?"

She shot a swift look at me. "Not these days. No. It takes a long time to learn those an' the men here haven't the time, what with fishin' an' shepherdin' an' gatherin' the peat an' keepin' their boats seaworthy. 'Tis awful harm the sun can do to a fishin' boat if 'tis left without being tarred."

At any other time her answer would have amused me, for on Cathair Mor it was the women who worked the hardest and the men who spent a great deal of time sitting on the low stone wall by the loch, smoking and gossiping. However, I wasn't in a mood for amusement.

"Perhaps someone *did* learn to play," I began hopefully.

"No. No one but —" She gave me a nervous sideways look.

"But my husband."

"Aye. An' Mr. Kilarran — the younger Mr. Kilarran. Mr. Shane, I mean. He used to practice a lot an' laugh at the noise he made. But that were long ago an' I don't think he's been playin' much where he's been for the past eight years. They do say no man plays the pipes out of their native land. Except for playin' for the Queen, for they do say she has her very own piper."

And was that all I had heard over the distance between Cathair Mor and Cathair Beag — a bit of playing? Had I been close, would I have heard discords and pauses in wrong places? Shane Kilarran amusing himself on the great bird-haunted rock, safely away from Scottish ears to whom the bagpipes played badly was unforgivable?

"But why do ye be after askin'?" Rosheen looked at me with a sharpness that hinted at suspicion.

"Because a little while ago I heard someone paying 'The Red Man' and the sound came from Cathair Beag."

She stopped cutting up pineapple and stared at me. "But ye couldna' have. That's the Laird's song — always the Laird's song — an' I've only ever heard him play it in the days before his father were dead. He weren't famous then. And grand it sounded, too, out on the moors. As if he were tryin' to tell all the world beyond the sea that he would one day be Laird. And he were . . . he were . . . the bonnie red-haired man."

Then, as if realizing that after what had happened I would not see Lewis in that light, Rosheen gave a little sigh and picked up her knife. "Don't ye go frettin' now about hearing anything from that place. 'Tis only a bunch o' rocks an' no one goes there, ever. No one can get on the place. What ye heard was the sea. That was all. The sea sings here. 'Tis the sea an' the seals with their big eyes that fool folks an' make them fanciful. They called them mermaids. 'Tis all nervous ye are, an' no wonder. But dinna go thinkin' there's pipes bein' played on Cathair Beag."

She glanced over my shoulder, and I saw the light of recognition on her gaunt face. "Why,

Morag, now! Come in, come in. What would ye be wantin'?"

Morag's plaid cape was of the Macdonald tartan, but as she bore no relationship to that clan, I guessed it had probably been given to a servant by a long dead Macdonald and had eventually found its way to Morag's long back. She wore a shawl over her abundant hair, and she, who was a tall, thin woman, looked like a giantess.

" 'Tis The Mullaine's wife I was looking for," she said and turned to me. "I was for thinkin' there's that old cottage of Hamish McInch's. No one's lived there nor wanted it since he died an' likely no one ever will. It'll no be in much of a condition, but Angus an' Jaimie an' the rest could do somethin' about that. And then, likely, we could use it for our weavin'."

"Take me!" I said and jumped down from the table.

Rosheen protested. " 'Tis rainin' somethin' bad."

"The place be only over the *creagach*. You know well, Rosheen, 'tis just there before ye get to the first heather slope by the burn."

I ran to fetch my raincoat, which was hanging to dry. In the pocket was a yellow scarf, still damp. I tied it over my hair. "Let's go," I said.

Morag hitched her great cape around her as Rosheen murmured that " 'twere no afternoon to go lookin' at places and no *sith* would spirit it away in the night if we were sensible and waited till tomorrow."

"*Sith?*" I asked Morag as we went out of the door and ducked our heads into the slanting gusts of rain.

" 'Twould be a good thing if ye talked like us," she said bluntly. "But never mind. '*Sith*' is a fairy; '*sithean*' is a fairy dwelling." Morag was always proud that she could translate from Gaelic into English so much more easily than anyone else on the island.

"And you believe in these things?"

"Oh, aye, maybe," she answered casually, as if afraid that by speaking the absolute truth and denying the immortals of the Hebrides she might incur their wrath.

We crossed the *machair*, and the buttercups and the daisies dropped with the deceptive weight of the light rain. The scent of sea tang and clover and thyme and wet earth was glorious. Morag strode like a man, pausing only when we came to the rocky place to help me over the slippery stones.

On a bank in front of a small stream was Hamish McInch's cottage. It was two stories high and listed slightly, like a drunken ship. The windowpanes were broken, the door hung by one hinge and the roof tilted.

When Morag pushed at the door and it

creaked open lopsidedly, so that we could just squeeze through, I saw that the rooms were dry and that the roof would probably only leak in one of the island's fierce winter gales. The place was empty of furniture and there was a dusting of blown sand on the floor. A litter of straw had drifted through the storm-smashed windows and a pile of rotting peat was stacked on the stove. Three enormous spider webs swayed in the draft.

" 'Tis likely, ye think?" Morag asked.

I said, looking about me, "It would be marvelous once it's whitewashed and the windows mended. But who does it belong to? I mean, there must be rent to pay."

She shook her head. " 'Tis Mullaine land, surely, hereabouts."

"But I can't just take over a piece of property."

She gave her rich laugh. "Is that what ye call it?"

"Hamish McInch must have relations."

"Oh, aye, in Glasgow. But he lived alone here until he was ninety. And he's been dead this four years and no one's been around askin' about it." Morag walked across the room, eying it critically. "That stove . . . We'll be havin' to get Dru to see it gives us a good fire for our tea." Then she went into the hall and stood looking at the staircase.

"Come on," I said. "Whether we can have the place or not, let's take a look upstairs."

The tiny rooms were dry except in two places where the thatch of the roof had worn away and dried salt spray lay like a thin gauze covering over the floor.

"This is where we can store all that stuff ye say we'll need. Angus will repair the roof; he's good at thatchin'."

"Yes," I said, "yes, fine." But as we left the cottage and tried, unsuccessfully, to close the door, I didn't dare hope that a place had been so easily found for my weaving scheme.

The rain was falling more heavily. "Aye, but 'twill be worse before it gives over," Morag said, looking at the western sky. "Then we'll be havin' a fine night."

We scrambled over the rough grass and the scree, the rain making little tattooing needles on our faces.

When we reached Mullaine, Morag said, "I'll be gettin' Angus busy on the thatchin' right away. 'Tis so little needs to be done."

Wherever she was, Morag would always take over the practical reins and, gratefully, I let her. She left me and went around to the back door of the Castle. I was quite certain that she could scarcely wait to tell Rosheen, over a cup of tea, that we had found the place for the weaving.

I crossed the Great Hall, sliding out of my

raincoat as I went.

"You're wet," said my son, trying to imitate my earlier manner to him, "and I'm not cross. Will you come and play Scrabble?"

He had little specks of white around his mouth. Rosheen had obviously been feeding him the meringues Antonia had taught her to make. "Lick your lips," I said.

He understood at once, grinned at me and licked. "It was lovely," he said. "All gooey and sticky inside. *Can* we play Scrabble?"

"I think that's a fine idea for a rainy afternoon. You can take my coat for Morag to hang up to dry. And my scarf. Then we can play at this table."

"Oh, not here!" Paul protested, waving my wet coat so that it dripped, as he had done previously, on the rose-and-gold Tabriz carpet. "Antonia will come along and want me to play her beastly piano."

"I promise she won't. All right, then, you say where we'll play. But take those things to Morag to dry."

In the end we played in Paul's bedroom.

After beating me at one of the games, Paul obviously decided that he had better not push his luck too far. He went to the window. "It's stopped raining. Can I go out again? I want to go see my seal. Do you think he'll stay?"

"I don't know, darling."

"I don't know what to call it."

"Call what?"

"Why, my place. Every place has to have a name, doesn't it?"

"We'll try to think of one."

He fidgeted, watching me gather together the scattered letters of our Scrabble game. "I really must go to that place," he said. "I left my scarf there. I tied it to that bit of rock."

"You can fetch it tomorrow."

"But it will get wet."

"And what kind of state do you think it's in at the moment?" I countered, laughing.

"Please, I wouldn't be out long. I really wouldn't."

I knew exactly how he felt on the island. There was so little to occupy a small boy who was used to television, cricket, football and friends who talked his language. He hadn't found a lasting interest in helping the islanders bring in their cattle and even the fishing expeditions with Rory couldn't contain complete delight. Popular as he was among the island children, he was a stranger who "talked odd," and that in itself isolated him. Yet he had the temperament to make the best of what was there; he never sulked or complained.

"Fine," I said. "We'll go together to Rinn's Place." But as I said it, I hoped he wasn't going through such a period of loneliness that even a grownup was a better companion than no one.

I made him put on his windbreaker, for the rain had cooled the air, and we set off on the short shore route. The sky was rich with a clear gilded light that suffuses a land immediately after daylight rain. As we passed them Jaimie's cows gave us their lowering look, lifting lazy heads from the rich green patch of grass.

I looked away to the southeast. Up on the highest eastern point of the Brenlorns it was said there were a few wild white cattle, that almost legendary breed of rare animals which ate at night and slept during the day. I had never seen one, but Morag told me, "Their horns turn upwards and inwards, and they have shaggy manes like lions. Ach, but they're beautiful."

I had asked in ignorance, "Why don't you catch them? They would surely be better looked after than up there and out in all the terrible weather you sometimes have here."

"Aye, but even if we could catch them, we could nae touch them. They belong to The Mullaine."

Lewis's wild white cattle, which he had probably forgotten existed . . .

XIV

We crossed the green valley, made for the narrow cleft in the rock and squeezed through. It had been cold walking along the exposed seashore, but here, sheltered from the winds, with the western sun pouring down and the tall cliffs cradling the tiny bay, it was warm. The sea had none of the gentleness of the air; it tore and ground at the rocks, pouring out white foam in great cascades.

Paul called above the crash of the water, "Rinn . . . Rinn . . ."

Whether the seal knew its name or whether it was making for the cove anyway, I had no idea, but suddenly it was there, plunging and gliding toward us. It heaved itself clumsily onto the rocky ledge, rolled over and lay with flippers folded.

Paul had gone across the beach to an opening in one of the rocks. It was too small to be called a cave but it was a good shelter, its overhanging shelf carved by the sea and the storms into a slightly downward curving line like half an umbrella.

"Look," Paul said.

Under the ledge was what at first appeared to be a pile of dry brown seaweed and a few pieces of rotting wood.

"*Look*." He was impatient at my lack of immediate interest. Then he picked something up out of the pile and held it out to me. It lay in the palm of my hand, cool to my touch, glowing like a jewel. Paul was leaning over my hand, eager for some wonderful revelation. "Is it precious?"

I said, saddened that I had to wipe the hope from his face, "No, darling. It looks like a huge emerald, doesn't it? But I'm afraid it's just a piece of broken glass from a bottle that has been rubbed smooth by the sea." I held it to the sunlight, and suddenly in its depth of rich steady green there seemed to glow a great beauty.

"I found this, too." Paul dived for a piece of wood roughly carved in the shape of a whale.

I said, "Some sailor must have begun making it and then in a bored moment thrown it overboard."

"Is it very old? You know, like things they always say they'll find one day at Tobermory?"

I heard him but I didn't answer, for at that moment I looked toward Paul's pile of flotsam, and I could see something that glinted through the seaweed.

"*Where did you get that?*"

I threw down the piece of glass and bent and picked up the thing that caught my eye, the thing that was mine, that I had lost at Mullaine Castle.

"Paul, I'm asking you. Where did you get this?"

He looked scared. "I've never seen it before. It's a ring. It's pretty, isn't it?"

I checked an impulse to say, "It's mine. I lost it last summer." Instead, I looked out at the waves licking a jagged line of rocks. "I wonder how far the tide comes in here?"

"*I* know. I watch it lots of times. Just a *little* bit creeps in. But it doesn't come up to my collection."

His collection — a piece of glass, a partly carved whale, some unopened tins of something or other — the labels were washed off — and this, that was mine.

"I'll keep it," I said.

He looked saddened.

"Paul," I said gently. "It isn't yours. You told me you hadn't put it where I saw it."

"But it was on *my* rock." He wouldn't remember it, of course, because I had only worn the ring once. It was so small that I could just get it on my little finger, and even then, it was tight.

Lewis had given it to me. Rubies and topaz, in an intricate setting, formed a circle around a small fire opal. It was an elaborate but not expensive little ring and I had loved it. The jeweler to whom I had taken it had told me that it was early Georgian and much too fragile to be made larger. He could, of course, reset the stones in a modern ring for me. But its beauty was partly in its setting. I thanked him and put it back in my small folding jewel case.

A year ago, when Antonia and Lewis and I were all briefly at Mullaine, I wanted to show it to my mother-in-law.

I remembered the day very clearly. It had begun badly. Lewis had flown into one of his rages because he had decided, he said, to buy Paul a particularly spirited horse someone in Mull had for sale.

"We'll keep it here and Paul can ride it whenever we come to Mullaine."

"Lewis, you *can't*. No one here can ride anything more daring than a donkey. We are only here for two weeks at the most in a year, and who would exercise the horse?"

My protest was enough to inflame him. I was crossing him again; I was preventing his son from enjoying all the privileges a child of his should have. White-faced, in that voice scarcely above a whisper which was far more terrifying than shouting, Lewis raged at me. In the end he didn't buy the horse for the simple reason that the owner decided not to sell.

On the day following the scene, Antonia arrived with some friends, for a week. Lewis had mentioned the ring. "Show it to Antonia. She might even know of a jeweler who could make it larger for you without damaging it." The rage was over and he was smiling and calm.

But my ring was missing from the jewel case and I could not find it anywhere. Lewis had seemed more alarmed than angry. "That's just the kind of thing you keep doing these days, isn't it, Clea?"

He was right. I became distraught after his furies and it apparently affected me so that I mislaid things, forgot dates, concentrating on my enormous efforts not to provoke him further. It wasn't easy to hold on to pride and the integrity of one's own opinions while a man tore all arguments against his own into low, seething strips.

Ice-cold, he had said on that occasion. "One of these days, Clea, you'll end up doing something really frightening. God knows what, but . . ."

Defeated, I had turned and walked out of the room.

From then on I took even greater care to try to remember where I put things, to check on dates. But the absent-mindedness persisted. I faced the awful question: Am I losing my grip on my mind? My answer to myself was vehement. I wasn't. But then came the further dreadful question. Did one know when one's mind was breaking?

One thing assured me. The police, the lawyers, all those engaged in that terrible investigation after Lewis's disappearance, had praised me for what they called my stability and I called, more truthfully, my determination not to let anything get me down and ruin Paul's life or my own.

For a year, then, an antique ring had been lost. Now that ring had reappeared, washed up all these months later on a beach on the far side of an island ravaged by storms and wild seas. It made no sense.

Had the tiny thing been carried by the sea from the northwest of the island to this southern tip, in the swirling of the great waves, the delicate gold tracery would have been crushed against the harsh rocks. So the ring had not been stolen by someone and fallen into the sea near Mullaine, to turn up here. Someone had placed it where it would be seen. Someone who knew it was mine? Someone who watched Paul *and knew that he came here alone?*

The cove suddenly became sinister.

I twisted the ring around in my hand, watching the glint of sea-washed stones. Who had touched it last, putting it on the bed of dry seaweed where Paul, with his little magpie mind for collecting "treasures," would find it and show me? Or, even, that I might come to this secret place on my own and find it?

Paul had gone over to Rinn, and the seal was wriggling toward him with the inherent curiosity of its kind. "Are you going to keep the ring?" he asked, watching me over his shoulder.

I said with forced amusement. "Darling, I don't think it would be much use to you. You couldn't wear it."

"Are *you* going to wear it?"

It was the last thing I intended to do. But I would show it around and watch faces. From now on I would suspect everyone of . . . of what? Perhaps of something someone knew without realizing its significance.

"Let's get back," I said to Paul, and as I moved away from the sea, I looked up at the cliffs. Nothing moved, no one appeared to be watching us. "Are there any caves around here?" I asked.

"I've tried to find one, because it would be fun," Paul said. "But there aren't any. There are only those little holes where the birds go at night." He chattered on, obviously unaware of my distress. "Rinn knows his name. When I

201

said it he flapped those things —"

"Flippers."

"— as if were clapping me. I want him to stay here."

"All right. You've staked your claim. But we're going now. You first." I put the ring in the pocket of my skirt and marched Paul to the cleft in the rocks.

As I did so I glanced up at the forbidding line of the cliffs. It was then that I noticed that halfway up there was a curious formation of stone, darker than the rest and forming a serrated circle. Differing rock formations usually ran in horizontal strata; this was odd, as if someone had climbed up, taken a brush and painted some huge sign on it. But no one had. It was quite obviously a freak circular formation of rock and it was shaped like a star. I knew then why it had been called on that ancient map, the Bay of the Dark Star.

We met only two people as we walked back over the rocks to Mullaine. Jaimie was tickling the brown behind of his cow as he urged him homeward and once, when I turned to look back, I saw Shane standing on a ridge of rock, his back to us. On a small island it was inevitable that everyone kept meeting, but I had an uncanny feeling that although he might not have been watching us at the cove, Shane had seen us leave the place.

When we reached the Castle, I sent Paul to clean up. Then I went to find Antonia. She was sitting at her dressing table, combing her hair upwards with slow luxuriant movements, so that it stood like a feathery snow-white halo around her face.

Her husky voice answered me. "Come in . . . Come in . . ."

I crossed to her side and held out the ring.

She laid the comb down on the carved Italian desk that served as her dressing table, then looked down at my palm. "It's pretty and old —"

"Lewis bought it for me, and last summer when we were up here, I went to my jewel case to get it out and show it to you and it wasn't there. You remember?"

"I remember your saying you'd lost a ring, but since I had never set eyes on it, how could I recognize it?" She looked up at me, her eyes puzzled and amused. "And now you've found it."

"This afternoon, down at that cove where Paul plays."

"How on earth did it get there?"

"That's what I want to know."

She leaned back in the elaborate Italian chair which she used as a dressing stool. "You lost that ring for a whole year and then found it right on the far side of the island? Oh no!"

"Here it is. And Paul can prove I didn't make the story up."

"I don't understand."

"Nor do I."

She stared at her reflection. The slender gold chain at her throat glinted in the light. "I remember that once a friend told me she had lost a very valuable ring and the insurance company paid up. Then a long time later she found it. Do you know where? On the floor. It had got caught up in the hem of her skirt and after a while became dislodged, and there it was." She glanced down at me. "You wore that skirt up here last year. I remember, because I thought what a lovely color it was, rose and grey with a hint of green."

"The ring did not fall out of the hem of my skirt. Paul found it on a pile of seaweed and I hadn't been near it."

"Paul. Ah . . ." she said thoughtfully. "You know lots of boys just pick up anything they find lying about and store it."

"Paul didn't."

"Judith dear, how do you know?"

"I just do."

Antonia rose and went to a cupboard and took out the crimson embroidered bolero she often wore in the cool of summer evenings at Mullaine. "What explanation have you?"

"Someone put the ring where Paul or I would see it."

"I doubt if it would seem important to Paul."

"He is collecting anything and everything in that place," I said. "But someone could have watched me on my way there and put the ring on the seaweed where one of us would find it."

"Oh, really, Judith! Who?"

"That's what I don't know."

She shook her head, returned to the dressing table and sprayed scent on her neck and hair. "Just because it's good for my morale up here," she explained.

I could see her small, light smile reflected in the mirror, and turned to the door. I should have known that Antonia couldn't help me.

"Judith."

I waited, hand on the heavy ancient latch.

"Dear, I seem to remember that you have been forgetful and inclined to lose things at times. You have, haven't you?"

"At times, yes."

"Well then, don't you think perhaps you could have had the ring all the time, perhaps in your coat pocket, and it dropped out today and rolled on to the place where you found it."

"No."

She sighed. "I hate reminding you, but there was that time when, I believe, you forgot to meet Lewis for lunch. And —"

"Yes. Apparently I did forget."

It was terrifying to be warned of possible lapses of which there were no memories. In that secret place where amnesia befogged the mind, who knew what had been said, been done? But I wasn't an amnesiac. All I had ever done during a state of emotional unhappiness was to mislay something or forget a date. Nobody was going to see that as a mental disorder.

Antonia was standing, waiting for me to speak. "What is it? You're looking so troubled."

I met her eyes without faltering. "I *am* troubled. But because of the discovery of my ring, not for any memory lapses I may have had. There's only one thing for me to do, I must ask everyone I can think of on the island if they have seen the ring anywhere."

"And they'll say no." There was a faint mocking in her voice. "Because they probably wouldn't notice it if it were adorning the horns of one of their cows. They've eyes only for the wool on their sheep and their salted herrings and their whiskey."

"That's very unfair. They are good people, proud and independent, and I like them."

"Oh, so do I," she said, "but I don't like wild Scottish islands as my daily dose."

"Go back to London, Antonia."

Sadness clouded her face. "You know I can't.

206

Not yet. Not until I have recovered my voice. And I will, Judith." Her eyes were full of hope and fear. "You don't doubt that, do you?"

I doubted it terribly and sadly for her. But I said, "Just have patience. That's all we can both have at the moment."

"Oh God." She flung out her hands, and her gesture was both dramatic and wholly sincere. "If I could see the lights of Covent Garden again and hear the crowds at the Metropolitan. I want to feel the coolness of flowers in my arms after a recital at the National Theatre and dinner afterwards and champagne. Judith, let's have champagne tonight — just the two of us. Draw the curtains and pretend that outside are the city lights."

"Yes, let's," I said.

We smiled at one another like conspirators.

XV

It was the night of Antonia's small party. Nobody felt less like sitting down with dinner guests than I did. But I knew that the island life was far more lonely for Antonia than it was for me. I had Paul and I could also enjoy talking to the island people. Antonia had nothing to say to them — not because she disliked them but because she was totally out of her depth, and the distance between their lives was far too great to be bridged by words. I had the additional bond with the islanders of the weaving industry that was soon to start on Cathair Mor.

Jock had taken me down to the loch in his cart that morning and arranged to collect the dyes and the various materials and equipment we needed. Then I sat beside him as he drove his lazy and beloved old horse as near to Hamish McInch's cottage as the dry-stone wall and rolling shelves of scree would allow. There, with the help of Duncan, who was waiting for us, we unloaded and stacked everything in one of the rooms. With Jock and Angus and Dru all working on it, the roof had been repaired and new windows put in — the island people could move fast when they chose. I had a feeling that the speed with which they helped to renovate the cottage they still called "Old Hamish's" was out of some silent sympathy they felt for me. Although we didn't speak the same language, there was trust between us.

I had planned that the women who were intending to join the group of weavers would all meet me the following morning at the cottage. In the meantime there was tonight to get through, and I didn't look forward to it.

I already knew Joe and Catherine Torrens quite well. They lived in London and had inherited a large house on Mull which they had turned into a summer home. I liked them, and in different circumstances would have enjoyed meeting them again. Antonia's other friends, the MacCallums, were charming, high-spirited and musical. Shane, the fifth guest, was, for me, the unwelcome one.

Had it not been for the ancient, muted tapestries decorating the stone walls of the western-facing drawing room and the deeply recessed windows looking out onto the vast stretch of sea and primrose light, we might have been seated in Antonia's London house, so sophisticated was the ambience.

We had dined well and were drinking coffee and liqueurs. Joe Torrens was asking Shane about the Middle East, and Shane was telling us, too briefly, about the bazaars and teahouses of Isfahan, the minarets and the mountains and the flowers of Iran. Catherine, always fascinated by travelers' tales, kept asking him questions, forcing him to tell more. I was fascinated also, and for a little while the tension I felt whenever I was near Shane disappeared and I enjoyed him as an entertaining companion.

"Did you get suddenly very tired of the desert?" Antonia asked with misleading innocence. "Was that why you decided on an impulse, as it were, to come home?"

Shane picked up one word of her question, quietly, almost casually, and answered that. "Desert? Oh, no. You've no idea what it's like there. Roses, ibex on the high slopes and apricots and mulberries for the picking." He smiled at her, but the real question she had asked him had not been answered. Shane was no man to be drawn against his will.

Antonia was far too gracious a hostess to thrash an unwelcome subject and she turned to the Torrenses and asked them about a new singer, a fine young contralto who had taken London concertgoers by storm. Antonia was always avid for news of the music world and the Torrenses and the Mac-

Callums filled her in with news that had not yet infiltrated Cathair Mor.

Catherine said suddenly. "You have a Celtic name, Mr. Kilarran."

Antonia answered for him. "Oh yes, he has. And do you know, his ancestors go right back to the High King of Dalriada? What was his name?"

"Conall," Shane said briefly, and tried to change the subject.

Antonia would not be diverted. "They ruled their island far more rigidly than we rule Cathair Mor today," she said.

"My dear Antonia, you don't," Shane said in a voice that was steel beneath pleasant casualness. "The islanders rule themselves. You can't conquer a Cathair man or woman." Completely at ease, he sat with Saturn purring on his knees. The cat's gleaming bronze back quivered with delight as Shane ran his fingers lightly over it.

And yet I sensed, as the conversation drifted on, that the ease was superficial. Hundreds of years of feuding seemed to be casting their shadow and I wondered if Shane had ever resented, as his ancestors had, The Mullaine's rule. But if that were so, why had he become Lewis's friend? Perhaps, at the beginning, it could have been expediency. They were two boys from the same world on an island that knew nothing of universities or the sophistications of great cities. And when they had both left the island, the one to follow music, the other as an engineer, the friendship might have remained out of habit.

There was laughter in the room and then quick repartee. I only half listened. How well did Shane and Lewis know one another during the years after they had left Cathair Mor? How often did they correspond?

When Shane arrived that evening, he had brought with him a present for Paul. It was a maze, made of ebony and pale-green soapstone. The players had to move two small, intricately carved figures to the center of the maze and the little man who got there first was the winner. It looked easy, but it was cunningly constructed, full of fake leads, sudden cul-de-sacs, paths seemingly pointed in the right direction only to lead nowhere.

I had watched Paul play with it earlier and heard Shane warn him that the little men mustn't collide or the game would have to be started all over again. Shane had said, "Your father and I used to play with one I had years ago."

I held my breath and watched Paul. He was moving one of the green men along a narrow ebony row. His expression didn't change nor did he speak. It was as if the word "father" had no meaning for him.

Quickly I had said, "It's very kind of you, Shane. It's so beautifully made."

He said to Paul, "Have fun. Goodnight," and left Paul's playroom.

I said vaguely something about "going to wash your hands, Paul, before dinner."

He studied his middle finger, licked it lightly and gave me a bright look. "I'm clean," he said.

I knew then that he hadn't been in the least upset by the mention of his father.

"Judith dear . . ."

They were all looking at me, their faces registering amusement and surprise. I gave a little jerk. "I'm sorry . . . What did you say?"

"Catherine was suggesting that you might like to go and stay with her in Mull. Just for a change. I'd look after Paul."

"Thank you," I said, hoping that Catherine would understand. "I'd like that very much, but I can't."

Antonia said quickly, "Darling, of course you can. You'll be as safe there as here, and Duncan would deliver you into their hands."

"But I've got work to do here."

"Oh, that!" Antonia waved a dismissing hand and turned to Catherine. "Do you know, Judith has got herself involved with some small project? She's starting a weaving project here.

That can obviously wait."

"No, it can't. I must get the women started."

Catherine said, "But that's marvelous. It's high time they had an interest outside their homes. The island will die unless something is done to give it some stimulus."

Antonia said, "It's dead already — for me, anyway."

Catherine only laughed. "You turn a jaundiced eye on anything that hasn't an opera house and newspapers with distinguished critics to applaud you."

Antonia agreed without resentment. "You're so right, I do."

Janet MacCallum said, "It's a beautiful little island and thank heaven there are still unspoiled places like this in the world. I could live here very happily for the rest of my life."

How easy people thought it was to change their life style, and so often how dangerous to try, unless will and character drove one. Janet was too soft and feminine for a simple existence.

"And so the weaving project is settled?" Shane looked at me.

"Yes," I said, surprised that he had asked.

"And you have great dreams, Judith?"

I resented the slight mockery in his voice. "Oh, no." I spoke quickly "I'm not competing with large commercial firms. This is a very small luxury business and my office in London will only sell the tweed to one exclusive couturier. That way, of course, the industry won't make a lot of money. I don't intend to corrupt the islanders."

A hint of amusement crossed Shane's face, but before he could speak again, Antonia asked him, "How long are you staying here? I mean, have you got any new projects lined up? Somewhere abroad, an exciting new building, a theatre, perhaps?"

"Nothing like that, I'm afraid. I have plans for work, mostly in England, but I intend to be on the island for some time, though."

Antonia gave him a long blue stare like a pretty cat trying to fathom something she couldn't quite grasp. Then her expression relaxed and she laughed. "Have you heard the story −" She plunged into an amusing piece of gossip about a well-known opera singer.

Whenever Antonia was around, conversation flowed, for she was mistress of the art. She did not make the mistake of bringing all the conversation back to herself, but at the same time I knew that everyone in the room was very aware of her. As we sat together, the impression remained strong that tension emanated from someone in the room and no amount of laughter and light conversation could erase it.

The guests left at eleven o'clock. The thin

moon watched through one of the high Gothic windows as we all left the drawing room and crossed the Great Hall.

It was a warm night, almost as gentle as a summer night in southern England. Antonia wandered with her guests down to the loch, where Duncan awaited them with the *Midir*. I stood just outside the Castle door, vaguely disturbed that Shane, who had already taken leave of Antonia, remained by my side.

I wanted to say "Goodnight" and leave him, but something held me there, a strong and disturbing power that I resented but against which I was powerless.

"So you have already found a place where your weavers can work?"

"Yes."

"You've staked a claim on Hamish's old cottage."

"I don't know about 'staking a claim.' It's simply that Morag showed it to me and suggested that since it had been empty for so long and was getting more or less derelict, it could be just the place for us. It seems that nobody cared about the cottage, so it would be perfectly in order for me to use it —"

"Being the Laird's wife, you can, so to speak, 'take over.' Is that it?"

"I wasn't thinking of myself in that way, I —"

He interrupted me. "And if you find after all

this trouble of putting the place in order, the cottage isn't available even for the Laird's wife? What then?"

"Then someone on the island must know and should have come forward and told me."

"Someone has."

"Who?"

"I have."

He was barely more than a shadow, for the moon was half hidden by a slow-moving cloud and we were just out of range of the blaze that came through the door from the chandelier in the Great Hall.

"That cottage," he said, "is on Kilarran land. You didn't know?"

"No." I added, startled. "And what's more, I simply don't understand the laws of this place. I thought that Lewis's family, as Lairds —"

"Owned everything? No, they don't. Perhaps Lewis never told you, but centuries ago, after some pretty bloody fighting, it was agreed that the Mullaines should be the Lairds but the Kilarrans should own certain lands."

"And this cottage is on that land?"

"Yes."

"Then," I said hotly, "when the old man who lived there died, why did you let it get derelict? Why didn't you restore it so that someone could have it as a home?"

"Because I wasn't here. And since Rory

writes letters rather as children do — you know the type: 'It's a nice day. I had salmon for dinner last night. I hope you are well' — well, since that was the kind of letter I received from him, I had no idea that old Hamish was dead and the cottage was empty."

"What did you intend to do with it when you returned and found it was vacant?"

He shrugged. "I've heard of no one on the island who is homeless."

"If no one else needs it, then please let me have it. My London office will pay the rent."

"I don't want rent."

"Now that you've told me I have no real right to it, I can't just take over."

"It seems you have." His tone was uncompromising.

"In ignorance. But please let's have the whole thing settled. My firm is spending money on dyes and any apparatus needed. I can't let them go into all that expense unnecessarily."

"My dear Judith . . ." He had moved into the beam of light from the Castle. The lines of his face were accentuated; the mouth smiled slightly but his voice was quite cold. "I doubt if 'this thing,' as you call it, this weaving experiment will ever be settled. Cathair women won't be ordered around, you know. At your first attempt at being 'lady boss' they'll walk out, back to their stone cottages."

"Is that a prophecy?"

"Not put exactly that way. But something may happen to spoil your scheme. And if it's not the women themselves, tiring of the idea, then it'll be – shall we call it a move of fate?"

"You want it that way, don't you?" His words and his manner annoyed and frightened me. "Why? I'm sorry if I seemed arrogant by taking over the cottage as I did, but I honestly believed it to belong to nobody."

He said, "There are very few things in life that have no ownership. The air, the sea. I can't think of anything else, can you? We don't even possess our own peace of mind, do we, Judith?"

I took a few steps away from him. He was too near, his words too full of meaning. From the distance I could hear laughter and voices calling "Goodnight." Only a green glen and a stretch of beach separated us, but the people down at the loch seemed to belong to another world. I had an uncanny feeling that if I shouted for help – though heaven knew why I would want to – there would be no one from the small stone landing pier or from Mullaine itself who would come to my rescue. It was as though Shane had woven a circle around us and we were invisible and inaudible save to each other.

I shivered. "I'm going indoors. I'm rather

cold. And I'm sorry if I annexed property of yours. But of course, I shall pay you rent. I leave it to you to tell me how much. Please put it in writing to make it legal."

"Goodnight, Judith. And I've told you, I don't need rent."

"But *I* need to pay it. I want to make something really good out of this project. Shane, please try to understand. *I need to work . . .*"

He had been moving slowly away from me. He stopped suddenly. "*You* need to work? That's fine! Then by all means, work. But I suggest you don't involve others who are perfectly satisfied in their lives. Contentment is a fine thing, and God knows there's little of it in the world today. And you are just going to take more away from a small, happy, unambitious community because *you* need to work."

I was not known to have a sharp temper, but to my complete surprise it flared up. "Is it really the islanders you care about? Or is it thwarting me, because . . . because, well, why? Shane, tell me the real reason."

"I've made it quite clear."

"Oh no, you haven't!" In that moment I felt as strong and unyielding as a judge.

"Then I'll tell you again," he said. "I see a group of women weaving tweed for the European market, watching the other islanders, with their already established industries —

Harris and Barra and Stornoway. I see rivalry entering as a result, and bitter competition. My dear Judith Mullaine, I doubt if you know what you are doing."

The silence between us lasted for a few long moments. Then he said in a curiously softened voice, "Yes. Yes ... Perhaps you'll win the women over and they'll work hard — not just for the satisfaction of what they're doing, but for you. You have a way with you, Judith — it's hard to put into words, but it's there, an irresistible thing."

I was his enemy and he was mine. Yet while he spoke something had been revealed behind the harshness of his condemnation. Perhaps his deeper self did not censure me ... or perhaps I had only imagined a sudden gentleness breaking through his inflexibility.

I felt reckless courage surge through me. "I wonder what you really mean because I don't believe it is what you actually say. I wish I knew. I wish I understood. I wish I could see why what I do mattered so much to you."

He said very quietly. "Because it is my island." And then he walked away from me.

XVI

I was in a dilemma. Two of Morag's grandchildren were hovering on the outskirts of the Castle waiting for Paul to come out and play. But he was avoiding them. He had entered one of those strange moods of secrecy children sometimes adopt during their lives when they want to go to a place of their own, a place they resent sharing. Paul had his. I knew that the mood would pass and he would come out of his reserve into wanting once again to run and climb and play with the island children. But for the moment his "special place" (*that* bay) and Rinn (*his* seal) were things he wanted to keep to himself.

On the other hand, finding my ring in the cove had frightened me and I wanted to try to fill Paul's day with other interests so that he would have no time to cross to that corner of Cathair Mor, so beautiful, secluded and ominous. Whoever had watched us then, would watch again, watch Paul . . . He would be safe with the children or with Rory. But how could

I chain an independent child? And whoever watched him had made no attempt to abduct him. For the moment, he was safe. *I* was the one who was to be ground down, subtly, slowly defeated.

In the end I took him with me to the Abbey to see Rory. I pretended I wanted to ask him if he had found the missing bagpipes. This would give me the opportunity to have a quiet word with him and ask him if he would take Paul fishing that morning.

The plan worked. Rory and Paul were going to a stream where the trout leaped snapping at the hovering flies. The stocky man and the small, slender boy set off for the trout stream singing "The Road to the Isles" at the top of their voices.

I had arranged to meet the women at Hamish's cottage that morning, and I was already late. But I detoured and went back to the Castle to fetch an overall I had forgotten to wear for the dye mixing.

Rosheen was at the end of the Great Hall and Antonia was with her. Because of the height and emptiness of the place their voices echoed against the stone.

They were talking about me.

"Then, if no one here plays the pipes, she must have imagined them," Antonia said, "and the light the other night she said she saw moving on Cathair Beag —"

"Now don't ye be worryin' yerself about that," Rosheen said, her duster whirling over the long refectory table. " 'Twill be all right, likely enough. The lassie has had a bad time and people as has had bad times do funny things."

"I know. I know."

"It's fine everythin' will be."

"Fine? Rosheen, you say things will be *fine* when my son has been accused of trying to murder his wife? When he has escaped in order — in order to *what*, Rosheen?"

"Till things die down, likely."

"But things won't die down. The police never let them. And he's my son."

"Likely as not," Rosheen was saying in her soft voice, "he'll be somewhere thinkin' things over. In the end they'll find that it was just an accident. The poor lassie can't believe that now. But the Laird, he has winning ways, he'll make them all see."

"Yesterday, Rosheen, at my dinner party, I could see my guests' minds working, wondering about it all. They're charming people, but they're human and naturally curious. It's horrible; it's part of my nightmare. Lewis . . . You know him, Rosheen —"

"Aye, all his life, that I have. An' he the bright-haired little lad who'd come to my

224

kitchen an' eat oatcakes with a lot of honey on them. And laughin', and sometimes kickin' the floor in his little tempers."

"Just child tempers. That's all they were. He had no evil in him. How could he?"

I could have crept away at that point, but I didn't. They were so certain that I was safely away from the Castle that there was no caution in their conversation. I stood, blatantly listening. I *had* to listen as well as watch, for at some time or other, someone would say something all-important. And who knew, it could even be Rosheen, who was not only a fine servant but, since Antonia had no friends on the island, her confidante also.

"If on that night," Antonia was saying slowly, "Lewis had just lost his temper and that was all; if Judith had exaggerated the attack and in actual fact the knife had caught her accidentally —"

"Aye, and it could be that way."

"But, Rosheen . . . oh, dear God, suppose, on the other hand, Lewis *didn't* attack Judith? All these strange things that have happened could be part of . . . part of some — how can I put it? — some twist in Judith's mind. I don't mean that cruelly, for I am fond of her. But people can change, become unbalanced. Suppose she —"

"She what?" Rosheen straightened, and as

she looked at Antonia, I shrank into the shadows of the round wall of the tower.

"She *wanted* Lewis accused? Suppose she wanted to —"

"Now why would she be doin' that?" I heard a rising indignation in Rosheen's voice.

"Perhaps because she wanted to be free and at the same time to keep Paul. Perhaps because she knew that Lewis would never let him go. And this was the only way —"

I left the shadows and made a movement toward them, words of furious protest rushing to be spoken.

But before I could say them and before they even saw or heard me, Antonia moved against a heavy chair and lost her balance. Rosheen sprang to save her from falling.

Antonia clung for a moment to the stocky woman. "I don't understand anything that's happening. I'm frightened . . . I'm so frightened. And there's something that makes everything even worse, although at the moment I don't understand why . . . Rosheen, why has Shane Kilarran come back just at this time?"

"Ach, but that's somethin' none of us know."

I turned and walked away, my footsteps so loud where they touched the stone slabs in between the golden carpets that both Antonia and Rosheen must have heard me. But neither of them called out to me.

I would have had to go past them and up to my room to fetch my overall. I left without it. If I got covered with all the bright dyes of the world, it didn't matter. Nothing mattered but the terrifying sense that something else had crept into my life. Now the story was getting around that I could have caused my own injury that night in London because I wanted Lewis accused . . . and there was nothing, *nothing* I could say or do to correct that suspicion. Except one thing: bring Paul into it, force a seven-year-old boy, whose memory had closed up because of a traumatic experience, to tell his story. That was something I could not do.

I reached the cottage where the women awaited me. It was a ragged day; the wind split the clouds and broke up the mists so that they hovered over the Brenlorns like a luminous web.

The little stream ran strongly over the rocks, and I saw a trout leap, gleaming, from the clean water. The door of the cottage, which had now had its broken hinge mended, was open and from inside came the sound of women's voices raised as if in anger.

I hesitated outside, with a sense of despair that they were wrangling even before the work had started. If this was to be the baptism of my industry, then Shane was right and it was doomed from the start. I seized hold of my

227

courage and walked in. The women were making so much noise that they hadn't heard me. They were grouped around the vats which held the dyes and it was Morag who was shouting the loudest.

One of the women was waving a long stick that was used for stirring the dyes. She called out something in Gaelic and flung the dripping stick furiously into the corner of the room. As she turned, she saw me. Immediately Morag, also, turned. "The dyes," she said, "they're ruined. All the fine dyes — just look."

A heavy, unpleasant smell of rotting vegetation hung over the room. The women made a pathway for me as I crossed to the vats. I looked into them. Immediately I started back, putting both hands to my face, staring at the mess that had ruined the pure greens and reds and purples of the dyes.

"What in the world has happened?" I swung around on them. "What is that hideous tangle of stuff in the vats?"

"Bog myrtle," Morag said. "It's smellin' like nobody's business."

"I know that. But how did it get there? *Who did this?*"

The eyes of sixteen women stared me out. Someone said, "Now how would *we* know? And why?"

"Them vats of dyes is now all spoilt," said

Jessie MacAllan, whose husband was a shepherd. "Ach, and what d'ye think we do now?"

I said furiously, "Before we think about what we do now — which really means starting all over again — I want to find out *why* it was done." I picked up one of the mixing sticks and stirred a vat of purple dye. A heap of soaked and tangled bog moss, dyed to a dirty black with earth and mud, clung to the stick. There was something menacing and evil about it. I dropped the stuff back into the swirling dye and walked along the line of vats. Every one of them was discolored by the stuff.

The scent of bog myrtle was not unpleasant up on the moors, but mixed with chemical dyes and some of the muddy earth that had been torn up with it, the smell was horrible.

"An' didn't I tell ye not to go leavin' the door unlocked?" Jessie said angrily to Morag. " 'Twas ye left here last."

"An' when do we lock doors here?" Morag demanded.

"Likely we should start, then," came a voice from the group crowding round me.

"I be thinkin'," a woman said, "that it could be one of Nessie MacKeal's brood. They're a wicked lot an' up to mischief, an' she not joinin' in with us here."

"Let's go out an' find out." Morag marched to the door.

"No." I stopped her "You can't go questioning people that way. It's as if you were accusing them."

"I'd have the hide off mine if I thought they'd done this," someone said.

"Ye'd best not to be too sure it wasn't one of ours," Jessie warned.

The argument and the guessing were swift and long, and wasted valuable time, but I understood the islanders well enough to know they would talk as long as they pleased, and all I could do was wait and try to think in my own mind who could have ruined the dyes.

"Why did ye leave the door unlocked, ma'am?" Jessie demanded, glaring at me. "I'm thinkin' it were *you* should ha' seen that it were all safe, like."

It was inevitable that in the end I would be the one accused of carelessness. I was the captain of this ship and so the blame was mine.

I had no answer. I went over to the boxes stacked in a corner with wool ready for dyeing. Tangled in with the top box lay muddy clumps of bog myrtle. Someone must have come loaded with the stuff, someone who wanted to ruin my project, someone who wanted the women to mistrust me. "If she can't safeguard our wool, then how can we trust her with our work?" Perhaps the intention was to scare them from working for me. Superstition ran rife on

Cathair Mor. They could confess to being Free Church of Scotland, Episcopalians, or any other religion. It made no difference. Woven like a thread through it all was that streak of paganism that saw signs and omens, believing in the mysticism of the seventh son of the seventh son, in magic rings among the heather, in "the Sight," as they called the ability to foretell the future.

I was tight with fear that one of them would start the others off with some talk of what had happened being "A Sign" — though of what, heaven knew.

I heard a sharp angry voice come from clear across the chattering and the arguments. "The wool came from our sheep. Now what are we goin' to do when winter comes? 'Tis ruined — that for the market and that for us."

"Aye, an' Jaimie needs a new sweater this winter."

"An' I'll have to tell Shamus an' likely he'll be mad at *me*. An' —"

"If you'll all please stop talking," I called, pitching my voice above theirs, "I can reassure you. *You* won't lose by this. Any loss will be mine or my company's. I promise I'll have wool for you for the winter."

"We shouldn't ever have let ye have ours."

" 'Tis all very well to say we'll get wool. But when? That's what I be askin'. The English

231

won't care when they send it to us, an' cold it is up here by autumn."

"You may not know me very well, but one thing I can tell you. You can trust me. Please . . . You'll get your wool, if I have to go to the mainland to fetch it myself." While I spoke I went to the next box of undyed wool. It was untouched. Morag helped me lift the box down and tried the one underneath. That, too, was perfectly clean. "There you are! There's enough wool in those boxes to start you off for your own needs."

"Maybe likely there is," Jessie agreed, peering over my shoulder.

"And now," I said, "the first thing we have to do is clean up. I'll ring through to London and get them to send fresh dyes and wool. It won't be from your sheep, but that's unimportant." I glanced down at the vats doubtfully. "Can I leave you to clear this all up? I can't think how you're going to get rid of that terrible mess."

"Ach, but that's easy," Morag said. "We'll dig a ditch in the side of the moor an' bury the lot."

"And be very careful to clean the vats thoroughly. There'll have to be a padlock on the door," I said. "I'll ask Duncan to go across to Mull and buy a couple for us."

I left the women to the horrible task of cleaning up and went out into the sun. A soft flurry of cirrus clouds was drifting across the sea, and the stream – the one they called "McInch's Burn" – made tinkling sounds as it flowed over the stones.

I knew that my first act was to contact London. Dyes must be flown to Scotland immediately and wool delivered. I had sufficient faith in Gerald Farrer's efficiency to know that he wouldn't let me down or spread around, more than was necessary, the fact that I was on the island. So many people must know by now or have guessed.

If we discounted children's mischief, which I did, then who had destroyed the dyes? Some blind hatred, some venomous wish to discredit me, was following me like a shadow. I came back to my suspicion that this morning's sabotage was no act of unreasonable vandalism but an effort to denigrate me.

Antonia was at her piano, playing softly. When she heard me she turned. "You're back very quickly. I thought you were going to start the women on their weaving."

"I couldn't," I said. And told her why.

She had swung the piano stool around and was sitting up very straight, watching me as I stood on the steps that led to the dais. "I can't believe it! It's so malicious, so ... pointless."

"No it isn't," I said.

She ran her fingers through her hair. People

here aren't like that — even the children don't damage property."

"I've thought of everything."

"Have you, Judith?"

I tensed as I saw her eyes narrow. I knew in that moment that the black fear that had walked with me on my way from Hamish's cottage was in Antonia's mind too: *Had I ruined the dyes? Without knowing it? "She is no longer a responsible person . . ."*

I knew perfectly well that Antonia was as upset at suspecting me as I was at sensing that she did. I said, "I've got to telephone London for fresh dyes and I'll have to find wool somewhere to replace the lot that is damaged. They only destroyed the first box —" I broke off. "They" sounded wrong to me. "They" did not hate me. But "One" did . . .

I turned to the door.

"Where are you going, Judith?"

"Out," I said. "Just out —" and escaped.

I walked on the lower slopes of the moors, wondering if I could report to the police this malicious act of destroying the dyes, since this was something the women had also seen. But how could I prove I hadn't done it? Who knew that at some time during the night a man — or woman — had crept out and dug up the bog myrtle and flung it into the vats? Who knew that that person wasn't myself?

234

Antonia's words slid into my mind: "I wonder why Shane Kilarran has come back at this particular time?"

Except for the lonely sound of a protesting goat, I was quite alone. I flung myself down and lay with my face in the heather. The air was scented with wild honeysuckle and bog mint; a lark sang somewhere overhead and the heather was rough and scratchy to my skin.

Here, on the empty moors, my thoughts fastened on a new fear, a new reason for the things that were being done. No one else, it seemed, had heard the bagpipes; no one else had seen the light on Cathair Beag; no one on the island had ever set eyes on my little Georgian ring. Everything had been done at a carefully chosen time and place when I was alone.

I was scarcely aware of the birds wheeling and screaming around the rocks. Time didn't touch me. I got up and wandered slowly, as if nothing troubled me and my life was sweet and easy and uncomplicated. But I walked like that because part of me was dazed with fear.

I took off my sandals and stepped over the wet rocks. The water was very cold and the seaweed slithered between my toes. I was thinking of Shane Kilarran and of his last words to me on the night of Antonia's dinner party: "Because it is my island."

Cathair Mor.

Once upon a time they had fought for it, the Mullaines and the Kilarrans; they had feuded and had killed for it. Mullaine had won. How much did that matter now? I knew that Lewis cared very little for his island and his title of Laird. His life was centered on the great concert halls of the world; his interest lay, as Antonia's did, in the cities. He came to Cathair Mor at the most twice a year, and even then he took little interest in it. I think his greatest pleasure, so far as the island was concerned, was to see that gaunt grey tower of his Castle rising up against the emerald of the loch and the purple of the distant Brenlorns. I think he liked to feel that here he could hoist the Mullaine flag whenever he wished and claim a small kingship. But it was a pleasure that soon bored him. Like Antonia, every waking moment he spent on the island out of duty was a kind of penance. Born on Cathair Mor, he had made the world his home. Lewis would never have fought to keep the island for the Mullaines. But it was possible that Shane Kilarran had chosen exile as an engineer rather than stay on the island as second to the Laird. Cathair Mor was "his island."

I stepped unthinkingly into a rock pool, scattering the tiny life in it. I remained, my feet in the water, staring into the silver misty distance without really seeing it.

My feet were sinking in the soft sea-saturated sand. I dragged them out and climbed over a rock and onto the dry shore. I watched a ship in the distance. It was probably taking tourists to Skye, far to our north.

I had to find out somehow if Lewis had the power to pass the island on to another family. As things were, if he was alive, he was still Laird. If he was dead, then Paul was the young Laird. And acting for my son, who seemed to love the island, I had no intention of handing Cathair Mor over to a Kilarran. Or to Antonia, who might find some way to take control of Paul because Judith Mullaine – deranged and distraught – could not be entrusted with the care of her son. Yet how could I be calm and reasonable when I had no idea where my danger lay? I was no heroine, but life had caught me up in a situation most people only read about. And, heroine or not, I had to cope and guard against the snare I hated most of all – self-pity. And walk with care . . .

XVII

One of the island's frequent prankish mists had crept in unexpectedly from the sea, blanketing the island. Paul was out with Rory, and although I felt he would be safe, I was anxious to find out where they were, for mists could be hazardous for the unwary.

Restless and overanxious that Paul had not returned to Mullaine, I made my way through the thick white atmosphere to Inverkyle Abbey. I pulled the heavy iron bell and waited. Jeannie came to the door. No, neither brother was in.

"Mr. Rory's after fishin'. He's been gone a long time, but he'll come to no harm, he knowin' the island as he does."

"I think Paul is with him."

"Then he'll come to no harm either, so don't ye go frettin'." She shook her head at me. "An' ye shouldna' be rightly out. It's fair thick. But there'll be sunshine later, likely." She nodded toward the invisible sky.

I thanked her and left, walking down to the loch.

The mist was patchy, and suddenly, through a faint clearing, I saw a figure huddled on a boulder which overhung the water. It was one of Rory's favorite places for fishing. Below him the sea was silent, as if tamed by the thistle-down softness of the mist. There was a ghostliness about the island and I felt I was in a dream place and watching an insubstantial man sitting, like a dark statue, on a stone.

One salient point registered. Rory was alone. I called to him, but the mist muffled my voice.

"Rory." I began to run, stumbled and fell flat over a lichen-covered rock. Grazed and frustrated, I got up and moved more carefully. "Rory . . ."

He heard me at last and looked up.

"Where is Paul?"

"I don't know."

"But he ran out of the house and said he was going to find you."

"That's right and then he saw Shane. And then the mist came down." He spoke his sentences like a child – short, simple, emphatic.

"Where *are* they?"

"Gone," he said. "They've gone."

My heart did a violent swing around. A bird dived in front of me, its wings outstretched, silent and bewildered.

"Birds hate the mist," Rory said.

"I know . . . I know . . . *Where have Shane and Paul gone?*"

"I don't know."

"But they must have said something. Please *think* . . . try to remember."

"Shane said something about the boat."

"In this mist?" A boat sliding from its moorings into that vast pearl-like space toward what? Toward whom? I clung to a vestige of serenity. "Rory," I said gently. "Just try to remember. Where did they say they were going?"

"I don't know. I thought I had hooked a fish and I wasn't listening."

But people on the island knew when the mist was coming. Shane must have seen the swirling in the distance — and yet had taken Paul with him to the boat.

"Paul . . . Paul . . ." The mist stifled my shout so that it came back at me like a blow wrapped in cotton wool.

I stumbled and slithered over the rocky place away from where Rory sat, running through the *machair.* Once I looked back. I had reached a place where I could no longer see Rory. I was in a hushed, opaque space where nothing and no one was visible.

"Paul . . ." Oh God, let him be safe!

Only moments later, I saw them. They were in the Kilarran boat, which lay gently on the sea that only such a mist could tame. I saw

Shane reach across Paul to the mooring rope.

"Paul . . ." My scream had something of the seagull's wildness in it.

I raced toward them over the sand, and their dim figures became more solid. As I reached the tiny pier Shane edged his way across Paul, who was sitting in the stern of the little boat.

My feet clattered across the slats of a jetty. Shane stood in the boat watching me. "We have a visitor," he said to Paul, laughing.

Out of breath, I bent down and reached Paul's arm. "Get out of there . . . quickly . . . quickly. Do as I say."

I could feel the small muscles of his arm tensing, resisting me. "It isn't time yet. I don't want to come home. It isn't home, anyway."

"And don't argue. Get out of that boat." My voice was shrewish; I felt terror clutching me.

"If you don't let go," Shane said calmly, "You'll have us all in the water."

I clung to my son with one hand and with the other I clutched the mooring rope. "Then will you please help Paul out of the boat?" I said to Shane.

"By all means. But I can't do that while you're holding on to him." He, also, hung on to the mooring rope, and we were like two people in some private tug of war.

The rope swung away from me almost imperceptibly, but it was enough to make me lose my balance before I could let go of Paul's shoulder. The little boat slid from me with the movement of the tide. In that split second I lost my balance. I cried out as I fell, but no one had time to save me. The ice-cold water met over my head as I crashed in the narrow strip of sea the swing of the boat had opened up between itself and the jetty.

I struck out and surfaced spluttering. Shane's strong hands pulled me into the boat. "That was a damned silly thing to do," he said, and tugged on the rope to drag the boat close to the pier. "Here, put your arms into that and go home and dry out."

"That" was a thick white sweater. "Go on."

I said, "Paul, you go first. Here, let me help you." Breathless and shivering, I reached for him. "Go on, get up on the landing stage."

"I . . ."

"Don't argue . . ."

"But I don't want to. *I'm* not wet. Let me stay. I want to stay. Shane was going to show me the engine."

I gave him a push. *"At once . . ."*

My tone startled him into obedience. When he had scrambled on the pier, I reached out and hauled myself up by his side.

Shane was watching us. The mist swirled around him so that his face was blurred. I heard him say, "You'd make a charming mermaid, if only you didn't shiver so obviously. Go and get dry."

The cold was seeping through my flesh, but I stood dripping on the pier. "Where were you going?"

"Oh, I don't know. Anywhere . . ."

"In this mist?"

"We had planned a sort of tour round the island and back just before the mist hit us. You know it comes down very suddenly."

"Yes, I *do* know. But if you had looked over to the horizon, you'd have seen it coming."

"Clever girl, I would. Now, do you want to catch pneumonia?"

I seized Paul's hand and began to run. The thick hairy wool of Shane's sweater irritated my neck and wrists.

Paul said, "Why are you so angry? I was only sitting in the boat with Shane."

"I'm not angry with you," I said and slowed down to a swift walk, holding on to Paul's hand — something which I knew he hated. "But I don't often give you firm orders, and when I do, please do as I ask without stopping to argue, because I have a good reason."

"What reason?" He withdrew his hand from mine, picked up a stone and threw it.

"It would have been madness to have gone out in this mist," I told him.

"We weren't. We were in the boat talking and

Shane said we'd have to wait till it cleared. Sometimes he said it goes as awfully quickly as it comes."

"From what I saw, he was loosening the mooring rope."

"Oh, he was only seeing that it was all right."

That's his story, I thought.

My sodden clothes clung to me; sea water from my hair dripped in rivulets down my back. There was nothing soft or comforting about Shane's sweater.

"I don't want to go home," Paul said. "Antonia will try to make me practice."

"No, she won't. Come on, please, Paul. You're dragging back."

"I'm out of breath and I've got a stitch in my side."

"Since you can outrun me every time we've raced, I don't believe a word of that. And if we don't hurry, I shall get galloping pneumonia."

After a pause and a few gasping breaths he asked, "What's *galloping* pneumonia?"

"I've no idea. But I warn you, if you don't hurry I'll get it. And it won't be nice for me or fun for you."

"You're pretty good fun usually," he said.

"Thank you," I told him dryly and thought that this was an ironic time for my imperturbable son to pay me a reluctant compliment.

We were both out of breath and finished our

journey back to the Castle in silence. The fear clutched at me that had I not seen Rory, I would never have known that Paul was with Shane.

And there was no one I could tell my terror to, not even Antonia, for I had no logical reason to fear Shane, except my own arguments that someone was harassing me. Shane's uncompromising behavior toward me made me feel he was the one I had to watch. I knew that my frantic nervousness over Paul's safety was accentuated by the fact that there was no one near me who would understand. And that was turning me into something approaching a hysteric where Paul's safety was concerned. Strength lay in keeping calm, I told myself with a wisdom I was afraid I could not apply.

I had a quick bath, and when I was dressed again I dried my hair vigorously with one of Antonia's monogrammed towels. I stood and looked at my reflection. People said, "You really are lucky to have that lovely heavy hair." If they saw it now, they would find no compliments to pay me. It looked like nothing more glamorous than tattered overlong petals of some drowned flower.

Rosheen came in with some coffee. "Ye drink that up an' quick." She set down the little painted tray with the coffee on it. " 'Twill do ye good."

I thanked her and gave her Shane's sweater to dry. When I had changed I went to find Paul.

Antonia was in the playroom with Paul. I heard her say, "And we'll send him over to Mull to the Torrenses' stables while you're away in London. Then he'll be in fine form whenever you come here and ride him. Oh —" She caught sight of me in the doorway. "Judith! Did Rosheen bring you up a hot drink? I told her to."

"Yes, thank you. She brought her own brand, laced with whiskey. She has never been able to understand that I hate the taste of it. But I drank it and it did warm me."

Antonia said lightly, "Oh, for the islanders, whiskey is the magic cure for everything. Your hair is still wet."

"There were no half measures about it," I said dryly. "I went right in and under. By the way, who is going over to Mull?"

"A horse," she said, "or rather, a pony. I'm going to buy one for Paul. It's time he learned to ride."

"Yes, he can ride. But not here. We won't be staying — I mean —"

"I know what you mean," she said quickly. "But, Judith, whether you stay a short time or not makes no difference. The Torrenses will enjoy looking after a pony and he can be brought over here whenever you come on holiday."

I was silent, wondering how Antonia could imagine we would ever return. Whatever happened in the future, and although the island was a beautiful place and I could have loved it, I knew that once free, I would never want to live here again. A fear as deep as mine could not be brushed off by time. A scar as powerful as the fissures in the great guardian cliffs of the island had formed inside me. I would come back to oversee the weaving, but I knew that I could never again bear to stay long on Cathair Mor.

I watched Paul flipping the table-tennis ball onto the bat. The tiny click of the celluloid was a light accompaniment to the conversation. Antonia was perched on a high stool that had been put in the room some few years ago for Paul to climb on and reach the top shelf of the games cupboard.

"If he has a pony," she said, "it will get him away from all this play with the island children."

"I *like* him to be with them. He needs young people. He'll have to wait for a pony until he's older and everything is . . . settled."

Paul tossed the ball up high, reached to catch it and missed. A lock of his fair hair hung over his forehead. "Why can't I have both? Going out to play *and* a pony?"

"You've never been as far on foot as a horse would take you, and you could lose your way," I said, wanting to keep off the fact that this could be one more attempt by Antonia at bribery — the pony for music practice.

"Couldn't you give Rory a horse as well? Then he could come with me and I'd be safe." He flashed an impish sideways glance at Antonia.

She flicked her skirt impatiently, like a Spanish dancer. "All right." She smiled at Paul. "And then perhaps you'll be a little nicer and please me."

He turned toward her, his eyes cool and very bright. "Aren't I nice to you?"

"Sometimes, darling. But not when you're obstinate and won't listen to those who know what's best for you. I've tried to explain to you in an adult way because you're an intelligent boy. And I do so hate nagging, so you really *must* listen."

"What to?" Paul asked.

"I want you to practice your music. It's for your sake, it really is."

He gave the small ball a mighty whack, flung down the bat and said, "I thought there was a catch in it. A pony for that awful piano. No, I won't. I won't! I've got a cassette in London and I can play what I want to on that. And I'll *never* like pianos."

Antonia had won so many battles with her enchanting smile. She turned it full on Paul. "But if practicing now makes you famous and earns you a lot of money when you grow up, like –" She flashed a look at me and stopped.

Lewis's name hung on the air.

If Paul noticed, he gave no sign. "*I* know what I want to be when I grow up. I want to be a farmer and have lots of sheep and cows and dig and grow things. *That's* what I want."

I checked an impulse to cry, "Hurray! He's not a Mullaine." And thought of my father and his love of the earth.

"Can I go and watch television?" he asked, as if the argument were over.

"Of course," I said.

He turned to look out the narrow window into the white mist and I knew that he longed to be out of doors.

Antonia left us, her heels clicking loudly. Paul gave her a moment or two before he followed her. He had learned to keep out of range whenever she was in her "Paul as a future musician" mood. Then he followed.

Suddenly alone in the room, I had an impulse to see Shane. It was as if I knew that at this moment I would have the courage to say what had to be said between us, and that if I delayed until we met again – tomorrow or the day after – my nerve would have weakened. I had to talk to him and watch and try to discover by a word, a look or a gesture whether he was the danger I had begun to suspect.

From somewhere above, I could hear the distorted sound of the television, then, after a few minutes of silence, the radio turned on. Paul had obviously decided that of two sophistications, both taken for granted by the cities, the radio here on Cathair Mor was the best.

I tied a scarf over my damp hair, collected Shane's sweater as an excuse for the visit, and went out. The mist had cleared, but I walked without confidence. I had no idea how to go about finding out what I desperately wanted to know. I was acting on impulse and trusting to instinct or inspiration – or both. It was quite possible that both would fail me.

Shane was in a small room with a high vaulted ceiling and a single stone-mullioned window. He sat at a large desk with neat piles of papers, and if he was surprised by my visit, he didn't show it. "I'm sorry about that dip in the sea, but boats sometimes have wills of their own." He looked me over. "You seem nicely dry" – he took my hand and felt it – "and warm."

Little needles of electricity spattered my hand and I drew it away quickly and handed him his sweater.

He tossed it onto a chair. "You've come at the

right moment," he said. "Jeannie is about to bring in tea. Let's go into my study."

He guided me across the stone passage into a room that was part of the hall planned as the monks' refectory. The walls were hung with lovely Persian prayer rugs and the floor was covered with a grey pile carpet that merged with the stonework so that it didn't seem out of place. There was a large sofa, comfortably cushioned. Every effort had been made by previous Kilarrans to give the place an atmosphere of warmth and home. The room had been cut in half and was out of proportion, too high for its size, comfortable enough while eyes were kept on a level, but the homelike atmosphere was lost, at least to me, as soon as I looked up to the distant vaulted ceiling and measured the height of the stone walls. Up where they met the roof, the room was a mass of shadows, like the Great Hall at Mullaine.

When Jeannie brought in the tea I saw the swift glance she gave us as if she were intrigued by my visit. The smallest thing that happened on the island would be mentioned and argued over. "The Mullaine's wife had tea with Shane Kilarran . . ." And the "How's" and the "Why's" and the "What's" would be talked over.

"The cake is homemade," Shane said.

"It looks lovely." I bent over and inspected it casually, outwardly calm, inwardly angry with

251

myself – now that it was too late – that I had come here unprepared, with no thought as to how to approach him for what I wanted to know.

We sat opposite one another in chairs so deep that I, who was small, longed to kick off my shoes and tuck my feet under me. But it wasn't that kind of meeting. It was going to be anything but cozy.

Shane broke the silence. "How is the weaving experiment going?"

"Surely you know? Someone sabotaged the dyes?"

"Oh yes, I heard. How stupid!"

"Was it?"

He raised his eyebrows as if the question needed no answer.

"I think it was part of some plan to discredit me among the women," I continued. "To say, in effect, 'She can't even keep the stores safe from vandals, so how can we trust her with our wool and our livelihood?' "

"I suppose the vandalism was by one of the women who is against this scheme of yours."

"Do you think so?"

"If I can remember a conversation we had," he said, "and expand it, then it's someone who feels as I do but carried the protest to a rather dramatic conclusion."

"It's not a conclusion, because I'm going

ahead with my plan," I told him. "But that's not why I'm here."

His smile was cool and polite. "I hoped it was a pleasant social call."

"Did you, Shane? I'm here because I've got to talk to you about Lewis."

"Ah!" He put down his cup and leaned back, and his eyes were wary silver in the light of the many great lamps scattered about the room.

"You know everything, don't you?"

"Everything?"

"About what happened. About Lewis and me . . . that night . . ."

"But how can I? How can anyone — except those who were there?"

"Two of us," I said, "and one missing —"

"Leaving you. Yes, Judith, I know all that."

I put down my cup. The tea was strong and refreshing but I didn't want it. Our conversation was going badly. I felt awkward and exposed, like a raw nerve. I got up, crossed to a beautiful walnut cabinet and stared into it at the strange collection of objects. Rory had told me about them on my first visit to the Abbey some years previously.

I looked straight into the fierce eye of a seventeenth-century silver sea-centaur, half horse, half conch shell. With my back to Shane, I had more confidence. "Do you know where Lewis is?"

"Isn't that a question the police should be asking me?"

The centaur had a long curling mane and hoofs that were lifted in preparation for a plunge.

"Do you know where Lewis is?" I repeated.

"No."

I swung around. "But he has been in touch with you."

Shane rose, picked up the tea tray, strode with it across the room and set it down on a table near the door. It was an unnecessary act and I knew he was playing for time.

"Yes, I heard from him," he said.

"*After* what happened that night?"

"I was in the wilds of Iran, away from cities, and the letter was obviously delayed. It was first sent to the office in Teheran and redirected."

"There must have been a date on it."

"There was no date and no address. The stamp, by the way, was an English one."

"What did it say?"

"No, Judith, I can't tell you."

"I want you to . . . I have a right . . ."

He said with sudden impatience, "Where do you imagine this cross-examination is going to get you, Judith?"

"I want to know where Lewis is."

"You don't think he gave me even a hint, do you?"

"To his trusted friend — yes he might. *Did* he?"

"And how do you know whether Lewis trusted me at the end, or not?"

"I don't. But I'm asking *you*. Shane, please, don't fence with me. I've got to find Lewis — or someone must. The police, his friends, his manager, his agent — I don't know who, but it's desperately important."

"Is it important to Lewis?"

"Perhaps," I said and came back and sat on the thick velvet arm of the chair. "Perhaps to him, too. That is, if he needs treatment."

"Treatment? What kind? Psychiatric?"

"Don't *you* think so?"

"What I think doesn't matter," he said.

"Oh, but it does." I tried to hide my clenched hands. "For God's sake, Shane, don't give me question for question. Someone is undermining —"

"Undermining what?" he asked softly.

I refused to say "My sanity." Instead I said, tense and angry and aware that Shane was too strong for me, "Everyone on Cathair Mor knows what happens all the time. The island grapevine is as strong as that telephone cable laid under the sea between here and Mull. So you know, because everyone here knows, that I heard someone playing the pipes on Cathair Beag; you know that I saw someone walking there one night. You know —"

"I know what the islanders are saying. Of course I do."

"Have they been hinting that the Laird's wife is a little mad? That she hears things, sees things? *Have* they?"

"Oh, for God's sake —" He swung on his heel, turning from me.

"When people don't want to answer, they resort to exasperation." I tried to stop my inner shaking. "Suppose you tell me what everyone says?"

"I don't listen to gossip, so I don't know."

"Shane, things happened exactly as I told them in court. I have scars and a police report to prove —" I stopped. To prove what? Antonia had said, *Suppose she wanted Lewis accused . . .* and there had been soft terror in her voice.

How could I prove that I was the victim and not the one victimizing? Until these past few days on Cathair Mor, I had been certain that everyone believed my story. Now it was different. Now the whispers and echoes of doubt had begun.

I moved away from the cabinet and leaned against the wall, hearing myself ask what I never dreamed I would ask any man. *"Do you hate me?"* Each word spoken as if it were heavily underlined. As soon as the words were out, I felt a tight, choking embarrassment.

256

"Don't answer," I said quickly. "It isn't important. Whether you do or not, it can't help me or really matter."

I thought, *And that's a lie. It does matter.* But for heaven's sake, why? I was not the kind of woman to think that everyone should love me or even like me.

Shane was saying, "I can give you a kind of answer to your question, Judith. You see, I try not to form violent feelings about people until I can claim I understand them — one way or the other."

"Then will you please tell me if the letter you told me Lewis wrote you was *after* the attack on me? You didn't answer that. Was it? Did he pour it all out to you?"

There was the faintest hesitation before he said, "No."

Within me a voice cried not to believe him. I felt that I was stone outside and fire inside, freezing and burning all at once. Even the room seemed to spring alive, as though someone's emotion — Shane's or mine — breathed life into it, a disturbing, paradoxically destructive life. I was caught in a battle I knew I couldn't win; and yet I was unable to retreat.

"You look cold," Shane said, "and the tea is still hot. Have some more."

"No, thank you."

He crossed to the small table by the door and

poured himself a second cup. "Then I will. Jeannie hates food and drink being left. She's like the Middle Eastern people in that way — to leave anything you are offered is an insult to the cook and the kitchen. So —" He lifted his cup lightly to me.

I moved to the sofa, leaning against it because suddenly the wall holding me up seemed to have dissolved and my knees shook. Yet my tattered courage forced me to go on. "There's a saying, 'My brother right or wrong.' Does that also apply to friendship? I mean, whatever happened, however bad it was, would you always find an excuse for . . . for what that friend did?"

"How can you expect me to answer a clear yes or no? One needs to know the unexposed facts — the truths behind the masks. So, my dear Judith, how can I reply to such a question without playing Solomon?"

"*Are* you playing Solomon?"

"God in heaven give me that wisdom! So far, I don't possess it."

"Then perhaps you are letting yourself be emotionally involved."

He put down his cup very slowly and came toward me. Then he stood quite still in front of me and the slanting light gave his face a harshness of deep shadows and heavy brooding lines. What an extraordinary difference the tilt of a head could make, changing character, altering the mask . . .

"If you ever came to know me better," Shane said from that dark shadowed face, "you would know that I never allow emotion to rule my reason."

"Then you are an exceptional man and heaven help anyone deeply involved with you."

"That's the comment that hits the jackpot," he said and laughed suddenly. "Judith, don't ask questions that make me sound pompous." For a moment there was a flash of kindness in his eyes.

"Lewis —" I said faintly, encouraged by that single, almost gentle moment.

"Ah, no," he interrupted me. "We won't go back to that argument."

There had been no argument, just questions that he had sidestepped, except for one where he had hesitated just a little too long.

I walked away from him to the door. "You haven't helped me," I said, "but then, I didn't really think you would."

"I'm sorry. Put it that my judgments are ruled by a sense of loyalty and a knowledge of facts. It's as simple as that."

I gave him a long look. Simple? He was as complex as a computer is to a layman. He defeated me.

XVIII

I would never have understood, had I not experienced it for myself, how, even when deeply and emotionally upset, and living in fear, people can do very normal things without effort.

Walking over the hillocks and hollows of the glen, I even bent to pick buttercups and held the cool yellow petals against my face. I needed desperately to talk to someone, but I had no friends of my own on Mull or, in fact, in western Scotland. It was already clear that Antonia could not be expected to be impartial, and anyway, she suspected that I was walking the razor's edge between sanity and madness.

There was a friend in London, considerably older than I, who was a wise and sophisticated woman. Barbara Jay had known Lewis, and although she had never told me so, I knew she disliked him. The more I thought about her as I walked toward Mullaine, the more I realized how good it would be to talk to her.

All I wanted to do was to "let go." I didn't

believe in the stiff upper lip philosophy. If weeping would end pain, then I wanted to weep, but on Cathair Mor no one must be a witness to my lost pride and constant fear. I would telephone Barbara from Mull, and for the next few minutes, as I entered Mullaine and crossed the deserted hall, I worked out in my mind what I would say to her.

In my room, I wandered about, touching things with vague movements, closing the flap of the antique carved bureau, putting away the elegant Hermès silk scarf I had worn when I went to see Shane. I paused as I folded it, telling myself that I hadn't worn it for Shane, but to give myself courage.

Again there came the problem that I must not leave the island on my own. I couldn't ask Antonia to go with me without explaining why I wanted to use another telephone rather than the one at Mullaine. Nor would it be wise to ask Duncan. There was only Rory, and if he came, I could take Paul also.

Rory never asked awkward questions. He accepted people as a child does, finding nothing odd in their actions, however strange they might seem to other adults.

As I crossed the gallery that ran along one wall, I glanced down into the stony vastness of the Great Hall. Music came with beautiful clarity from Antonia's sitting room. She was listening to a recording of herself singing an aria from *Bohème*. When she listened to music, and particularly to one of her own recordings, Antonia lost all sense of time and place. She was "magicked" by her own voice, and I knew that it would be safe for me to telephone Inverkyle. I wanted no questions asked, however kindly, as to why I had to go to Mull.

Jeannie answered me, and soon Rory's soft Scottish burr broke the waiting. "Judith? Do you want me?"

"Yes. Are you free for a short while?"

"I have all day," he said. "At the moment I'm going through my father's stamp album. I must show it to you — some of the stamps are very rare."

"I'd like to see them sometime," I said, and then went on quickly, anxious to get the question and the answer over before Antonia at Mullaine or Shane at Inverkyle could overhear us, "I have to go to Mull. There's a very important telephone call I must make. To my office," I added with truth. "But you know I mustn't leave here without an escort. Would you come with me? I'd be so grateful."

"Of course. Do you want to go now?"

"Straightaway."

"Fine. I'll meet you at the boat."

"And I'll bring Paul."

It was all so easy. No one saw us leave, no one was down at the loch when the motor of the little launch burst into life and I slid the rope off the mooring post.

The sea between Cathair Mor and Mull was calm as we glided away from the shore. Paul loved to lean over the side of the boat as it left the tiny jetty and watch the jungle of weeds and the tiny silver darts of sea life that shot away from the vibrating bow of the *Midir*.

"There's an eel and . . ." Paul yelled, "and a crab and . . ."

I grabbed his heels as he seemed about to turn a somersault into the water. He sat down, eying me with reproach.

"All right," I said lightly. "It's just that I don't want you to have a watery grave."

"I can swim." He looked up at me. "Would you *mind* if I fell over into the sea?"

"I'll give you the answer you gave me. You can swim. But yes, I would mind because —" I stopped. I couldn't say to a seven-year-old boy, beginning to clutch at his independence and his manhood, "Because I love you and the current might drag you away."

Paul was watching me. "I know," he said and turned back to watch the swirling water. "You'd hate it if you didn't have me."

It was his way of putting what I was thinking. Suddenly I laughed. He was so normal, so healthy that he knew, without words, that I loved him.

He was staring back at Cathair Mor. "Shane says that along that high cliff there" – he pointed – "there's lots of weed in the sea and it's so long you could get caught up in it and drown."

"And if he had gone out and run on the rocks in that mist, that is exactly what might have happened to you." I sounded angry. I felt angry.

"But we were going to wait till it cleared. I told you. Shane said it would and it did."

He turned his head to watch a school of porpoise, leaping clear of the sea, their black triangular fins shining in the light. I looked across at Rory. He had his back to us. His unruly hair was blowing in the wind made by the *Midir*'s speed and his broad hands with the red-blond hairs steered a straight course for the place where the island boats always moored.

We had to walk quite a way to a large house that was now open as a hostel for tourists. The warden and his wife were responsible for a small bird sanctuary and it was at their house that visitors could telephone. The village was some distance away and I was quite certain that there was no one among the dozen or so tourists wandering over the stony beach who could be a danger to us. I explained to Rory that according to police instructions, he must keep himself and Paul within sight of me while I called London.

"Of course." Rory gave me his vague, charming smile. "Antonia told us that you had to be watched."

The way he put it gave me a small shock, but Rory was completely without guile, so I knew they must have been the words Antonia had used to him. *Just watch Judith. She does strange things . . .*

I went into the house, and Kathleen and Lovat Camus greeted me with pleasure. I assured them that I had had tea and asked if I could use their telephone to make two London calls. They must have wondered why I had traveled all the way from Mullaine to call London from their house, but they led me to a little room littered with files and account books.

I sat down in a swivel chair and asked the operator for Barbara Jay's London number. I was in luck. Barbara was home. The preliminary greetings over, I told her why I had called. I spoke rapidly, trying to give her a clear picture as speedily as possible. The line to London was at its best indistinct and at its worst like a relentless thunderstorm, and since we were in such a remote part of the island, contact was liable to break off at any moment. "Shane arrived on the island just after I came here," I said. "Of course, that could be coincidence — everyone would say that it was. But I'm not certain. All I know is that the awful question is in my mind all the time. Is he on Cathair Mor to watch me?" The wires crackled.

"Judith?" Barbara's voice came clearly. "Are you still there?"

"Yes. I can hear you fairly well."

"Why should this man be on the island to watch you? Why suspect him? After all, if Cathair Mor is his home —"

"I haven't told you everything, but I must. Have you time to listen? I mean, have you got people there — friends?"

"I'm quite alone here, my dear, and I'm ready to listen. Tell me — just tell me."

It didn't take long, in spite of intermittent cracklings on the line, to tell her of the things I had seen and heard without anyone else being present, so that in each case there was only my word for them. Barbara encouraged me with small interjections to let me know she was still on the line and listening.

"Have you told the police any of this?"

"How can I, when I have no proof? Even Antonia, who is an honest person, and kind, believes that I'm in a state of some neurosis."

"You mean Antonia thinks you are cracking up under the strain?"

"No. It's worse than that. She thinks that

266

I might have been a little mad all along — that I injured myself in order to implicate Lewis."

"For whatever reason?"

"Why do people do odd things? She may think we had a quarrel and I wanted to harm Lewis professionally. Or that I suspected another woman or — oh, there could be a dozen reasons. But I don't believe any of these occur to her. I'm sure she thinks that I am unbalanced — insane, if you like."

"Oh, Judith!" I heard her spurt of laughter.

"Nothing is ludicrous when you're *in* it," I said desperately. "I know how Antonia feels about me; I can see her mind working. She thinks I'm making up all these stories of things I see and hear in order that my original story of Lewis's attack sounds believable. She fears it may all be part of a kind of insane compulsion."

"And you can't go to the police because you have no proof — no one else is around when they happen?"

"That's right. Barbara, I've *got* to have proof."

"I think there is only one thing you can do — play for time, and be strong, Judith dear. Because it's obvious that someone is trying to break you down mentally but doesn't dare to harm you physically."

"But I *am* being harmed! If it can be established that the whole tragic affair was my doing, that I really am unbalanced – I'd be an unfit mother and they'd take Paul from me."

"For heaven's sake, the authorities don't just listen to a few rumors and act on them. If you'll only wait and stay strong, proof will come. These people usually outstep themselves."

I listened eagerly to her words. "Oh, Barbara, please tell me if that's what you would do. Just wait . . . ?"

"Go about your daily life, take an interest in the weaving project you wrote to me about. Watch over Paul, but for his sake and for your own, don't let anyone see you are frightened."

"You've done me good," I said. "Thank you."

"Call me if you need to talk to someone, just ring. And, Judith, hold on hard to the fact that you've not only got yourself to protect, but Paul."

I shot a look through the window. "He's outside on the beach with Rory. Looking for treasure. He thinks every bit of wood is from some marvelous shipwreck, and a piece of glass bottle a jewel!"

Barbara laughed. "Leave him his dreams, and join in them, if it gets you away from fear. Goodbye, my dear. Ring whenever you need me."

No amount of atmospheric crackles on the line could prevent the warmth and concern in her voice from reaching me. When I had replaced the receiver I went to the window and watched my son with Rory. They were throwing stones into the water, making them skid across the little waves.

I inquired at Oban the cost of the call and made a note of it on the pad at Lovat's desk. Then I rang my office in London and explained about the accident with the dyes. I took full responsibility. "I should have had a lock put on the door," I said, "but nobody locks doors on the island, so I didn't dream that anything in the cottage we are using was in danger. I suppose there are vandals everywhere."

Gerald Farrer was understanding. The sum involved in sending a fresh lot of dyes was comparatively small for such a large company. But I undertook to have a lock on the cottage door before the next lot of dyes arrived. As far as the ruined wool was concerned, I made my own arrangements from the Scottish end, writing to a supplier in Glasgow.

Before I left, I took a longing look at the shelves of books. One lay open on the window seat. I picked it up. It was a book of verse by the poet Rilke. I read:

Perhaps all the dragons of our lives are princesses who are only waiting to see us once beautiful and brave.

269

The essence of every fairy tale — the symbol of the courage which overcomes danger. Courage was what I needed so badly.

XIX

Back on Cathair Mor, I left Rory and Paul and stopped at Morag's cottage to tell her that the new consignment of dyes would be coming soon. She was delighted and her small grand-daughter hopped around us on her now beautifully straight legs. I had bought her some sweets in Mull, and although she clutched them happily, stuffing them two at a time into her mouth, I knew that as soon as I had left, Morag would take charge and dole them out to her in healthier rations.

Morag's cottage was some way west of Mullaine, and crossing the rough foothills of the Brenlorns, I passed Logan MacRobert's cottage. I was surprised at the loudness of the voices inside, for the people of the island spoke softly. Someone was saying angrily, "All that oil! 'Tis the Mullaines will benefit. Not us."

Old Murdo's thick cackle drowned the rest of the sentence. "Ach, an' ye think the Mullaines will take the prize in oil, do ye? But 'twill be someone else, someone wi' more right to it . . ."

The islanders always spoke Gaelic among themselves, but Murdo had used English. I could make a fairly good guess why. He had probably been standing near the window of the cottage and seen me approaching and wanted me to know how the villagers felt about the oil. What oil? It was obvious that drilling was about to start somewhere near Cathair Mor because the islanders would not be interested in anything that did not directly concern them.

Surveying for oil had been in operation around the coast of Britain for some time, and the huge oil companies and the government had been locked in argument about controls. I had only scanned the many newspaper reports because I didn't understand the technicalities. Now, however, it seemed that all of us on Cathair Mor were involved.

I almost ran the rest of the way to Mullaine.

Antonia was sitting at the drawing-room window, which had been enlarged from its original medieval slit to give a splendid panoramic view of the sea. There was a magazine on her lap but she was making no attempt to read it.

"I've just overheard the men in Logan's cottage discussing oil," I said, breathless from my run. "Do *you* know what it's all about?"

"Oh yes." Her eyes shone. "And now, apparently, does the island. Oh well, it will give them time to get used to the idea."

"What idea?"

"One of the companies has been surveying for oil out beyond Skerryvore and the result is exciting. There was a slump for a while in these oil projects, but it's building up fast now. With multimillions going into drilling, naturally there's tremendous competition among the huge Western companies and the governments concerned." She laughed. "But that's something we are not concerned with. We just reap the benefit."

"We?"

"You and I and . . . Lewis." There was a glow of excitement in her eyes; she seemed to have forgotten that when Lewis was found, there could never again be anything into which we could enter as associates. Some odd quirk of wishful thinking caused her to link our names together. At the same time I had to know exactly what she meant.

Without taking my eyes from her face, I asked, "Antonia, please tell me. What is it in all this that concerns us?"

"Just that the oil rigs out in the Atlantic will make us rich and no government can interfere because this is our island."

"How can it make 'us' rich, and why are the islanders angry about it? What does it have to do with them?"

"Everything." Antonia's eyes were brilliant with a kind of secret joy. "With the Torran Rocks to the south and Iona a tourist attraction to the north there's only Cathair Mor that can be considered as a kind of halfway place for the men and the supplies and the mini-submarines they'll be using. It will mean enormous changes."

"How long have you known about this?" I demanded.

She looked surprised at the tone of my voice. "Some weeks."

I held back the pertinent comment that she might have told me and not let me hear it at second hand. "The people are going to hate it," I protested.

"They'll have to get used to it. And anyway, it will bring in revenue in the way of shops and industry in general. The whole pattern of the place will change. The men on the oil rig will want a place to come to, to relax and spend their money. Houses will be built near the loch, which they propose to open up. Cathair Mor will be rich. Think, Judith" — she gave a luxurious little sigh — "of all that lovely money rolling in."

"For whom? For the Mullaines."

"The islanders will benefit too. They'll have a better life."

"They already have a way of life they love."

274

"Oh, Judith, don't be so obtuse. What have they got now? A bit of fishing, a bit of farming on their wretched little crofts, complete isolation from other people."

"But they're content," I protested. "They're a small community who know and understand and like one another. This drilling for oil will involve them in the rat race."

Antonia asked softly, "Are you really the one to criticize me? After all, *you* are bringing an industry to the island. Weaving."

She was right. But I still felt I had an argument, for mine was a small island industry. The oil rig in the Atlantic would involve rich outsiders — and possible ultimate corruption for the people here. "I wonder how, in future years, Paul will feel about the despoiling of the island?"

"I doubt if he'll care. Paul will have his profession."

I ignored still another effort to introduce the controversial subject of music. Instead I said, "It's a paradox, isn't it? This lovely island will live — and die — if this project ever goes through."

"It must go through."

I went to the window and looked out over the glen with its splashes of color, to the distant loch, serenely blue. The heather and the fern and the speedwell would all disappear. The lovely curls and ribbons of copper-colored sea-weed would be crushed by bulldozers, the barnacle geese and oyster-catchers would be scared away. Even the kestrels, whose great wings soared over the Brenlorns, would speed to lonelier places in the more northern islands.

"Surely the authorities can do nothing without Lewis's consent?"

"But since he is not here, *I* make the decisions," Antonia said. "You know that. It was explained to you at the time of your marriage, Judith dear. While Lewis is alive — but absent from the island — I control everything. Only when he is dead ..."

"Yes?"

"Well, in that case, you know Paul inherits Cathair Mor. But Lewis isn't dead. I would know if he was." She watched me closely. "Judith, *I would know!* Lewis is alive . . . somewhere. I can read doubt on your face, but you must believe me. Mothers know instinctively if anything has happened to their children."

"Do they?"

Would *I* know if one morning I found that Paul was missing from his bed? Would I know by intuition the moment when someone might whip Paul away from wherever he was — on the moors or in the Bay of the Dark Star with his seal?

Antonia was saying, "Well, now you know

about the oil and I'm glad you do. I thought it better not to tell you with all this . . . this other worry hanging over you like a cloud. I had a feeling you might be upset about it in case the island would be spoiled. But that's progress, Judith, and there's so much money in this for us all." She flung out her arms in an excited, embracing gesture. "Luxury, Judith . . . lovely luxuries in exchange for the use of the island by the oil people."

"Oh, Antonia, you have your luxuries."

The joy went out of her voice. "Have I? If this deal doesn't go through, what will I have in the future? Heaven knows when I'll sing again. Oh, I pretend I will, but if I'm honest, I have the same doubts as the doctors. There's money from recordings, but this oil project will make that seem like little bits of gold dust. This is *business*, Judith, real business . . ."

"And the destruction of an island."

She said with an unusual spurt of anger, "Why don't you join the conservationists and revert to Victorianism?"

"I'm sorry," I said. "But in a way, I have an interest too. Through Paul."

"Paul will thank me for making him rich."

My answer came in a flash. "I thought you wanted him to become rich through the fame of his musical genius."

She said lightly, "Well then, let's leave Paul

277

out of this. There's Lewis. I know my son. When he returns – and he *will*, Judith – he'll be delighted with what I have achieved."

"You should have told me," I accused her. "It's really nothing to do with me, as things are. But it might involve me –"

"It can't," she interrupted steadily. "It can't unless Lewis is . . . dead. And I've told you, I know he is not." She was watching me, and suddenly she caught her breath in a small, horrified gasp. "Oh, Judith, no! You can't be hoping that he is . . . You couldn't be *that* – oh, that cruel!"

I turned on my heel and walked away from her.

She came after me and caught my hand. "I'm sorry. I shouldn't have said that. But I don't understand anything. I start thinking awful things, fearing . . . oh, fearing. Stop me, Judith, stop me having these thoughts."

I said hopelessly, "How can I? I have awful thoughts too . . . and fears."

She put both her hands up to her face, closing her eyes. I had a feeling that she was asking herself whether she should be frightened *of* me or *for* me.

Then, with an obvious effort, she dropped her hands and her expression changed, lost its despair and strengthened. "They tell me it will be difficult getting British engineers with offshore marine experience," she went on. "There's a kind of wild competition going on to get them again. Millions of pounds are being spent and the race is to get the oil out as fast as possible. So they'll speed up any signing of a contract."

"It's one thing to talk of producing oil and another thing to find it."

"How cautious you are! Of course they'll find it. The rich companies don't spend millions without being certain of a huge return for their money. The ocean bed is a mine of wealth." Then, again, her calm deserted her. She made small distracted movements, touching her hair, the silk collar of her dress, the slender gold chain around her neck. "Everything must come right, Judith. Lewis. The oil. Everything in life is balanced, isn't it . . . *isn't* it? I mean, you touch the bottom of a well and then all you can do is rise up again. We've touched that rock bottom, Lewis and I. And now all that's left for us is to rise again."

I was silent, thinking, *She has left me out. But of course, that's the way it would have to be.* If Lewis was the winner in the end, then it was I who must be the loser.

The telephone bell rang, and as if it were an escape for her, Antonia flew to answer it.

Mullaine became suddenly oppressive. I escaped, not knowing where I wanted to go and not really wanting to go anywhere, for the eternal mist that bedeviled the island was creeping up again. I walked slowly across the *machair* and saw that Murdo's door was open. I went through the gap in the dry-stone wall and knocked on the door.

"Come on in, *mo ghaoil.*"

I entered the kitchen, with its own thick brand of fog caused by Murdo's foul and ancient pipe, and as an excuse for calling, asked him how he was after the fire.

"Oh, it didna' hurt me. I've been after thinkin' I'd clear oot they newspapers an' the fire did it for me. But it saved me my treasures."

"Treasures?"

He gave me a long, sly grin. "An old man's, that's all."

"I was passing Logan's cottage and I overheard you talking about the oil."

He took up his pipe and drew on it, letting out a cloud of smoke. "Oh, aye?"

"I heard you say that there's someone who has more right to the oil than the Mullaines."

"Oh, aye?" he said again, maddeningly.

"Who did you mean?"

He shook his head. "Now how would I be knowin' anythin' at all aboot it?"

I ignored the wide innocence of his watery

blue eyes. "But you do, otherwise you wouldn't have said what you did." I leaned toward him. "Murdo, what did you mean?"

He chuckled. "I'm oold, an' maybe I get mad when they don't listen to me, so I says somethin' that'll make them sit up. 'Tweren't nothin' at all."

I tried another tactic. "I once heard that you had second sight."

"Ach, The Sight. Aye, likely I have."

"Then can you foresee something . . . something about the proposed oil? Is that it?"

I had touched his vanity. He leaned forward, digging at the bowl of his pipe. "That's it, mebbe. There's strange things'll be happenin' not so very far off."

"What things?"

He shook his head. "The Sight didna' tell me everythin'. But ye'll see, *mo ghaoil,* ye'll see . . ."

"Murdo!"

He crossed to the window. "Ye'd best be gettin' back, or the mist will catch ye."

I was defeated and I knew it. I was perfectly certain they had all been discussing the oil when I heard him in Logan's cottage. Whatever it was Murdo knew was giving him a secret delight that he had no intention of sharing with me.

The mist was floating as if on a tangible breeze. I decided that I would have time to look in at Hamish's cottage and check the dyes and the wool before the white cloud blanketed out the island. I walked along the shore, turning inland where the little stream ran into the sea.

Duncan had repaired the door with a bolt he had acquired from somewhere. "I didna' even ha' to go to Mull for it," he had told me with pride.

But the shock of the ruined dyes was still with me and I was anxious. I peered in at the window and saw the looms, standing where the men had set them up, and the boxes of wool, as we had arranged.

Reassured, I left the little patch of weeds and wild grass that crept up to the walls of the cottage. The white sea cloud had floated behind me like a lurking stranger and I could scarcely see further than my outstretched arm. I knew that common sense should have warned me to turn back once the mist had settled on the edge of the water. That was always the warning. When it reached the waves, only those who knew the way blindfolded could ignore it.

The way up from the shore to Hamish's cottage had been a climb, so that returning in such limited visibility meant that every step had to be watched. The cliffs fell almost sheer to the shore and the sea made no sound. I should have been used to the frequent white uncanny hours when the island became invisible, but I was not.

The one thing that reassured me was that Paul was indoors, for I had heard the *cling* of the table tennis ball as he practiced, hitting it against the wall of his play room.

It wasn't far from Hamish's cottage to the Castle, but I walked warily, pausing and lifting my head to try to see a landmark. But there was none. No round tower of Mullaine thrusting into the sky, no crofter's cottage, not even a goat or a cow to prove to me that I was not alone in this primeval world.

The thrust in the middle of my back was so powerful that the cry I gave was a startled scream. I had no time to steel myself against the sudden blow or to try to fling myself inward. I hurtled sideways into thick white space.

My frantic outstretched arms sought to grasp something as I fell, but felt only the rough cliff face that seemed to have neither handhold nor foothold. Then my right hand, still stretched out, came upon something soft and cool. Instantly my fingers tightened and my fall was checked — it must have lasted only a matter of seconds. Had it been longer, I would have been killed. I was flung against the wall of rock and felt the hardness of a ledge beneath me. But my legs were over the side of the lifesaving rock and my balance on it was as precarious as if I had been on a ladder without foot support. I swung my legs violently inward and the rock above the ledge caught my knees and almost bounced me back over the edge. I grasped a thin wind-dwarfed bush growing in a cleft in the rock, and it held. It was my lifeline, and I edged my legs onto the ledge and lay quite still, my heart thudding.

Below me the sea was silent. Above me nothing moved. But something had . . . some-*one* had . . .

I lay, stunned with fear, and strained my ears listening for a footfall or a scrape of rock, for it was possible that whoever had sent me hurtling over the side was capable of climbing down and attacking me again. I was by no means safe — unless, with the mist that had now become merciful, my attacker had believed that I had been flung the full drop of the cliff and was killed. My only hope was to remain silent until, listening for a sound from me, and hearing none, he would be assured that I was dead.

I looked down. Scattered over my skirt were the broken heads of the little sea pinks which dotted the face of the cliffs. I must have grasped them in falling. I stretched my limbs very cautiously. I was bruised but no bones were broken. At the same time I had no idea how I could save myself. I could see neither how far I had fallen nor how distant I was from the sea below. Until the mist cleared I did not know which way I dared move.

And whichever way I went, if I could manage to move at all — up onto the top of the rock face or down to the shingle beach — *who would be waiting for me?*

Who? Who . . . ? I heard the single questioning word in the loud beating of my heart. Who was the piper on Cathair Beag? Who was stalking me, awaiting his opportunity? I thought, lying there, my clothes damp with the mist, my limbs tense with fear, that perhaps the things that had happened had been a plan building up to this moment when an attack on me could be made and a mist would conceal the attacker.

And the result of an inquiry would be that I had accused an innocent man; that I had been behaving strangely and finally, in a moment of despair, had killed myself.

I could not remain indefinitely on the ledge of rock. I had to call for help. Now that shock was wearing off, I realized that whoever had attacked me would not be able to see where I had fallen any more than I could see him. In a way, my dangerous position was my security. If I called out, perhaps a crofter, searching for a lost sheep or a wandering cow, would hear me. And whoever had tried to kill me would not dare to show himself if an islander came to my rescue.

I called, straining my voice against the muffling mist. I called three times, but no other voice broke the silence. I was getting colder, and the dampness of the rock on which I lay was seeping through my clothes.

Then, out of the blankness around me, I heard a dog's deep bark. It came three times, and a voice followed.

"Is anyone there?"

"Rory!"

"Where are you, Judith?"

"I'm down here . . . on a ledge of rock. Get help. Please, get help . . ."

"Are you hurt?"

"I don't think so. But *get help*."

I peered upward through the mist and saw a moving shadow above me. "If you aren't hurt, then you can get to the top easily. The mist is clearing and you aren't far down. Can't you see? Look!" A faint movement, like a small dark patch of mist, floated above me.

"I can see *something*."

"That's my hand. Just wait, I'll come down and help you."

"No, don't. Do as I ask, please. Get help."

"We won't need it. Don't be frightened, Judith. I won't hurt you."

I heard him give an order to his dog Lufra and after that came a few little grunts, typical of Rory when he was making any effort. Then I heard the scrape of heavy shoes against rock.

"It's not – a bad place – to have – fallen," Rory called between mumbling and panting. "But you shouldn't have been walking in this."

This was no time for explanations. I lay still and saw above me a pair of feet, then stocky legs appeared too near my head.

"Be careful," I called. "You're close above me and I can't move out of your way. The ledge is very narrow, though I can't see the edge."

"The mist is actually clearing," Rory said. "It seldom lasts long. But down there, where you are, the cliff holds it in. That's why I can see better than you can."

"Rory, you nearly stood on me!"

"Don't worry, lass. The ledge is longer than you think. I'm just feeling my way. I can see you. I won't step on you. I've fished from this ledge many a time."

The feet worked their way to a shoulder of the cliff just past my head. I craned around to watch. Then Rory was there, clinging to the rock face and looking down at me.

"You're sure you're not hurt?"

"No." I moved each limb to show him. "Just scared."

"It's a good thing I came along when I did, isn't it? Or you might have thought you could climb down on your own, and it's at this place that the sea comes right up to the cliff." He shook his head slowly. "And the dear knows what would have happened had you tried to climb down." He leaned back, still regarding me solemnly. "I don't understand why —"

"Rory, get me out. Just don't talk. Help me, please."

He took my hand, but too gently, so that I couldn't rely on his weight to support me. He said, "Lying there with the mist around you, and your hair falling over the rock, you remind me of the story of Enya in the legend — you know the one? She used to lie on deerskins and sing to a golden clairsach. I have one. It's like a small harp —"

"Get me off this rock, for God's sake."

"I'm sorry," he said sadly and put out both his hands and drew me up carefully till I stood beside him.

I leaned back against the cliff face and breathed a sigh of relief. I could see now that the ledge was wider than I had imagined as I lay on it helplessly horizontal.

"Now," Rory's voice was suddenly brisk, "I'll go first and you follow. Put your feet exactly where I do. Just 'step into my shoes,' as they say." His little giggle was curiously reassuring.

"I'll do just what you tell me," I said fervently.

"It's not hard if you know the way."

I followed carefully, peering up into the mist to see his handholds, putting my feet exactly onto small jutting pieces of rock Rory found; gripping with damp cold fingers a small ridge here, a tiny strip of a ledge there. If this was what they called an easy climb, then every real climber, tackling difficult rock faces, was reckless and every mountaineer utterly mad. As I followed Rory to the top, I clung, feeling each indent and swell of rock against my body, too scared of releasing the sensation of solidity against my body to look beyond Rory just above me, and knowing that it was fatal, if one were frightened, to look down.

An opalescent glimmer had broken through the mist and I knew then that we were almost at the top and that my fall hadn't been nearly so far as I had imagined. But that didn't lessen my intense fear, because the plunge to the sea was steep and deadly and whoever had made that violent thrust at my back had not reckoned on the ledge saving my fall. Whoever he was, he could be gloating now at the sight that would meet a passing fisherman when the island was clear again. Judith Mullaine lying on the boulders just above the sea line, or floating, drowned and tossed by waves. Guilt-laden, dead by her own hand.

A few last tentative movements, some grunts from Rory, and he held out his hands to pull me the last foot or two to safety. I stumbled onto the top of the cliff and lay there for a moment. One hand was bleeding and my skirt was torn. But I was alive. Lufra's feathery tail flapped against my face.

"You'd better come along down to the Castle and get dried out," Rory said.

"I fell into the sea because of my idiocy. Now I'm tossed over the side of a cliff." My voice was high with a hysteria I was trying hard to control. I felt lightheaded with the paradox of relief and fear. I walked a few shaky paces, Lufra bounding by my side, and then I had to stop and lean against Rory.

He put his arm around me. "Are you all right?"

"Yes, if only my legs would stop shaking."

"You were frightened."

"Dear heaven, you can say that again!"

"But what made you come this way?" he asked, his arm still firm around me.

"I wanted to make certain everything was all right at Hamish's cottage — the looms are there and I feel responsible."

"You shouldn't walk near the cliff top when there's a sea mist. In winter sometimes great boulders break away in storms. You probably slipped on a loose rock."

I didn't choose to talk about it — I trusted no one.

The Castle tower rose, its crenellations looming like a great shadowy crown. I said, quickening my step, "Only minutes ago I wondered if I would ever see Mullaine again . . . or, in fact, anything. I suppose when the mist cleared, *someone* would have seen me and I'd have been rescued. That's what imagination and fear does for you – it can only see the worst."

Rory drew me close in a shy hug. "Everything will be all right, Judith, in the end. It's wretched now, I know, and . . . and terrible. But it will soon be over."

I jerked my head back to look at him. The emerging sun, gilding the mist, gave his face a luminous quality. "What do you mean?"

As I watched, a closed look came over his features. He gave me a small, secret smile. "I know things – some Scots and Irish do. I told you, don't you remember? Sometimes things of the future are clear to people with The Sight. It's like knowing that the old tales of the Hebrides are true – that immortals live and are visible to some people and that –"

He was edging away with embarrassment at what he had let slip out. I interrupted him, ignoring the slide into talk of the immortals. "What do you think you know – or *do* know?"

He shook his head. "Nothing . . . oh, nothing." He giggled nervously. "I talk nonsense sometimes, Judith."

"But you know something that involves me. *What?*"

He gave me his sunny smile. "It's just that, somehow, I know that you'll be all right in the end. That's all."

"I was so nearly not 'all right' when you found me just now," I said, and suddenly made a decision to tell him the truth. "Rory, just listen ... I'm not joking or imagining anything. Someone came up behind me on that cliff and pushed me."

He stared at me, open-mouthed, but in spite of his seeming amazement, I saw wariness in his eyes. After long thought, he said, "You know, Judith, it could have happened. Yes, it could. I know Logan was out looking for a cow. Perhaps that was what knocked against you in the mist. Yes, I'm sure that was it." He sounded triumphant.

I drew away from him and walked on, limping a little because my right ankle suddenly began to hurt. Rory had given me a curious evasive prophecy. I knew that if I insisted that a human hand and not a cow's rump had pushed me, he would start to talk of "faery mischief." Reason and magic were intricately woven in Rory's mind and I could not rely on anything he said.

We entered the grounds of Mullaine. I was safe, but I was almost as tense as when I had lain on the cliff. Once again I had no witness to who had been stalking me out there. Would anyone believe that I hadn't been merely foolish in venturing out and had missed my step and fallen? That was what the islanders would say. And Antonia? What she would believe turned me ice-cold inside.

It would be hard and clear in her mind. Antonia afraid that by design or insanity, I was implicating Lewis . . .

Rory's arm was resting lightly on my shoulders. I shrugged it away as gently as I could and stopped by the rowan tree near the Castle lawn. "Thank you for what you did. Would you like to come in for a while? Antonia will be around and you could have a drink with her while I change out of my damp clothes."

Rory said "No" very quickly. Antonia scared him too much.

The chandelier in the Great Hall was as yet unlit, for the mist was clearing and the western sun was emerging in soft radiance. As I went up the stairs, I could hear Antonia and Paul talking in the drawing room. I went past them and to my room.

I had a quick bath and changed, and then, sitting at the dressing table combing my hair, I tried to think whom I could tell — or rather, whom I could tell *who would believe me* . . .

Barbara? Yes. But she was five hundred miles

away and her faith in me was out of affection, and that would not help me in the realistic world of witness and fact.

Elbows on the dressing table, chin on my hands, I said to my reflected face, "I've got to save myself – *for* myself and for Paul."

I could go away without even the police knowing, pack essentials and leave. To my mother in New Zealand. To Barbara's holiday villa in the South of France. Anywhere ... anywhere.

A sense of excitement shook me. I would take no one into my confidence, but in the early hours of a morning I would slip out with Paul, take one of the launches and cross to Mull. From there – My thoughts pulled up short and my excitement died. It was an impossible plan. For one thing, a woman, a child and some luggage, however little we traveled with, could not get to Oban on the mainland without being seen. There would be no way of getting there at night, and in the daytime the search would be on for me. My attempt to escape might lead to a new inquiry, new questions, new doubts about me. I was cornered, here on Cathair Mor. The Castle of Mullaine was no longer my sanctuary, it had become my prison. And I was completely helpless to do anything about it.

I must be my own protector on the island.

There must be no more wandering over the hills or by the sea unless there were islanders around, perhaps cutting peat on the moors or down by the loch mending their nets. Wherever I walked, I must be the one to seek company, distant and unaware maybe, but within safe call.

Then I thought in despair, *But I can't live like that . . .*

XX

Antonia wore a dress of soft ruby wool. Her hair gleamed like frost and her heavily embroidered silk bolero was patterned in crystal beads. I wore my favorite leaf-green dress. Lewis had once said, "If you wear so much of that color, you'll grow into a tree one day."

When I went down to join Antonia, she said, "My dear, do go and put on one of your necklaces."

"I only brought the topaz with me, and I don't know why I did that because it's rather elaborate and only really suitable for formal occasions."

"The topaz will be charming, the dress is so plain . . . though you can wear it with your pretty figure."

Antonia and I had been invited that night to the Abbey for dinner. I wanted to go — not that I thought I would enjoy myself, but I needed to watch Shane with the security of people around me. He had become a kind of obsession in my mind. *How much is he involved?* He

296

frightened me. And yet, in a curious way, I felt some power in him that drew me.

I even asked Antonia a little later as we walked across the glen to Inverkyle, "Do you like Shane?"

She thought for a moment before replying, and then she gave an odd little laugh. "*Like* him? My dear Judith, Robert taught me never to trust a Kilarran, but I hope I'm civilized enough to be sociable with my neighbors. He has a strong personality. I doubt if he likes us much, either. You see, Judith, both you and I married Mullaine men, and old bitterness dies hard."

"But this is the late twentieth century. Hundreds of years have passed since the fighting and the hatred —"

"Robert always said of Shane's father that though he was charming and gracious, he hid his dislike behind every smile. The pride of ownership of land and title, he used to say, is the strongest pride there is. The Kilarrans will never forgive us in their hearts."

"But Shane's life and work isn't here —"

"His roots are, and his home." She shivered. "Just think of it, Judith. It's June, and here we are wrapped up in coats."

"We could be wrapped up in coats in London," I said, "and it's a lovely evening."

I looked back once and saw Paul at his

window watching us. I said, without thinking, "I hope Rosheen keeps an eye on him."

"Judith, you really mustn't worry so much. Paul is perfectly good. He'll go to bed when Rosheen tells him." Her voice became lightly teasing. "Don't go catching Rory's complaints about the 'little people,' or whatever he calls them, stealing away human children. Paul's a bit too big for them, for all their supposed magic."

She knew perfectly well that Rory's tales were very far from my thoughts.

Lichens and mosses made rich emerald patches in the glen and little clusters of blue speedwell were as vivid as if the sky had dropped chips of itself there. The ancient stone of the Abbey glowed, the columned porch with its carvings appeared, in the evening brilliance, as almost too splendid for the tiny island home of two ill-assorted bachelors.

As we stood in the nave, giving Jeannie our coats, Shane came out of the covered cloister on the right to greet us. He was in ordinary clothes, but as he led us into the living room, Rory appeared in full formal dress. He wore a kilt of the Kilarran colors, blue and grey and crimson, and a black velvet jacket. With his bright hair and his fine straight legs, he looked impressive in spite of his lack of height.

Antonia was carrying on an easy, social conversation with Shane, and had I not known how she felt about the Kilarrans, I would have thought a close and sincere friendship existed between them. We went together into the large drawing room, which had windows looking out onto the smooth green lawn and the flowers of the cloister. Over the stone fireplace was a heraldic carving of some fabulous creature. Rory saw me looking at it. "A salamander," he said with obvious delight that I had noticed something belonging to the unreal world that he so loved. "And all those twists and turns of carving are meant to represent the fire and the flames surrounding it."

He had told me about it on my first visit to the Abbey, but had either forgotten or wanted someone to talk to while Antonia spread herself elegantly in the chair Shane had drawn up for her. She was reminiscing, laughing at some amusing memory long before the two island men had grown up and gone their ways.

The room was comfortably furnished and the color scheme was conventional, rose and old-gold brocade – I wondered how many of the great houses of Britain had those same colors, as if such grandeur needed a uniform in fabrics. The ceiling had been lowered by wooden beams and crossbeams filled in with squares of heavily carved oak. I doubted if Shane or Rory had changed a thing in their lifetime here, or if, indeed, their parents had. The room savored of the grandiloquence of Georgian ancestors.

Antonia was asking Shane about his travels. Didn't he feel the cold after those hot Middle Eastern countries?

"I'm immune." He laughed. "And those Middle Eastern countries can be very cold in winter, particularly so in the places where I often worked, far outside the cities."

She watched him over the rim of her glass. "Do you ever want to go back?"

"Oh, possibly."

I bent down and stroked Lufra and he sat up, his eyes like brown velvet. I went on stroking the beautiful head and the great dog laid its muzzle against my knee.

"He's twelve," Rory said to me. "And when Shane came back after all these years, Lufra knew him. Isn't that odd?"

I nodded, listening to what Antonia was saying to Shane. "I know I'll sing again. I tested my voice — oh, very carefully — the other day and it didn't hurt. It will be so wonderful. But then, you understand. You travel the world just as I do. It gives one such a sense of freedom to know that you can be in San Francisco or Tokyo or Sydney within a day — two days." She sipped her drink. "Once you have tasted travel, as we know it, I'm sure one could never settle down — not, at least, on an island."

"And the other morning," Rory was saying to me, "I saw a golden eagle . . ."

I made an effort to be interested. I *was* interested; it was a joy when eagles returned to the eyries of the North. At the same time I was more intrigued by the way Antonia was trying to find out what Shane's future plans were.

He was saying, "It's the old story, you know, Antonia. A man who has slept with a goose-feather pillow under his head can never really rest. We have goosefeather pillows here at the Abbey."

The light, apparently inconsequential conversation flowed on until Jeannie entered to announce dinner.

The dining room at Inverkyle was another part of the Abbey that had never been finished. Here again the end wall was covered with ancient and magnificent carvings and the floor was black marble. There were two gables, and the height of the room did not give it the pleasant intimacy needed in a dining room, lit as this was by wall sconces.

Rory drew out one of the tall carved oak chairs for me, and Shane said, as if reading my thoughts, "One of these days I'll have the ceiling here lowered. It's one of those things I've never got around to, for we have so few guests and the dining room seldom gets used." He glanced at Rory. "Sometimes Jeannie tries to urge him to ask people over from Mull. But he doesn't."

Rory said, taking his seat at the end of the long table, "I don't want people to dinner. I'm never lonely here. I have all the people I know on the island and lots . . . lots of people you don't see. They talk to me, you know, when I'm alone. Lufra hears them too."

The dog raised his head, watching us. In the room's light, they seemed so similar, Rory's head and the setter's glossy coat. Even Shane's dark hair glinted in the crimson-shaded sconces.

Dinner was simple but excellent; the wine good, the fish freshly caught, the strawberries sent over from hothouses on the mainland.

Antonia said, laughing, "You eat well – for two men on their own."

"Should bachelors eat bread and cheese?" Shane parried. "Shouldn't life be as good as we can make it? That's my belief, anyway."

"And mine. But here –" She shuddered. "Shane, you can't possibly think that living here is making the most of life."

"Why not? I am a Scot and Scots love their land. This is my island and I'm part of it. It would never take up all my life. Yet it's here – like the roots of a tree stretching far beyond where it stands, but remaining the focal point. Inverkyle" – his eyes had no dreams in them;

they were alert and aware — "is me and I am Inverkyle."

I doubted if anyone noticed the sudden start I gave because I covered it up by leaning back in my chair.

The conversation had changed and Shane was telling us a story of an adventure in Iran. Then the talk turned light and impersonal, and Rory put in little spurts of information. I had never noticed him at ease with Antonia and it was curious how seldom he spoke to Shane and how he watched him, shyly, covertly.

In a lull in the conversation, Shane turned unexpectedly to me and asked me how the weaving project was going.

I looked at him calmly across the wide space of the hearth between us. "I'm waiting for fresh dyes."

Antonia said, "I do so hope it's going to work, because if not, I'm afraid Judith's office in London will hold it against her."

"It will work," I said, "if only because the women here are glad of a diversion."

"Your office will pay the labor costs?"

"Of course. Good tweeds are very fashionable now."

Antonia gave a low laugh and adjusted the embroidered collar of her bolero. "I give it two years, no more. And then the women will be back in their crofts brewing tea and gossiping, with their looms packed away again under those awful unbleached linen sheets they have, until the winter, when they'll start weaving cloth for themselves. And how dull it is – all browns and dark blues and black –" She gave a small impatient shrug. "I only hope they'll appreciate what Judith is trying to do for them."

Shane asked softly, "Do people appreciate change?"

Antonia turned to him, laughing. "You obviously do. Your life is spent enjoying change. And so is mine. Oh, to get back to my own world!"

Rory crossed the room, his kilt swinging. Antonia and Shane scarcely noticed. They were talking about a city they knew well. Venice.

"Is there anywhere more beautiful?" she asked. "I sang *Bohème* in the Fenice Theatre there. All that gilt and pink plush just suits the place . . . and the attendants in their wigs. Strange, isn't it, that here we sit, on a lonely island talking of some past gala night in Venice. Oh . . ."

We all started, for suddenly a great sonorous sound of crashing metal nearly deafened us. A bell was being tolled immediately above us. Antonia flung up her hands, shielding her ears.

Shane shot up out of his chair. "For God's sake, does he want to bring the ceiling down?"

"Who?" My voice was drowned, but Shane swung round and said, "Rory . . . sounding that bloody bell." His face was dark with anger, but before he could reach the door, Jeannie came running in. "Mr. Rory's gone to the tower, and it's not safe. We never let him do that. I don't know why —"

Shane brushed her aside and rushed out. Antonia took her hands from her ears. "I never knew you had a bell in the tower here."

Jeannie, hovering in the doorway, said, " 'Twas put in — oh, sometime, so they say, when Prince Charlie landed on Eriskay. 'Twas goin' to be a grand welcome. But it no came to anythin'. 'Twas said a way ago that Mr. Shane's father wanted to ring it after the Great War, but 'twas unsafe — 'twasn't hung properly and the door to the tower has always been locked."

"And now," Antonia said quietly, for the tolling of the bell had ceased, "Rory has found a way to open that door."

Jeannie shook her head, smiling fondly, as if he were an errant son. "Aye, he gets into mischief. But there's so little here for him to do, an' he bein' childlike, an', mebbe, because ye're here, likely he's showin' off."

I heard quick angry strides on the stone floor of the porch and then Shane came scowling into the room. He turned first to Jeannie. "Did you know about this?"

"About what?" She was a tall woman and looked him levelly in the eyes.

"That he managed to remove — or someone removed for him — the heavy padlock my father had put on the belfry door."

"Oh, nae, naebody would —"

"Somebody has," Shane retorted. "Rory was up there sounding that bell, which could have crashed through the porch, and if anyone had stood underneath, killed them. The unutterable fool! Where is Dru?"

"He's gone down to help Murdo pile his peat, now that the shed be repaired. But I'm sure Dru wouldna' have risked nae accident."

"For Rory, Dru would do anything." Shane swung around on me furiously. "And do you know where that lock is at this moment?"

"How should I know?" I asked, startled.

"Fastening the door of the cottage you intend to use for the women's weaving job. For God's sake, has nobody here got any sense?"

It was my sneaking feeling that Shane was right that made me answer almost humbly, "I'm sorry, but I can't think that Duncan used the padlock from here. I asked him to get one from Mull."

"Well, he didn't. Dru saved him the journey. Rory has just admitted it." He turned impatiently away as his brother appeared.

His velvet jacket was dusty and his hair

tousled, as though he had had to crawl up some difficult way to get to the bell rope. "It was just done for fun," he said like a child. "It sounded fine, didn't it? They'd hear that over in Mull."

"And they won't hear it again." Shane was in a black fury. "Of all the bloody silly things to do."

Antonia sat listening, a little smile on her face. "Well, talking just now of diversions, that was certainly one. I can't say the bell is particularly musical."

"I wonder it could sound at all after the rust of centuries," Shane said less angrily. "All right, Jeannie, you can go. I'll see Dru later."

"You know, Shane," Antonia said, "that bell could be quite useful in future."

"Not while I'm here."

"But what Rory said is quite true. It could be heard as far off as Mull, and it's what is wanted here. One of these days there's going to be a storm or some kind of disaster and all the islanders might be needed to cope. The bell would summon them, just as it was put there to do."

Shane sat down and leaned back his head. "The struts that hold up the belfry are rotted. The thing was never properly installed — if it had been, we wouldn't have been deafened down here when it rang."

"Have you ever heard it before?" Antonia asked.

"No," Shane said. "No one living has ever heard it."

"Until now," Antonia said softly.

I said, "I'll ask Duncan to get me a lock from Mull tomorrow and you must have yours back."

Shane looked at me with polite, cold eyes. "Thank you, but you may as well keep it. Fixing another lock where one is already in place is rather a waste of time and energy. I'll get another for the belfry. But" – he turned to Rory – "don't ever go up there again. I'm sorry" – he addressed both Antonia and me – "for that episode, but if you hadn't been here when I found that padlock missing, I'd have created far greater hell."

Antonia laughed. "I'm sure you would. Poor Rory. He really was trying to amuse us."

Rory had recovered from Shane's anger. "There's something else missing," he said, "and *I* didn't do that."

"What?"

"The set of bagpipes Lewis gave me. I put them in the chest by the cloister door, you remember?"

"Perfectly."

"Well, they're not there. Judith was with me when I looked."

Shane poured more coffee into our green-

308

and-gold cups. "You probably took them out to try them again and can't remember where you left them."

"But I *didn't*. I haven't touched them, and I know they *were* there."

Shane seemed to hesitate. Then he got up. "All right. Let's see."

As he went out, Antonia also rose and crossed to a harp standing in a corner of the room. "I'd forgotten," she said, reaching out to stroke the faded gilded wood. "Years ago, Rory, when your father was alive and I was up here with my husband on a holiday, I used to play that and sing to it. Did you know" — she turned to me — "that the piano and the harp are two instruments I learned when I was young? I don't play either well, but sufficiently to find the right notes." She pulled a carved stool forward, sat down and touched the strings. "It doesn't feel as if anyone has played it for years. What a shame! It's a lovely instrument, so much softer than a piano."

Shane entered, carrying bagpipes. He laid them down on a table.

"Where did you find them?" Rory's mouth was open in amazement.

"Where they were all the time, where you said they were not. In the chest by the cloister door."

"But they *weren't!*" Rory and I spoke simultaneously, using the same words. I added, "We went together to look. Did he tell you that I came over to find out if they were still here because —" I hesitated, glanced at Antonia and collected my courage. "It may not seem to make sense, but I heard someone, about a week ago, playing the bagpipes on Cathair Beag."

For a moment no one spoke. And then Shane said, "Sounds are deceptive here, Judith. It was probably someone over on Mull."

"It wasn't. It couldn't be," I said sharply, far more angry at Shane's disbelief than at Antonia's. "I *know* the sound came from there. And whoever it was, was playing the island song, *this* island song, 'The Red Man.' "

"Well, it's a free country. He can play what he likes," Shane said too airily and turned to Rory. "You'd better put those pipes somewhere upstairs — by the cloister door isn't the wisest place, with all the rain and the winds that howl through this place in winter."

From the brocade stool by the harp, Antonia said softly, "You used to be able to play the pipes, Shane. Why don't you try?"

"Because I have too much consideration for my guests' ears. I'm no musician." He sat down again in the large chair, stretched his legs and began rubbing Lufra's glossy back lightly with the toe of his shoe.

Antonia struck a few strings on the harp. "Do

310

you know, I've almost forgotten how to play it. That's dreadful, isn't it? Give me an easy tune to try, someone."

Rory said, " 'The Skye Boat Song.' "

She nodded, and sat for a moment looking at the strings. Then, tipping the harp toward her, her snowy head bent, the crimson of her gown glowing richly against the worn gilt of the harp, she began to play.

At first she plucked many wrong notes, but she kept on, touching the strings, and eventually she mastered the melody she wanted. Over and above the soft music of the strings, I heard her voice. At first it was little more than a hum, and then I heard Rory give a little gasp of pleasure, for she was playing the music for one of the loveliest and most haunting of the Celtic legends. Slowly the muted hum of her voice gave way to distinct notes and words:

"How beautiful they are
The lordly ones,
Who dwell in the hills,
The hollow hills . . ."

Very softly, without straining her voice, she sang the theme song from *The Immortal Hour.* Ordinarily the song was not for her type of voice; it was too fragile, too pitched to a fey, almost offbeat quality. She continued to sing

311

very softly, her voice husky and missing notes. Yet the effect was part of the strangeness of the song.

The room gave a stage effect to the scene. Out of one window I could see a single lamp that illumined the cloister; out of the other, there were the Brenlorns, half lit by moonlight.

I felt there was about the setting and ourselves, a timelessness — almost a sense that I had been plunged into some world far from reality. Hundreds of years of legend and superstition were crowded into that pillared room and I sat enchanted, listening.

Suddenly, as if a rock had been flung through that web of magic, the music stopped with a hoarse cry: "I can't. I can't sing . . ."

The harp swayed a little before it settled itself. Antonia started to her feet, crossed the room and sat in the chair near Shane. Her face was strained and furrowed with distress. "It isn't any use. It's gone, it's all gone."

"It was lovely," I said. "That song —"

She said, her voice fierce and hoarse, "How can I go through life humming a song? And when I tried to open up my voice, I couldn't . . ."

Shane rose, saying quietly, "Suppose you just have patience a little longer? You told me you had orders not to sing for — six months, was it?" He touched her shoulder as he passed.

"There's a very good adage about timing every-thing, not rushing fate, or you lose the way that's set out for you. Now let's all have a brandy. Or would you like a liqueur?"

"Brandy, please," Antonia said in her broken tones.

Shane looked at me. I shook my head. "No, thank you."

"Come along," he said lightly to me, "a brandy would perhaps relax you."

"I'm quite relaxed."

He said nothing, but he poured me out a drink also, and as I took it he said, his head bent, his eyes meeting mine too keenly, "Why are you afraid?" and then turned away, making it not so much a question as a statement.

Antonia was saying huskily, "It really was foolish of me to burst out like that. Of course I've got to be patient — that's what the doctors told me. I shouldn't have tried my voice out just now, but seeing the harp there was too tempting." She put her hand to her throat and cleared it cautiously. "You see how hoarse just that little effort has made me. But I'll get through all this. And you — all of you — will have to come to my first recovery concert, even if it's halfway round the world!" She smiled too brightly at us.

Rory said dreamily, as if he hadn't been listening to her, "It's a beautiful song, that one.

My grandmother used to sing it to me long ago. She came from way beyond Braemar. It was she who frightened me with her stories of the maze."

I turned toward Rory. "What maze?"

"The one that had been in our family for ages. But I hated it, because she scared me with her tales. Shane found it when he came home and began going through the cupboards and desk drawers." He grinned shyly at me. "I keep everything, you see, but Shane throws things out. He has such an ordered mind; I haven't."

"Shane gave Paul a maze, a most lovely one," Antonia said. "We were playing with it yesterday when Judith was out. You heard, of course," she went on speaking to Shane, "that Judith nearly had a very bad accident. She slipped and fell in the mist. That clever dog of yours and Rory found her."

"You didn't hurt yourself?" He turned to me.

"The fates or the angels must have been on my side," I said lightly to Shane, "because all I had were a few grazes and scratches. A ledge of rock saved me."

"Ours is a dangerous coast. You should treat it with respect."

"Oh, I do. Only I didn't reckon that the mist would come in so quickly."

"Shane thought that since we didn't want

that maze, Paul would like it," Rory said brightly.

"It's a very valuable present to give a small boy," Antonia said. "It's really quite beautiful."

Rory warmed to her interest. "My grandmother told me the story of the labyrinth — you know, the Greek legend of the maze, about people being trapped in them and never finding their way out. I used to have nightmares about it."

"But it has charming stories also," Antonia told him. "There's a maze in the grounds of Hampton Court Palace, and in Victorian times, having one in your garden was a status symbol. So the old horror story doesn't apply any more. Paul is fascinated by it."

I sat very quietly, holding the brandy glass in my hands. The evening had been strangely equivocal, as if everything that had been said or done had a second meaning. Yet we were all seated comfortably, friendlily, in a lamp-filled room.

Antonia began telling us about a concert in San Francisco where they brought onto the stage a star made entirely of white roses. I had heard the story before and my attention wandered.

Someone said something that started a chain of laughter around me. Even Lufra, ears twitching, gave almost inaudible barks, as if caught by the merriment. I had no idea what had amused them, but during my wandering moments the atmosphere in the room had changed completely and was now lightly social. We talked of places and people, foreign cities that both Antonia and Shane knew, and mutual friends of their families who lived on the mainland of Scotland.

At eleven o'clock we left, Shane walking back with us across the glen, luminous in the three-quarter moon. A light breeze blew our hair.

At the Castle door, Shane turned to Antonia. "One day I shall hear you sing again."

"Thank you. Yes, I promise you will." Their hands touched, and my mother-in-law, looking up at him, had the moonlight like a kind of silver rapture on her face.

XXI

I left the castle about ten o'clock the following morning to go to Hamish's cottage to join the women. I had some designs with me and some swatches of color Thorburn's had sent me.

Paul sat on a mossy hump of ground, hugging his knees and staring ahead of him. I knew that look on his face only too well. It was almost as vague, as dreamy as Rory's usual expression, but it was deceptive. It hid intense concentration. When he grows up, I thought, people will be deceived by that look, and a little amused. Then he'll break his dreamy silence and startle them with some powerful thought that has been possessing his mind.

He saw me, looked up and said, "Can I go and see Rory?"

"Don't you think you should wait until he suggests taking you with him? He may not want to fish today. Couldn't you join the children down on the beach?"

"Oh, but I don't want to go fishing."

"Then what do you want to see Rory for?"

His deep-blue gaze was very steady. "I want to ask him if he'll take me in the launch to fetch Rinn."

I said, laughing, "What for? To show him where you live?"

Paul was not amused. "I thought I could keep him on *this* side of the island."

"But why? You like your bay."

His eyes shot away from me. He unlocked his fingers from over his knees and rolled over onto his stomach. "I want to bring Rinn here. I thought I'd ask Rory if we could take a rope and sort of tow him. Or perhaps, if I took lots of fish, he'd follow the boat round."

"Darling, you can't take him from a home he has chosen for himself. Leave him there — it's not far for you to walk if you go by the cliffs."

He said, head turned away from me, chin on hands, "But I *want* him *here*."

I sat down by his side, laid my designs and the swatches of colored wool beside me and said, "Paul listen to me. You have your own home now, and when you are adult you will be able to choose where you live. Would you like someone to come along and haul you to a place where *he* wanted you to go, and you didn't?"

"No, but I'm human."

"And a seal and any other animal, mammal or bird, my dear, has a right to choose its own place."

"If I brought him over to this side of the island, he might like it better."

"Or you might lose him for good. I'm sure Rory has told you abut Eilean nan Ron –"

"It means the Seals' Island," he said, bright with his learning of Gaelic from the children.

"Well then, even if you could drag Rinn from the place where he is happy now, he'd probably swim away to Eilean nan Ron and you'd never see him again."

He turned over and looked at me, mutiny on his face. "Why don't you want me to have Rinn here?"

"Why do *you* want him here?" I countered.

He shrugged his shoulders. "It's nicer this side."

"But that little bay is lovely, it's small and isolated. I thought that was why you adopted it, because you could make it really yours."

"I don't want to go there ever again."

This wasn't a slice of childish willfulness. I said, alarm curling inside me, "Why are you suddenly afraid of that place?"

He didn't answer me.

"Paul, *why?*"

"I'm not afraid of anything."

"That's silly. Everyone is afraid of something – even grownups. I am." *Dear God, I was!* "So you must tell me why you've turned against that bay."

He got up and began to run away. Over his shoulder, he said, "Then I'll never see Rinn again, and it's your fault. Because I won't go back there."

I could have run after him and kept him by my side, interrogating him until he gave in and told me what was the matter. I didn't. It was only a short time since his traumatic experience in our London house. There was already a shutter pulled across his mind. Paul was not normally willful, nor was he more disobedient than any other child. But there was at the moment some delicate imbalance due to shock and I must not tear through his thoughts by force, for that way I might do irreparable harm. "Give him time," the doctor said. "He doesn't need psychiatry. He's a very balanced little boy." Give him . . . time . . .

I watched him skipping away to where Morag's granddaugther and Jaimie Mac-Donald's three sons were sprawling across the rocks, peering into the pools and fishing out anything that interested them. With the children he was safe. But making my way over the flower-spattered grass to where the women awaited me, I wondered whether it was fear that had ruined his "secret place" for him. I would have to find out, although for the moment I had no idea how to go about it.

★ ★ ★

Morag's welcome was as kind as always, and she shot me the smile that softened her gaunt face. But the rest of the women, sitting and standing around, were not in the least welcoming.

I greeted her, and then in order to please them, said it again in my very badly pronounced Gaelic: *"Ciamar a Tha?"* —

I was met with barely a murmur of response.

"The dyes will be coming any time now." I spread the drawings and the swatches on the table. "I've simplified the designs a little and I thought you might like to choose which one you will do first. And here are the colors."

They moved almost reluctantly toward me. Morag, by my side, said, "They're angry, so they are."

"Why? What have I done?"

"Ye've done nothing, *mo ghaoil*. But it's the oil — that's what they won't have."

"Morag, please tell them . . . tell them in Gaelic so that they can understand better. Tell them that I dislike the idea of industry and upheaval and all the ugliness that will result from opening up the loch. Please, tell them I'm on their side over it."

"Aye, if ye feel that way, then I'd better. 'Twas ye, too, they thought was wantin' the oil men here. Ye bein' The Mullaine's wife."

"But I don't! I have only just heard about this

project. Look, I'll go outside and you call me when you've explained to them. Tell them I can do nothing."

I left them, pulled the door shut behind me and sat outside in the warm sun, listening to the humming of insects and the rippling of the clear water of the burn. I knew that I might have to wait some time, for this would be another example of the islanders' love of argument and of meetings.

After about a quarter of an hour Morag came out, "They were after blamin' ye for the oil – like I said, ye bein' wife of The Mullaine. But I've given them a hard talkin' to, that I have. An' now they're wantin' to get on with the job of weavin'."

"My tower of strength," I said softly and took her rough hand. "Bless you, Morag. What would I do without you?"

"Likely there's times when ye'd not know whether ye were comin' or goin' with these women. 'Tis obstinate they are if they think someone's tryin' to give them orders."

I found the women bent over the scrubbed wooden table where I had left the designs and the color swatches. They gave no hint that they had been accusing me unfairly among themselves, but I sensed a greater interest in the weaving project.

Only, as I was about to leave, one of the

women asked, "Will ye be comin' to the meetin' tomorrow?"

"What meeting?"

"Why, about the oil, of course. They must know fine well that we'll be havin' a meetin' an' fightin' it all the way."

"They" – meaning, in the absence of Lewis and the clearing of my name, Antonia.

"Yes, I'll be there," I said. "Though you mustn't expect me to take sides. I'm just a visitor."

"Aye." A look of compassion crossed the weathered face. "We know that well."

I left them at the cottage, cleaning and preparing the looms, their soft voices like the murmur of the sea.

Shane was coming away from the Castle as I crossed the lawn. He saw me and stopped and waited for me to reach him. "I was told that you had gone to see the women. I suppose you've heard about the proposed meeting."

"Yes."

"I've been discussing it with Antonia."

I asked unhappily, "But is there anything *to* discuss? I understood that it was all settled and it was now only a matter of Antonia's signature."

"I wouldn't say it's so easy. But we'll see tomorrow night."

"Nobody has told me yet where the meeting is to be held."

He asked in surprise, "Why? Are you coming to it?"

"Of course."

He looked at me thoughtfully. "Oh, but as you say, of course. You will have a great stake in it in future, won't you, Judith?"

"I shan't be here."

"How can you be so certain of that?"

I sensed a challenge in his voice, and anger stirred. "All right, I'm not certain of *anything*. I'm just hoping, that's all."

"After starting the women on their scheme —"

I interrupted, still angry because I could detect a touch of censoriousness in his voice. "I'm not abandoning them. I wouldn't. Wherever I am, I'll always be in charge of this project, and if they want advice I'll be around — at least —"

"At least?"

I said faintly, "Well, no one can ever be sure of what's going to happen in the future. I mean, I hope I'll be around ... I *must* be around ..."

"Yes," he said vaguely, and looked away over my head into the smooth mother-of-pearl sky. "Well, then, I'll see you at the meeting."

He left me, moving with agility over the rock-strewn shore. As I watched him I began to speculate about him and his life in the Middle

East. He had talked a little to us about the wild and lonely places he had sometimes found himself in. He must be so used to dealing with people whose life style, religion and temperament were vastly different from his, I was quite certain that he would always cope with situations. And I knew, without any doubt, that he was coping with one here, on Cathair Mor, although exactly what it was I had no idea. I felt antagonistic and yet curiously drawn. He frightened me and excited me, and I hated both sensations.

These weeks on Cathair Mor had shown me how isolating was fear that had to be hidden because there was no one to share it with. I knew as I crossed the great Hall that the best ally I could possibly have had would have been Shane, because he was strong. And yet, I felt he was the last person I could go to for help and advice.

Antonia and I were lounging in cane chairs in the sun. There was a heaviness in the air and the edges of the sun were blurred, a sure sign of weather disturbance.

Tiny midges plagued us, and brushing them away, Antonia said, "There's thunder around and I'm being bitten by these beastly things." She flapped her hands and pulled a blue chiffon scarf over her hair.

Paul was down on the beach with Rory, who

was cleaning out the wheelhouse of the Inverkyle boat. I leaned back in my chair, suffering the midges because my thoughts were heavily occupied. I asked, "Has Paul mentioned to you why he no longer wants to go to his bay?"

"He did tell me some silly idea of bringing the seal round to this side of the island. But he won't find anyone who will use the launch for such a harebrained idea. Anyway, I wouldn't think too much about it. He probably waded into the sea for something he saw — you know how Paul has been looking for treasure ever since Rory told him about the galleon sunk off Tobermory Bay. He could have seen a piece of driftwood or something and tried to get it and a wave knocked him over. I'm sure it's as simple as that."

"That's not like Paul. He'd pick himself up and try again."

"Well, it can't be anything human to frighten him because it's a very tiny bay and there's nobody there but Paul."

"There's just one way to it," I said, "through a narrow fissure in the cliffs. Someone else could have found it."

She turned her face toward me, and for a moment our eyes met and we both knew what the other thought. Then Antonia said with more than a touch of impatience. "Of *course*

326

nobody else is there — how could they be? Paul told me with great glee that the cleft in the rock leading to that place is so narrow, you can scarcely see it from a distance."

"*He* saw it."

"Well, he's a sharp-eyed little boy and thin enough to wriggle through anything."

"I got in there, too. And so did the men who came to search for him. Antonia, whatever frightened him is important, and I know one thing. If he decided to go to the bay again, I wouldn't let him."

"He may quite easily go there without telling you."

"I hate the idea of keeping tabs on him, but I'll have to, without letting him see I'm watching him."

"Oh, Judith, there you go again. Full of fear. And for what? Because a small boy has grown tired of playing alone in some isolated bay." She bent and set her glass down on the cane table. "*Can't* you understand that it's your own mind creating these fears? *Yours,* not someone else's actions." She glanced away from me as though what she was saying was making her both embarrassed and unhappy. "When Lewis — oh yes, let's say his name . . . when Lewis brought you to meet me that first time in London, I thought, She's just what I would have liked for him. She's attractive, she has a charming speaking voice, she has a sense of fun and she is essentially unneurotic. Thank God for that last! But I no longer know. I'm fond of you, Judith. I want you to be happy and safe. I'm *sure* you're safe, but you aren't happy. Or —"

Or *sane* . . . I supplied the essential word for her, but silently. Aloud I said, "How can I be happy? Surely it's not neurotic of me to be anxious because my husband tried to kill me and has disappeared, and because the police, a most reasonable group of men who would never alarm without cause, have warned me to stay here? In this case, being afraid is not neurotic. And nothing that I've told you has been imagined. You must believe me. Someone . . . someone —" I broke off, because the expression on her face hadn't changed. I was fighting a losing battle of words, of pleading for belief and trust. I leaned back in my chair. "Oh, what's the use?"

"If you'd only let me help you!"

"You can — by believing me."

She turned her face away. "Of course I believe you."

And that was a cautious, cowardly little lie because she was afraid of what I might do — lose my temper, become violent, break with sanity . . .

She was walking away from me, and I watched her push through the low branches of the rowan tree, her hands held out as if she were blind. I saw her lean against its trunk and lay her head on her arms. A sudden picture crossed my mind's eye. Antonia, standing triumphant on a concert platform, acknowledging the wild applause; Antonia wearing her favorite dark-rose gown, her hair glistening and yellow roses in her arms. Antonia, on top of the world, a great singer with a great pianist for a son . . . I blinked the picture away, got up and went to her.

The low branches of the rowan tree rustled softly as I parted them. Antonia was weeping softly. I put my arms around her and laid my face against hers. There was nothing I could say to comfort her, but for one moment I felt her weight against me.

My frustration dissolved. She was, after all, as bewildered and frightened in her way as I was in mine. "It won't always be this bad," I said gently, and hoped she wouldn't ask me how it could improve.

She didn't. She turned on me almost violently. "I don't know. Oh, I don't! I once talked about touching rock bottom, and then finding there was no way to go after that but up. There *is* another way, though . . . and that is *to stay at rock bottom.*"

"Then we'll keep each other company," I told her, "because I'm not that far off myself."

She leaned her back against the tree and looked at me. "If I could lose myself in my career, it would be easier. But I can't, and so . . . I have nothing. And if I find, when I do sing, that my voice isn't as it was, then I'll never, I'll *never*, be a poor singer standing on some small platform, smiling at ragged applause. I'll find another interest. Paul . . ."

"No," I said quickly. "Not Paul. Neither of us must use him for our own release. That's something I'll fight you over. So don't even try." As soon as I spoke I felt sorry for the rising indignation in my voice. I said more softly, "We're both under stress at the moment, so let's leave the argument, shall we?"

She moved out of the shadow of the delicate fronds of the tree. "I've said it so often, Judith, but I do mean it. You are in many ways like my dear daughter. And yet — oh, and yet we behave as if we had nothing in common." She shot me a wavering smile and walked away, saying as she went, "We could have been such marvelous friends. But people change. I suppose it isn't their fault — any of us can get ill, physically or mentally . . ." Her voice trailed off as she crossed the lawn.

I was alone. I wanted close friends to talk to; I wanted laughter and the little superficial, but delightful, pleasantries of everyday city life. Scenic beauty and crystal-clean air were all very fine for a holiday, but one needed to be born and bred on this lonely island for it to satisfy all the aspects of life.

I moved out of the shadow of the tree and went down to the beach. I needed the comfort of someone simple and honest and uncomplicated. Here, on Cathair Mor, only one person was close enough to me to give me that, and that was my seven-year-old son. I ran across the *machair* to the shore. The children were playing among the scattered boulders, and Shane sat watching them. He was so still that he might have been carved out of the stone that matched his brown sweater and gave a faintly burnished look to his profile.

"Paul hasn't been over to see his seal for a couple of days," Rory said from behind me.

I gave a start. "You must have sprung out of the air, because you weren't in sight a moment ago."

He laughed. "You passed quite close to me, Judith, and you didn't see me, did you?" It always pleased him to be able to surprise people, as if it gave him a power over his own inadequacy. "I was lying flat on the grass over there, listening to the bees looking for honey in the buttercups. I was trying to understand what they were saying."

I didn't feel like being involved in one of his fey conversations. "Has Paul said anything to you as to why he no longer wants to go down to the bay?"

"No."

Shane, hearing our voices behind him, turned.

Rory said, "We've been saying that Paul doesn't go any more to that bay he found. You remember, I found its name on an old map we had. The Bay of the Dark Star."

"Well," Shane replied easily, "he's probably bored with it."

"Oh no. Not with his seal there. He wants me to take the launch over there and feed the seal with fish so that it'll follow us round to the loch."

"Then you'd better tell him that seals can find their own fish quite easily without having to follow a boat as bait." Shane rose.

I said quickly, "We're disturbing you, I'm sorry." I spoke out of the curious shyness that was beginning to overpower me whenever I was with Shane. It was a stupid remark, but there was no way I could unmake it.

"Oh, you're not disturbing me. But I do have work to do."

"Work *here*, on Cathair Mor?"

His quiet eyes met mine. "Indeed I have. There's the meeting to discuss the oil project."

I said with sudden insight, "And *you* are arranging it?"

"Put it," he said, "that I am to cope with the practical side. I'm making myself responsible for having enough chairs and benches for those attending — and that's more or less the whole population here. Jock's cart will collect the things from the cottages and bring them over."

"Who is to be chairman?"

"I am," said Shane, and made it a quiet exit line as the first rumble of thunder shook the air behind the hills of Mull.

XXII

The islanders' protest meeting over the oil project was held during the day. Any gathering called on the island was always a lengthy business because it was a change from routine and every crofter and fisherman was going to make the most of it. On the other hand, they knew that it must not drag on into the evening because nothing must prevent the small but very necessary herring fleet from sailing for the night fishing.

A large empty shed on Kilarran land was to be used for the meeting. It had once been a storage place, but now that the motor launches made easy runs to Mull and back, there was no longer any need to store food or grain.

The shed stood near the eastern end of the loch and looked directly toward the pinnacles of Cathair Beag.

The afternoon was wild and not in the least like a summer's day. The men had swept the shed and put in the chairs and benches, and some of the villagers brought stools with them, hugging them against their thighs and striding over the heather in twos and threes.

I had not been invited to the meeting, and I understood why. I was not involved. But soon after Antonia left the Castle, angry and defiant, wearing a sky-blue dress and with the light of battle in her eyes, I decided to go too.

As I paused at the door of the shed, I heard a voice behind me say, "Aye, an' if it isn't The Mullaine's bonnie wife."

I turned and saw Logan.

"So ye be comin' to the meetin'. But 'tis no place for ye. Likely we'll be fightin' before the meetin's over."

"Since you are apparently all agreed in not wanting the island to be involved in the oil interests, I can't see what you're planning to fight over."

His laughter went out on the wind like the blare of a trumpet. "Oh, there be one or two who see money in it." He took my arm. "Likely there'll be fightin', too, among them as is up there" – he pointed heavenward – "I mean, them as lives in the Castle and the Abbey."

"I suppose Mr. Kilarran is on your side?"

"He is an' that. An' I wouldn't want him for an enemy."

We entered the huge shed together. The warmth generated by the crowd of tightly packed people, plus the fish smell that always hung around the herring men and the fumes from their pipes, hit me after the cool, clean air outside.

Logan found me a chair near the wall. I sat down, noting with relief that it would be easy to slip out if the meeting got too heated, too long or too dull. Not that, with Antonia and Kilarran as opponents, I imagined the latter would happen.

Antonia was on the platform, and as I caught her eye I thought I saw an expression of annoyance cross her face. Shane was standing, talking to two crofters, and Rory was seated cross-legged on a wide but not very safe-looking window ledge. Lufra sat by Dru's side, eying a brown-and-white sheepdog.

I looked about me. Everyone I knew by sight was there, and many whom I didn't. They all seemed to be talking, but because most of it was in Gaelic, I could only guess that they were planning to fight to the last to defend their island. At least, that was what I thought until I heard raised voices and a fist lifted. I saw Duncan take a flying swing at a black-bearded man. Someone cried out; someone else laughed.

Shane, who was facing the room, saw the incident. He turned away from the men to whom he was speaking and banged his fist on a table on which lay some papers. There was immediate silence. Then Shane said, very quietly, "If anyone wants to fight, will they please go outside. This is to be a meeting, not a brawl." He added something in Gaelic. It was brief and final.

Whatever had caused the heated argument faded. The men and women settled themselves on the chairs, stools and benches and turned their faces politely toward the platform.

Antonia put up a hand and fluffed her hair; Shane went to her side at the table. The meeting was open.

It wasn't easy for someone used to the southern English voices to understand all that was said. But what was all too obvious was that Antonia resented Shane's mastery of the meeting.

After he explained why they had all come there, he said, "Mrs. Mullaine will now give you details about the oil project. Please listen to her carefully, and remember one thing. Everyone here has a right to voice an opinion. After Mrs. Mullaine has spoken, I will speak. After that, the meeting is open for everyone. This is your island and it is up to you to take a personal interest in everything that is happening."

"And I hope that is exactly what you will do," Antonia said as Shane sat down.

She spoke well, using her tremendous ability

to control an audience. She painted what she thought of as a glowing and irresistible picture of Cathair Mor as a place reborn, with money pouring in from the opening of the loch and the renting of it to the oil moguls; the shops, the houses that would be built, the increased communications with the mainland. She opened her arms, not too theatrically, but sufficiently to encompass them all. "It will change our lives."

"Aye," called a sour voice from the back of the hall. "Aye, that it will. Ye'll get the money an' we'll get them from London wi' their fancy ways. I'm tellin' ye, ma'am, we won't be dictated to by they —"

"Aye, that we won't" came murmurs from around the room.

Antonia's eyes flashed fire. "*You* are telling *me* what you will and won't do? Remember, please, that while my son is . . . is away, this is *my* island, and if I choose to sign a concession that the oilmen can open up the loch and add any amenities that might come to the island, that is *my* right . . ."

Someone shouted, "The *bodach* wouldn't ha' done that."

"I know enough Gaelic," she retorted angrily, "to realize that you are talking of 'the old man,' by which I presume you mean my husband, the late Laird. How dare you refer to him like that."

"Aye, we dare because that's how he were. An oold man an' a fair one."

I sat crouched in my corner, aware of swift glances my way. I knew what they were thinking: *But if The Mullaine who attacked her is dead* she *is the one to have the say.*

If Lewis was dead . . . I looked about me, wondering if any of them knew something I did not know. Perhaps one of the men, wandering over the moors or by the shore, had seen someone following me, seen someone entering Hamish's hut, heard the bagpipes playing the island song. Muted protestations from all around me rose to a small uproar at something Antonia had said.

Once again Shane silenced them. "Your turn to speak will come. But first, have the grace to listen."

He sat down and Antonia continued. This time she changed her tactics. She lost her imperious authority and began reasoning. "It will open up business for all of you." She had been throwing her voice in order to be heard at the back of the place, but its staying power was limited. Her tone had become husky. She took a deep breath and continued with an effort. "Your fish will be wanted for the men on the oil rig, your eggs and poultry. The men coming off duty will want amusement somewhere nearer than Oban. We can supply it here.

There could be a cinema and an inn —"

"— an' lock up yeer women while the oilmen roll by," shouted another voice.

"How do ye know that The Mullaine will agree wi' ye?"

"Of course he will. He wants benefits and good living for the islanders as much as I. And —"

"An' what if The Mullaine ne'er comes back? Then the little lady there will be the one to say."

"Aye, an' what does she say?"

I shut my eyes tight and counted ten, waiting for someone else to speak and release me from the turned heads and the questioning eyes.

Antonia came to my rescue. "The Mullaine *will* come back."

It was Rory, of all people, who asked, raising his voice in nervousness to a little squeak, "Then he'd better come quick, hadn't he?"

For a moment Antonia was at a loss for words. She was no more certain than I was, or anyone else for that matter, exactly what Rory meant by his obscure question.

It was Shane who answered. "I think we are getting from the point. Mrs. Robert Mullaine is acting Laird here. It is she to whom you must listen."

Someone said, "An' I ken fine ye won't be listenin'."

340

"On the contrary, I'm listening hard," Shane said. Then he turned to Antonia, who had sat down. "May I put my point of view?"

She shrugged. "If you think you have one that opposes mine."

"Oh, I have."

And Shane had. Just as he had opposed my weaving project, so he opposed the scheme for renting the loch to the oil company. But here he had a real issue. He put before his audience a far clearer picture of what the offshore oil rigs near Skerryvore would mean to the islanders. He talked of a possible helicopter landing, which would disrupt not only the islanders in their low-built cottages but all the wild life of Cathair Mor. He told them that the oil companies were tough, that they would make the most of the concession; that the islanders wouldn't just be losing their peaceful lives, their fish and their wild life, but their entire island. "If you want riches, then you only have to work harder. It's in the sea and in the soil."

While he spoke, Antonia sat rigid.

The audience delighted in interrupting. "But how do ye know there's oil there? Maybe there isn't. Maybe it's just talk."

Shane said, "They don't start to negotiate unless there has been a major oil find out there." He jerked his head toward the west. "I have read that a scientific survey has been made. Their greatest headache at the moment is the hiring of an oil rig. But they'll get it because of the money involved. And then they'll start on Cathair Mor. I can talk to you about permanent platforms, mini-submarines, landing strips; about the special school for deep-sea divers at Fort William. I could even read you out of this." He rapped the table with a bunch of cuttings in his hand. "It's a very advanced proposal for exactly what is done when an oil corporation starts its activities. What it all adds up to is that the whole project will despoil our island, our beaches, bring restlessness and dissatisfaction along with the money. Do you want that?"

"Aye," said a little man, "I do. I'll turn my croft into a shop an' they can come an' buy their cigarettes an' their chocolate an' anything else they want. Then me an' my *cailleach*" — He nudged his thin wife — "will be rich an' we'll buy a hoose at Oban."

Shouts surrounded him. "Whist, Sandy, ye oold fool. They'll no be bringin' ye anythin' that the government won't then be takin' away. 'Twill be The Mullaine, if he comes back, or someone at the Castle, who gets rich. Nae us."

The islanders were prepared to argue the point for hours on end. I stayed for a long time. *I must listen because it could affect Paul, through me. If Lewis is dead* . . . Every time the lovely

342

windy air breathed and stirred through the open door, it brought a longing to escape. But I remained, remembering that like it or not, I was involved. Once, after a particularly inane exchange between Sandy and Logan, I made a move to get up, and as I did so, caught Rory's eye. I must have imagined it, for he had no reason to want me there, but it seemed that he shook his head very faintly at me.

I felt a reluctant admiration for Shane. He was cool, concise and practical. He was also very determined that the islanders' point of view should be made absolutely clear to Antonia.

The man called Sandy MacAllister was the enemy in their midst. He shouted, once, "Ye've been away for eight years. And likely ye'll no be stayin' here. What's all this to ye?"

Shane answered in a voice that, although quiet, could be heard all over the room. "Wherever my work takes me, whatever place I am in, this is my island."

I shot Antonia a swift look. She had tensed, and her hands resting on the table were tightly clasped. I had a feeling she would have liked to hit him.

Logan spoke, his voice carrying to the beams of the great barn; Dru spoke; the Malcolms and the Bruces and the Robbies added their protest. Sandy MacAllister was a lone voice joining Antonia.

Every point was repeated and repeated again, until Shane, exasperated, stopped the meeting. "As you all spoke, I made notes. I have them quite clearly before me. There's no need for repetition. You know Mrs. Mullaine's proposals for opening up the loch and making a helicopter landing strip. You know my reactions and you know your own. If we go on and on repeating ourselves, we'll just get into some mad merry-go-round."

Someone near me whispered, "She won't get very far makin' her millions out of the oilmen. If it comes to it, we'll sabotage the whole damnty business."

I recognized the throaty chuckled behind me. Murdo answered in a stage whisper, "Ye're wastin' yeer time. There won't be no oilmen comin' to Cathair Mor."

"What d'ye mean?"

"I'm no tellin'. But just ye wait. An' it won't be that long, likely."

Antonia was on her feet "Don't you *want* a higher standard of living? Don't you *want* progress?"

Like a heavenly choir, rehearsed to an infinite degree of unison, they roared, "No!"

Nothing, of course, was resolved. I left as Shane summed up. I remember thinking as I slipped out, *There should have been an impartial chairman. Shane is partisan.*

He took over control of the meeting and I felt both a certain fascination and faint quivers of alarm. Not even Antonia was able to stand against that quiet, masterly determination.

I went and sat on the low wall, hearing the murmuring of the Gaelic voices behind me as the people strolled reluctantly out of the barn. I was on Shane's side in the arguments, and I admired his calm control, but that didn't stop my fear of him.

Before I could assemble my reactions to the meeting, he joined me on the wall. "Well, now you know what they are like when they have a meeting. Round and round we go, hitting the center of the argument and then returning to the outskirts of the circle and starting all over again. They love the game."

"But the possible result isn't a game."

"No." He became grave. "It damned well isn't. Antonia will get her way."

"Oh, Shane, no!"

"Well, who can stop her?"

"If Lewis comes back . . ."

He said quickly, "Why didn't you speak up? Paul is involved, you know."

"How *could* I say anything? If I agreed publicly with the islanders, can you imagine how Antonia would feel? I couldn't do it to her —

she had too many against her as it was. We've had our argument, she and I. It was not for me to add to it there."

"Well, Antonia has the power to sign that concession, and she will. Whether you like it or not, my dear, you'll be a rich woman."

I didn't miss the thrust of cynicism in Shane's remark. "As far as you are concerned, you think I'm just making a token protest in order to keep any popularity I have with the islanders. And you're quite convinced I'm secretly on Antonia's side. You think that for money I'd welcome the destruction of a beautiful and private island."

Shane said nothing, but looked at me intently.

The islanders were calling to us as they left the shed in twos and threes, and each time they said "Goodbye" Shane paid them the compliment of answering in Gaelic, *"Oidche Mhath."*

I should have left him, for there was nothing more we had to say to one another. But I stood there like an infatuated adolescent. It was hard for me to stay, but harder to leave. I was "magicked"; caught, as I had been some years before, in Lewis's thrilling web. Now a different kind of man trapped me by his inflexible personality.

I heard myself say with sudden shyness, "I'm really waiting for Antonia."

"Well, there she is."

She came out of the barn, the pugnacious Sandy by her side. I knew, by the swift, imperious sweep of her hand as she talked, that she was angry and was reviling the short-sightedness and obstinacy of the rest of the islanders to this, her only ally.

"What is going to happen now?" I asked Shane as he turned from another friendly *"Oidche Mhath"* to Logan and his pretty wife.

"Either the Mullaines will become very rich," he said, "or the whole thing is a dream Antonia will waken from. The bubble of great expectations could burst here with a bang, but with little more than a whisper when the British public read of it in a small paragraph of their daily newspapers."

"You think it will burst?"

"My dear girl, how do I know? I'm putting the possibilities before you."

"Shane," I said, "the islanders have no power to stop it."

"Oh, that isn't the way it must happen. I doubt if you know anything abut the oil round our coasts."

"I don't."

"It's mortgaged up to its neck — and beyond. If the Arabs lower the price of oil, then ours won't be the miracle we've made it out to be."

"So the deal might not go through?"

He shrugged.

"Why didn't you tell the islanders this?" I said hotly. "It would have given them some hope that they could keep Cathair Mor the way it is."

"The new discoveries of oil round our coasts are full of vast political and financial ramifications. Do you really imagine that the people here can fully understand them? Much more sophisticated observers are confused by the situation."

"I suppose you're right. But that's because the islanders would just set themselves firmly against grasping it all."

He laughed. "At least you're beginning to understand them."

"I like them. They're proud and honest and content."

He looked at me in surprise. "Well! Well!" For a moment his expression softened. Then he said briskly, "You'd better hurry. Antonia is looking our way and I think she is waiting for you."

It was a cool dismissal and I resented it. "Antonia is too angry to care very much if I walk back with her or not. I think the reason she is watching us is that she's afraid you might persuade me to your side."

"I thought you were on my side, anyway."

"She probably thinks you're trying to turn me into something more than just a passive objector, into speaking at meetings and inciting the people here to some violent demonstration."

Again he laughed, throwing back his head so that the sun glinted in his eyes, turning them to points of silver water. Then, abruptly, he stopped laughing. "I thought I understood people. But you puzzle me."

"There's nothing subtle about me."

"In the light of what I know and see and hear — dear God, that's an understatement!" he said with unexpected violence. "Damn it to hell, you're as subtle as a pretty animal stalking his prey in the dark, mewing like a kitten and ravaging like a tiger."

"And where does that quotation come from," I lashed at him.

"It's original. Mine own." He turned on his heel and walked away from me.

I watched him go. *This is ridiculous! Shane always wins by leaving me. Next time it will be different. I'll walk away first.*

Shane had stopped to speak to Morag, who was on her way down to the shore with a basket, probably in search of driftwood for kindling.

"Shane . . ." I called after him.

He turned to me. "Uh-huh?"

I said, my thoughts rushing to be

spoken, "If I were subtle —"

"Leave it, Judith. Forget what I said." He stood his ground, watching me walk toward him. "It's always better not to overdo attempts at understanding."

"It's better still," I persisted, "to clarify something that seems to be muddled. If I had been subtle, nothing that has happened *would* have happened. I'd have been more clever. I'm sure that other women would have handled Lewis differently and —"

"Since I seem to have touched a raw spot, then go on. And what?"

"There would have been no trouble — no attempt on my life, no ruin of Lewis's career. Another woman would have perhaps let Lewis have control of Paul, have let him grow up to take part in wild parties and watch wife-swapping. Because Lewis is brilliant and gifted, perhaps any other wife would always have given in to him all the way."

"I doubt if your differing views over Paul was the complete reason for the problem. A single strong center of disagreement between two people eventually fans out and extends to other differences. I'm pretty certain that if Paul hadn't been there, your marriage would have broken up in the same chaos. You'd have found some other reason —"

My face flamed at the shattering injustice of

his remark. I felt a sudden angry strength as I faced the tall suntanned man. "Talking about what happened is still horrible to me, but there's only one thing I want you to know. I can't think why, because it shouldn't matter. Perhaps it's because I loathe one-sided criticism and so I have to explain."

"I think it would be wiser not to."

His clipped comment made me doubly determined. "Shane, listen, just *listen*. And then you can go and we'll never speak of it again." I took a deep breath because my lungs seemed empty, like a vacuum, in spite of all the sweet air around me. "One of the very last things Lewis said to me that night was that he had married me because he wanted a malleable wife — someone who would give him a son and then let him do what he chose with him. I was to produce Paul, and when he grew out of babyhood, hand him over as if he were a child I never wanted. He wasn't interested in Paul until he was old enough to talk and be trained Lewis's way. I was then no longer necessary."

"On the contrary," Shane said, "I told you that Lewis wrote to me. I can only guess that the letter was sent, perhaps, a few days before that final crisis. In it he poured out his feelings for you. It was so torn with hopeless emotion — if you like to put it that way — I made a vow to myself that I would tell no one. But I will . . . I must because you've got to know how Lewis felt about you."

"I know. Oh, I know . . ."

"But you don't. And I intend to quote. I have a good memory and I'm making nothing up. Lewis wrote: 'Judith married me because I was a famous figure. There's no ambition in a woman more powerful than to marry for the satisfaction of reflected glory.'"

I sat there for a shocked moment, aware that the lie could not be disproved. I had no defense, because what had happened was known only to Lewis and me.

Nevertheless I couldn't stop my indignant protest. "You judged me on Lewis's words. I was condemned, wasn't I, before you even met me? There's nothing I can do about that."

Shane was frowning into the distance. "I'm sorry, Judith. I shouldn't have told you that. It doesn't help anyone, and I'm not usually given to speaking so freely. And I can give you no explanation. Just put it down to — oh God, to what?"

"Shane — *where is Lewis?*"

If I had hoped that my sudden question would throw him off guard, I was totally mistaken.

"I think the very last talkative islander has now left the barn," he said, looking away from me. "I must lock up. It's a habit I've caught from the townsmen." Then he turned and touched my face with a strange, intimate, tender movement. "Don't try too hard for an understanding I can't give you, Judith."

This time I left him with a spurt of speed. Antonia had disappeared and only a few fishermen were strolling down to the loch.

My way lay past Murdo's cottage at the edge of the Inverkyle Abbey grounds. Murdo himself was squatting on a wooden box, looking like an ancient seer, his hair grey and tousled like ruffled pigeon's feathers. His gnarled hands were whittling away at a stick.

He looked up as I passed. "So they didna' gi' ye a chance to say a word at that meetin'. 'Twas too bad, an' ye bein' the Laird's wife, like."

"Oh, I was just part of the audience. And I don't feel that anything anyone said could make any difference. I mean —"

"I ken what ye mean. 'Tis The Mullaine's mother signs the forms that takes the rights o' our island frae us. That's the thinkin', so ye say."

"Yes, that's what *I* think — and I'm afraid we all think."

"But I'm tellin' ye, lassie, all o' them there, except one, was after gettin' it all wrong. Just one o' them knows it won't be that way, the way they all think it be."

"What *do* you mean?"

He gave me his long, sly grin. "Just that they're all after thinkin' wrong."

"Murdo," I urged, "who is it who knows — or thinks he knows — differently?"

He tossed the stick away, snapped his penknife shut and leered up at me. "Just him who kens rightly that the real Laird won't be havin' strangers here and kens, too, where The Mullaine be hidin'."

Something suddenly blotted out the weak sun above me, and my head shot up instinctively, as it always did these days at unexpected sounds or movement. The fine outspread wings of a kestrel shadowed my face for just an instant, but as if it hurt me physically, I drew quickly back. Murdo saw me and chuckled. "I'll mind he be lookin' for his mate."

"Who knows where my . . . husband is hiding?" I was shouting the words, for Murdo had left me with a speed no one would have guessed his old legs could manage. *"Who knows?"* I shouted after him again.

Murdo turned. There was a distance of coarse grass and windbent bushes between us, but I heard his voice quite clearly. "Don' ye be frettin' or fearin', lassie. As I tell ye, there's one as knows where the Laird is. An' one that knows the one that knows. Ye ken?"

"No, I don't." I called after him as he began walking backward to his cottage, grinning at me as he went. "Murdo, don't go . . . please."

He was at his door, gave it a heave with his bony old bottom and then, with lightning speed, was inside. The door was closed firmly before I could reach it. I was quite certain that however hard I hammered, Murdo would pretend to be deaf.

It was clear that he wanted to throw out hints to me of some secret knowledge. He must be enjoying the sense of importance it gave him. Antonia had once called him, impatiently, "an inquisitive, interfering old man." Yet even the most insignificant fact could be an important pointer to the fears that menaced me and the future of my son.

A single charcoal cloud hung over Mullaine, and I walked the other way, down to the beach. I knew Antonia well enough to realize it would be better to keep out of her way for a while.

The tide was out, and except for the single stationary cloud over the Castle, the evening had a bloom of lavender over the Brenlorns and pearl over the sea. I avoided the wet boulders where the carragheen moss grew and walked as near to the sea's edge as I could. The waves teased the wriggling life in the rock pools and in the distance the porpoise leaped and played in the blue-green sea.

In the quiet, with only the cry of the disturbed sea birds and the wind like an arm around my shoulder urging me on, one thing was becoming clear. When I first returned to the island, all was silence so far as Lewis was concerned, now the whisperings had begun, with people flinging out hints because they bubbled inside with a secret they thought they knew. Rory. Murdo.

But never Shane . . .

XXIII

For the next two days Antonia turned life at the Castle into a battleground between herself and the people of the island. Shane was her chief antagonist, but Rosheen, Duncan and I came in for sudden torrents of resentment because we hadn't supported her at the meeting.

Duncan took it all with a Scottish calm; Rosheen simply shook her head and said in her gentle Gaelic voice, "Aye, but she's bonnie, even though she's angry wi' us."

And Antonia was "bonnie." The unconcealed boredom which she displayed at Mullaine had subdued her vitality. Now, with almost everyone against what was vitally important to her, she became swift and vivid in anger and exhausting to live with.

She knew perfectly well that since I sided with the islanders, I could not have spoken at the meeting, but that fact did nothing to ease her bitterness toward me. How *could* I sit by and let them form a voluble army against her? Whatever I felt personally was unimportant; I should have defended her. She was my mother-in-law; she had done everything she could to make this difficult time pleasant for me. Words like affection, loyalty, duty were bandied about wildly.

It wasn't easy to remain silent, to avoid being embroiled in argument. But I knew she wasn't really attacking me for my silence at the meeting. She was venting on me all her store of bitterness and shock at the loss of her voice and fear for her son.

Perhaps if I had lost my temper and we had had a shouting match, she would have felt better. But I was too tense, too haunted by my own fears to have energy left to fight her. And if I had done so, it was possible that although she wouldn't openly accuse, me, that, too, would be seen as a sign of my unbalance. So I held on to my temper and my patience against all the contrary urges, and in the end, she stopped trying to needle me. Instead she spent most of her time in her sitting room playing over and over again some of her own records. The tension lasted two days. Then one evening I passed her room and heard a recording of her singing from *Bohème*. Immediately my deep compassion for her triumphed and I went to her and begged her to understand.

"Nothing of what has happened affects my feeling for you. Please see that. Just because I disagree with your policy for Cathair Mor doesn't mean that I'm your enemy. People have to disagree. Nothing can ever work if they just blindly nod acceptance to what everyone says."

She must have been feeling terribly lonely, for she seized on my effort at reconciliation and we even managed to laugh together.

It was Shane, though, who dominated my thoughts. I didn't want to feel that way. I lived only for the moment when the police would find Lewis and I could return, free of fear, to London. Yet wherever I was — walking down to the loch to watch the herring fleet return, supervising the washing of walls and floors in Hamish's cottage before the weaving began, or just lying sleepless in bed — Shane dominated my mind.

One late afternoon while I was playing with Paul, Antonia called from the doorway, "Judith? I'm going over to Mull to see Joe Torrens. Will you come with me?"

The afternoon was cool and she wore a beautiful loose-weave coat of grey-and-pink wool, the collar turned up around her face.

"The fresh supplies of dyes should have arrived by now," I said. "They were being sent by air to Glasgow and it's possible that they're at Mull waiting for instructions from me. Yes, I'll come. Then if they're there, I can arrange for Jock to bring his cart and collect them from the jetty." I turned to Paul. "We're going to Mull. Would you like to come with us?"

He shook his head. I made a guess that if I were going with someone else, he would come. But he was always slightly on edge with Antonia, for he saw, like her malevolent shadow, the hated Bechstein grand.

"Then, if Duncan is free," I said, "why don't you take him with you to your bay and see if anything exciting has been washed up on the beach."

"No." He hunched his shoulders tightly, rejecting my light touch. "I don't want to go there."

"Your seal might miss you."

"No, he won't. Seals don't miss people."

I heard the little note of nostalgia and longing in his voice. "Won't you tell me what has turned you against the bay?"

"Nothing has. I . . . I just don't want to go there."

"But —"

"And I don't want to talk about it." He ran from me to the edge of the lawn, where Saturn was trying to push the football with one curved paw.

I left him and went to fetch my coat. As I entered my bedroom I heard a sound outside on the lawn. Antonia was there, pushing at my lattice window. "You'd better shut it,

Judith. It looks like rain."

I closed it. Then, before I joined Antonia, I went to find Rosheen, explaining to her that I was going with Antonia to Mull. "Please keep an eye on Paul."

"Ach, an' sure I will." She showed me a large shallow tin of brown honey-smelling toffee. "I've made this for the laddie. He'll like it weel."

"He'll love it," I said.

Antonia had already telephoned Joe Torrens and he would be meeting us with the car when we arrived on Mull. On our way over she explained the reason for this visit.

"I need a man's view of what is happening about the oil," she said. "Oh, I know my lawyers and my accountants are working on it with the oil company, but they are in London; they can't be expected to understand the feeling against me here. Joe knows the Hebridean people, he can perhaps give me some help as to how I can win them over."

Secretly I knew that neither Joe nor anyone else would ever be able to help her influence the islanders. I remembered what Shane had said at Antonia's dinner party: "You can never rule a Cathair man or woman. They rule themselves."

Shane again . . . The little boat cut through the green water, sometimes plowing into an

361

unexpected high wave. I thought of something I had been told as a child. "Count the waves, Judith. Every seventh one will be higher than the rest." I never discovered whether this was fact or fancy, but certainly, during our ten-minute journey to Mull, waves came at intervals, sluicing to the tip of the bows. Cathair Beag rose to our right, its savage cliffs topped by pinnacles and crowned by the ever-circling halo of sea birds.

Antonia disliked the journey and sat hunched in her coat, staring toward Mull. I enjoyed every moment, I loved the dip and sway of the *Midir* and the swish of the sea; I loved even more the brief sense of freedom it gave me to be away from Cathair Mor. For in spite of its wild beauty, it was — as it had been from the moment I had set foot on it after leaving the hospital — my prison, and I couldn't free myself of that fact.

Antonia broke our silence, saying thoughtfully, gazing at the sea as if it were her enemy, "I don't believe Shane is really against this oil project. He's an engineer, and so it's probable that he knew, through his connections in Iran or from engineering friends, that a company was interested in getting permission to drill in the Atlantic."

"But he really has no say."

Antonia shook her head. "So it appears. And

yet I can't get rid of the idea that he is more deeply involved in the island than we know."

I sat, feeling the cool sea spray on my face and icy qualms inside me. It was possible that *I* understood. I half closed my eyes and saw it like a picture across my mind's eye. Lewis signing away the right to his island for the sake of the three most important things to him — his good name, his great career and his son. So much to receive for a wild stretch of land he had never really loved . . . It had become like a relentless discord in my mind: "Help me prove that Judith is unbalanced and that she lied in court. For that, I will give you Cathair Mor."

Shane Kilarran's island . . .

After less than ten minutes on the green-and-silver water, we were there.

"Mind ye hold on," Duncan called. "I'm turnin' to land."

Joe met us with the car, apologizing for Catherine, who had gone to Edinburgh.

We drove first to check that the dyes had arrived. Antonia waited with Joe while I made arrangements for them to be taken to Cathair Mor, where the cart would pick them up. Then we drove to the Torrenses' large stone summer house.

Antonia poured out her problem and her anger over drinks. "They're so insular they can't see that they'll *all* benefit," she cried.

Joe shook his sleek fair head at her. "You can't understand, can you, my dear Antonia, that it's impossible to link up two entirely different civilizations — and that's how I see you and the islanders. You're poles apart, and poles can't meet on common ground."

"Then I'll have to go ahead without their approval."

"I'm afraid that if you antagonize them, there will never be any happiness at Mullaine for you."

"Oh, but when the money comes, I won't *be* at Mullaine ever again."

He looked at me. "And Judith? And Paul? Have you thought that you may be making the place alien for them too?"

I said faintly, "Joe, remember the circumstances. Will I ever come here again? And . . . and what if Lewis returns one day, after . . ." The words "after a prison sentence" choked inside me.

"Oh God." He rubbed his hand with an embarrassed gesture across his chin. "Of course —"

"*Of course he'll come back,*" Antonia interrupted, "and he'll be delighted with what I have done."

"Face it." Joe's voice was quiet and uncompromising. "If they find Lewis, it will be years before he sets foot on Cathair Mor. I'm sorry to be harsh, but you have to accept the truth — however terrible it may be."

"Oh no." She sat up very straight, her hands clasped in her lap. "You're wrong; you're quite wrong. When they find Lewis, he will make them understand and —"

"And what?" Joe asked.

"They'll free him, of course. There'll be fresh questions asked and the truth . . . will . . ." Antonia faltered and looked across at me.

I got up from the pretty low Victorian chair I'd been sitting in and crossed the room. In a wrought-iron stand were Joe's collection of shepherds' crooks, some beautifully carved with the heads of birds and fish. I looked at them with a frantic intensity, as if I had been ordered to memorize each one.

Behind me, Joe was saying gently, "Don't stay dreaming in never-never land, Antonia. Lewis has got a hell of a lot to face when they find him, and you will need your strength for yourself and for him."

"Oh, he won't need a prop. Because, as I've said, the truth will come out at last."

"I'm afraid the truth has already come out."

"That's where you're wrong."

I turned around and looked at her. For a moment our eyes held, and hers faltered first. "I can't say anything now, but you'll see. Oh, Joe, you'll see."

He got up, flung up his hands helplessly and said, "What I think we all need is a drink and a change of subject."

Antonia seized on his suggestion as if she knew she had gone too far. The Torrenses liked me, and whatever she might tell them in confidence, she didn't dare say in front of me, "Judith did it . . ." At that her courage failed.

Antonia had been called a fine actress as well as a great singer. She showed this talent in that awkward moment while Joe poured drinks.

"Do you know what I read yesterday?" Her voice changed and became light and excited. "It was in one of the London papers sent on to me. There was a news report that eight hundred million pounds will be earned by the North Sea project in a year's time. Isn't it exciting? The same thing could happen out here, beyond Skerryvore. Just think —"

"I am," Joe said and handed her a martini.

"It really doesn't matter to me that the islanders are against me, but Paul might want to visit the island when he grows up. So I suppose I'll have to find a way to win the people round. I would hate him to feel unhappy whenever he goes there."

Joe laughed suddenly. "My dear, it will make no difference what anyone feels. You've already made up your mind to sign. So why come to me?"

"I just wanted someone to be on my side," she said slowly and quietly.

The laughter left his face. "I know. It's lonely for anyone to have a great decision to make. Believe me, I can understand, and so does Catherine." He got up and bent and kissed Antonia's cheek. "But you'll survive, darling. You're the surviving sort."

Back at Mullaine, I left Antonia at the door and went around by the tower and the rowan tree to the kitchen entrance. Paul was sitting in the rocking chair with Saturn on his knees, and Rosheen was teaching him some Gaelic.

"How are you?" *Ciamar a Tha?* . . . "I am well" – *Tha gu math* . . .

Laughing and twisting his tongue, Paul tried unsuccessfully to copy her soft singing words.

Reassured, I left them and went to take off my coat. Antonia was in my room. She had my Hermès scarf in her hand. "You dropped that just outside the door."

I took it, thanked her and turned as a shaft of sunlight burst into the room. "The rain kept off," I said. "It's going to be a lovely evening." I crossed the room and pushed the window open.

The pane was smooth to my touch, but there were marks on it. Puzzled, I traced them with my finger. They were letters written backward on the outside, so that in my room they were easily readable to me. One word . . . one name. CLEA.

I swung around. "Antonia, look."

She joined me, and watching my finger outline each letter, gave a small, choked cry. "Your name . . . Lewis's name for you! Oh, Judith."

I leaned weakly against the wall. "You were standing out there waiting while I put my coat on. You told me to close the window, and there was no mark on it then. I'd have seen it if there had been."

She shook her head, her eyes bright with fear.

"And when we returned I went straight to the kitchen. I didn't come in through the front door. You came directly to my room to bring me the scarf. That's right, isn't it?"

She nodded.

"*So who wrote my name?* Because *I* didn't, and I'm quite certain you didn't. Who came to the Castle while we were in Mull?"

With both her hands clasped over her mouth, Antonia shook her head.

"It's obvious," I said. "Whoever came thought that I would enter my bedroom first. He — or she — never reckoned on your coming. And if that had happened, when I called you to see my name there, it would have looked like just one more thing that I might have done myself to incriminate Lewis. Only *you* came in here before me and you can prove I wasn't near the window."

She sank down on my bed, and in the evening light her face was suddenly drawn and old. "I can't . . . I won't believe . . ."

"Then you must," I said. "Here's proof. Whoever did this made the slip I never dared hope he'd make. He? She? I don't know. I don't even dare guess. Can you?"

She made no attempt to answer or even let me know she had heard. Her body was trembling and she pulled the big collar of her outdoor coat around her as if she were cold.

"You believe me now, don't you?" I asked desperately. "You must, because this is proof. Proof, Antonia . . ."

She gave a sharp, husky cry and started to her feet. Then, without a word, she fled from the room.

I flung the window wide, trying to push away my own name. Outside, the great cloud had widened but there were rips in the sky where the blue showed through.

Someone could be out there in the larch wood. The branches of the trees waved in the taunting wind but nothing seemed to move lower down between the rough red trunks.

Had the window remained open, whoever had scratched CLEA on the pane could have climbed in. I paced my room, wondering what

I would have found. My name scrawled in lipstick on the mirror? Something I prized missing? A threatening note?

Paul was clattering down the stone passage and I ran out to him. "When you were playing outside, did you see anyone come to the Castle — anyone at all?"

"No." He began fidgeting. "Rory is waiting for me. He said that when the sun was off the burn, we could go looking for trout. And it *is* off."

"It won't be for long," I said, "there's another patch of blue sky. But never mind that. Are you *sure* you didn't see anyone round the house?"

"No . . ."

This time I thought I heard a faint hesitation in his voice.

"Then did you hear anyone — or any unusual sound?"

He frowned at me. "No. And now can I go and fish?"

I wanted to hold him there in the Long Gallery until I had made certain that his moment's hesitation meant nothing except impatience with me. "Where are you meeting Rory?"

"Just outside. He said he'd fetch me."

I still made difficulties for my son. "It's nearly dinnertime," I said.

"Oh, we won't be *really* fishing. Rory just

wants to look at the burn and see where the trout are. There's a big one, he says, that hides under a rock."

"Where is this place?"

"Just over there." He pointed vaguely.

"Paul, don't go too far away." Then I said again, lamely, "It's nearly dinnertime."

He gave me another of his clear-eyed looks. "You said so, and I won't be far."

"Rory will be with you?"

"Yes," he said and was away, hurling himself down the stairs. I heard his running feet across the Great Hall and then the heavy creak of the door opening.

I couldn't hold him back, he had a right to his freedom, and I comforted myself that Rory would be with him all the time. And if someone had wanted to kidnap him, they would have done so at the bay.

I fought against what I had so nearly suspected, telling myself that if Paul had seen someone, he would have admitted it. His hesitation before answering was surely because of his eagerness to join Rory.

Suspicion was like a freak wind. It came and hit at you and shook you off balance. But I needed to stay steady and not be swung off my feet by fear. I must not play into the hands of my own suspicions or go after Paul, asking and insisting: *Did* you see someone? *Are* you telling me the truth? *Did* you hear something? Words remembered from the past crashed through my brain again. *That way, madness lies . . .*

But the name scratched on the pane of glass was real. Apart from the attack on the cliffside, this was the strongest reminder I had that someone was trying to destroy my sanity or my life — which one, did not seem to matter; opportunities were seized when they occurred.

I closed the window and secured the catch. Then I went to my dressing table, sat down and laid my fingers over the mauve shadows under my eyes. The world of the emotionally hurt adult is enclosed; no one else can ever really reach it; that was why I felt so alone on Cathair Mor.

I could change all that. I could show my friends, the police and the public — who must have read the news of Lewis's attack avidly — that someone wanted my physical or mental destruction.

I could show them the pane of glass and say, "This is proof, isn't it? Look, only my husband ever called me by that name. And no one here — except my mother-in-law, who saw for herself that I couldn't have cut my name on the windowpane — knows that my second name is Clea."

I ran to the door and dragged it open and flew down the stairs to the telephone in the stone alcove beyond the Great Hall.

The place was deserted, and mingled with the smell of ancient seasoned stone, I was aware of Antonia's scent, as if she had passed that way only seconds earlier.

I lifted the receiver. There was no burring sound, not even the crackle of atmospherics. The line was dead. I wasn't surprised. The telephone link between our island and the mainland was often unreliable. I had known times when both the Castle and the Abbey were out of touch with the mainland.

Rosheen was preparing lobster, and Duncan was seated on a stool by the open kitchen door shelling peas.

"The telephone isn't working," I said.

"Ach, and I'd be no surprised at that!" Duncan said.

"The mistress made a call this mornin'," Rosheen said. " 'Twas a long one — I heard the *cling* when she put down that receiver thing."

"Maybe 'twas so long it bust the line," Duncan said and roared with laughter.

"I've got an important call to make —"

"They'll nae mind if ye go to the Abbey an' use theirs."

"Oh, I can't do that," I said quickly, and then as quickly changed my mind. "Yes. Yes, I will. Though theirs could be out of order too."

"Likely," said Rosheen. "I mind the times

when it breaks down, that thing. And 'tis when we want it most."

I ran across the yard at the back where in the past horses had been stabled. Rory would be out with Paul, but Jeannie would be preparing dinner even if Dru was not there. And Shane? I didn't care. I would be safe at the Abbey with Jeannie around. And I had to contact the police.

XXIV

The heavy bell pealed through the Abbey, rumbling and echoing into the high vaulted roof. I waited. Nobody came. I rang again. Then, when there was still no answer, I went around past the line of dark guardian pines to the back of the Abbey.

There was no reply to my sharp knocking there, either, and when I tried the handle of the door, I found that this, too, was bolted. There was no one at home at Inverkyle, and a lesson had obviously been learned from the havoc done at Hamish's cottage. The people of Cathair Mor now locked their doors.

I looked at my watch. It was half past six and Jeannie would surely be back soon, for there was dinner to prepare. I remembered how Rory had told me that left to himself, he allowed meal times to become flexible but that it was different now Shane was there.

I wandered a little way inland, keeping the Abbey in sight, and sat on a mound of grass almost surrounded by the rosy violet of early bell heather. Above me a bird sang and in the distance I could see the savage cliffs of Cathair Beag and the wings of great birds soaring above it.

At the sound of a footstep I turned quickly.

Shane said, "I went to find you at the Castle."

"And I came to find someone at the Abbey. I'd like to use your telephone if I may. Ours is dead."

"It happens all the time," Shane said, "either to one or the other. Of course you can make a call from our place — always providing ours is working."

"There's no one at the Abbey."

"You haven't heard? Another meeting has been called, and this time just for the islanders, without Antonia or you or me."

"To talk over the oil?"

"Of course. Jeannie and Dru have gone. But I found Rosheen and Duncan in your kitchen preparing dinner. They had refused to go to the meeting out of loyalty to Antonia."

I clasped my hands tightly around my knees. "You wanted to see me?"

"To show you something. I should, perhaps, have let you see it before." He took a sheet of paper from his pocket and handed it to me. "I planned to keep it to myself, but I've changed my mind. You remember, I received a letter from Lewis . . ."

I said, as he hesitated, "Before — as you put it — the crisis? Yes."

"But that was only half the information I had had from him. Here is the rest."

He waited, watching me as I unfolded the sheet and then held it limply in my hand.

From far away I heard the bleating of sheep and then the light, formless jingle of the bell Jaimie had hung around the neck of his cow, Enya. It was another world.

"Well, aren't you going to read it?"

I looked down at the page. On it was typed:

This is my sworn statement. I did not attack Judith. She harmed herself in order to have me blamed. She wants complete control of our son, but she is no longer capable of looking after him. God help her.

There was no beginning to the letter, no address at the top and no signature.

I dropped the piece of paper onto the grass as if it had burned my fingers. "I don't believe Lewis sent this. He can't type."

"I typed it."

I said faintly, "You mean . . . you took it down from his dictation?"

"More or less, yes."

"So first he wrote a letter telling you why, according to his theory, I married him. Then

377

. . . this!" I asked shakenly, "Where did you two meet?"

"We didn't. He telephoned me while I was still in Iran. He was obviously in a state of great shock."

"Where was he?"

"I don't know. All I know is he told me he had to talk to someone, and he chose me. God knows why, for as I once told you, I'm no Solomon. I can't give judgment. But Lewis needed to make a statement to someone. I took down what he said, that's all. Then I typed it." As he spoke, Shane picked up the piece of paper from the grass when the wind was teasing it.

"Why didn't you show this statement to the police?" I demanded.

"What good would it have done?"

"They could have traced the call."

"To me — in Iran — from heaven knows where? I wasn't even in a city when Lewis contacted me. And by the time I got through to London and Scotland Yard, even had I wanted to, Lewis most certainly wouldn't have been at the place from which he telephoned me. He was on the run. You must know that."

"Was it because of Lewis that you returned here so unexpectedly?"

"Why should it be?"

"In order to . . . to see for yourself, to prove

378

to yourself, that Lewis was telling the truth. And to —"

"Get one thing straight, Judith. I'm an engineer; I don't throw a big job up in order to come and look at a friend's wife. I returned because my work was done. It was as simple as that."

"By not going to the police, you could have destroyed valuable evidence."

He asked quietly, "Evidence in favor of . . . whom? You see, *I* don't know the truth. *You* do."

But you're not impartial, I thought. You're still Lewis's friend and he has your loyalty. "Where is Lewis?" I was keeping my eyes on the tanned lean hands folding the paper.

He turned on me in sudden anger. "You accused me once before of knowing where he was and of being in contact with him. Let's ignore that. There is, however, something *you* can tell *me.*" Meeting his eyes, I thought, *I would hate to lie to him.* "*Did* you invent this story of an attack? Injure yourself? Did you cause a man to be accused unjustly?"

"You must be mad to think —"

"Let's say that in moments of high emotion we are all capable of a little madness."

"A little? Slashing myself and gashing my head so badly that I was in the hospital for weeks?" My voice sounded terrible — high-pitched and breathless. *"I want Lewis found."*

"Fine, so do I. And if I could, I would take you to him. I would watch you both while you talked it out. That way, and only that way, would I know the truth. Face to face."

"The telephone –"

"Ah yes, you want to use ours. But that may be out of order too. We'll have to see."

"I must contact the mainland. Something has happened that proves everything . . . *everything*, Shane. And I must call the police."

"What?" He had been watching my face. Suddenly he gripped my shoulders. *"What has happened?"*

"You're hurting my arms."

"Judith, what has happened up there at the Castle?"

His eyes were as hard as steel on my face. I turned my head away with a shattering fear that he was about to ask, "What have you done this time?"

"You're hurting my arms," I repeated faintly.

He let go immediately. But when his hands fell to his side, I found that I was trembling. "If you want to know why I must call the police, it's because I want to tell them that while Antonia and I were over on Mull this afternoon, someone scratched my name – Lewis's name for me – on my window."

" 'Clea,' " he said softly. "Oh yes, 'Clea.' "

380

"Do you know anything about it?"

"If you think I go cutting names in windows — For one thing, you need a diamond to do it and I don't possess one. For another, why should I?"

A diamond? Of course. That was how glass was cut, I thought. Lewis had a single diamond in a ring he had inherited from his father. He had had it taken out of its setting and kept it always in his note case as a talisman. Lewis's amulet . . .

I heard my own voice, faint and very frightened: "Lewis is on the island. He is, isn't he? And you know where."

"Why the devil do you keep asking that?"

"Because I believe you can take me to him — and I want to face him, but with others around, because I'm no longer brave where he's concerned. Shane, I must see him!"

"You probably will. But not through me."

I cried out as he turned to walk away, "Why are you so against me?"

"It's the other side of the coin, Judith," he called. Then he paused, turned and came back. "I'm an uncompromising devil. But then, I've had to be. I move in a harsh world among tough people. I should be more gentle with you — in different circumstances I would have been."

He walked very quickly away from me across

the heather. I sank limply down where I was and felt tears sting my eyes. I seldom cried now. The emotions that tore at me since that terrible night were too strong for tears.

"So this is where ye are, lassie." Morag's voice came out of the quiet around me. "An' we wonderin' when the weavin' be gettin' goin'."

Her brisk voice was like a shower of cold water over my stinging emotions. I sat up and brushed my eyes.

"Ach, and for why are ye cryin'?" 'Tis not right for someone sae bonnie to be juist sittin' around cryin'."

"I'm sorry. I must look a mess. But —"

"Whist noo. Don' go tellin' me aboot it. I ken. Everybody kens aroond here. 'Tis fair awful what happened tae ye. But ye're safe here wi' us. An' there's the weavin'."

"Morag, I'm not going to let you down. The weaving project will go through. It's just that — well, things aren't proving easy at the moment. Give me a day or two, please."

"Aye, an' we do — *that* we do!" I struggled to my feet, and she gripped my shoulder. "Dinna cry, lassie. The Good Lord gave us the earth to enjoy, an' that's a fine thing, I'm thinkin'." She turned, saw two of her grandchildren disappearing with flying feet over the hill, and strode with long mannish steps to retrieve them before they fell into a bog.

I had no idea of the time. But something in Morag's calm, unsentimental words calmed me. I knew that I couldn't now go to Inverkyle to telephone. Too much had been said between my asking if I might call from there and Shane's abrupt exit. And one evening and one night more would make little difference. No one could erase my name from my bedroom window. It would be there tomorrow for Inspector Hartwell to see.

Antonia didn't appear for dinner that evening. I played half-heartedly with an egg mousse and even less enthusiastically with a fresh lobster salad. Paul, who hated lobster, ate sausages with the relish of a starved urchin.

I decided that I would take Duncan with me in the morning and go to Mull to call the police from there. I would have to trust Antonia to support my evidence, although the more I thought about it, the more I wondered if she would side with me against Lewis. She was fond of me, but Lewis was a son she loved. I faced the fact that I was on my own — and the more so if Shane showed the message from Lewis to the police.

I was drinking coffee and playing Scrabble with Paul, but all the while I was asking myself the question: How did I know that Shane himself hadn't made up the whole story in order to harass me further? The simple answer was that I didn't know.

I would have to fight for Antonia's support and I had better make certain of that immediately. I purposely missed an easy word in the Scrabble game, tossed my losing letters on the board and said, "You've beaten me."

"You could have put 'bang' there," said Paul. Then he gave me his wide grin. "You let me win that game, didn't you?"

"*Did* I?" I laughed. "Well, it's time you went to bed. Why don't you take the radio up to your room and listen for a bit? I'll come and see you later."

I left him packing up the Scrabble set, blessing fate for giving me an independent and reasonable child.

The rich Hebridean "gloaming" was dying into black night as I went along the stone passage and up the worn, narrow stairs in the tower to Antonia's rooms. The silence was intense: there was no sound — neither of music nor of the typewriter.

I knocked twice and called her name: "Antonia?"

Then I tried the handle of her door. It opened. Her sitting room was beautifully neat, the yellow cushions unruffled, the damask curtains undrawn against the night. I looked into her bedroom. That, too, was empty except for

Saturn, who was curled up on her blue velvet day bed.

I looked into the dining room, the library; I went to the head of the stairs, which gave a clear view of the Great Hall. Antonia was nowhere. I ran to the kitchen.

Rosheen was tidying up. Aye, she had seen the mistress go out a while ago. She was wearing that long dark cloak which the islanders had woven for her all those years ago as a wedding present and which she always left at Mullaine. Nae, she hadn't said where she was going.

There was only one place I could think of and that was Inverkyle Abbey. And since she had no interest in Rory, she must have gone there to see Shane.

To tell him . . . what? About "CLEA" on the windowpane? Or, having first shown me the supposed message from Lewis, had Shane sent Dru to ask Antonia to call at the Abbey, since Mullaine was too dangerous for conversation between them because I was there?

Inactivity was unbearable. I raced to the heavy door and closed it behind me with a boom that echoed back at me. I ran, giving no thought to what I would say when I saw them, Antonia and Shane, and perhaps Rory, knowing only that I must do something to release the tension I felt. Whatever truth might emerge, it had to be faced.

Oh God, came my blinding, despairing prayer, *don't let it be Shane.* And yet I knew, even as the prayer tore through me, that there could be no one else ... but Lewis himself. And Lewis was not on the island.

XXV

He was there, standing quietly under the dark pines, as if waiting for me.

Shane.

"Where are you going in such a hurry?"

I gave a terrible shudder, as if a bullet had hit me. He had been so still, so one with the straight black trunks of the trees that the shock took the last ounce of breath out of me.

He was patient. He waited until I could speak.

"Shane . . . where is . . . Antonia?"

"I don't know."

"But she's not in the house, and there's nowhere else on the island she would visit."

"Rory is sitting by himself with a rather hideous china shepherdess Jeannie broke, and a pot of glue. Jeannie herself and Dru are most likely in their own sitting room. I'm here. So –"

"Then where *is* Antonia?"

"I don't know. Why don't you just go back and wait?"

"Because I'm frightened."

"Of . . . ?"

Desperate, I was no longer cautious. "You . . . Antonia . . . Lewis . . . or someone I don't yet know."

Shane bent his head, and I knew that my face was just visible to him in the last strip of dying light. "I'm frightened too," he said.

"*You?* Oh no!" I tried to laugh. The sound came as a cry caught in my throat. "What have you to fear?"

"You," he said.

It was so outrageously incongruous that I just stared at him.

"I'll even tell you why I'm afraid." He put up his hands and cupped my face almost gently. "Because you stay in my mind; you walk through my thoughts. God in His heaven, what have we done to one another?" He dropped his hands.

The earth seemed to sway under my feet. I reached for the trunk of the nearest pine tree to steady myself. "I've done nothing to you."

He said in a voice so changed that its harshness shocked me. "Oh, not directly. But don't you understand? Lewis never lied to me."

"Perhaps nothing was important enough to lie about when you were together."

Shane said in a low tense voice, "Go back, Judith. Do you hear? Go back to

Mullaine and stay there."

"I want to talk to you."

"One of us, my poor mixed-up girl, must stay sane."

"I must find Antonia."

"For God's sake, *go!*"

I turned and fled.

When I reached the Castle, I searched it again. I could not find Antonia. I had a frantic thought that perhaps she had been mistaken for me and was lying injured, as I had so nearly been, among the great boulders on the shore. I ran to find Duncan, and asked him to go out and search for Antonia.

" 'Tis likely that she's gone to talk to some o' they as is agin' this oil scheme," he said. "An' she'd be mightly mad at me if I went lookin' for her."

I hadn't been in the tower room since I had gone there to relive in memory my life with Lewis. This time I crossed straight to the window. A half-moon lay on its back, silver and supine, while the clouds played over it. Only the tops of the trees moved with the wind and in the distance the cottage lamps shone like pins of gold. It was quite likely that Antonia, determined to win the crofters sufficiently to her way over the oil concession, was going from cottage to cottage, using her charm and her lovely smile to convince them. I went down to the drawing room, where Rosheen had lit a small fire because the evening was cold.

Shane filled my thoughts. Every word we had spoken, every lift and fall of our voices was clear in my mind.

Shane . . . I put my hands over my ears and tried to shut him out. But I could not.

Antonia returned in about an hour. Wild relief swept over me when I heard her coming up the staircase from the Great Hall, and as she passed the drawing room, I shot up out of my chair and opened the door.

She stared at me, startled, her face drawn, her eyes made enormous by dark shadows. Her hair was disheveled and she clutched the dark cloak around her as if she hoped it would make her invisible.

"I was so worried," I said. "I didn't know where you were."

"I went out . . . for a walk."

"You? Walking?"

"Yes. And now I'm tired. Goodnight, Judith."

Just as I had fled from Shane, so now Antonia fled from me.

I let her go, knowing that however much I tried, she would tell me nothing more that night.

It was difficult to sleep. The curtains were

closed over the window where my name could never be erased unless I deliberately smashed the glass. I knew that I must call Inspector Hartwell in the morning and ask him to come to Cathair Mor. And I knew he would come, for his last words to me had been, "If there is anything that seems suspicious, call me and I'll fly to Scotland. *Anything*, Mrs. Mullaine."

But I could not have summoned him for those things for which there were no witnesses. Now I had Antonia, and I had sufficient faith in the Inspector's knowledge of people to know that even if she swore that I had not been within sight of her all that afternoon, he would know that she was lying.

By late morning, or the afternoon, he would be at Cathair Mor, and I would tell him of those other things and dare him to believe that they were figments of my imagination.

At some time in the early hours, something woke me. I started up, heart beating, and looked about me. The door was still closed. But leaning on one elbow, I heard voices somewhere below. The little bedside clock pointed to half past three.

I got out of bed, stepped into slacks, pulled on a sweater and opened the door. I went along the gallery, and turning to the main staircase, found Paul halfway down, hugging his knees and with his head tilted, obviously listening.

"Darling, what are you doing out of bed?"

"I had a nightmare and I was coming to find you. I thought you were down there."

I put an arm around him and felt him trembling. But as I drew him toward me, he pulled away and raised a white stunned face. "It's Antonia and Shane. And they're talking about . . . my father." He dropped his head against me and burst into violent tears.

I let the torrent flow for a few moments, then I raised his head, felt in my pocket for tissues and gave them to him. He wiped his eyes and blew his nose. With my arm still around him, I realized that this was the breakthrough. He had spoken of his father for the first time since the night Lewis left.

For Paul to cry was a rarity. There were two urgencies: one to comfort him; the other to walk in on Antonia and Shane together at the unlikely hour of half past three in the morning. It had to be something they considered so secret, they could not discuss it openly, and because of that, I knew it had to concern Lewis.

I drew Paul close as the weeping ceased. "Listen, darling, and try not to be upset about it. Your father has gone away, and it may be for a long time. Will you be very good and help me?"

"How?" he asked cautiously.

"By just going back to bed and waiting until morning. Then we'll talk about it."

He huddled against me, obviously cold and frightened. "I don't want to go back to bed."

"There's nothing to be afraid of. I'm here. And Rosheen and Duncan and —"

"I want to talk *now*."

It was urgent that I join the two whose voices I could hear in the drawing room. But first I had to listen to Paul, because the floodgate was open and damage could be done if I checked what he had held back for so long.

From my vantage point on the stairs, I had a good view of the Great Hall and it would be easy to intercept Shane when he left. Paul was my first consideration. I had to let him talk.

"All this time," I said, "since I was injured and taken to hospital, you haven't once mentioned your father. Why, Paul, why?"

A shudder ran through him. I sat quietly, wondering how best to cope with a child's traumatic experience. I had to trust to love and instinct. "Paul, just tell me, darling. Did you actually forget your father?"

"Yes — No — I mean —" He broke off and bent his head, staring at his hands plucking at the cord of his dressing gown.

The great shudder he had given must have been the breaking down of the barrier that had blocked his memory of Lewis. Now there was remembering, and that pained and disturbed him.

"It was all sort of ordinary here — you and Antonia and Rory. And yet it wasn't. Some of the boys at school have fathers who just go away. I thought — I don't know — I sort of couldn't remember the bit in between Father being there and not being there. And then —"

"Then what?"

He curled himself up, pressing into me as if he wanted to hide. "There was a man . . . out in the bay. He was watching me over the top of a bit of a cliff. It's silly, isn't it, but he made me scared. I only saw half his face."

"You didn't know the man?"

He shook his head. "But it was awful, because he made me remember something —"

"What was that?"

"That night when . . . when you . . ."

I waited. Again instinct told me that Paul had to say it, had to voice the thing that had been enclosed behind the shutter in his mind.

"That night when you were hurt . . ." He glanced quickly over his shoulder as if afraid that someone might be standing behind us on the stairs.

I thought, feeling sick with fear, It *was* Lewis . . . there at the bay. Lewis watching his son. But Paul hadn't seen his full face and so the protective barrier had not collapsed at the sight of him. More than ever I fretted to rush down and break in on the conversation in the room below.

Paul said, suddenly, "It's all right, isn't it?"

"Everything is all right."

"And I won't have to go to that bay again?"

"Darling, of course not."

"That man —"

"He won't hurt you, I promise you that. Whoever he is, he won't harm you."

And, dear heaven, he won't!

"Now," I said, "will you go to bed — I'll come up to you a little later."

"But I *told* you. I heard them talking downstairs about my father. *Is* my father here, on the island?"

You didn't lie to a child. I said, "Paul, I don't know. But I must see Antonia and Shane. It's very important. Get into bed but keep the light on and wait for me. I'll come up as soon as I can."

"All right," he said.

His matter-of-factness was like a light illuminating everything. He had come out of that traumatic state, and had reacted to the shock with his usual courage.

I kissed him with such a fervent thankfulness that he drew a little away from me; he was never one for emotional outbursts.

"Go to bed," I said again in a brisk voice, and

gave him a little push.

When he had climbed back up the stairs, I raced in slippered feet to Rosheen and Duncan's bedroom. I rapped on the door and roused them.

When Rosheen came out, wrapped her dressing gown around her, I said, "I'm sorry to disturb your sleep, but would you please go and sit with Paul until I come back? I don't know how long I'll be, but I don't want him to be alone."

She gave me a puzzled stare. "Aye, of course I'll go to the laddie, but what − ?"

"Rosheen, I don't know. I just don't know what has happened. But it's something that may be urgent. Please just go and sit with Paul."

"Aye, that I will. Dinna worry." She gave me her wide smile.

I thanked her and ran along the gallery from the servants' quarters and down the staircase to the small drawing room. I could hear Antonia's voice and then Shane's.

I pushed open the door.

Antonia was leaning against the cushioned end of the sofa. Her back was to me, but in her long dark cloak and silver hair lit by the lamps, she looked as if she were playing a great dramatic role.

I asked in a voice I hoped sounded nonchalant, "Is there anything being said that I should hear?"

Antonia swung around. Her eyes were enormous and very afraid. Shane, too calm, too remote, asked, "What do you want to know, Judith?"

"Lewis . . . You've been talking about him, haven't you?"

"You're damned right," said Shane.

"Then, since it concerns me, please let me in on the conversation."

"Antonia will tell you."

"*No!*" she shouted, using the whole force of her voice. Then she put her hand to her throat and shut her eyes in pain. "No, no," she said more softly. "Shane, this is between ourselves. I've promised you —"

"You've promised nothing," Shane said. "How could you? He's your son. But it's come to the point — and you know it — when you've got to be honest with Judith. Or shall I tell her?"

She edged her way as if she were suddenly old and tired, and sank on the sofa. "You tell."

Shane said to me, "You'd better sit down too."

"I'll stand." It was bravado, because my legs were already shaking. But whatever I had to hear, I wanted to make a show of courage.

"What is it I should hear?"

"Antonia knows where Lewis is."

She cringed as I looked at her.

"No," she cried. "Judith, believe me. *No!* I haven't known all the time. Only just after . . . after . . ." She floundered.

"After what?"

She said faintly, as if her voice had almost given out, "After Lewis saw Paul at the bay. That was when it happened. Lewis believes that Paul recognized him, although he was quite a distance away."

"So he was there all the time."

"After he escaped from Cathair Beag. That's where he first went, so he told me. But he couldn't exist there, with no food and very little shelter."

"And he could live, without *anyone's* help, at the bay?"

"Fishing. And with the burn for drinking water. And . . . and at night he used to . . . to take things."

"From the crofters, you mean?"

She nodded. "No one here locked their doors and the islanders sleep soundly in this air. He took only small things — parts of a loaf of bread, an egg, milk . . ."

"And then Paul saw him."

"He couldn't risk being recognized, even by his son. So he came here to me late one night.

Judith, he was desperate and he told me everything."

"*What did he tell you?*"

"The same as he told Shane over the telephone. You wanted freedom from him but you had to keep your son. So you —"

"I know," I said harshly. "I injured myself. And Lewis has been building up a case against me to convince you, and the courts, that I am unbalanced."

"He is my son. I was so sure he wouldn't lie to me."

"But he did," I said quickly. "And you knew yesterday afternoon that he had lied to you. You saw my name on the window and there was proof that I couldn't have done it because I hadn't been out of your sight until I went to find Paul and you went straight to my room with my scarf. And no one else here, except you, knew that Lewis always called me Clea when we were alone."

She rose and began walking agitatedly up and down the room. "Yes, it's true. I believed him until I saw the name scratched on the windowpane. But I had to know —" She paused and swallowed as if her throat pained her.

"To know what?"

"The truth, Judith. I tried to find Lewis . . . I went to the place where we had met before, but he wasn't there . . . he wasn't anywhere."

I glanced down at the pair of practical shoes she kept at Mullaine. They were muddied and scraped. "You went all that way to the bay?" I asked unbelievingly.

"No. Lewis always met me in a gully on the moors. But tonight, when he wasn't there, I was terrified that he was lying somewhere injured, or ill. I had to talk to someone −" She paused and looked at Shane. "You were his friend, and the only one here who could help me. I roused Duncan" − she turned again to me − "and he went to the Abbey and asked Shane to come. I said to tell him it was dreadfully urgent. It was − You see, I didn't dare go to the police, and someone had to help me find Lewis."

While she was talking, it flashed through my mind that my past "forgetfulnesses," my mislaying things, had all been carefully planned. Lewis had been steadily building up a case against my sanity even then, quietly planning for the day when he would be free of me and have his son. But the plan had misfired. His impatience and his rages had destroyed him.

"Now you know, don't you?" I said to Antonia. "It was Lewis working to destroy me. And you know what he wanted. Everything his way − the sun and the moon and the stars. His music, his wonderful life − and Paul. But not me. His responsibility was toward his career and his son; he had none left for me. Women flocked to him, he could take his pick of them. So, somehow, without damaging his image, I had to be eliminated."

"Oh God! Oh God!" She threw her head back and gave me a long, despairing look. "Please believe me, Judith. *Believe me!* I wanted to be fair to you because I'm fond of you. I could never have harmed you."

"We're wasting time," Shane said curtly, "and there's little to spare." He was frowning as if impatient with both of us. "Suppose we keep to the salient point."

"The salient point," she cried and flung her cloak onto the sofa, "is that everything is crashing about me. This morning I heard that the oil project will probably come to nothing. They are by-passing Cathair Mor. Pipelines will carry the oil direct to the mainland, and —"

"For the moment," Shane cut in harshly, "damn the oil!" He moved away from us. "It's late, but I'm calling the police."

"*No!*" Antonia rushed at him. "Shane, please find Lewis first and let me talk to him. You must at least do that. He's my child . . ."

I was looking out the tall window that gave a view of the loch and Cathair Beag in the distance. The night was very black except for one moving light. "It's there again, on the rock. Look . . ." I cried to Shane.

I saw his head turn. Then he moved. He was across the room and out the door in what seemed a single stride.

"Judith, please understand . . ."

I heard Antonia's voice only from a distance, for I was racing after Shane.

There were swiftly running footsteps behind me. "Please stop . . . both of you . . ." Antonia managed to throw her voice in a long, despairing cry of words. "For God's sake, let him be. Don't hound him. Hasn't he suffered enough?"

"No." The answer came clear and sharp from the far end of the hall. Then the door opened and a draft of night air blew in as Shane disappeared.

Out in the cold darkness, he heard me following him and stopped. "Don't be a little fool. This is something I have to do, and I don't want to be responsible for you, too, in the middle of the night."

"It will soon be dawn, and I'm coming with you. There isn't any argument."

"You're right. There's no time for that." He seized my hand roughly. "Come on, then."

His fingers were tight around mine, dragging me on, taking no notice of my frantic efforts to keep up with him as I stumbled over the rough coarse grass. We raced across the *machair*, and the island was silent and primeval except for our rushing footsteps. The sea lay quiet, wrapped in its own sleep.

I managed, with the little breath I had, to gasp, "You can't land at Cathair Beag. Lewis told me he was the only one who had found the way."

"He found it with me," Shane said. "But I'm not taking you in the boat. You can stay down by the loch and wait."

"I won't."

Shane said, very quietly, "I rather like being obeyed."

"Then I'll disappoint you."

We reached the jetty where the two launches lay. The water was black and the red dawn streaks in the eastern sky did not yet touch our island.

Something moved in one of the boats. I stopped. Shane put an arm swiftly around my shoulders as if to shield me.

"Hello," said Rory Kilarran. "I knew you'd come."

XXVI

"What the hell are you doing here," Shane burst out.

"Waiting for you."

"Oh, for God's sake, go back to bed," Shane said impatiently. "We've got enough on our minds without you playing hide-and-seek."

"I know where you're going, but I've got something to tell you that makes all the difference. You don't need to go looking for Lewis. He's not important now."

"He is, and we're not playing games," Shane retorted. Then, more gently, "Go back home, Rory."

"I've got something to tell you," he said again.

"It can wait till morning."

"It can't. If you know what *I* know, then you won't need to go looking for Lewis."

Shane paused. *"What do you mean?"*

Rory had climbed onto the jetty and was perched on the bollard, looking up at us. "I've been looking for Lewis too. You see, I saw a light on Cathair Beag, just as Judith did,

404

though I don't think anyone else believed her. I kept going to look because I guessed there was someone there."

"Then why the hell didn't you say?"

"I was afraid. After what he did to Judith, he could have killed me if he knew I'd seen him. But tonight Lufra was missing, I think he was after a rabbit, and I went to find him. I saw Antonia — and she never goes walking. I wondered what she was doing because she was carrying something bulky under her cloak. So I shut Lufra up and came out and found her again and followed her. I guessed she was taking food or something to Lewis — there's no one else she'd be visiting on the island. She was waiting and getting upset, and she began to cry and sort of wander about wildly, falling down and picking herself up."

"And when she fell, you didn't go to help her?" Shane asked.

"No. Lewis could have been somewhere around."

"Well, and then?"

"Antonia went back with whatever she was carrying to the Castle and I supposed I'd better go home to bed. It was then that I saw the light, a flashlight I think it must have been, shining on Cathair Beag. I knew then where Lewis was hiding. He'd probably left the place where he was before because he was scared of being seen, and gone to the rock." Rory gave a small sly grin. "Do you know what I did?"

"No, but you'd better tell me."

"I took our launch and went over there. I went right round the island and found a dinghy tied up to a rock in a tiny bay. I knew that it must be the place where Lewis used to go when he was here as a boy. I just untied the boat and let it float away."

"So all this time the dinghy must have been somewhere hidden off Cathair Mor, because that's where Antonia went to him with food."

"No one ever visits that southwest corner of the island," Shane said. "It's just a mass of cliffs — great basalt columns nobody would dare to try and scale."

"And the police never gave a thought to the fact that he might return to the island; they were certain it was too dangerous."

"That dinghy," Shane said, "was obviously the one missing from Carsaig." He frowned at Rory. "Why didn't you come and tell me all this instead of taking things into your own hands?"

"Don't you *see?*" Rory insisted. "I worked it well. Lewis can't get off the rock. He'll die there without food and water."

"Dying is the last thing we want for him," Shane retorted. "The truth comes first."

"But it doesn't matter any longer. All this time we've thought he was important here —

that he was Laird. But he's not. He's *not* the Laird of the island."

"What the devil do you mean?"

"What I say. Lewis is not Laird," Rory shouted. "And I know who the real one is — by birth and everything."

"Who?"

"I am," said Rory.

The first ray of the sun glowed thinly in the eastern sky, and somewhere behind us in the trees the dawn chorus began. Rory's red hair blew about wildly; his eyes were brilliant, like a fanatic's.

"Didn't you hear what I said?" he asked with the first note of impatience I had ever heard in that gentle Scottish burr. "I said —" He broke off and took a deep breath, as though his momentous news needed all his strength. The single sunray touched us.

In that second before Rory spoke again, I heard my own voice:

> " 'And *I* am Laird of Mullaine',
> The red man said."

I spoke from a kind of hysterical compulsion. Three devastating emotions forced the words from me — shock and fear and mental weariness.

Only Shane was unimpressed. I saw, in

those moments, his strength, his ability to put first things first.

"You two can talk about it here," he said to us, "but don't either of you get in my way," and leaped into the boat.

"Wait, I'm coming," I shouted.

He looked up at me. "You're crazy. Stay where you are."

"I said I'm coming." I leaned forward to lower myself into the launch.

Shane reached up to push me back. I caught his wrist and hung on to it. Then I took a stride forward and fell inelegantly into the boat.

"What in the name of heaven do you think you're doing?" Shane exploded. "You could have landed in the sea for the second time in a few days. That was damned silly."

"So was trying to keep me back."

Rory stepped down immediately behind me and the *Midir* swung wildly with our sudden weight and movements.

"I've got to come too," Rory said. "Listen, please. Oh, just listen. I've got a story to tell you."

"Keep it until later."

Rory shot forward and wrenched Shane's hand from the engine starter. "No, I won't. *Can't you understand?* Lewis is stuck on Cathair Beag. I freed the rowing boat he had tied up there." He gave a small, high giggle. "He's caught — so there's time, there's all the time in the world, for you to listen. And you must. Lewis isn't important. *I* am. I've got proof, you see, that Lewis isn't Laird."

"I doubt if you could read a genealogical table even if you saw one." Shane sounded angry and impatient. "So, for God's sake, let's get going. We'll talk about who is Laird later."

"I found proof of what I'm telling you when Murdo's shed burned down. You remember . . ."

Shane looked at me. I was sure he, too, recalled that that had been our first meeting and the beginning of our mutual suspicion.

He asked Rory, "What has Murdo got to do with this?"

"Everything. If you'll just let me speak," Rory pleaded.

Shane lifted his shoulders in resignation. "All right. What do a few more minutes matter if you've really done what you said you had?"

"I've told you. There's no escape for Lewis."

"Go on, then. But make it quick. There's a job I've got to do."

"Oh yes," Rory said sadly. "You've always had that."

"Come on down here." Shane drew me into the tiny saloon and we sat together on a cushioned seat. Shane's arm rested along the back not touching me, yet curiously protective.

409

Rory squatted on the steps. "Antonia's husband, Robert, had an affair with Mother. It was before Lewis was born — and before you were born. Did you ever hear about it?"

Shane answered matter-of-factly. "If Mother had such an affair, I doubt she would have gone about telling the world. So, no, I didn't know. And I don't think I very much want to. Now, shall we get on?"

"No." Rory leaned forward, swaying with the boat. "There's a letter explaining everything. It's important."

"We'll see it when we get back," Shane said.

"Oh, but I've got it with me." He felt in his pocket and handed a folded sheet of paper over to Shane. "I knew you wouldn't listen to me unless I had some proof to show you. It's Mother's letter written to Robert Mullaine telling him about me. *Me!* Murdo told me he has another letter and he says he'll produce it for a sum of money."

Shane was reading the letter quickly. "Yes, by God, yes. You're right. It's all here, in my mother's handwriting."

I remained silent, an outsider in this most personal revelation.

"It happened at a time when Antonia was away singing."

"I gather that."

"And Father was also away on business,"

Rory said. "So Robert Mullaine and Mother were thrown together. I suppose they were both bored."

"And so they had an affair. According to this letter, Mother was having Robert Mullaine's child and wrote to tell him so. But he never received it — or was it that Murdo stole it from Father's desk?"

"No." Rory shook his head vigorously. "Murdo told me he kept it."

"A little case of blackmail should the necessity arise?"

"Yes. Mother wrote those two letters to Robert while he was in London. When he did not reply, nor come to the island to see her, she was quite certain that he was deserting her. Your father, Shane, was returning from abroad and Mother had made a decision. She would never tell anyone the truth. I was to be brought up as your real brother. But I'm not . . . I'm not . . . I'm a Mullaine, and the eldest."

"Well," Shane said, "apparently deserted by a lover and with a returning husband, what else could she do?"

I asked in a small voice, "Why didn't she telephone Robert? Surely she could have done that safely from the Abbey."

"There was no telephone link with the mainland in those days," Shane said. "I wonder what happened when Robert returned to the island

— which he used to do for a few weeks every summer? It must have been hard for Mother, and more than hard if she had really loved Robert. But how she felt — how either of them felt — is something we shall never know."

"And *I* never really knew my father," Rory said. "He was always in London. I think I was about three years old when Lewis was born."

Shane was looking at Rory as if he had never really seen him before. "Yes, there are so many likenesses. The hair, the forehead, the eyes — all more Mullaine than Kilarran."

"Do you know where I kept the letter?" Rory asked with one of his little giggles.

"No. But does it matter?"

"I took the lock off the belfry door at the Abbey and hid the letter on a ledge behind the bell. If Murdo came looking for it, he'd never find it there."

I sat up straight. "That's the lock you gave Duncan for Hamish's cottage door."

"That's right." He reached forward and took the letter from Shane. "I'll keep this and I'll show it to our lawyer." He lifted his head, and there was a radiance about him. "All my life I've been nothing. And now I'm something. I've been something and someone all the time."

Shane said quietly. "A lot of scandal is going to be raked up if you insist on going to court."

"But I *do*. Nobody ever takes any notice of

what I say. Now, at last, they'll have to."

As he looked back at the wild island I asked, "Shane, what will happen?"

"We'll have to see. If Rory is registered as my father's child, and I'm certain he must have been or the secret would have come out long ago, then I don't know how he stands in the law. I hope it doesn't come to that." He turned to Rory. "Don't you think that you could be content just to know that you should be Laird and leave it at that, without bringing the whole thing into the courts and the press? You know and we know. And perhaps one day, when he's adult, Paul can know."

Rory's face fell with disappointment. Cathair Mor was his universe. To be the red-haired Laird of the island song and to be acknowledged as such was his Celtic heart's desire.

I felt sorry for him because I knew that in the end Shane's advice would prevail. He was strong. He could assert his influence without any great effort. And I was glad, not for Paul's sake as the future Laird, but for the sake of the island. No place, however small, could be controlled by a man who lived in dreams and was incapable of making decisions.

"Why didn't you tell me about all this earlier?"

Rory said plaintively. "Because I really *did* think that Lewis might be somewhere on the island and if he knew I had seen him or that I got too near where he might be, he could have done to me what he nearly did to Judith. He might even have killed me. I had to wait until he was found."

Without comment, Shane started the *Midir*'s engine.

Rory asked, "Aren't we going to . . . to talk about it? There's got to be some sort of plan."

"The only plan I can see at the moment is finding Lewis," Shane said almost violently. "Heaven forbid that I should ever again be such a blind fool!" He shook his head vigorously and looked at me. "I was clinging to a friendship formed before I was old enough to make judgments. So many years separated us by then, that there was nothing to destroy the illusions. I'm sorry." Then, calm and strong again, he said, "Go back, Rory, and take Judith with you."

"No," I said. "What you've just heard concerns your family. What you are about to do concerns mine. I'm coming with you."

"Then *you* go," he said to his brother. "It will be quite enough for me to have to cope with Lewis, if Lewis is really there on Cathair Beag."

"Oh, he is," Rory said, "and *I'm* coming. And you can't stop me. No one can."

Once, as we crossed the strip of sea to the

great rock of Cathair Beag, Rory broke our silence. "It's like they said in the legend. Only the 'hollow hill' — the place of magic where the dream would come true — was just a little cave beyond the bay."

"Paul's bay," I said softly. "Where he saw his father."

"Good God!" Shane turned to me. "Who told you that?"

"Paul, just before I walked in on you and Antonia tonight. It must have been a terrible experience."

As the little boat's engine purred, I explained to Shane. "I don't know how Paul will take this shock of remembering. I've never seen him cry as he did."

"That's fine. It's a release," Shane said quietly. "That son of yours is very normal and uncomplicated. Don't make difficulties and delve into subtleties with children. They're tougher than you think. And they recover far more quickly than we, with our twists and turns of sophistication. Now hold on, both of you."

The launch rocked crazily as we rounded the jutting corner of Cathair Beag where the waves were as savage as the cliffs they battered.

"We'll never land here."

"No, we won't. But once past this corner there's a place — Ah! I can just see it."

"You'll tell Lewis that I'm the real Laird, won't you?" Rory asked. "You see, if he knows he'll be so mad —"

"He has many more important things to be mad about," Shane told him. "Now just stop talking while I try to find the beach — it's the size of a pocket handkerchief, anyway, and these rocks could rip the boat to pieces if I make a wrong turn."

It was almost impossible to see how the *Midir* could find a safe way between the vicious rocks. I watched Shane swing the wheel with slow, wary movements, heading to what looked like a formidable barrier of rocks.

"Why are you turning here?" I called to him. "I can't see a beach."

I had no idea whether he answered me. If he did, the pounding of the waves took his voice away. I sat holding tightly to the rail, feeling every lift and swell as the sea attacked us.

We had now slowed to a crawl and were sliding eel-like toward the tall, columned crags of Cathair Beag. Quite suddenly, in a narrow opening, I saw a tiny beach that was little more than a sandy patch between the rocks. I held my breath as the *Midir* slid toward it, waiting for the moment of impact between the little boat and the guardian boulders. Imagination leaped ahead, visualizing us all being flung into the boiling sea.

"When we get there — *if* we ever land," I shouted above the turmoil of the water, "there's no way anyone could climb those rocks. They're absolutely straight and I can't see any footholds."

"Nor can I," Shane called back.

The little boat shuddered as he turned the wheel quickly to avoid a collision with the basalt blocks scattered in the sea. I stared ahead of me, searching the pinnacles of Cathair Beag for any sign of human life. I could see none.

"Lewis can't be here. I mean . . ." what I meant was never said, for suddenly we slid into shallow water and the sea beneath us was crystal-clear. I remembered how the police, searching for Lewis, had circled the island and could find no landing place, and I said shakily, "If the police had only searched more thoroughly, they'd have found this beach."

"You flatter it," Shane said coolly. "It's a small strip of sand and I'm certain that at high tide it isn't even visible. I first saw it one day when Lewis and I were sailing round Cathair Beag and he pointed to this spot and said, 'You see those vicious teeth of rock? Well, if you're clever you can navigate between them, and there's a strip of beach to land on.' I suggested we try it, but —" The crash of a wave behind us took his voice away.

"But what?" I shouted.

"Lewis told me once was enough. He wasn't going to tempt that devil place — as he put it — again. 'One slight swing of the wheel and you'd be torn to pieces, boat and all.'"

"And so nobody dreamed —"

By my side, Rory said in a singsong voice, "Nobody dreamed either, Judith, that I was the real Laird." His voice, in the sudden peace of the shallows, was curiously high and sweet, like a child who had seen his wonderland.

Our shoes were sturdy, but the sea licked our ankles as we leaped ashore. One by one we landed on the half-moon of beach.

I followed Shane up the narrow beach, my feet sinking into the soft sand.

"Stay where you are," he called back.

"Where are you going?"

"For the moment, I've no idea." Head lifted, he seemed to be waiting and watching for a movement above him.

The great basalt cliffs were split into long columns, like those I had seen at Fingal's Cave on Staffa, where I had been taken as a little girl. Clefts and fissures cut into the cliffs, and I said, "Perhaps a man *could* climb to the top. We came right around the rock, didn't we, and that's why we can't see either Cathair Mor or Mull. This must be the place Lewis found."

Shane ignored me. He put his hands to his mouth and his voice rose, deep and clear, above the sound of the sea: "Is anyone there?"

A cloud of startled birds rose, shrilling in agitation, some diving at us, the rest circling the rock — white and grey wings stained crimson with the dawn.

Rory caught my arm. "What are we doing, Judith? Lewis will just have to stay here. He can't get away. No one could swim in this water, and out there" — he gave a little giggle and jerked his head seaward — "the porpoises have probably found the rowing boat and are having games with it." He left my side and touched his brother's arm. "Don't let's stay here —"

Shane shook off the restraining hand as he would shake off the antics of a tiresome puppy. "Rory, either stay here and keep quiet, or go back to the boat."

Rory stood defiantly facing his brother. "I won't do either. Now that you know who I am, *I* will —"

Shane seized him and marched him to a little part of the beach where there were no rocks. "Now, are you going to keep quiet? Because if you're not, I shall have to land you flat on your back here. I promise you I can do that quite adequately so that you'll be no more nuisance for quite some time."

"Stop quarreling!" I cried to them.

"No one is quarreling," Shane said without

taking his eyes from his brother. "I'm just demanding to be left alone to do what I have to."

Rory turned away. "You don't understand, any of you. It's important to me that I'm Laird — but no one listens."

"We'll all listen in good time," Shane told him more gently. "But this is priority number one." He turned back to the cliff and raised his voice again, calling, "What do you want to do up there, starve to death?"

The gulls and oyster-catchers and curlews all resented us, swooping the air around us brown and white and black against the lightening sky. We waited. Then when the birds had settled on their ledges, something moved near the cliff top. I held my breath.

"Come down, Lewis," Shane shouted.

The movement far above us ceased; the dark figure disappeared for a moment. Then we saw him again. He was making his way slowly down the rock face, sometimes visible, sometimes hidden in the gullies. He could not have heard what Shane had shouted to him at that distance and against the roar of the sea, but he must have recognized us, for halfway down he paused, crouching on a ledge as narrow as that which had saved my life on Cathair Mor.

It was Lewis. The fiery hair, blown wild in the wind, the narrow face, the gesture with the hands that I had seen so often, fingers curved as if poised over the piano keys, but reaching now for holds on the cliff to steady himself.

I cried his name, but the east wind took my voice away.

That same wind carried his forward to us. "You're wasting your time because I'm not coming any closer."

"Don't be a damned fool," Shane shouted.

I knew by the turn of Lewis's head that he was looking at me. "You, Clea, why don't you tell them the truth?"

"I have."

Lewis moved cautiously, climbing a little nearer to us. A piece of rock broke off and slid with a soft thud onto the beach.

Rory said, "He's really coming down. Shane, he is. And I'll have to tell him about the letter."

We ignored Rory's bursting, excited words. The minutes of standing there, the cliffs like a formless cathedral, held a macabre tension. Lewis had paused again, crouching on a lower ledge. This time his voice came clearly to us: "You know none of the facts — my wife has seen to that. But I won't be caught until I've proved her guilt. Yours, Clea . . ."

"Come down and talk sense."

Lewis turned his head toward Shane. "So she's won you? You believed me when I talked to you on the telephone. But now —" He broke off and slid a little on the ridge, clung for a heart-stopping moment and then found a foothold. He remained there, leaning back against the cliff face, and looked down at his hands, crying in a high-pitched staccato, utterly unlike the voice I knew, "Oh God, my hands! If they are ruined for music, she'll die a dozen deaths. I can promise her that."

"Stop the dramatics and make a move — upwards or downwards. Whichever it is, you haven't a hope, so you may as well choose the sanest way, and join us."

Lewis had been flexing his fingers, then, as if reassured that they had not been injured as he slid on the slippery ridge, he seemed to relax. "Well, Clea, what next? For you, I mean?"

He had moved close enough so that his every word came to us clearly. I called to him, "Please understand. I never tried to hold you to marriage, and even if you had left me, you would have had the right to see Paul. You must believe —"

"I am. By remaining here."

"Then I'm coming up," Shane shouted.

"Stay where you are," Lewis called. "But send Clea. If she can climb, we'll talk here — or *I'll talk* and *she* can listen. If she can't climb, then she'll slip and slide and fall, my poor little wife, and it will be a case of tragic accident or perhaps of suicide, while of unsound mind. Or

422

guilt . . . And only your word, Shane, if you try to betray me. But you won't. And Rory won't, because — Look at him . . . he's afraid of you, of me, of the whole damned world. Send Clea up here."

"No," Shane called. "She's not trying any heroics while I'm around." He went to the cliff and reached up, feeling for ledges.

"Don't go up there," I cried.

Behind me, Rory laughed. "It *is* almost a legend, isn't it? It all began because Lewis was near the bay, the one I showed you, Judith, on the map: the Bay of the Dark Star."

Shane had begun to climb.

"You won't reach me that way," Lewis's voice still had the high, emotional pitch. "You have to zigzag up and you don't know how."

My body felt like ice in the windy dawn. The great rock was suddenly wreathed in a sunburst of flame. Rory put a hand through my arm and began to ask me if he had ever told me the Celtic story of the sea gulls. I shot away from him as if he had struck me. "Just keep quiet —" I hissed at him, but didn't take my eyes from Shane.

It was all exactly as I had thought; I said vehemently to myself, as if we were two people arguing, *I told you so . . . I told you this was what was happening.* Lewis, hiding on the island, spending those terrified, lonely hours working out ways to destroy me. Anything . . . anything that came into his mind. *Make her see things; make her hear things that nobody else sees or hears. ("Clea hears things, sees things . . . that's the beginning of madness.")* And then, on that misty afternoon, finding a new and fool-proof way to get rid of me. A thrust in the back, a fall to the sea below. An accident in the fog, or a suicide — it wouldn't matter what the coroner had decided. Lewis would have been free of me and free to tell his story, backed by his mother's report on my strangeness.

"Why the hell did you marry me?"

The words came above the turbulence of crashing sea. I remained silent too long. Lewis shouted with wild urgency. "Well, why did you?"

"Because of love," I said, but my voice was too soft and the wind took it away. Anyway, it was a hollow answer — it no longer had any meaning.

I saw Shane slip on the cliff again, and cried out to him, "Don't risk your life. It makes no difference now."

I doubt if he heard me, and even if he had, I was wasting words. He would obey only his own urge.

I subsided into a frantic, immobile fear. It was madness for Shane to have put himself in such a vulnerable position below a desperate man, and yet I felt a kind of awed admiration.

Rory's plaintive voice came from behind me. "I know what's going to happen. Shane will get all the credit for finding Lewis. All my life, it's Shane who has won. But *I* found Lewis first."

"Antonia found him first," I said. "Or rather, Lewis went to her."

"But she'd never have given him away. So it was really I —"

I let him go on talking and heard nothing. I was watching the ledge where Lewis crouched with Shane just below him. The men were on the sea birds' territory and the cormorants and the gulls wheeled and shrieked around them. Suddenly a huge bird swooped low.

"An eagle," Rory cried.

The tip of the splendid wing slapped across Shane's face and he jerked away. As he did so, he lost his balance.

I screamed.

At the same moment Lewis's arm swung down. I watched in horror. *Let him be safe. Please, God, let Shane be safe* . . . a child's prayer.

And answered. For Lewis did not sweep Shane to his death. Instead he seized his wrist and steadied him until he found a foothold again. Then, as Shane leaned in safety against the rock, Lewis let go.

Rory said in an awed voice, "Did you see

that? Lewis saved Shane's life."

I could neither answer him nor move. Rooted and appalled, I watched the men — like antagonists who had found a comradeship in a momentary danger.

The eagle, like the defending ruler of a kingdom, swooped again. A wide brown wing swung in an arc; the hooked beak was etched against the grey cliff. The picture had changed in a flash. It was now a bird and a man who were in conflict. The feathered body shadowed the sun's light; the swoop downward was swift and elegant. I saw Lewis's arm hit out at the bird; I heard Shane, who had been reaching upward again, call out a sharp warning. He was too late. The bird circled the pinnacle of rock, and with another terrible and beautiful swoop, dived again. The huge wing struck Lewis.

He flung his hands up to his face, and the movement made him lose his balance, as Shane had done minutes before.

Shane hoisted himself onto the next ledge, clawed desperately for a higher handhold, just as Lewis's body, slender and small-boned, rocked sideways, tilted and keeled over.

The cry came — a long-drawn appalling sound echoing among the crags and mingling with the screams of the birds. Unlike theirs, his was the sound of the terror of a man sighting death.

XXVII

Shock suddenly made me lose all sense of hearing. I was in a limbo without sound, unaware even of movement, until suddenly Shane was climbing down to the beach, shouting, "Rory, get help. Go on – go on!"

"Where?"

"To the island."

"But who shall I ask?"

I turned in amazement, incredulous at Rory's foolish question. There was a glint in his eyes, and I knew then that he didn't want to go. If Lewis was injured, then Rory wanted delay. He wanted it to be too late to save him.

Shane was scrambling down the cliff, taking chances with his own safety in an effort to reach the place, hidden from us, where Lewis must have fallen. Then, Shane, too, became hidden.

I ran forward, squeezing between clefts in the long basalt columns. Lewis lay curled up as if he were asleep and his head was bleeding. Shane turned and looked beyond me to Rory, who had made no attempt to move. "We need a stretcher and ropes. Get going . . ."

"But I don't know where." He moved toward us and stared down at Lewis. "He's dead, isn't he?"

I thought for a sickening second that Shane was going to hit him. "No, he's not dead. Now, for God's sake, go."

Rory looked up and gave Shane a strange, wide grin. Then he just stood there, shaking his head.

I said quickly, "You go, Shane, and take Rory with you. I'll stay here. Go and get help. Don't argue — there's no time."

The spaces between the columns of rock were scarcely wide enough for one person to pass another, but I edged around Shane and went to Lewis's side. "I must stay with him," I said.

"I don't want you to be here alone."

I said impatiently, "It doesn't matter what you want. Someone has to remain and *I want to.*" I knew that I couldn't trust Rory. He would be unpredictable.

Shane gave in. Argument wasted valuable time. I watched him edge back between the rocks, pushing Rory before him.

Shane turned suddenly, took off his coat and threw it toward me. "Better cover him with this."

Shane had wrapped a large handkerchief over the wound on Lewis's head. Now I laid the coat over him and pulled out my own handkerchief from the pocket of my skirt. It was pathetically small to help stem the bleeding, but it was all I had.

I lifted Lewis's head very gently onto my lap. His fingers were scratched and the nails torn. I folded his hands underneath Shane's coat for warmth and then I sat, my eyes scarcely moving from the break in the cliff from which I could see the wild water churning around Cathair Beag.

The great rocks sheltered us from the wind that soughed around the pinnacles above us. I wasn't afraid, for Lewis could no longer harm me. I watched the *Midir* pass by the narrow opening in the cliff and then saw only the sea.

Lewis's face with its fine bone structure, had a curious nobility. I bent toward him. "It's all right," I said. I whispered the empty words as if to give myself comfort, for I was certain that Lewis couldn't hear me.

The sky was lightening rapidly. The sun had lost the red glow of dawn and was turning pale yellow. The birds rode the wind, coming into sight at the very top of the cliffs, their wings spanning the space between the columns, then disappearing.

Waiting was an eternity. I wondered if Paul

was asleep. I knew that now, whether he was sleeping or waiting for me, he was safe. I would need to go carefully with him, but in the end it would be all right. Paul would face what he had chosen to forget and had been forced to remember; he would be upset for a while and then, healthy with childhood, push it all away from him with the excitement of a football game or swimming contest.

Lewis stirred. I saw his lips move.

I bent down, saying softly, "Don't try to talk."

"K.333 K.333." His head moved restlessly and I felt a moment's fear that he might regain full consciousness, and in spite of his injuries, find sudden frenzied strength and attack me.

K.333 – Mozart's B Flat sonata – Lewis's favorite music. Even in unconsciousness he was in his own world. I watched his fingers move, and went on praying that he would not open his eyes until Shane returned.

In a wild, hysterical moment I thought, *Suppose no one comes back for us . . .*

They arrived in the two launches. One carried four men, a stretcher and ropes. Dru MacColl and Shane were in the Abbey boat, and it was they who took Lewis to Mull, where an ambulance, telephoned for by Shane, was waiting to drive him to the hospital at Salen.

I sat crouched in the stern of the *Midir* as it

plunged through the high waves back to Mullaine and Antonia.

The great stone tower stood stark and medieval against the paling sky. After centuries, it was no longer the seat of the Laird. The islanders would no longer speak of "The Mullaine" but of "The Kilarran," although to the proud and insular and independent people of Cathair Mor, precisely who owned their island counted for little.

I found Antonia in her own small sitting room, curled up uncomfortably in a chair, her hands twitching in a troubled, restless sleep. She opened her eyes and looked at me. Then she sat up slowly, as if her limbs were stiff. "You . . . don't have to tell me. Lewis . . ."

"He was on Cathair Beag."

"*Was? . . . Was?*" Her eyes were overbright, as if, when I found her, she had only pretended to sleep.

"There has been an accident. Oh, no one was attacked," I added quickly as fear darkened her face. "Lewis was on the cliff and a bird swooped down. He tried to avoid it and lost his balance."

"Oh-h-h." The sound was a moan drawn out of her shock and pain.

"They've taken him to the hospital at Salen."

She shot out of her chair. "I must go to him." She brushed past me and then turned. "He's

dead ... my son is dead." The moan came
again, wild and keening and lonely.

"Antonia please ... listen to me. He was
alive when they carried him to the boat. I
saw —"

She swung around, put her hands to her ears
as if to shut out the vague comfort I could give
her, and disappeared into her bedroom. I heard
her speaking on the telephone.

In a matter of minutes she returned, saying
in a tranced voice, "I must go to him ... I
must be there ... I've just called Catherine and
she and Joe will meet me at the jetty on Mull."
She seemed to be fighting for every word she
spoke. Then she turned, looking at me with
her dazed eyes, hesitating as if trying to make
up her mind. "Will you come too?"

"Of course, if you want me."

"I do." She reached out and put her arms
around me in a sudden, swift gesture. "I'm
sorry. Oh, Judith, I'm so sorry. I knew when I
saw his ... his name for you, Clea, written on
the window that you couldn't have scratched it
there. No ... no, that's not true. I knew —"

I tried to stop her. "It's not important any
longer."

"Oh, but it is. I have to clear my mind of all
the muddle of thinking, the fear and the ...
the not knowing what to do. I can only do that
by talking. And I have to tell you, Judith, I

432

have to. I knew, you see, before I saw your name there on the window; I knew when Lewis told me he wanted to prove to the courts that you were . . . you were unbalanced and unfit to look after Paul. That's when I realized — although I didn't dare face it — that he was doing these things to you. I know him so well and I read his eyes as he told me — they were lying eyes because *he* was lying. It tore at me, Judith, but what could I do? What *do* you do when it is your own son? Judith, help me, help me, please." The words rushed out like a flood, wild and distraught.

"I think we'll have to help one another," I said and kissed her cold cheek.

Dru was waiting with the *Midir* at the loch, but Rory was there also.

He seized Antonia's arm. "Have you heard? Has Judith told you?"

She eased her arm away without answering.

I said quickly, "Not now. Please, not now," and pushed him aside as Dru helped her into the boat.

"But she says she knows," Rory called in triumph. "And she doesn't mind. It's wonderful —"

"*Not now.*" The tone of my voice silenced him.

When we were away from the jetty where

433

Rory stood watching us, Antonia seemed to become aware of what had been said. She asked, like someone speaking in her sleep, "What was he talking about? What is so wonderful? What *could* be?"

"Just something that happened to Rory personally. Nothing that's important at the moment."

She was in a state of shock and accepted my unsatisfactory answer without interest.

We crossed the green water as the sun rose, and the Torrenses met us at the pier on Mull. With their usual thoughtfulness they had brought both their cars, "because," Catherine whispered to me, "we thought of asking Antonia to stay with us for a while. But you will probably want to get back to the island, and so will Shane."

"Thank you," I said, and blessed Antonia's friends for their thoughtfulness.

The *Midir* had been tied up at the jetty to await our return, the *Lennonan* had already taken the men who came to help back to Cathair Mor.

I remained in the car when Antonia went into the hospital. Catherine went with her, and when she came out she drew Shane aside for a moment. Then they stepped back to the car and Catherine told us that she would remain at the hospital with Antonia. She hesitated, bent and laid her cheek lightly against mine.

"It's all right, honey. I'll cope," she said softly and then, with Shane, went back through the hospital doors.

Joe and I sat without speaking and I was grateful for his silence. After a few minutes Shane came out into the courtyard and I opened the car door quickly. His face had a strange, remote gravity. He said quietly, "I think you should go back to Mullaine, Judith."

"Lewis . . . ?"

"He died in the ambulance."

I heard my own cry: "Oh God!" And yet, there had been no longer any hope for Lewis in his life. He could not have lived without the great concert halls, the adulation. To have it end this way was his only liberation.

Shane got into the car and sat next to Joe as we drove in silence back to the jetty.

Dru was waiting for us, and although he remained silent, his expression asked the question.

Shane said simply, "It's over." And Dru understood. He climbed down into the *Midir* and started the engine.

The sun had risen sufficiently to cause a strange and lovely circle around the island while we in the boat were still in the tall shadow of Cathair Beag. I felt as if we were speeding toward a gilded halo.

435

Shane spoke first, breaking the poignantly close silence between us. "When I arrived from Iran, it was different. I was troubled for Lewis. Then I met you and I was troubled for you. You complicated my thoughts."

"I'm sorry."

"I don't really think you are. And you don't need to be. Understanding people is difficult enough, heaven knows! I was harsh with you because you bewildered me. It's no excuse, but it's the best I can give."

We were sitting outside and the wind was cold and the sun too brilliant. Later in the day it would rain. I didn't care.

"It's strange," I said. "It came out in different ways, didn't it – the unbalance . . . Lewis's wild tempers, Rory's life of dreams . . ."

"You scarcely knew Robert, did you? He was a difficult man. It's said, you know, that if Robert hadn't been impossible to live with, Antonia would never have been the great singer she was. Her work and her tours were an escape. But she would never admit her marriage was a failure."

"I shouldn't have left her," I said suddenly. "Shane, I should have waited at the hospital to be with her."

"No. She needs someone who is not emotionally involved. Catherine is perfect. Give Antonia time to grieve and to sort out her feelings."

436

He was right. I closed my eyes against the bright sun. When I looked again, Shane was watching the herring fleet come home and Dru was steering the *Midir* toward the loch.

As we neared the island Shane touched my hand very lightly, and I knew that he, too, felt the entry into that golden circle that lit Cathair Mor like a benediction. We looked at each other without speaking. I was content to wait.

ABOUT THE AUTHOR

Anne Maybury lives in Knightsbridge, London, and says she "can only work in the stimulus of great cities." She is a full-time author who gets much of her inspiration for her books from her travels in England and abroad. She is the author of such popular books as *Jessamy Court*, *The Midnight Dancers*, *Ride a White Dolphin*, *The Terracotta Palace*, *Walk in the Paradise Garden* and *The Jeweled Daughter*.

THORNDIKE-MAGNA hopes you have enjoyed this Large Print book. All our Large Print titles are designed for easy reading, and all our books are made to last. Other Thorndike Press or Magna Print books are available at your library, through selected bookstores, or directly from the publishers. For more information about current and upcoming titles, please call or mail your name and address to:

THORNDIKE PRESS
P.O. Box 159
Thorndike, Maine 04986
(800) 223-6121
(207) 948-2962 (in Maine and Canada call collect)

or in the United Kingdom:

MAGNA PRINT BOOKS
Long Preston, Near Skipton
North Yorkshire,
England BD23 4ND
(07294) 225

There is no obligation, of course.